About the Author

C.A. MacRae was born and raised in Manchester, England. From a young age she found a love for storytelling. A creative person by nature, she attended Art College to pursue her passion. In 2004 she met with Carolyn Reynolds, the Executive Producer of Coronation Street, over a script she wrote. Years later when life enabled her, inspired by Carolyn's words, she researched and wrote the Gemini Complex, The Cabal, the first book in the trilogy of the Gemini Complex. C.A. MacRae is very passionate about humanity, nature and the world we live in. Her passions are the key to the meaning behind her writing.

The biggest threat to our planet Earth is the greed of Man.
Man alone has caused the destruction of the environment on land and within our oceans and along the way precious life. It's time to make amends, before we all lose this beautiful Earth, our home.
C.A. MacRae

Gemini Complex

The Cabal

C. A. MacRae

Gemini Complex

The Cabal

Vanguard Press

VANGUARD PAPERBACK

© Copyright 2021
C. A. MacRae

A CIP catalogue record for this title is
available from the British Library.

ISBN 978 1 784658 24 3

In this work of fiction, the characters, institutions, events and places are
either entirely fictitious or a figment of the author's imagination. Any
resemblance to actual events or persons living or dead is entirely
coincidental.

Vanguard Press is an imprint of
Pegasus Elliot MacKenzie Publishers Ltd.
www.pegasuspublishers.com

First Published in 2021

Vanguard Press
Sheraton House Castle Park
Cambridge England

Printed & Bound in Great Britain

Dedication

In Memory of Doris and Flo (angels without wings).

Acknowledgements

I have a heartfelt obligation to mention the following people for their support, encouragement and knowledge.

Roddie MacRae, thank you for your love, support, belief and endless knowledge.

James MacRae, thank you for helping me with your outstanding graphic design talents, the cover of the book reflects the complexities of the contents.

Dianne Nice, I am sending you a huge hug to heaven. Thank you for your encouragement, comments, support and friendship. I miss you dearly.

Donna Stapleton, thank you for your friendship, encouragement and proofreading my first draft.

Randy Cameron, thank you for proofreading and your invaluable input.

James at Greenwood Military Aviation Museum, Nova Scotia, Canada, thank you for your knowledge on the Brisfit.

Carl Kumpic, thank you for your knowledge and suggestions.

To the best parents a child could hope for, James and Doris Dowd thanks for making me believe I have a writing talent.

Team Pegasus a huge THANK YOU!

Facts

The Gnostic Gospel of Mary exists; the papyrus scroll was discovered in the late-nineteenth century. It was purchased in Cairo in 1896 by a German scholar, and then taken to Berlin.

Gnostic religion derives from Jewish Christian beliefs, originating at the end of the first century Anno Domini in early Christian and non-rabbinical Jewish sects.

The Cathars were a Gnostic revival movement, which appeared in the Languedoc region of the South of France in the 11th century. Amongst the Cathars were Perfecti the divine ones. They were highly respected by many of the local people, leading a life of austerity and charity. They travelled in pairs and ministered in an apostolic fashion.

Catharism acknowledged women as preachers; they were given the greatest opportunities for autonomous action since women were found as being Believers as well as Perfecti. They were able to administer the unique sacrament for the Cathars called consolamentum.

In 1208, Pope Innocent III initiated the Cathar Crusade and endeavored to end Catharism with a secular alliance of the French Crown employing noblemen and foreign mercenaries to destroy the Cathars. The Holocaust of Albi, Toulouse, Beziers, Carcassonne, Fanjeaux and Foix followed. In 1243, the last of the Cathars retreated to the Cathar fortress of Montségur. It was besieged from May 1243 to March 1244 by troops of the seneschal of Carcassonne and the Archbishop of Narbonne. On the 16th of March 1244, two hundred and ten Cathars were burnt alive near the foot of the fortress.

The Knights Templar (Christ's Soldiers) was a Catholic military Order founded in 1119 and existing until 1312. Templar knights were the most skilled fighting units of the Crusades; they wore distinctive white vests with a red cross. However, non-combat members of the order formed as much as 90% of the order's members. The order derived from humble beginnings; this was short lived as they gained a powerful advocate in Bernard of Clairvaux who in later years became Saint Bernard. He was a leading church figure primarily responsible for founding the Cistercian Order. Having Saint Bernard's blessing the Templars became a favored charity throughout the Christian World, receiving land, money, business and noble-born sons from families who were eager to help the fight in the Holy Land.

The Templars were exempted from the order of obedience to local laws by Pope Innocent II's papal bull (official order), Omne Datum Optimum. This meant that the Templars were not required to pay taxes, could pass freely through all borders and were free from all authorities except that of the Pope. This helped their rise; 90% of non-combat members managed a large economic infrastructure, developing pioneering financial techniques that were an early form of banking in its own network. They bought and managed farms and vineyards, built massive stone cathedrals and castles. They were involved in manufacturing, import and export, had their own fleet of ships and at one point they even owned the entire island of Cyprus. The Templars arguably formed the world's first multinational corporation.

Link between the Cathars and Templars

Bernard of Clairvaux wrote the rules for the Knights Templar and was the key to their financial success.

He traveled to southern France in June 1148, and his preaching there helped strengthen support against the peace-loving Cathars who were now deemed as heretics.

The Cathar fortress of Montségur in the South of France was rebuilt after 1204 by a nobleman called Raymond de Péreille who had Templar connections (the castle builders). Under Raymond's protection, Guilhabert de Castres, Cathar Bishop of Toulouse, set up a centre for Catharism at the fortress around 1232, where the last of the Cathars took refuge until March 1244.

The Knights Templar were deemed as heretics as they had broken away from the Catholic Church. On 13th of October, 1307, King Philip ordered the arrest of all Templars in France. They were tortured and burnt at the stake. Thereafter Pope Clement V instructed all Christian monarchs in Europe to arrest all Templars and seize their assets. He issued the papal bull (order) Pastoralis praeeminentiae on 22nd of November 1307.

Speculation

On the night of the 15th of March 1244, a small party of Cathars with two Perfecti (the divine ones) were aided by a Knights Templar guide to escape from the fortress of Montségur (a death-defying feat to say the least; the fortress was built at an altitude of 1,207 meters above sea level). They descended the steepest walls and cliffs of the fortress to escape their death.

It is said the Cathars accumulated wealth, which may have included the Holy Grail, yet they were non-materialistic people. It is also said on the night of 15th of March 1244, the escapees escaped with the Holy Grail. Could the Holy Grail have been a Perfecti with the bloodline of Jesus Christ?

The Knights Templar have also been heavily linked to the Holy Grail.

Prologue

Mary nodded her head. "Yes, I am sorry, I'm struggling with my appetite."

"It has been a very eventful day for you… well, it has for us all," said the duke.

Dr Goodman shook his head in agreement with the duke's words.

"Mary, when I told you, that you were going to witness greatness and feel greatness earlier, I meant every word I spoke. Fate, prophecy and a little collaborating have deemed that you are now, Lady Mary Tavistock. Your pa and ma knew you were not their blood daughter, as my father and mother knew my sister was not theirs. You were both separated at birth." The duke took a deep breath expecting some form of reaction from Mary.

Mary did not flinch at the duke's words; all she could do was sit and listen.

"It was easier to keep your anonymity that way, so you could both remain safe. You are identical to your sister and therefore separating the two of you made matters easier so that we could protect you both and the bloodline. It's important now that you carry on through life as Mary, as she can no longer be Mary, even though I know, Flo is very much alive in you. This is your calling." The duke paused once more.

The words of the duke were hard to digest and only made little sense, but she felt a deep sense of hurt, knowing her parents knew all the while that she was not their blood child and never told her. Mary's tears started to well, as a wave of untold sadness struck her heart with an incredible innate sense of not belonging. Loss and grief engulfed her mind, albeit, aware that her tears were about to fall, she fought the compulsion to cry.

"Please, eradicate all your questions from your mind and tongue, for your own safety. The less you know at this moment in time, the safer you will be. Your life could depend on this. You need to focus on the here and now." The duke placed his hand on Mary's.

Dr Goodman looked on with compassion in his good eye. "Tomorrow, Mary, I will be taking you to Portu Satis Tuto, where there will be others like you, and many that will protect you. You will be safe there. Your training will commence and in time many of your questions will be answered."

She gulped with apprehension. "Are there people wanting to harm me?"

"Yes, Mary, it is our belief." The duke clutched her hand, and then released his grip, in an effort to emancipate Mary's dread.

Her expression remained the same: one of shock and horror. "Wouldn't I have been best just keeping my anonymity? And who is wanting to harm me?"

Dr Goodman answered, "I am afraid the answer is very complex. It is impossible for me to give you an answer, right now."

Her expression changed to one of utter confusion.

"Mary, you need to rid your mind of these questions. All you need to think of right now is apple cinnamon pie," the duke jested. "The here and now."

Mary had a look of disbelief as if she had not been sitting at the table hearing the words spoken, she could hardly grasp the conversation that had just occurred. Now it seemed that the duke was making a mockery of her safety — *Apple cinnamon pie. What kind of brainwashing was this?* she asked herself.

"Would you like a piece? Mrs Thorpe made one especially for Alexandra, it's her favorite… Mmmmmmm, I think we should skip the main course and eat dessert," the duke smiled.

Dr Goodman piped up, "Sister Crouse has led me to believe it's one of your favorite foods to eat, too!"

"Yes, Ma's apple and cinnamon pie… except she is not my Ma, is she?"

"Your ma will always be your ma, as your pa will always be your pa. Time and your heart cannot change what the past provided for you. However, it is very important now that you honor your new identity." The duke clasped Mary's hand. "Your own happiness lies only in knowing who you truly are and making peace with it."

Mary's eyes widened. "But I have no idea who I am any more."

Dr Goodman piped up with deep sincerity within his voice, "It's very important you comprehend His Grace's words, for they are very wise words."

"Thank you for your wise words, Your Grace, but if you do not mind me saying so, I feel very overwhelmed with the words spoken and I cannot possibly eat a morsel of apple cinnamon pie. All I feel inside of me is a huge sadness in my heart and a feeling of not belonging. I have no idea of who I am or why I have been put on this blessed earth." Mary tried to hold back her tears but they flowed, regardless. Her lips trembled in the defeat of her efforts to stop her tears from falling. "I, I would like to be excused." She did not wait for a reply, but backed up her chair, and made a run for the door and opened it in great haste.

Chapter One
The Climb

March 15, 1244
Mount Montségur, South of France.

The darkness had formed around Bertrand Raseire of Rennes le Château. He was on a rescue mission of the utmost importance, as he thrashed his way through the brambles with diminished vision, cursing underneath his breath when the occasional thorn snagged the skin on his face. He had fought in numerous battles and survived against many a sword even when hundreds of his kin had been killed in action. He was a seasoned warrior of the bloodiest of battles. Yet, here he was battling against the brambles and it felt like the brambles were winning. "Ouchhh," he whispered as he unhooked a thorny branch from his eyelid. "I could lose an eye," he muttered. Bertrand was sweating profusely underneath his leather jacket despite the cold, damp air in the valley where the moon lit the Château of Mount Montségur like a beacon.

Bertrand's first mission was to make sure he was undetected by Marshal Guy de Lévis and Captain Croix's soldiers who patrolled the low grounds of Château Montségur by the Papal Order of Pope Innocent IV and King Louis IX's men.

Lord Raymond de Péreille was counting on him and his expertise in alpinism. Lord de Péreille of Montségur surprisingly had managed to negotiate an amnesty for his soldiers, against the odds. Much to his amazement, even more surprisingly he had also been given a fifteen-day truce for the peace-loving Cathars he had fought so incredibly hard to save. Lord de Péreille had convinced Marshal Guy de Lévis that he needed that time to sway the remaining two hundred and fifteen Cathars to renounce their faith. "Surely it was essential to end the Inquisition peacefully? So that it can be remembered that way," he had suggested to Marshal Guy de Lévis. Although deep within his heart he knew very well none of the remaining Cathars would recant their faith but he needed that time for Bertrand Raseire to return from his Knights Templar mission in Khwarazm, Greater Iran. He was the only person he knew that could successfully climb the steepest side of Mount Montségur, a terrain he had practiced on before he climbed Aneto, the highest peak of the Pyrenees Mountains at eleven thousand, one hundred and sixty-eight feet. Mount Montségur was a mere three thousand, nine hundred and thirty-seven feet but what made this climb extra special was that it had to be done at night with no aided light but the moonlight and then descended by novices, one being pregnant. He knew Bertrand was the only man for the job and he was more than capable of defying the odds when they were stacked against him.

Bertrand stood at the foot of the east side of the mountain, staring up at the imposing site of rock fascia as the full moon shone down, casting shadows on the deep crevices he had once climbed. He was focused on finding his first anchor in the dihedral rock formation, where two planes of rock come together. He had practiced his dihedral climbing several years ago on this very part of Mount Montségur where the rock formation cornered. It was excellent training for practicing the most difficult rock-climbing technique of stemming. His body tension had to be trained. His stomach and back muscles had to be strong and responsive; to contract and relax at appropriate positions of climbing was the key to this climb. Bertrand had kept his lean muscular body strong, toned and conditioned, despite the battles.

He needed to be fully focused and not to take his attention off the rock formation or his body movements for one second to prevent falling. Even though the dihedral climb was the hardest climb of Mount Montségur, it was the safest, as the corner would shadow Bertrand so he could climb undetected, fully focused on the rock and his body movements.

Bertrand turned and gazed at the burning tar braziers of Marshal Guy de Lévis's army. They were burning brightly just two hundred feet away from him. It was crucial that he made the least amount of noise possible. Albeit he knew he had to most likely replace several anchors to secure the rope for his descent to abseil back down the mountain. Somehow, he hoped the soldiers would be distracted enough with their nightly banters and rituals not to hear his noise. Bertrand took off his jacket and hid it with his sword amongst rotting leaves and stepped into his rope harness, and threw his knapsack on his back with the coiled line. He chalked his hands and placed his palms against the rock, bowed his head, closed his eyes and prayed for his safety.

When he opened his eyes, he caught sight of his first anchor and began his ascent. He placed his hands and feet wide apart from each other, using them like suckers, climbing with the left foot and right hand and the right foot and left hand, smearing his feet by pressing the soles of his shoes into the rock, and using his fingers like claws, palming, on both sides of the rock fascia. It was going to be a hard climb as the rock was not as dry as he would like but he was confident he could do it as he secured each move on the rock.

Chapter Two
Au Revoir

Dianne clasped Théodore's hand in distress. Am I the only person here fearful? she thought. Her azure blue eyes were glazed and her olive skin paled.

Théodore cupped her petite clasped hand with his and rubbed it with his other hand, in aid to calm her. "Calm your soul, Dianne, we will survive this night." He smiled, although he was deeply saddened by his thoughts too. Even though Bishop Marty had done everything in his power to help Dianne and himself come to terms with what had to be done. It had been extremely difficult saying goodbye to all the sweet, wonderful people he would never see again. Many of them had helped him become the very man he became but he had said his heartfelt goodbyes that night, after having the last supper of breaking bread and drinking red wine. He had hugged each one for dear life; his tears had flowed from his azure, blue-colored eyes, while he kissed their cheeks.

He turned to look at Dianne, she too was shedding tears and sobbing with distress; her slight frame shuddered with the tremors of grief. Grief not yet warranted.

It was incredibly hard coming to terms with not seeing their smiling faces again, not having in-depth conversations about anything and everything. No more laughing, singing, fishing, and eating together. No more fun game nights, and praying together, no more solace in the silence. All two hundred and fifteen of his kin were going to sacrifice their bodies just so Dianne and he could survive. Bishop Marty had brought him some comfort with his words. Bishop Marty had been like a father to Théodore. He had assured him that his soul would meet his and Dianne's soul once again. "Someday," He had said. "So, you must look after your soul, you only have one. It can never be taken away from you, like the life you have here on earth can. Be kind and loving, and always take much time out of your day to reflect and feel the light within you. A light that burns so brightly."

Those words comforted him somewhat. However, he remained a little confused as to why Dianne and her unborn baby and he were the only ones being rescued. Bishop Marty had told him they would find out one day soon, after Arnaud de Miglos knew they were no longer in danger and they had survived the Inquisition. "You are hope on earth," Bishop Marty said.

Raymond de Belvis, Etienne Boutarra, and Paul Louis Caraman circled around Dianne as Bishop Marty hugged her for the last time. Tears were streaming from her eyes uncontrollably and each Perfecti knew they needed to calm Dianne down in order for her to survive the descent.

"Dianne, you and Théodore are God's hand on earth. It's very important you calm your soul, for if you do not, you and your unborn baby will not survive this night, nor will Théodore. Calm your soul, child, and tune your mind into the light that burns so bright inside you. This light will always protect you. Feel the warmth, peace and love it brings, and hold it dear to your heart and mind. It will never leave you. All of your kin gathered here have no fear of tomorrow. For tomorrow will bring freedom, where their spirits can freely roam." Bishop Marty's eyes twinkled as he smiled. "Even fly, within this beautiful land, where the eagles soar high in the vast blue sky, the songbirds sing the sweetest tunes, nestled within the trees as the leaves rustle in the warm breeze and the stream trickles into the flowing river. Where the dew-drenched grass tastes so wholesome to the goats grazing in the field. This is our home, the place we love the most and a place I will never leave. Come back one day, dear child, when it is safe and visit me, you shall find me here. It is not 'goodbye' but so long for now." He kissed her head of strawberry blonde hair. "Now, Arnaud will take you to the ledge. It is vital that you do what he tells you to do."

Paul Louis Caraman piped up, "Just be mindful, Dianne. It's what you do best." He smiled gleefully. There was no sadness within him. As Dianne looked at Raymond and Etienne, they too had joyful expressions on their faces.

Raymond's soft voice uttered the words, "We are ready to leave this life. It's our time, Dianne, and we will be leaving it with our kin. Hand in hand we stand united and our souls will be released before a flame of Pope Innocent's, can scorch our flesh."

"I will come back as a white cat, so please feed me well and give me a comfortable bed," Etienne jested.

"What about Limoux and Maurina, who will look after my cats, after tomorrow?"

Etienne commented, "They will find you, do not worry."

Arnaud placed his bulging knapsack on his back.

"Arnaud, do you have the chalice and scriptures wrapped well?" said Bishop Marty with concern in his voice.

Arnaud placed his hand on Bishop Marty's shoulder as an act of reassurance. "Yes, just as you have wrapped them... do not worry, they will be safe. I will carry out your wishes."

"May the good God be with you, Arnaud."

Arnaud released his hand and bowed his head; he then walked over to Dianne and Théodore. "It's time to go. Bertrand has almost reached the top shelf and we now need to be ready at the ledge. God will be with us so do not fear the dark oblivion for we only carry the light," he voiced with assertiveness.

Bishop Marty spoke with jubilation, "Go, Vibrant Lights, our love will be with you, we will sing on your descent. The Pope and King Louis's men will be too focused on our harmonious tones, so that if you make a noise louder than you should, they will not hear you."

The four men, dressed in their white linen robes with natural rope ties, turned and joined the rest of the two hundred and eleven Cathars that had congregated waiting for them underneath the candlelit chandeliers. Bishop Marty, Raymond, Etienne, and Paul Louis joined them; they made their way to the west wing of Château Mount Montségur. Dianne turned for one last look with her blurred, teary-eyed stare that quickly turned into a white light haze from her vision of all the Cathars dressed in their white robes and skull caps. They began to sing 'Lo Boièr' and walked outside to the west ridge. It was not long before their voices were echoing down the mountain and resonating through the valley.

Dianne was completely and utterly calm on her descent of Mount Montségur, despite entering a mist. She was mindful of every move she made while listening to the harmonious, relaxing tones of her kin.

Chapter Three
Ablution and Sacrifice

March 16, 1244
Mount Montségur

Pierre-Roger de Mirepoix walked up to the Château's large arched wooden doors with a heavy heart; he had brought with him the news Bishop Marty needed to know to move forward, although to him death was not a way forward. Before entering the Château, he turned and took in the breath-taking view from Mount Montségur as he scratched his bald head then rubbed his round belly. *This view will never seem the same from this day forward,* he thought. A tear welled in his eye. How he had wished for this day not to come, but it had, and he arrived with it.

Dawn was not far off as the trees of the valley bathed in the mist and a glimmer of the sun's rays started to shine. Mirepoix knew it was not going to be long before the valley's mist would dissipate only to be replaced by smoke, a deathly scent and sight that would stain his mind until his dying day.

He knocked on the right large wooden door of Château Mount Montségur and announced, "It's Mirepoix."

A small wooden door within the door opened and Mirpoix's amber-blazed, brown, teary eyes met a pair of green jubilant eyes. Something he did not expect to see.

"Come," said Etienne, "Bishop Marty has something he would like to give you."

Mirepoix stepped inside the Château to see every Cathar smiling — men, women, and children glowed with happiness as he walked to Bishop Marty; there was an air of peace and excitement at the same time, something Mirepoix found hard to comprehend and profound. *Do they not realize their demise is imminent*, he thought?

Bishop Marty stood with open arms, as Mirepoix met his embrace.

"Do not look saddened, Mirepoix, our journey in this life has come to an end. We all know that. However, my kin and I will begin a new journey, this day. A journey filled with light, where there is no sorrow, no pain, no darkness, no suffering, no hatred, only love, joy and laughter."

Bishop Marty released his hug; his azure, blue-colored eyes, gazed sternly at Mirepoix as his lips smiled within his long white beard and moustache. "Have they arrived safely?"

"Yes. They have reached Rennes le Château. I have just received Arnaud's dove. He's following your instructions before they head for Miglos."

"Good... now, for all your hard work and faithfulness I would like to reward you." Bishop Marty handed him a heavy knapsack. "Inside this sack holds the key for you and your family to make a new life, for after today, I feel that the King's men will take ownership of your Château and you will be left with nothing. It is not your faith or belief being sacrificed here today, it's ours. Therefore, it is only right that you shall live a good life from this day forward. Lord de Péreille has been given his heavy sack of freedom too. Promise me you will make every day of your life count, and live life to the fullest, and seek the beauty in the day.

"I will try," Mirepoix answered.

Bishop Marty commented, "Do and you shall have a happy, wonderful life from here on."

Mirepoix was reluctant to take the sack but Bishop Marty closed Mirepoix's fingers with his hand so that Mirepoix would clasp the sack.

Bishop Marty insisted, "You must take it, it's rightfully yours, no one else's."

Mirepoix gripped the heavy sack.

"Now, promise to me you will do what I ask of you?"

Mirepoix's eyes glazed with tears as he spoke softly, "I promise." He sniffed and sighed then shrugged his shoulders before he spoke. "I already know the answer to my question, but I have to ask this question anyway. Is there anyone here that wishes to renounce their faith?"

Bishop Marty asked Mirepoix, "What is the answer you already know, Mirepoix?"

Mirepoix managed to produce a flat-lipped smile before answering with the word. "No... no Cathar here wishes to renounce their faith."

"Your answer is correct. Now, you had better place that sack on your back, otherwise Marshal Guy de Lévis or Captain Croix will be seizing that too."

Mirepoix placed the knapsack on his back and let out one almighty sigh. "They are ready for you."

Bishop Marty smiled. "And we are ready for them. Lead the way."

Bishop Marty followed Mirepoix, and two hundred and fourteen Cathars followed singing jubilantly, two by two, hand in hand, passing the barricade of soldiers on either side of the walkway as they made their way down to the base of the mountain. The scent of tar became evermore present with each step they took.

Captain Croix dismounted his horse and greeted Mirepoix with a nod. His skeletal features enhanced his cool demeanor as his cold, curt tongue sliced the air. "For the last time, does anyone here wish to recant?" he shouted.

"They do not," Mirepoix answered.

"Are you sure?" Captain Croix asked with a glint of humanity in his cold brown eyes that almost looked black.

Bishop Marty replied, "They are sure."

He took a large sigh. "Well, I was not expecting that... God damn you!" Captain Croix sighed, then commanded, "Tar them!"

A soldier stood wearing oversized gauntlets held a large hot tar brush he stood at the foot of a humongous wooden spiral, constructed from large freestanding logs. Each one becoming a little taller in size as it reached the center of the spiral. Tarred kindling had been placed in between the logs so that when the fire was lit it would blaze quickly.

The soldier tarred Bishop Marty with a large black cross on the front of his white linen robe, all the while Bishop Marty did not flinch, it was as if he was no longer present in his body, but his body remained motioned all the same; each Cathar followed suit.

A second solider directed Bishop Marty to climb the log steps to the center of the wooden spiral where the old man took his central position. He clasped his pendant of a white unicorn, which hung around his neck. Then he stared up at the blue sky and started to sing as each Cathar, hand-in-hand, took their position on the spiral and clasped their pendants of animals and flowers of Mother Earth. They too looked up at the sky and sang their hearts out.

Captain Croix shouted out, "Raise the flame!"

All the soldiers that were positioned three feet apart around the perimeter of the wooden spiral, raised their torch; each soldier stood motionless and expressionless.

"Ignite the fire!" Captain Croix commanded.

The torches were lowered and flames began to rise. Each soldier stepped back many paces to safety, staring at the flames all the while.

Captain Croix mounted his horse once again and shouted above the billowing flames, "God bless your souls, every one of you! Viva Angelina!"

Chapter Four
A Violent Murder

The 31st of October 1897, was an exceptionally cold, dark, eerie night in the quaint town of Coustaussa in Southern France as Priest Raymond Belvis stood outside his church entrance, locking the doors. He was not sure whether it was his old bones that made him shiver or the mystique of Halloween. He nervously turned the key, looking behind him as the barrel of the lock clicked. His pupils began to dilate as he stared at a man walking towards him. Placing the keys in his cassock pocket he turned and stood still for a short time, not recognizing the man. As the man drew closer, an expression of relief appeared on Belvis's face. "Bonjour, Cross, I didn't recognize you without your cassock on. Why are you not wearing it? Have you fallen foul of Bishop Rolland?"

Cross didn't answer. He just stood shivering in the cold air, taking his last puff of a cigarette, then throwing it to the ground and stomping it out.

He knew why Cross was not wearing his cassock; he had been decommissioned by Bishop Rolland for the second time in 1892 and had not been seen since. He was curious as to why he'd not seen him for eight years.

Belvis declared, "Well, it's too cold to be standing out here... I know where there's a warm fire, a bottle of Banyuls and a good ear." He tapped Cross' shoulder. "You can tell me all about it as long as you don't smoke in my house." The two began to walk to the presbytery. Cross shrugged his shoulders, still not speaking a word; this was unusual to Belvis, as Cross was never stuck for words. In fact, Raymond suspected it was his words that had gotten him into trouble with Bishop Rolland and the very reason he was not wearing his deacon's cassock now.

They entered the presbytery; Belvis locked the door behind him and applied the chain lock. Cross' stare caused Belvis to react. "One can never be too careful these days. Come warm your hands and heart by the fire in the kitchen."

They entered a sparse kitchen with a crackling fire.

"Would you like to put more wood on the fire while I go and get a bottle of Banyuls from the cellar?"

"Oui (yes)," replied Cross, "but no wine for me."

Raymond looked thoughtful as he stopped reaching for the second wine glass on the shelf. He placed a glass on the table and continued to walk down to the cellar and pulled a wine bottle from the wooden crate. When Raymond arrived back in the kitchen, Cross was stood by the fire with a lit cigarette shaking in his hand. He decided not to ask Cross to put the cigarette out.

"Cross, God has given you a life to live, so it's important that you do that in the best way you can. He understands your hopes and fears; it's time to make the right decisions in your life... Now, why have you come to visit me after all this time?"

Cross, twenty years younger than the seventy-year-old, frail priest, threw his cigarette in the fire. His vagabond look seemed to intensify the coldness in his brown eyes as he clenched his fists before answering; his thoughts of aggravation were clearly visible. "I have come to ask you about the parchments and list of names with bearings I delivered here on the 29th of September 1891."

Raymond looked shocked. "I have difficulty in remembering what I was doing last week, never mind seven years ago... I know nothing about the parchments, nor the list of names with bearings; I do remember you delivered a sealed package to Bertrand Raseire, not to me... You should be asking him this question and maybe Boutarra, or Caraman."

Cross smacked both hands on the sturdy wooden table, creating one almighty thud. "I know it was sealed, I resealed it with Rolland's stamp. I was only able to glance at the parchments at the time and thought my translation read, 'Jesus of Nazareth married me, Mary of Magdalene, for I was the one he loved the most' She bore his children in Gallia Narbonensis, that is Narbonne today from where the Divine Gnostics originally derived during the 1st Century Anno Domini. The list of names of Divine Cathars and parchments are proof the Divine Gnostics are the

Holy Grail, I am sure of it. Do you know if these parchments were the same parchments Bertrand Raseire found in his church?"

"They couldn't have been, because the parchments he found were only small and do not mention Mary of Magdalene; they are rather cryptic, I have seen them. However, I do believe there are bearings within the writing. It sounds like Raseire's parchments guided him to the parchment you are talking about. If your translation is correct, well, that would change biblical history or not as the case may be."

Cross ran his fingers through his long hair. "Exactly! The names made no sense to me at the time, as I questioned my translation. However, thereafter, Bishop Rolland was bequeathed 2,200,000 francs in his own name from Saissa Cacatier of Coursan. So when I confronted Rolland about the truth of the parchments, coordinates, the Cathars, the money and the list of names, Cacatier being one I can remember, he denied the absurdity. He then decommissioned me for my insubordination and preposterous claims of blasphemy against the church and demoted me to be no more than a footman to him." He smacked the table, aggravated by his own words. This time the thud caused everything to vibrate that lay on the table. "I am sure you know the truth behind the parchments and that's why I am here. This matter has been haunting me for eight years; I need that list of names and coordinates."

Raymond looked pensive. "I had no idea that there was a list. That explains why Raseire, Boutarra, and Caraman took the package upstairs that day." Raymond sipped his wine and savored it before swallowing. "After what you have just told me, I am very tempted to take this matter further, above Rolland's head." He turned to place his glass down on the table, then walked to the window in contemplation.

Cross yelled, "That would be a mistake!" As he hit Raymond full force on the back of the head with a pair of iron fire tongs.

Belvis fell to the floor and was completely stunned by Cross's action. He staggered to his feet, fell to the floor once again and eventually turned and asked, "Why… why do you hurt me?"

"I need that list and I am sure you have it. Tell me where it is. Then I will be on my way. You'll never see me again." Cross dragged the priest away from the window and sat him in the armchair by the fire.

Raymond placed his left hand on his head as it hurt so badly. His hand felt wet; he turned it to see his palm covered in blood.

Cross squatted down in front of him, swapped the fire tongs for a hatchet and looked Priest Raymond Belvis in the eye. "Now once again, where is the list?"

Raymond placed his hands down on the arms of the chair as he looked in horror at the hatchet, trembling in fear. "I... I told you I don't know anything about a list and that is the God's honest truth." Raymond saw his opportunity to dash to the door and pushed Cross, knocking him to the floor.

Cross quickly stood in reflex and threw the hatchet at Raymond's head, who fell to the floor immediately while blood gushed out from his head with velocity, causing a fountain of blood as he lay motionless.

Cross checked his neck for a pulse... The priest was barely alive and yet he began to crawl to the window.

Cross shook his head in disbelief and shouted, "You should be dead by now!"

He hit Belvis hard in the head with the hatchet in a frenzied attack thirteen more times, shouting, "Die, die, die!" Eventually he stopped, shaking with the adrenaline pumping through his body as he fumbled for a cigarette. "Holy shit, that was painful for both of us." He lit his cigarette and took a few puffs to control his shaking body; he then crouched down and laid Belvis flat with his arms crossed on his chest. He stood over the body and calmly spoke. "It's a pity you had to die this way, you were the one I liked the most." He smiled. "I think we both agree that killing this way in the future is not for me. I think I had better start studying toxicology, it's Bishop Rolland's turn for the hatchet." He laughed. "That's figuratively speaking, he deserves a poison that causes the most suffering a person could endure while still living. Now, to look for that list." He tossed his pack of Le Tsar cigarette papers and his cigarette butt close to the edge of the fire and shouted the words, "Viva Angelina!"

Chapter Five
The Retribution

On 25th of March 1898, in the courtyard at Carcassonne Cathedral (Southern France), Bishop Rolland paced up and down; he was impatiently waiting for dawn to break to meet Cross. Jean Pierre Martin Rolland had developed a taste for grandeur; he was a man from humble beginnings, the first child of ten, born in the quaint fishing village of Saint Valéry en Caux, with its white chalk cliffs and pebbled beach. Rolland knew what it was like to go hungry; he grew up fatherless from an early age.

His honesty was more than questionable, he'd acquired riches by any means possible, and 'morals' were just a mere word to him. Finally, the sun began to rise, gradually metamorphosing the darkness into vibrant shades of orange as Cross appeared like clockwork. "Bonjour Monseigneur Rolland."

Bishop Rolland did not answer. Instead, he lifted his hand for Cross to kiss. Cross bowed and kissed his hand.

Rolland acknowledged Cross to stand by nodding his head. "You made a terrible mess of the assassination on Belvis but I will put that down to inexperience. However, whatever possessed you to write the words 'Viva Angelina' on a cigarette paper and leave it by the body? Are you out of your mind?" He shook his head. "Why leave evidence? Do you know how hard I have had to work to erase your name from the list of suspects?"

The clean-shaven, manicured Cross stood with his mouth open as he began to answer but before he could voice a word Rolland scoffed, "Did he confess?"

Cross' cold brown eyes stared into Rolland's stern blue eyes. "You were right. He was going to see the Archbishop of Toulouse about you and Raseire. So, I carried out your orders, except killing him was a little harder than I had anticipated." Cross knelt. "Please forgive me, Monseigneur Rolland?"

Bishop Rolland nodded his head and did not answer but tapped his hand on Cross' shoulder, for him to rise. Cross did so.

Rolland smiled sardonically. "You may resume your normal duties with me."

Cross looked excited at the bishop's words. "My clerical duties as Deacon?"

Rolland's portly face frowned. "No, as my footman; you still need to prove yourself after your insubordination. This way, I will be able to keep my eye on you. Now, I am very parched and I'm in need of my bitter lemon tea. I'll be in my study."

Bishop Rolland turned and walked away. Cross immediately clenched his fists and whispered, "A bitter lemon tea, coupled with curare, that's what you really need, enough to cause paralysis and then a slow painful death." He headed straight to the kitchen, animated with his plan in hand. He had planned the bishop's death for some time and visualized his contorted, panic-stricken expression many times. It was time Rolland paid his penance for all his wrongdoings against him.

Finally, the day had come. He stood outside the door of Bishop Rolland's study with a pot of potent, poisonous, bitter lemon tea, cup and saucer placed on the most ostentatious silver tray money could buy. He knocked on the medieval wooden door and did not wait for an answer as he entered the study. Rolland was quick to correct him. "Cross, how many times must I ask you to wait for an answer?"

"Many. I am sorry, Monseigneur Rolland, I am so glad to be back, it slipped my mind. I have your bitter lemon tea." Cross knew he should wait, but he had previously just walked into the study, just to see if he could eavesdrop on a conversation, or see any intriguing papers Rolland was working on. Cross placed the silver tray on Rolland's desk, glancing at his paperwork whilst doing so.

The bishop was staring all the while at Cross' every move. "I see there are no candied orange coins on the tray; chef knows full well that I like the bittersweet stimulant in the morning — it sets me up for the day. Now go, get me my candied orange coins and bring me another pot of tea."

Cross leant forward to pick up the tray.

"No, no, no leave this one here," Rolland scoffed.

Cross walked to the door, bowed and walked out of the room. He closed the door, all the while the adrenaline was pumping within his body with anger and anticipation of the harm he was about to inflict on Rolland.

He returned to the study with a fresh pot of bitter lemon tea, cup, saucer, and candied orange coins. He knocked on the door and waited for an answer, knowing there might not be one.

Rolland was silent. A wry smile appeared on Cross's face as he opened the door. He was faced with Rolland's contorted face and outstretched hands. He placed the tray down on the large ostentatious bocote wooden desk and calmly voiced his despair. "Monseigneur Rolland, what is wrong with you?"

He leant into Rolland's face, lifted Rolland's left eyelid and looked into his eye concerned; Cross's facial expression turned to one of delight. "Your eyes are telling me you can't move, which means you can't talk. I'd say you are pretty helpless right now, and yet you are aware of everything that is going on and guess what? You're going to stay that way till the day you die. I shall see to that with my daily dose of vengeance. In the meantime, I shall search your study until I find exactly what has made you very, very rich." He poured himself a cup of bitter lemon tea and placed three candied oranges on the saucer, sat in the Queen Anne oxblood leather chair and put his feet up on the bishop's desk, sipping the tea and munching on the candied orange coins, savoring the flavors. "You're quite right, I feel an incredible uplift."

Chapter Six
An Ostentatious Funeral

On the 3rd of December 1901, at the Monastery of Prouilhe, Cross entered Monseigneur Jean Pierre Martin Rolland's bedroom, just as he had done for the past forty-five months. However, this day was a little different from the rest.

Cross smiled as he gazed at Bishop Rolland who sat in his wheelchair staring out of the window at the sunny blue-sky day. Cross sneered, "I hope you don't mind but I've decided to switch things up a little today, seeing as I have no further use for you and I have pressing matters I must attend to." He placed his face right in front of Rolland's face and smiled menacingly. "I must say how excited I am; instead of administering you with your daily dose of curare, which keeps you ohhhh so quiet and still, I'm going to test out my skills at administering aconite." He laughed in Rolland's face. "If you are really lucky, today will be the day you die." He grinned. "Would you like that?"

Bishop Rolland's eyes widened in horror.

"I see the curare is starting to wear off, I had better get to it." He uncorked a small green-colored glass bottle, tipped the bishop's head back and poured the liquid down Rolland's throat. "Now, this is what's going to happen to you; the aconite will interact with your cardiac cells, they will not be able to repolarize and eventually this will lead to a heart attack. I do hope that it's not too long, for my sake more than yours. I have lots to do and little time to do it in."

At four p.m. Bishop Rolland took his last breath as Cross watched him pass away. He was pronounced dead by the doctor of Prouilhe at four thirty p.m. Cross looked on tearfully. The very minute the doctor had left the bedroom, Cross crossed Bishop Rolland's arms on his chest, as he lay on the bed. He then bellowed out, "Viva Angelina!"

On the 9th of December, at ten a.m. the city of Carcassonne was the subject of an impressive, ostentatious funeral, where two mitered abbots, seven bishops, five hundred priests accompanied by the Archbishop of Toulouse, military and civil authorities paraded in the city. Cross walked alongside Deacon Tournebouix from Castelnaudary and Limoux, Priest Boutarra from Rennes-les-Bains and Priest Adrienne Bertrand Raseire from Rennes-le-Château, all the while not a word was uttered the whole duration of the ceremony.

Cross eventually broke the silence in the courtyard of Carcassonne Cathedral. "So, Boutarra, have you been selected as Bishop of Carcassonne?"

Boutarra smiled wryly. "Archbishop Arnajud-Raymond Gauti would never select me. He considers my views outrageous and deplorable, so maybe you should be asking Raseire, he's nearly as old as me." Boutarra chuckled.

Cross stared at Raseire who stared back, he then stared back at Boutarra. "I can see why Gauti finds your views outrageous. I would even go as far to say that they are preposterous; the ancient languages of Basque, Celtic, Punic, and Hebrew all derive from an ancient mother language that's identical to Modern English. Whatever gave you that idea?"

Boutarra scoffed, "Clearly you have not read my book."

Cross raised his eyebrows with ignorance. "Your Dromlech tour, what is that all about?"

Boutarra shrugged his shoulders in dismay.

Deacon Tournebouix answered. "It's a circular tour of the mountain ridges around Rennes-les-Bains, I'll take you on it one day and show you the meeting point of the Tectosages."

Cross looked baffled. "What do you mean by Tectosages?"

Raseire ridiculed, "They were one of three ancient Gaulish tribes!"

Cross replied calmly, "That makes a lot of sense now. Well, you seem to be a man who knows a lot about everything. So, Raseire, have you been selected as Bishop of Carcassonne?"

"Don't look at me for an answer but if I was a betting man, I would say the odds are against me. Hell will freeze over before I am made Bishop of Carcassonne."

Cross stared intensely. "Seriously, I hear that de Saint-Martin is going to be selected. Archbishop Gauti can only speak highly of the priest."

Raseire's expression turned to one of puzzlement. "Priest de Saint-Martin, I have not heard the name."

Boutarra butted in, "He's from Vésoul; he's never had a district, he's based in Rome."

"I still haven't heard of his name."

Cross declared, "Oh, you will."

"That sounds threatening, and how can a priest become a bishop if he's never had a district?" Raseire shook his head with dismay.

Cross shrugged his shoulders. "I am just warning you, that's all. Your extravagance has been duly noted, so be prepared for it to come to an end. They know about you purchasing five separate plots of land at Rennes-le-Château in the name of Marianna Fanjeaux, the woman you live with."

Chapter Seven
A Senseless Killing

On the 5th of October 1902, at six p.m. in Fontfroide Abbey, Narbonne, South of France, Christina Cacatier cried out in agony on the altar of the chapel, as Dr Goodman and Nurse Crouse felt joy within their hearts, but looked on with trepidation. Priest Bertrand Raseire, Priest Etienne Boutarra and Bishop Paul Louis Caraman of Portu Satis Tuto knelt beside the altar, praying as a bright warm light surrounded it.

"Breathe deeply through your nose, Christina, and out through the mouth," Nurse Crouse spoke softly but sternly, with a mild German accent. "You are nearly there with your second baby."

Dr Goodman asserted in a well-spoken Bavarian voice, "Pant if it's too painful to breathe deeply, Christina."

Christina leant back and pulled her knees into her chest to open up her pelvis.

Nurse Crouse adjusted the birthing cover. "The baby is there, Christina, I can see the head. On your next contraction take a deep cleansing breath, chin on your chest, now… I want you to push gently and exhale with your push."

Christina cried out, "Ahhhhhhhh," as she exhaled, lifted her chin, took a deep breath and placed her chin back down and voiced, "Ah, ah, ah, ah." She then breathed deeply.

"You're almost there, cleansing breaths, Christina." Dr Goodman reassured her, "The head is almost out."

Christina cried out once more, "Ahhhhhhhhh."

The baby slipped into Nurse Crouse's hands. She then placed the delivered baby in a towel and wiped away the membrane from the baby's airways. She tapped the baby's bottom to stimulate a cry. The baby let out one huge cry and fell silent.

Dr Goodman smiled from ear to ear. "You have another girl, Christina, monozygotic twins, identical twins. Congratulations."

"Muscle tone is good, heart rate good, reflex good, good color on the body with bluish hands and feet and baby has a good strong cry." Nurse Crouse smiled with relief. "Now you need to push again on the next contraction to deliver the placenta, Christina. Then you may hold your babies."

Christina smiled, pale with tiredness, her strawberry blonde hair tousled over her face as she panted and pushed with all her might. "Ahhhhh!"

Dr Goodman placed the placenta in a bowl and covered it.

Nurse Crouse placed one of the newborn baby girls in Christina's arms. "She's your first born, what are you going to call her?"

"I am compelled to call her Mary, although the meaning of her name is beloved, bitter and rebellious. She will always be dearly loved, although I am hoping she will not be bitter and rebellious." Christina peered into the baby's eyes. "Mary has a different shaped iris on her left eye."

Dr Goodman peered at Mary's eye. "So she does."

He then walked over to the other baby, held by Sister Crouse and peered in her eyes. "Well, you will be able to tell them apart by their left eye."

Sister Crouse chipped in, "Mary does not seem to want to suckle. Would you like to name your other baby, hold her and see if she is hungry?"

"Yes," Christina declared.

Dr Goodman took Mary and turned to show Priest Raseire, Priest Boutarra and Bishop Caraman. He made the sign of the cross on Mary's forehead with his forefinger.

Nurse Crouse placed the younger baby into the arms of Christina. She said, "My daughter shall be called Florence; the meaning of her name is blossoming in faith and in belief." Florence suckled for a short time and then fell asleep.

Christina looked upwards with her striking blue eyes at the huge, glowing gold crucifix, while sat up in bed. "Thank you, Lord, for my healthy baby girls. They shall know who their father is one day."

Nurse Crouse smiled with joy. "Christina, you need to rest. Your babies are content." She outstretched her arms, picked up baby Florence, and then passed her to Bishop Caraman. He made the sign of the cross on Florence's forehead with his forefinger.

Sister Crouse wheeled Christina and her bed out of the chapel, saying, "I'll be back shortly."

The dark sandstone walls of Fontfroide Abbey were lit with huge medieval torches, as Sister Crouse pushed Christina to her bedroom. By the time they arrived Christina was asleep. Sister Crouse did not have the heart to move her from one bed to the other and so she left her in the bed she lay in. She turned and smiled, viewing the warm honeycomb-shaped bedroom with its maple herringbone floor before closing the door. As she began to walk up the dimly lit corridor, she noticed a manly-looking nun walking towards her carrying a pot of tea and toast on a tray.

Sister Crouse instantly tucked her chin in which made her look portlier than she actually was. "Can I help you?" she asked with curiosity.

The nun spoke softly. "Yes, Father Raseire asked me to bring this tray, after the birth of the baby."

She looked at the nun suspiciously and repeated the word, "Baby."

"Yes," the nun said.

"Christina is sleeping and will not need any tea and toast at this moment in time, you may go and enjoy them yourself." She stared at the nun through her black-rimmed, goggle-like glasses that emphasized her brown, glaring eyes.

"Very well." The nun turned and walked in the direction from which she came, while Nurse Crouse waited until she disappeared out of sight. She walked quickly back to the chapel where the four men were very much beguiled by the twins.

"Father Raseire, could you answer my question, please?" Nurse Crouse asked with concern.

Raseire looked confused. "I will try."

"Did you ask for tea and toast for Christina?"

Raseire scoffed, "No, I did not."

Dr Goodman looked on with horror in his eyes.

Nurse Crouse shook her head in disbelief. "I thought something was not quite right, the nun had cold, dark brown eyes that looked lifeless as if there was no soul within his body. Oh, I say this because the nun was a man. I am sure of it."

Raseire asserted, "We need to get to Christina immediately."

Dr Goodman affirmed, "You stay here with the babies, Nurse Crouse and I will make sure Christina is all right."

The two hurried to Christina's bedroom. The door was closed as Nurse Crouse left it. When they opened the door, the tray of tea and toast lay on the floor untouched, next to Christina's bed.

They hurried to Christina. Dr Goodman felt for her pulse, over the carotid artery, placing his index and middle fingers on Christina's neck.

His albino eyes started to water. "I… I can't feel a pulse, nein, nein, nein!" He then placed his right ear above her left breast, listening for a heartbeat. He looked up at nurse Crouse and uttered the word, "Nein." At the same time, he placed his palm on Christina's forehead and gently tilted her head back and lifted Christina's chin so her mouth was open. He positioned the heel of his hand in the middle of her chest, just below the nipple line and situated his other hand on top. With his arms straight he started pumping his hands with pressure and releasing pressure, making sure Christina's chest rose, before he applied the next quick compression. He pushed thirty quick compressions and then took two puffs in her mouth, then started pumping his hands again. He shouted out to Nurse Crouse, "Why?" He nodded his head while repeating the procedure several times before collapsing, kneeling to the floor and sobbing.

Nurse Crouse, teary-eyed, spotted a small amount of blood on Christina's chest. She removed the white cotton cross over nightdress from Christina's left chest and noticed a small amount of blood on the surface of her pale skin. "There's a puncture wound over her heart. What could have caused her heart failure so quickly?"

Dr Goodman shook his head. "I am not sure, but I promise to find out and make sure whoever has done this suffers. The babies are in grave danger; we need to relocate them immediately. Bishop Caraman must return to Portu Satis Tuto with Christina's body."

Chapter Eight
Battle of the Wills

Priest Arnaud Tournebouix and Cross hiked through the mountain ridges of Rennes-les-Bains. Cross was not there for Tournebouix's running commentary of Boutarra's Dromlech circular tour or to discuss the meeting point of the Tectosages. They were of no interest to him. He had an ulterior motive. He wanted to know much more about Raseire. Bishop de Saint-Martin had gone quiet on him, now that the trial had been held; there had been no word from Rome and he did not like the silence.

The 1st of February 1915, was particularly warm in Rennes-les-Bains for the time of year although the grass was still blighted by Old Man Winter.

Tournebouix stopped to look at the view of the wintery valley with Cross trailing behind him. He took a deep breath in, savoring the clean, crisp, infused air with the scent of spruce trees before exhaling out. Cross was panting to catch up; he was only thirteen years older than the lean, muscular Priest Tournebouix but his age had begun to show.

Tournebouix called out, "You need to hike more often, Cross, and breathe in this wonderful fresh air God has created for us." He took another deep breath and exhaled slowly as Cross arrived, gasping, trying to catch his breath.

Tournebouix commented, "You can smell spring is in the air."

Cross sniffed a little, it's all he could manage as he placed his hands on his hips, slowing his breath and looking around him.

Tournebouix gazed around mesmerized. "I truly love this place. Here you can stare up and see the Mountain of Horns and look down on Alaric's Grave. Sixty million years ago all of this area was abundant with Poekilopleuron, Ampelosaurus, Struthiosaurus, and Telmatosaurus."

Cross seemed a little puzzled. "Were they ancestors of the Tectosages?"

Tournebouix chuckled, "No, I am talking about dinosaurs. Would you like to hear about them?"

"I'd really like to hear about Raseire; do you know if he has heard from Rome yet?" Cross replied.

Tournebouix's smile depleted. "I am really not at liberty to say."

Cross cupped his chin with his right hand then rubbed the sweat off his forehead into his dark blond hair. "Well, how about I tell you what I know and then maybe you will trust me enough to tell me what you know."

Tournebouix did not react and so Cross continued, "I think we will both need to sit down for this." Both men sat on the dry grass.

Cross continued, "This is what I know so far. On the 19th of January 1909, Bishop de Saint-Martin sent a letter to Raseire, informing him of his new appointment as Priest of Coustouges. Outraged, Raseire resigned from his duties as Priest of Rennes-le-Château on the 29th of January. Bishop de Saint-Martin persecuted Raseire, wanting to know where Raseire got his money. He was hell-bent on breaking him to find out. In defiance Raseire set up a temporary chapel in the conservatory of the Villa Bethania, leaving the new priest with an empty chapel."

"Yes, I remember this, the battle of the wills," Tournebouix acknowledged.

Cross smiled wryly and continued, "Bishop de Saint-Martin was infuriated by Raseire's actions. So he took Raseire to court on three charges, on the 16th of July 1910. Raseire was ordered to appear on the 23rd of July at the Carcassonne court to answer the charges. He did not appear. He was ordered to appear again on the 23rd of August; it seemed he was having trouble getting legal representation and so the date was changed to the 15th of October, where once again he was not present but his lawyer was. The court deferred judgment to the 5th of November.

Tournebouix nodded his head. "How do you know all of this?"

Cross rolled his eyes. "I work for Bishop de Saint-Martin from time to time and delivered most of the letters to Raseire's house. I also have a photographic memory."

Tournebouix scratched his bald head, feeling a little awkward.

Cross raised his eyebrows and continued. "Raseire finally attended court. He was not convicted of the first charge (trafficking the masses), but he was found guilty of culpable negligence in his accountancy procedures. The second charge and the third charge of disobedience followed because he continued to traffic the masses, even though he was told not to. He was sentenced to withdraw to a retreat house and undertake spiritual exercises for ten days. They ordered him to do this within two months of the present date. He also needed to present Bishop de Saint-Martin with detailed accounts within one month. On the 17th November 1910, he was advised in writing by T. Person, the Dean of Couiza, indicating he had ten days to appeal."

"He appealed, but he was too late. Why, I really don't know." Tournebouix acknowledged.

Cross' brown eyes narrowed. "Yes, he appealed on the 30th of November. De Saint-Martin had great satisfaction in knowing his sentence had already begun on the 28th of November. On the 5th of December, he was informed he was no longer allowed to say mass under any circumstances. On the 17th of December, Raseire failed to produce his accounts. Instead, Raseire's lawyer sent a letter of appeal against the judgment to Rome. Does he have friends in high places there?"

"It sounds like he has, but I have no idea who that can be. Priest Boutarra would certainly know more than I. I do know that the congregation of the Holy Sacrament judged the case obscure." Tournebouix furrowed his eyebrows.

"Yes, they did, Rome had not resolved the matter and the case was handed back to the bishop, much to his pleasure, back to the court of Carcassonne. On the 9th of March 1911, C. Pyre, Vicar General of the court of Carcassonne, acknowledged that Raseire had a doctor's note from Dr S. Raou, declaring that Raseire's ill health did not permit him to undertake the spiritual exercises at the retreat house, and therefore, he could not carry out his sentence for his accountability on counts two and three."

Tournebouix pulled out a blade of dry grass and started to chew on it.

Cross continued, "However, Raseire does manage to write to the court providing receipts already accepted by the court and a certificate from the mortgage registry on 13th of March. As to his total expenses of 193,150 francs, he would try to vindicate what expenses he could but he had not bothered to save receipts for more than two years. Altogether he sent sixty-one documents and asked for their return, as it was essential for his personal security. Do you know why that would be?"

Tournebouix pulled the blade of grass away from his mouth. "I'm not sure, but it sounds like he had to provide the receipts to someone else who would harm him if he did not have them. Very ominous indeed."

Cross nonchalantly replied, "Yes. Raseire then sent another letter on the 25th of March to Pyre explaining the money he had received originated from various incomes, funds from collection boxes, including Rennes-les-Bains, a lottery, his brother's generosities, sales from postcards and his collection of one hundred thousand postage stamps, the occasional sale of furniture and income from lectures of the history of Rennes-le-Château, giving him an annual income of 1200 francs from 1885 to 1910."

"He's quite an entrepreneur," Tournebouix jested.

"I would even go as far as to say he's corrupt. You see on the 4th of April 1911, Montserver, Clerk of the Court, stated that Raseire's reply was very deficient. He wanted to know what documents he had used to calculate the annual income of 1200 francs from the collection boxes. The figure Raseire stated would have roughly meant he would receive 23 francs per week. Montserver also wanted to know the dates of his brother's largest donations. He also stated that the sequence of documents he provided gave a total sum of 36,000 francs. There was still a discrepancy of 161,150 francs that were unaccounted for."

Tournebouix lifted his eyebrows in shock. "That's a lot of money. If Raseire had that much money, why was he taking money from the collection box at Rennes-les-Bains? More to the point, why was Boutarra letting him take it? It does not make sense."

Cross smiled wryly. "It does if Boutarra was in cahoots with him."

Tournebouix's green, beady eyes narrowed with thought.

Cross continued to talk. "On the 6th of April Raseire hit back, writing a letter to Montserver expressing his disappointment relating to the information he had provided. He stated he had not kept accounts from collection boxes; however, he did state his brother's donations were received between 1895 and 1903. He asked why he, as priest, had been required to submit such detailed accounts, that were normally only required when there's a commercial bankruptcy. Bishop de Saint-Martin saw Raseire wriggling out of his clutches, so he had to change tactics. On the 9th of April, he launched a Commission of Enquiry to resolve the issue and guess what?"

Tournebouix shrugged his shoulders, then answered, "They did not really progress any further."

Cross produced a sardonic grin. "They did, much to Ussat, the president of the commissions, and to the bishop's delight. He did not accept Raseire's accounts and explanations on the 9th of May. I believe Raseire was really getting tired of the whole situation; he called it a 'witch-hunt'. On the 14th of May Raseire replied, stating he was not prepared to submit to any further interrogation. Ussat made yet another request for information, which occurred on the 7th of July. Surprisingly, Raseire provided some of the information on the 14th of July. He declared the total cost of building Villa Bethania to be 90,000 francs and informed Ussat the work had commenced in 1901 and was completed in 1903. However, the entire estate was in the name of Marianna Fanjeaux. Thereafter, there were no further requests for more details; they had finally found some mud that would stick to him. So without further ado, the commission began to write its report. Their verdict was that Raseire had used church funds personally rather than through the bishop's office. Worse still he used the funds to build Villa Bethania on land that was owned by his housekeeper, Marianna Fanjeaux. He was deemed to be a serious problem, having taken money that had come from the diocese to enrich his own life, with no benefit to the community. However, they never found out where the large sums of money came from."

Tournebouix furrowed his eyebrows. "I was totally unaware that such proceedings had gone on." He took a bottle of water out from his backpack, pulled out the cork and sipped from the bottle.

Cross continued to talk. "On the 5th of December 1911, the court held a session, though neither Raseire nor his lawyer attended court. He was declared contumacious and overtly defiant of authority and he was judged as such. The court stated that 36,000 out of 197,150 francs had been spent on the church; the rest had been spent on costly constructions with no useful purpose, on land that did not belong to him and was not even built in his name. He was found guilty of improvidence and mismanagement of funds in his care. He was sentenced to three months suspension, but indefinitely until the goods of the church were returned."

Tournebouix commented, "I can't imagine how I would spend 161,150 francs on my own personal use."

Cross chuckled, "Oh I can... Anyway, Bishop de Saint-Martin could only validate the sentence for six months. He was furious about that and Raseire's appeal to Rome, which was sent immediately after the sentence had expired. Raseire was not as clever as Bishop Rolland."

Tournebouix looked puzzled once again. "What does Bishop Rolland have to do with this?"

Cross sniggered. "Tournebouix, you surprise me with your naivety... Bishop Rolland was bequeathed 2,200,000 francs in his own name from Saissa Cacatier of Coursan around the same time Raseire amassed his wealth, except it was not in his own name as Rolland's bounty was. If it had been, then Bishop de Saint-Martin could not have taken him to court or persecuted him as he has done. Do you know why they were rewarded with huge amounts of money?"

Tournebouix, feeling uncomfortable with the question, did not answer; he placed his water bottle back in his pack, stared Cross in the eye and stood. "We need to be getting back."

Cross stood. "Sure. I would like to see the Devil's Armchair on our way back if that's all right?"

"Yes, of course." Tournebouix smiled as he started walking, feeling relieved Cross was not pushing him to answer the question. "The Devil's Armchair is quite an attraction for some strange reason; it's well over five thousand years old, yet it has the Swiss cross engraved on it. I have my suspicions that the Swiss and Swiderians are kin and the Swiss flag symbol dates back a lot further than the 13th century."

"Interesting, but not quite as interesting as to where Raseire's money came from. Do you know Bishop Caraman? I think he's part of Raseire's alliance."

Tournebouix seemed shocked at Cross's comment and repeated the name. "Bishop Caraman... are you saying Priest Paul Louis Caraman of Alet-les-Bains, has been made a bishop?"

Cross rubbed his head. "Priest Caraman has disappeared from the diocese. There does not seem to be any mention of him anywhere or of

Bishop Caraman, but we both know he exists." Cross tutted with disapproval. "You really don't know anything about Raseire, do you?"

Tournebouix laughed. "I didn't but I do now."

Cross looked away annoyed, then turned back with a sardonic grin on his face. "I think we have earned ourselves a little tipple, Raseire's affairs are certainly enough to drive one to drink." He chuckled as he took out a small silver flask from his pocket and twisted the lid. "Well, that's my excuse and I am sticking to it. Would you like to try some Brugerolle cognac? Bishop Rolland gave me a few bottles of it before he sadly passed away. It's very soothing." Before Tournebouix answered, Cross took the flask and raised it. "Here's to your good health, my friend." He pretended to swig the cognac and gasped, "Arrrr, if it's good enough for Napoleon it's certainly good enough for us." He handed the flask to Tournebouix, who looked indecisive and did not take it. "It's bad manners, Tournebouix, not to toast my good health."

Tournebouix smiled and took the flask from Cross. "Well, if you put it like that how can I refuse?" He raised the flask and announced, "Here's to your good health." He took a few gulps of the cognac, then sipped a little more and savored the taste. "It's very smooth, although I am not sure it warrants the price." He handed the flask back to Cross.

Cross reacted by shaking his head. "No, no, no, have a little more. It will probably be the first and last time you have it. I have nearly finished my last bottle and it's far too expensive for me to buy."

Tournebouix took a few more sips and handed the flask back to Cross. He took it, turned the top on the flask and placed it back in his jacket pocket. The two started to walk down to the forest towards the Devil's Armchair in Rennes-les-Bains.

"Oh, that Brugerolle cognac is rather strong, it's numbed my throat," Tournebouix remarked.

"Do you know much about the Cathars?" Cross asked.

"A little. Castle of Montségur is just beyond Rennes-le-Château. On a clear day you can see the castle. They were dualists with Jewish-Christian beliefs, like the gnostics from the 1st century AD and because their beliefs differed from the Catholic Church they were deemed as heretics and slaughtered." Tournebouix appeared engrossed in his own thought.

Cross broke the silence. "Yes, Pope Innocent III initiated the Cathar Crusade together with King Phillip II, in 1209. Pope Honorius III, and Pope Gregory IX continued it and Pope Celestine IV finished it, so he thought. I am amazed that all three kings of France, Phillip II, Louis VIII, and Louis IX authorized French Catholic soldiers to torture and kill peace-loving people. Why? Well, the Cathars were affiliated with Mary Magdalene. Like the Gnostics before them, they assigned more importance to the role of Mary Magdalene. She was after all the one Jesus loved the most. The Gnostics helped to spread the words of early Christianity and Mary's spirited role as a teacher which contributed to the Cathar belief that women could serve as spiritual leaders, too."

Tournebouix shook his head. Cross looked sternly at Tournebouix. "Do you believe that Mary Magdalene came ashore to Saintes-Maries-de-la-Mer? That's just forty-seven hours of walking time from here."

"There is no conclusive evidence that she did, so I do not believe she did. Although we do know Mary Magdalene was a spiritual leader and the Catholic Church would not approve of having any woman as a spiritual leader."

Cross grinned. "I do, I am sure of it. The Cathars and Gnostics in France were evidence of that. I have also been very privileged to glance at a parchment that acknowledges Mary's very existence of being here. Anyway, I'll continue with the barbarous treatment and murders of the remaining three hundred and ninety-seven Cathars, who retreated to Mount Montségur in 1243. They were peaceful people, non-materialistic. They believed in 'Thou shall not kill'; they did not eat mammal meat — only fish, fruits, nuts, and vegetables. They believed if they ate mammal meat their spirit would no longer be pure, as the animal killed had a spirit entrapped in it and the entrapped spirit would become entrapped in their body. They loved cats and had lots around them, frequently kissing them. Their homes were called 'The House of God'. Raseire's church has the words 'This is God's House, The Gate of Heaven' written above the entrance to the church. All very fitting to Cathar beliefs, if you are asking me."

Tournebouix looked a little puzzled. "I am not so sure about that, h-h-h-however he has many c-c-cats and only eats fish. I... I am f-f-f-finding i-i-i-it d-d-d-d-difficult t-t-t-t-to s-s-s-speak."

Cross continued with passion and conviction in his voice. "What I find most interesting of all is that there were divines within the Cathars. I believe these divines are descendants from Jesus and Mary Magdalene, the Holy Grail itself." Cross stopped walking and looked at Tournebouix for a reaction. He continued walking with his brow-furrowed.

"P-p-p-please c-c-c-c-continue, C-c-c-cross, y-y-y-your t-t-t-thoughts a-a-a-are i-i-i-interesting."

Cross, a little flummoxed by Tournebouix's reaction. He collected his thoughts and continued walking and talking. "These divines were called 'Perfecti or the perfect ones'. Their name was given to them by Bernard of Clairvaux, who was instrumental in acquiring the recognition of the new order of the Knights Templar, and formed the rules for the fighting Cistercian monks." Cross stopped walking, Tournebouix, too. "Don't you find it interesting that St. Bernard knew about the divines of the Cathars? I believe he created the Knights Templar to protect the Perfecti. After all they were Christ's soldiers."

Tournebouix suddenly started to wheeze. Cross did not take notice; he was far too passionate about his findings. "The Perfecti were in direct communication with God, their prayers could reach God's ear. They were God's hands on earth, they healed the sick and instigated miracles. Does this sound familiar?"

"Y-y-y-yes… J-j-j-jesus p-p-p-erformed m-m-m-miracles, b-b-b-but a normal p-p-person c-c-can pray and r-r-r-reach God's e-e-ear!" Tournebouix's wheeze turned quickly into panting.

Cross grinned and continued to talk. "You are on the ball. On the 1st of March 1244, the Catholic forces captured the Castle of Montségur, the Cathars were offered lenient terms on the 3rd of March if they surrendered; they did not surrender. After all, they were the only ones left of their kind. I suspect they did not believe in the leniency that was being offered, with just cause. So, they requested a two-week truce in order for them to consider the terms. On the night of the 15th of March, two Perfecti, one Crednti Cathar, and a guide from the Knights Templar descended the castle wall of Mount Montségur; a death-defying act brought on by desperation. It was said they had the sacred parchments, written by Mary Magdalene. I have glanced at a fragment of the parchment."

Tournebouix bent his body to touch his toes. Cross looked on nonchalantly. He knew why Tournebouix was bending.

"Are you, all right?" Cross asked with insincerity.

Tournebouix breathed deeply and stood. "N-n-n-no, I-I-I-I a-a-a-a-am f-f-f-f-feeling o-o-out of-f-f-f-f b-b-b-b-breath." He looked baffled but shrugged his shoulders and voiced, "W-w-we m-m-m-must m-m-make h-h-h-haste. Please continue, I think I k-k-k-know where this is leading... Y-y-y-you think the p-p-p-parchments the Cathars w-w-were carrying w-w-were the s-s-s-same p-p-p-parchments R-r-raseire f-f-f-found in the c-h-hurch of S-s-saint Mary M-m-m-magdalene."

"It would make sense, it's totally possible for them to have made their way to the church, it takes ten hours on foot. I know, I have done it." Cross combed his hair back with his fingers. "Although the parchments that Raseire found were too small, I think they were clues as to where the Sacred parchment was with the list of bearings and the names of the Perfecti. Nevertheless, I cannot make much sense of the link between the bearings and surnames, all except one: Cacatier of Coursan and Saissa Cacatier, Bishop Rolland's wealthy widow, the one who bequeathed him 2, 200, 000 francs. However, the bearings also seem to be linked to Black Madonnas around the world in places where the Templars worshiped."

Tournebouix looked puzzled. "F-f-first of all, s-s-s-surely the church was not built at t-t-that time, in 1244?" He stopped again to catch his breath, placing his hands on his shoulders and taking deep breaths. "S-s-secondly... when did you g-g-glance at the s-s-s-sacred parchment and the list of b-b-bearings... with s-s-surnames? T-t-thirdly." He stopped talking to take in deep breaths.

Cross continued. "Firstly. The original church dates back to the 8th century, but it was most probably in ruins when the Perfecti hid the parchments. As to when the list of names and bearings were hidden there, I don't know, but it was most likely when the Holy Inquisition of the Knights Templar was rampant. It makes sense to hide the cryptic parchment in a Catholic church, for the church would not be searched; also, it just goes to show how desperate the Pope felt threatened by the Perfecti. He had thousands tortured in the most horrific ways and killed thousands and thousands of innocent people. Why? Because they had different religious beliefs — and heaven forbid, the Perfecti threatened many beliefs and the Holy Bible, it would need to be re-written. The religious beliefs of the Knights Templars had never changed. They were Christ's soldiers; the very men that were originally fighting Cistercian monks were no longer fighting for their Pope. Pope Clement V knew why, he had the Templars interrogated, tortured and killed.

"Why? Because they knew the Templars knew the truth and were protecting the Perfecti, the divine ones of Jesus's bloodline. So, Rome devised a plan to interrogate the Templars. They did so, but to no avail. So they killed the Templars in France and deemed them as devil worshipers. King Philip IV was glad to help, it was his chance to erase the huge amount of debt he owed to the wealthy Templars, plus he could acquire their riches too. God must have been furious. On 18th of March 1314, King Philip had Jacques de Molay, the Grand Master, and Geoffroi de Charney, Master of Normandy, the last known Templars in France burnt alive. They were placed on the scaffold on an island in the River Seine in front of Notre Dame de Paris. Molay appealed to the true living God, who is in Heaven, warning Pope Clement V and King Philip that within a year and a day they would be obliged to answer for their heinous crimes in God's presence. They both died within the year." Cross did not answer the rest of Tournebouix's questions; he stared at him in a sinister way. The two were now deep in the woods of Rennes-les-Bains, where the decaying leaves had lost their vibrant colors, although, they were still abundant on the rocky terrain. "Looks like you need to hike more often, Tournebouix, and breathe in this wonderful fresh air God has created for us."

Tournebouix rolled his eyes and bent his body to touch his knees and muttered, "I really don't feel well. E-e-everything i-i-is b-b-blurred and g-g-g-greeny y-y-yellow."

"I think you need to sit down. I can see the Devil's Armchair from here, you only have a few more steps to go." Cross hooked Tournebouix under his arm with his hand, and bent to the same level as Tournebouix, to make eye contact with him. His dark brown, malevolent eyes looked into Tournebouix's green, exhausted eyes. "I will help you, my friend, you need to sit down."

The two stood up slowly. Tournebouix began to hobble from lack of oxygen as Cross supported his every step. Cross eased Tournebouix into the armchair and giggled. "I must say it's rather fitting for a Catholic priest to be sitting in the Devil's Armchair." He tilted his head to his left shoulder and stared at Tournebouix until he took his last breath. Cross crossed Tournebouix's arms on his chest and bellowed out, "Viva Angelina."

On the 18th of October 1915, the Congregation at Rome finally delivered their judgment on Priest Raseire, thus Bishop de Saint-Martin removed Raseire's suspension. Thereafter Raseire was never reinstated as Priest of Rennes-le-Château.

Chapter Nine
The Confrontation

On 22nd January 1917, eight years to the day when Raseire was supposed to become the new parish priest of Coustouges, Cross knocked on the door of Villa Bethania. There was no immediate answer as he gazed around the large lush manicured cottage garden of Priest Raseire. He was surprised to see so much green for the time of year, it was as if winter had never arrived. The late morning sun had started to make him sweat as he wiped his brow with a neatly folded handkerchief. There was no answer; he decided to peer through the arched window next to the door. As he did so, a large white cat with sky-blue eyes, gazed back at him. He smiled at the pretty cat and in return for his smile the cat hissed at him; his steadfast glare at the cat, left it unfazed. A larger white cat with green eyes and long hair suddenly joined the first cat, it too hissed. Cross scowled and knocked on the door once more. A petite, middle-aged woman with olive-toned skin and kind brown eyes peered around the door. The two stared at each other for a short time.

Cross interrupted the silence. "It's me, Marianna, Deacon Cross, except I am not a deacon any more."

Marianna looked Cross up and down, then all of a sudden, her face lit up with recognition. "Ah, Cross, I did not realize who you were without your cassock and you have grown your hair long; you look like a charlatan."

Cross appeared a little baffled by Marianna's words. He questioned, "A charlatan?"

Marianna smiled. "Well, that's not entirely what I was meaning to say, but you do look different with that basin haircut, it detracts from your handsomeness. I much prefer you with short barbered hair." She opened the door and two silver long-haired cats ran out, hissing at Cross on their way past him. "The cats don't seem to like you, Cross," Marianna teased.

Cross smiled. "I think it's because they sense I don't like them. Well, it's not so much that I don't like them, it's because they make me sneeze and give me hives."

Marianna looked Cross in the eye and stared at him in silence for a short time before she spoke. "So what brings you to Villa Bethania, after all these years?"

"I've come to see the Abbé and congratulate him on his triumph," Cross asserted.

"Triumph!" Marianna ridiculed.

"Yes, it was triumphant in the end. He won the battle against Bishop de Saint Martin — the battle of the wills."

"He does not see it as a triumph, he's lost his church. You had better come in; I am sure he will be happy to see you after all these years."

Cross walked over the threshold of the door and was instantly hit by the aroma of baked goods. "Mmmmm. freshly baked bread. There is no mistaking that aroma."

Marianna smiled and jested, "I am afraid it's salmon en croute, we are having it for lunch. If Ade is happy for you to stay for lunch, then I'll set another place at the table. He's sitting in the conservatory; I'll go and tell him you're here."

Cross closed the door behind him and looked around the sparse hallway, with its magnolia-colored walls and blue and cream-colored decorated forget-me-not floor tiles. He was surprised, expecting it to be opulent, given the fortune Villa Bethania had cost. He turned around to look at the two cats sat on the windowsill, staring at him, watching his every move. He hissed at them, they in turn hissed back and dashed down the hallway.

"Oh, my goodness," Marianna scoffed as the cats almost ran into her. "Limoux and Maurina, you two will be the death of me one day. He's happy to see you, Cross, would you like to stay for lunch?"

"Yes, please. It's been a while since I have eaten a tasty meal." He rubbed his stomach in jest.

"Very well, I'll set you a place at the dining table. Adrienne would like to see you in the conservatory. It will be far easier if you walk around the kitchen garden to the conservatory, rather than tread mud through the house." Marianna looked down at Cross's muddy shoes.

In turn, Cross looked down and spoke, "Yes, of course, which way is the kitchen garden?"

"Out the door and to your right."

Cross opened the door as the two grey cats entered the house, both hissing as they ran past him. Marianna shook her head and laughed watching Cross close the door. He muttered, "God darn cats," as he began walking through the manicured gardens, smelling the scent of magnolias and pine trees. He turned the corner into the kitchen garden and instantly he could see Priest Adrienne Bertrand Raseire busily pruning a plant in the conservatory. He stopped for a short time and stared, and whispered, "Viva Angelina," tapping on the window to distract Raseire.

Raseire looked up and stared at Cross, then smiled and jested, "I didn't recognize you for a minute, you have grown your hair yet have a bad haircut." He stared at Cross for a while who was dressed in a cream woven woolen suit and held his hand out to shake Cross'. "It certainly has been a long time since I have had the pleasure of your company."

Cross shook Raseire's hand. "It most certainly has been too long. I am afraid I could not come to visit you, due to a conflict of interests with Bishop de Saint Martin. He occasionally employs my services as an errand boy, and pays me generously."

Raseire laughed. "Errand boy! You're dressed exceptionally well for an errand boy. Anyway, you are more than fifty years old. The last time we talked, you warned me I would know Priest de Saint Martin's name very well and that he would become bishop. How did you know he was going to be such a thorn in my side and Bishop of Carcassonne? Do you have friends in high places?"

Cross raised his right eyebrow. "That was purely speculation on my part." He shrugged his shoulders. "Anyway, congratulations on winning the battle of the wills. It took you eight long years, but you defeated de Saint Martin. Rome favored you in the end. You must have friends in high places." He smiled his sardonic smile with his thin lips and slightly tilted his head to the left-hand side.

Raseire laughed once more. "It would appear that they are not high enough, otherwise I'd be back in my church where I belong."

"Nonsense," Cross scoffed.

Raseire looked flummoxed.

Cross sat across from Raseire on a rattan chair. "I think they think it's time for you to take it easy; after all you're sixty-four years old."

"That's exactly Marianna's sentiment too. I guess it's time to accomplish my other goals." Raseire smiled as he continued pruning the hibiscus plant.

Cross narrowed his dark brown eyes. "What are your goals now, if you don't mind me asking?"

"Well, self-preservation for one; two, Marianna would like an automobile, so I am going to need to pave the road to Villa Bethania and learn how to drive. I would also like to build a twin tower to the Magdalena tower. I plan to build it to the east of the existing tower."

Cross furrowed his eyebrows before talking. "Twin towers, why?"

"Because there should have been two in the first place, the Gemini towers of Magdalene."

"You must still have a tidy sum left in savings if you are going to do what you say." Cross took out his silver flask from his jacket pocket and screwed off the top. "I want to toast your good health and happiness and can't think of a better way to do it other than sipping on the citrus flavor of Brugerolle cognac." He pretended to swig the cognac, and then handed Raseire the flask.

Raseire took the silver flask and sipped the cognac. "To your good health and happiness too." He sipped it once more and handed the flask back to Cross. "I can certainly taste more citrus than usual."

"I agree, the aged cognac really brings out the citrus flavor, it's from Bishop Rolland's vintage stash." Cross smiled falsely. "Talking about Bishop Rolland, I hope you are going to be more cautious with your income like he was. He had his main donations bequeathed to him in his own name, like the two million francs he received from Cacatier of Coursan."

Raseire's dark blue eyes narrowed. "How do you know the name, Cacatier?"

Cross laughed in jest before answering. "I know much more than you think, my friend. I know that Rolland received many large amounts of money. Why? Because he knew a secret, the same secret you know." He took a deep breath then voiced the words, "Perfecti, the divine ones."

Raseire's olive-toned skin paled; he repeated the word "Perfecti."

"Yes, that is what I said. I know they exist, but I don't know where. I have read the previous correspondence between you and Bishop Rolland. The most interesting piece was part of the Sacred Parchment, confirming Mary Magdalene and Jesus had children. With it was a list of names and bearings, the two connect to each other and yet are centuries apart. It is my belief the Cathars left a parchment in your church on the night of the 16th of March 1244. The parchment they left was coded so it would only be revealed to a certain sect. Once the code was figured out, the message it revealed would unveil where the Sacred Parchment was." His eyes narrowed. "The Templars a century later added a list of surviving Perfecti names and bearings, written on parchment paper, they wrapped them around the Sacred Parchment. The bearings would lead to the location of the surviving Perfecti. All was still hidden from the world until you found the cryptic parchment hidden in your church. I want to read the rest of the Sacred Parchment. Do you have it?"

Raseire frowned and thought a while before he answered. "I still have the coded parchment which was found while renovating the church. You can read it if you like. However, I do not know about the Sacred Parchment or the list of names with bearings. Rolland had the connections, that's why he received far more money than I ever did."

Cross gestured no with his head and mocked, "Why are you still receiving money then?"

"I don't need to answer that question. I think it's time you went on your way. Marianna can feed your fish to the cats." Raseire stared at Cross, angered by his questions.

"I am sorry I have offended you, I just thought I could help in some way. That parchment and the list of names are worth a fortune." Cross looked sorrowful.

"You have most certainly offended me and the only way you can make it right is to go." Raseire walked over to the conservatory door and beckoned Cross to walk through. "Au revoir," he scoffed.

Cross still looked sorrowful as he walked out the door with clenched fists, like a scorned boy. Raseire watched Cross as he turned the corner of the cottage garden.

Minutes later, Marianna walked through the connecting villa door to the conservatory, looking for Raseire and Cross. Priest Raseire was still pruning the hibiscus plant. "Where did Cross go?"

"He had to go, literally."

"Why?" asked Marianna with a dumbfounded look on her face.

"Because he had outstayed his welcome and there shall be no more questions on the matter, Marianna."

"Very well, Ade Raseire, your lunch is ready."

Raseire pouted. "I'm sorry but I have lost my appetite, my lips are tingly and my throat is numb all of a sudden, I must be coming d-d-down with a cold. S-s-save it for t-t-t-t-tomorrow."

Later on in the afternoon, Priest Raseire sat on his veranda enjoying the tranquility. He suddenly began to gasp, almost choking on his red wine. So, he rose to his feet and bent his body forward as he spat out the red wine, hoping to find relief. There was no relief; the slight exertion had made his breathing far worse. He managed to shriek, "M-ma-r-i-a-na," as he collapsed to the floor and drew his last breath.

Chapter Ten
A New Beginning

On the 10th of November 1918, it was a cold grey-sky morning. The Werneth hills were draped with sheets of mist and only the peaks could be seen. Daylight had dawned, though you could hardly tell through the variance of greys. Flo shivered as she sat beside her father, clinging to a bench for dear life. Her father was on a mission and time was of the essence. The cart filled with supplies roared as he drove the four horses hard.

Flo's voice rattled as the cart shook on the road. "The roads are incredibly muddy and treacherous, Pa, all because of being neglected for many years. The war has certainly seen to that."

Her father, focused on his mission only, did not respond.

"It has rained for so long. I cannot remember the last time I saw the sunshine, Pa, can you?"

"Nah, I can't, Flossy," he replied.

"The sun is shining in my heart today, Pa." She gazed at her father to see if he was smiling too, but he was totally engulfed with concentration. If the sun was shining in his heart today, he was certainly not showing it. His high cheekbones, pointed nose, and steel blue eyes, defined his hardened exterior.

Yesterday was the first time since before the war that she had seen him smile but at the same time she had noticed tears welling in his eyes and before they started flowing, he had made himself scarce. The celebrations were a bittersweet experience for him; he was riddled with a guilt that was pushing all he loved away, a guilt that was futile. The war had wounded him deeply.

Although Flo was only sixteen years old, she could see the war had torn her father apart. Somehow, he had blamed himself for the loss of his beloved sons, Richard and Archibald. There was no consoling him, the more anyone tried, the harder he pushed them away. He was punishing himself and falling into darkness but he just could not see it. Flo feared for her ma's happiness, for she was the one that he pushed away the most.

Just at that moment, the cart's front wheel hit a large pothole in the road. Flo screamed, "Ohhhhhhh, Pa!" as she lost her grip on the bench and was catapulted from the cart. The front left wheel was partially submerged in a deep muddy hollow, it rolled out as the rear left wheel followed before the cart came to a halt. Luckily for Flo, the ground was soft as her delicate body rolled in the mud uncontrollably. The ground and the sky seemed to blend into one to her conscious eyes. Finally, her tumbling stopped. She lay there dizzy, delirious and incoherent, and for a moment her thin, frail figure looked lifeless. The stillness in her sky-blue eyes misled her father, who started to panic. Was he to lose another child?

"Oh God, please don't take her too." His fingers fumbled as he unbuttoned her coat. "Flossy!" He placed his ear to her heart and listened for a heartbeat. "Ohhhhhhh, thank you, Lord," he said as he looked up at the sky, with tears in his eyes.

Flo soon came around as her father gently tapped her face a few times. "Flossy, wake up, wake up!" he spluttered, guilt-ridden.

Flo's eyes rolled, as she began to regain her vision, focusing on her father's piercing blue eyes. She was very much aware now of what happened, how she felt and might have looked. Her voice was weak. "P... Pa, what are we going to do?"

"What are we going to do?" The concerned and guilty look turned into one of puzzlement. "What do ya mean by 'what are we going to do', lass?"

Regaining her normal tone of speech, she said, "My clothes, Pa; they're all wet and muddy." She pulled on her bonnet that lay around her neck. "Look at the state of me."

Her bonnet was drenched with mud and there was barely any sign of it ever being white.

"Ahhhhhh, lass, your clothes will wash, and so will you for that matter. As long as there are no broken bones, that's all I'm worried about."

Flo could feel no pain but only despair. She was not fit for her first day of work at Chandringham House now.

"My only concern reet now is can ya walk, Flossy?"

"I think so, Pa, but right now all I feel like doing is wallowing away the day in this mud. Can you pick me up on your way home, Pa?"

"Ah, Flossy, what would be the good in that?" He shook his head with disapproval. "Take my hand and I'll help ya up!"

Flossy held her muddy-gloved hand out, her father clasped it and pulled Flo up. In an instant she stood up, her head hung low. She was no longer the proud girl that first stepped onto the cart at the beginning of the journey. Her father supported Flo with a tight grasp on her left arm while walking to the cart. Just as they reached the cart, Flo turned and looked at her father with a despondent expression and tearful eyes. "Pa, could we turn back? Please, I can't go looking like this!"

"Nay, Flossy. There's little time left. I need to get the supplies to Mrs Crabtree on time, or else I'll feel her wrath and you'll not step foot in Chandringham." He wiped the fallen tears from her cheek. "Flossy, stop worrying your pretty little head. Sometimes the best thing ya can do is not to think, wonder, or obsess. The cogs in your brain right now are clicking away; they're working that hard. I can 'ear 'em so just breathe and have faith that everything will work out for the best. Mrs Crabtree will take one look at ya and have ya cleaned up in no time." He smiled with sincerity in his eyes.

"Is there any semblance to your words, Pa?" she asked with doubt in her eyes.

"Eh, Flossy, you and ya posh words. I haven't a clue what ya mean."

"Any truth, Pa, I have heard Mrs Crabtree is a very cantankerous person, is she?"

"Na, lass." Ned shook his head as he smiled.

Flo stepped up onto the cart, as her father loosened his grip and let go of her arm.

"What on earth is Mrs Crabtree going to think of me, Pa? If only I could turn back time and cling on harder to the cart. I would not be in this state now, Pa." Flo shivered not only with the damp air but also with maimed pride. She no longer clung to the cart as if her life depended on it. So what if she was thrown off the cart once more? It would be no more embarrassing than how she felt now. Starting to concentrate on her breathing, she no longer gazed at her father or the ever-changing scenery that Mother Nature created. Instead, she sat withdrawn from all that surrounded her, staring at her muddied gloves as her strawberry blonde hair fell in her face. The cart found its own momentum and her body rocked in time.

Chapter Eleven
Nemo Me Impune Lacessit

Ned glanced at Flo's bedraggled body. "Don't worry, Flossy, like I said before, Mrs Crabtree will have ya cleaned up in no time and you'll be as good as new. So, pull yourself together, girl."

"I can't imagine that, Pa. I can only imagine Mrs Crabtree taking one look at me, nodding her head with repugnance, then turning me around and sending me right back from where I came. Then I can see all her other maids standing behind Mrs Crabtree laughing in the background and poking names at me. Ohhh, I can feel the humiliation now." Flo sat silent for a while as she clenched her fists.

Ned looked at Flo, then shook his head in disagreement; he then turned his attention to the road with a stern look on his face.

Flo piped up, "So what? So what if they call me names? You and Ma have always taught me that names would never hurt me and no matter what, I will live on. So, I'm going to stand up for myself and what is right, my exterior state is purely accidental. I'm a victim of circumstances. So I must pull myself together and overcome all the negative thoughts I have." She smiled. "Pa, you are soooooo right! I'll be cleaned up in no time and look as good as new."

Ned grinned, still keeping his eyes on the road.

Flo grabbed the corner bench of the cart, lifted her head and infused herself with pride once again. She looked up. Her jaw dropped as she viewed the golden gates of Chandringham.

"Oh, my goodness, Pa!" Flo hollered with joy.

The mist surrounding the lower part of the gates enhanced their golden glory.

"Wooooowww!" Flo muttered the words, "Are we in heaven, Pa?"

Flo's father chuckled. "Ah, lass, I think that fall 'as gone reet to ya 'ead!"

Flo was still aghast, as the cart pulled up to the gates and drew to a halt. Attached to either side of the gates were two sandstone turrets that stood almost symmetrical, lavishly designed, each one topped with a golden urn. On the lower tier of the turrets another golden urn was centrally placed and below the urn an inlaid circular lookout window with tracery stone embellishment denoted the splendor. Below each lookout window was a brightly lit doorway. Flo was surprised to see that each lantern was electric. "Look, Pa, they have electric! Even at the gatehouse."

"Ah, lass, they do. It's been 'ere for the best part of two years now."

The right turret had a small lodge attached to it. "I wonder what it would be like to live there, Pa?"

"I dunno," said Ned.

Flo's eyes marveled and for a brief moment, a thought adorned her vision. She could just see herself spinning around in a turret, her dress outstretched.

Just then an old, frail man stepped out of the right-turret doorway. He was smartly dressed in a double-breasted, brass buttoned, navy blue overcoat with gold braided epaulets and a matching navy top hat with a gold trimmed badge on it. Flo squinted, trying to make out the words underneath the coat of arms on the badge. The gatekeeper walked closer to the cart; it was only when he stood next to Flo, that she could make out the words.

"NEMO ME IMPUNE LACESSIT," she mumbled to herself. What does that mean?" She had never seen such words.

Flo's father stepped down from the cart and walked over to the gatekeeper. The gatekeeper smiled. "Mornin', Ned, and what a good mornin' it is!"

Flo's father replied, "Mornin' to ya, Jim, it's a bittersweet mornin' for me."

"Aye." With a sorrowful look in his eyes Jim said, "I can only imagine Ned. Sorry to hear about your lads. They were brave men. Without the likes of them, well, we would not be standing here, free, today."

Ned seemed lost for words and could only reply, "Aye."

Jim neither smiled nor frowned; his lips drew a straight line. "So, what have we 'ere, Ned?" he shouted as he walked around to the back of the cart.

"Mrs Crabtree's order, Jim. Our Flossy is also starting work today as a housemaid."

"Oh, is she?" looking Flo up and down.

Flo just sat there nonchalant, as Jim walked around the cart jingling his keys, emphasizing that he was the enforcer of those who passed through the gates of Chandringham. Jim stopped and lifted the grubby canvas enough to see the cart was filled with wooden crates marked carrots, eggs, potatoes, and parsnips.

"Right, Ned, all looks good back 'ere, you can never be too careful." He strolled back to the front of the cart and looked right at Flo. "Although I cannot say the same for your Flossy. Eh, lass, did ya not wash today or for that matter all week?" Flo looked saddened by Jim's remarks, but what else did she expect?

Ned quickly came to Flo's rescue. "Nay, Jim, ya know us Dwyers have our pride. We wouldn't step a foot in Chandringham House looking like we had just had a mud bath unless there was a perfectly good reason for it."

"I'm all ears, Ned," Jim scoffed.

"Flossy shone earlier this mornin' like a shiny new button. Unfortunately, the road 'ere was hazardous and Flossy took a tumble. Thank goodness in soft mud. So please, Jim, cut the girl some slack!"

Jim sighed demeaningly. "I can't... she can't enter Chandringham looking like that, Ned."

"But, Jim, Mrs Crabtree needs these supplies now, this minute. If I don't get them to her now there will be hell to pay."

"Not my problem," Jim said with a wry smile.

"It's not now, Jim, but it will be later when Mrs Crabtree finds out ya were the delay with the supplies arriving, note that word deellllllaaayyy. Good God, man, have a heart!" Ned's glare was full of disdain.

Jim pondered for a moment, rubbing his long skeletal forefinger over his lips. "Aye, you're right, man." Jim jangled his keys once more while walking spritely over to the huge golden gates that dwarfed him. He then selected a huge key from the ring, placed it in the large keyhole of the left gate and turned it. Flo could distinctly hear the mechanism of the lock click. Jim then walked towards the left turret and opened the door with a shiny brass key. Closing the door behind him, Jim was momentarily out of sight. He became visible on the other side of the gate, lethargically lifting each gate's drop rod. Ned stepped back onto the cart and sat beside Flo. She wondered if Jim had any strength left to open the huge gates.

"Pa, do you think he'll be able to open those huge gates?"

"Aye, lass, he can, but at what speed, I do not know. I better go and help push 'em open, otherwise, Mrs Crabtree will not get her supplies til suppa time at this rate." Ned stepped off the cart and pushed the right gate open. All the while Jim had only partially opened the left gate. Ned then took charge in opening the left gate fully, leaving Jim standing in the middle of the road.

"Thanks, Ned, these old bones are wearing out."

Ned, feeling sorry for Jim led the horses past the gates. He then pulled the left gate to and then helped Jim pull the right gate until it was ajar.

"See you shortly, Jim."

"Aye, that you will. Good luck, Flossy, with Mrs Crabtree; by heck, ya are going ta need it!"

Jim shook his head in disgust.

Luckily, Flo was hearing Jim's words but not listening, her curiosity consumed her thoughts. She spluttered out the words, "Mr... Mr Gatekeeper, Jim, what do those words mean?"

Jim's was momentarily puzzled.

"On your hat — NEMO ME IMPUNE LACESSIT?" Flo said.

Jim looked rather shocked with Flo's question, then his pupils seemingly started to constrict. "That's a secret, lass, for them that have knowledge of what it means."

Flo looked dumbfounded but the cogs started to turn in her brain. "What kind of answer is that? A secret. Why would those words be in plain sight for everybody to see if they were a secret?"

Jim tapped his nose with his forefinger and smiled before replying. "Folk don't like young women that ask too many questions and you're asking too many questions, lass."

Ned did not take any notice of the question or answer, he snapped the reins and the cart started to roll.

Ned and Flo were rolling towards Chandringham. Flo was more curious than ever now, and needed to know the answer. "Pa, my curiosity is getting the best of me. Do you know what the words 'NEMO ME IMPUNE LACESSIT' mean?"

"Eeeeeeee, Flossy, that fall has gone to your 'ead! I only know the King's English. They must be Latin words or somethin' of the like, somethin' to do with the duke's coat of arms. Only the toffs know what Latin means, Flo."

"Do you think Jim would know?"

"Nay, Flo, he's no toff, don't worry ya pretty little 'ead."

Chapter Twelve
Golden is Chandringham

Chandringham was now visible. Flo's eyes widened and she gasped, "Wow, Pa, what a spectacular vision that is being bestowed on us. Chandringham is more glorious than I have ever pictured!"

The fog had begun to clear, as a huge ray of sunshine shone through the clouds directly onto Chandringham House. It made the surrounding area look rather dark. The ray of sunshine emphasized the roofline, decorated with urns that were topped in golden finials. All the window frames were gilded gold, even the stonework looked gold.

Flo smiled with glee at the opulent splendor that was bestowed before her. "My goodness, Pa, it looks like Chandringham is made out of gold."

Ned nodded and took a moment to reply as he was viewing the splendor too. "Eeeee it does, lass, the Lord is shining on the old girl today."

"Pa, this has to be a sign. A sign that all is going to be golden and good from now on. I am sure of it." Flo sniffed the crisp clean air.

Ned smiled but did not reply. Life for him would never be the same without Richard and Archibald.

The cart rolled closer to Chandringham. Flo caught a glimpse of a body of water. It reminded her of a recurring dream. Her excitement and nervousness paused while she dwelled. Ned thought Flo was showing a sign of being nervous, for she was silent. He glanced at her, studying her stilled expression of thought. He had no idea of her torrid recurring dream, one that she was reminded of only last night. Every time, the dream started with the same deep, dark, serene water, that bubbled ever so slightly, giving nothing away of the fraught torrid battle that lay underneath; a battle to live. Flo, detached from the victim, looked on at the young woman with long golden hair just like hers, fighting for her life as the aggressor played with his prey pulling the slender body deep down then releasing his grip. When the woman drew close to the surface, the predator pulled her back down. Her clenched fists thrashed against the predator for dear life, her eyes wide and mouth shut. She pushed past, reaching for the surface then gulped as much air as she could before being dragged down again by her long golden locks. The woman's strength became drained as she gulped the water and a state of delirious calm set in. Her sky-blue eyes were wide as she stilled within the water.

"Eeeeeeee, Flossy, Flossy." Ned interrupted Flo's thought. Ned looked at her once again, there was no way he would let the moment go unspoken. "I hope you're a good swimmer?"

An expression of sheer puzzlement veiled her face. "Why do you say that, Pa?"

"Cause just look at what's in front, lass, what do ya see?"

Flo's eyes were now wide open and her mouth aghast with amazement once more. "The huge opulent golden house now appears to be floating on a lake. However, the lake has created a mirrored image of the magnificent golden house of Chandringham, may I add with exceptional clarity, despite a central towering fountain. It doesn't get much better than this, Pa, does it?"

Ned smiled. "Na, lass, it doesn't."

"I see what you mean now, Pa, by hoping I was a good swimmer. It looks like I will need to swim to Chandringham."

"Eeeeeeeeee, it's not a lake, lass, it's a pond and I think it's around a thousand feet long," said Ned proudly.

"It's the longest pond I have ever seen and for that matter that's the tallest fountain I have ever seen, it's towering over Chandringham. The fountain looks like it touches the sky, the angels." Flo paused as she felt a lump in her throat. "Our angels, Pa, Richard and Archibald."

Ned smiled at the thought; he was going to miss Flo's interpretations of the wonders of the day.

"Pa, how deep is the pond?" She took a large gulp, with her eyes like saucers.

"Not too deep, lass."

His answer seemingly calmed Flo as she smiled. "It really does look like Chandringham is floating on the pond."

Ned chuckled. "Aye, lass, it's quite an illusion. Ya would think ya could swim right up ta the house." Ned sighed deeply. "Ohhhhhhhhhhh." Flo was credulous to his word. He knew she would question other folk, but he felt that she believed every word he spoke. Little did she know he was harboring a huge secret.

Chapter Thirteen
A Stench So Foul

The cart approached the servant's entrance. It was quite a contrast to the opulent grand entrance with its huge sweeping stone staircase, decorative balustrade, and newel posts topped with rearing lion statues that Flo had seen on the duke's coat of arms. Ned pulled slightly on the horses' reins and shouted out, "Easy." The four horses slowed; their hooves no longer made a loud clattering noise on the cobblestone courtyard ground. In contrast, Flo's heart started to beat faster now, with her nervousness. Ned pulled on the horses' reins harder this time and gave a further command. "Whoa!" The cart then rolled to a stop.

"Ohhhhhh, gosh my heart is pounding so much it feels as if it is going to jump right out of my chest."

Ned turned and looked at Flo as he stepped down from the cart. "Reet, Flossy, calm down and wait 'ere while I go and see Mrs Crabtree."

Flo nodded yes as her skin paled underneath the mud on her face.

Ned turned around as he walked through the doorway. "Now then, there's no need for the collywobbles, Flossy."

Flo nodded once more as Ned closed the door. She could not speak; her mouth was that dry. Her thoughts were racing through her head. *I can't let Mrs Crabtree see me like this. She'll take one look at me and what will she think? She'll think I am careless.* A trail of a nasty odor had now activated Flo's sense of smell. Flo sniffed the air and looked dumbfounded. She whispered the words, "Do I smell?" Flo sniffed her left muddy arm; she could not smell anything, but wondered why all of a sudden she could smell the nasty odor. The scent had aroused her senses so much so that just to make sure, she sniffed her right arm. "Pooooooohhhhh." Flo was engulfed with a vile stench that seeped through her pores, she flared her nostrils; her stomach wrenched and she gagged. She could no longer control herself and tried to vomit,

"Urghhhhhh," but nothing came out of her mouth. "Oh, dear Lord!" She looked around hoping to see a horse trough. "Where can I bathe? I'll not step a foot in Chandringham like this. Oh my!" The cogs in her brain were clicking so fast and hard that Flo's head started to hurt. Her heart pounded and any second now she thought she would self-combust. She cupped her hand over her left temple to ease the pain. It was not working. She felt faint and her vision started to blur... Her inner voice commanded her to close her eyes, *Inhale, inhale even with that stench? Yes, needs must.* It was the only way she could calm down. *Concentrate on breathing.* Two short shallow inhales, was all she could manage the stench was so intense; *exhale*, "Ahhhhhhhhh!" *Breathe deeply*, "Ahhhhhhhhh." Flo had started to calm her inner sanctum, despite the smell and her thoughts. She spluttered out the words "Ohhhhhhhhhhhh, I will still be alive no matter whatever happens." Opening her eyes widely, she realized that Nivek or Siwel one of the leading horses had dumped a huge dung on the cobblestone. Relief ran through her body. Looking up to the sky, "Ohhhhhhhhhh thank you, Lord!"

Just then, the left door of the staff entrance opened, leaving the right highly polished black door with an impressive lion's head brass doorknocker closed. A short, portly, proud-looking woman was immaculately dressed in a black taffeta high-necked dress, with auburn-colored hair, styled in a Psyche knot, she stepped out onto the cobblestone courtyard. She stared intently directly at Flo. Flo, sensing her stare, plucked up the courage to look into a pair of kind, olive-green eyes. "So your pa tells me, you're lucky to be in one piece." Flo wondered how to reply. "Yes, M—M'lady."

Ned stepped out of the doorway. "Florence, please refer to me as Mrs Crabtree," her words, crisp and concise.

Flo uttered, "Yes, M'lady, I mean Mrs Crabtree."

Mrs Crabtree smiled, her button nose twitched, the stench quickly distracted her from her thoughts. Her nostrils flared and her nose guided her eyes to the precise location. Her kind eyes were transformed to a demonic glare, so much so it looked like her eyeballs were going to pop out of her eye sockets.

"Ned Dwyer!" She spoke with a loud, demeaning tone. "I have asked you to bring me supplies for our kitchen not the garden!"

75

Ned replied with a shallow voice, "Yes, Mrs Crabtree, it's unfortunate."

Flo could now see why this small, portly woman induced pure fear in the bravest of men.

Ned proceeded to say, "I'll get reet to…" but before he had time to finish his sentence Mrs Crabtree intervened. "Cleaning the manure up!" she scoffed as she pointed with her forefinger in an upward motion. Using her finger to indicate the word 'silence!' Her voice softened slightly. "However, I'm in need of the kitchen supplies immediately, Mrs Thorpe is desperate for the flour, in particular. So time is of the essence here. Ned, you'll need to take a sack of flour to the kitchen immediately, then clean up the manure." She pointed her forefinger to the right. "George is working in the miniature garden today. He'll be the closest gardener to direct you to a wheelbarrow."

Aptly timed, the right rear horse lifted its tail high enough to expose a pulsating anus. Mrs Crabtree exclaimed, "Ohhhhhhhh Lllllloorrd!" She had overcome one stench and she certainly wasn't going to wait around to be paralyzed by another. "Ned Dwyer! Can you keep your horses under control?" She looked at Ned with a pug face and then turned to Flo. "Come on down, Florence, before you start smelling worse than you look."

Flo sheepishly stepped down off the cart and wished the ground would open up a hole, just big enough so that she could step right into it. She did not dare glance at her father; all she could do was stare right at the ground.

Flo followed Mrs Crabtree through the opened door and stomped her feet on the doormat. She could no longer smell the odor of the manure; instead, a pleasant mild scent of pine infused the air. The scent calmed her a little, it reminded her of Christmas, of a freshly cut pine tree. She began to notice the decorative floor of black and terracotta tiles set in a diamond-checkered pattern with a rectangular terracotta tiled border. The floor had an uninterrupted sheen; it must have been recently cleaned. Flo noticed dry mud falling on the entrance mat from the bottom of her boots. Should she say something? Could she say something? Her mouth was so dry, but somehow, she plucked up the courage to speak. "Mrs Crabtree," she spluttered.

"Follow me, Florence, we need to get you cleaned up, immediately." She did not give her a glance.

Flo stopped in her tracks, she blurted out, "But, Mrs Crabtree, I need to take my boots off. I'll be making a mess on this clean, clean floor if I don't."

Mrs Crabtree turned to look at the trail of dry mud on the doormat. She looked into Flo's eyes. "Well spotted, Florence. Be quick about it." She lifted her head and clasped her hands in front of her torso, to reinforce her words.

Flo bent down immediately and slid off her muddy gloves, placing them on the floor. She clumsily bent to untie her laces. Her fingers and thumbs were not working in unison. She was very much aware that Mrs Crabtree was watching her every move. Finally, Flo managed to untie and loosen her laces. She then balanced herself by placing her right hand against the wall while pulling off her left boot. The corridor was narrow enough for Flo to take a step to the left and to pull off her right boot. Flo had noticed the wall color was magnolia, the same color as Ma's living room. She smiled to herself as her right boot came off. She was rather pleased she did not make a fool of herself by falling over while standing on one leg. She nimbly picked up her gloves and boots and looked Mrs Crabtree in the eye.

Mrs Crabtree gestured her approval with a nod. "Right you are then." The girl clearly had common sense, although she was overly nervous. That was only to be expected — Chandringham was intimidating to so many, she thought.

Ned had found his way through the door with a sack of flour on his back. His boots were rather muddy too. He stomped his feet on the entrance mat before he proceeded to walk. He realized that Mrs Crabtree and Flo had not made much progress down the corridor and that Flo had taken off her muddy boots. He then looked down at his and shrugged his shoulders. "Should I take the flour directly to the kitchen, Mrs Crabtree?"

In a decorous tone, she replied, "Yes, Ned, that's what I just said." She did not turn around but carried on walking down the corridor with Flo following. Mrs Crabtree turned right into a corridor. Before Flo followed, she glanced quickly at her pa and mouthed the words, "Bye for now, Pa."

Ned did not have time to reply as Flo had turned the corner. A lump in his throat appeared before he could voice any words. He gave a huge gulp to rid the lump and his steel blue eyes darkened with sadness. His beautiful baby girl would no longer be in his daily life.

Chapter Fourteen
Mud Does Not Stick

Flo walked briskly behind Mrs Crabtree, turning right once again. They were faced with a steep, narrow, stone-descending staircase. The walls seemed shabby and the decorative tiled floor was no longer visible. It was quite a contrast from the palatial exterior. Mrs Crabtree's portly figure moved rather quickly. Flo had to quicken her step to keep up. They finally reached the bottom. Flo's ivory cheeks were now a blush, amongst the grey cracked mud on her face. Mrs Crabtree turned left and took a few more steps, turned right and then opened a dull navy-blue door. "Right, Florence, this is your room. You'll be sharing it with Elsie. The right bed is yours and there's a fresh jug of water and basin for you to wash in. Your cupboard is also on the right, of course. In it, you'll find two uniforms, two face cloths, and two clean towels. Elsie will be with you shortly and will instruct you of your duties."

Relief struck Flo and she replied, "Yes, Mrs Crabtree, and thank you for sparing me any ridicule from any other staff members. For that, I am truly thankful." Flo smiled at Mrs Crabtree and she smiled back. She then turned on her heels and walked towards the doorway and closed the door.

Flo looked up at the white painted ceiling. "Oh, thank you, Lord." She quickly took a look around the room. It had relaxing pale green walls, a central window, with two identical metal bedsteads either side of the window. Her bed did not seem to have many blankets, unlike the bed next to it. Flo, for a brief moment, wondered if she would be warm enough in the night. She quickly distracted her thoughts and set about the task in hand, placing her boots and gloves underneath her bed, then undressing, down to her underwear. She poured some of the water into the basin as she did so; she caught sight of herself in the mirror. The mud had dried and cracked around her face. She resembled an old, wrinkled woman with grey skin. Flo smiled and flashed her perfectly, formed white teeth. As she did so the mud cracked a little more, revealing more of her ivory skin and rosy red lips. Flo soaked the face cloth in the basin and lathered up the coal tar soap. Its sharp, distinctive, fresh scent cleared Flo's nasal passageways. She gently rubbed the mud off her face and out of the front of her hair. In no time at all she was clean and fresh-faced once more. Flo smiled in the mirror with approval. There was a knock at the door, then the door opened. She was a little shocked, not expecting the door to open immediately. A slim, freckled-faced girl stood in the doorway. She was wearing a long blue dress with a white pinafore and a white frilly cap with red strands of hair dangling down from each side of the cap.

"I am Elsie. Are you not ready?" she asked with a hastened voice.

"Errrrrrrr no, I'm Flo. I just need to put my uniform on," she sheepishly answered.

"Reet well, you best get a move on. There's a lot to be done and little time to do it in. I'll give you some help." Elsie opened up the cupboard door and pulled out Flo's uniform. "Here you are, best get to it then."

Flo started to dress, while Elsie looked rather shocked at the color of the water in the basin and face cloth. She then noticed Flo's mudded coat, boots, bonnet, and gloves.

"So, I must point out, we have very high standards here at Chandringham. Mrs Crabtree says that 'Cleanliness is next to Godliness'. Your standards are well falling short of that, Flo!"

Flo was taken aback by Elsie's comment. "I took a tumble off my pa's cart and landed in the mud. I was as clean as a whistle when I stepped out of the house earlier this morning, honest. I'm lucky I am standing here now, and have no broken bones, honestly, cross my heart." Flo made a sign of the cross with her forefinger, sweeping downwards from her head to her stomach and then sweeping her forefinger completely across her chest.

"Oh well, that's bad luck and good luck, I suppose, at the same time." She looked rather dumbfounded as she curled her lower lip onto her upper lip and her brown eyes were almost cross-eyed. Flo wondered if Elsie knew how funny she looked and had to hold back her chuckles.

"I'll clean ya boots while you finish dressing." Elsie picked up Flo's boots and poured more water in the basin. Using the same cloth Flo had used on her face she proceeded to clean her boots with it.

Flo, now dressed, needed to fix her hair. "Oh no. My hairbrush. For that matter, my case!"

Her look of dismay in the mirror perplexed Elsie enough for her to turn around and face Flo. "Ya case?"

"Yes, it's still on Pa's cart."

Elsie smiled. "I'm sure ya pa will leave it with Mrs Crabtree, don't worry yourself unnecessarily. You can use my brush, for now, that's if you've got no nits?"

Flo's mouth dropped wide open with her dismay. In turn, Elsie smiled with her eyes.

"Just kiddin' ya! It's in me cupboard on the top shelf."

"Ohhhhhhhhhh thank you, Elsie." Flo opened the cupboard door and picked up a large paddle brush, untied her elastic band and brushed her long, golden, curly, locks of hair.

Elsie finished cleaning Flo's boots. "There ya are! They're as good as new." Leaving no time for Flo to answer, she added, "Reet, I'm going to get rid of this water. When I return, you'll be done, eh?" Elsie did not wait around for an answer. She turned, and then she was gone.

Flo placed her frilly white cap on her head and smiled at herself in the mirror. There was a knock and once again the door opened before she could answer. Flo was surprised to see Mrs Crabtree. "It's nice to see you are all cleaned up, Florence. Your father has asked me to give you this case."

"Ohhhh thank you, Mrs Crabtree." Flo took the case and placed it on her bed.

Mrs Crabtree scanned the room. "I take it Elsie has come and gone?"

"Yes, Mrs Crabtree, she's gone to empty the water, it was black." Just then the door opened and Elsie stepped into the room. She took one look at Mrs Crabtree and produced the same dumbfounded look on her face as she did earlier, curling her lower lip onto her upper lip and her brown eyes became almost cross-eyed. This was obviously a look Elsie produced often. Flo had better get used to it.

Mrs Crabtree turned and stood with her back against the wall so that Flo and Elsie could see her face. "Elsie, the duke needs the study fire lit before you do anything else. His Grace will be engaging in a meeting right after his breakfast. So, you had best get a move on. Flo, follow Elsie's lead and learn all you can today."

"Yes, Mrs Crabtree," Flo replied.

"Elsie, don't forget to show Florence where Mrs Bloom is in the laundry. Those muddy clothes and face cloth will need a good soaking before they get up and walk away on their own accord. Then proceed with your normal duties."

"Yes, Mrs Crabtree," Elsie eagerly replied.

Mrs Crabtree smiled, turned and walked out of the doorway.

"Reet, Flo, you don't need to get your uniform dirty, so you are best turning your clothes inside out and then bundling them up to take to Mrs Bloom. We need to be quick. So, follow me," Elsie commanded.

Flo smiled, nodded and bundled up her muddy clothes with the face cloth inside them. Elsie had walked out of the room before Flo grasped the bundle safely.

Flo followed Elsie eagerly, turning left out the doorway and up the stone staircase. A staircase that had stood where centuries of time had passed, but time had left its mark and caused ripples on the stone treads, through many servants making their path. It was now Flo's turn to make her mark. She wondered how significant that would be in a metaphorical sense. Elsie walked at a slower pace than Mrs Crabtree, to Flo's relief. The stairs were steep and she could not hold onto the handrail for fear of dropping her bundle of muddy clothes over her clean uniform. They reached the top and turned right into a narrow corridor painted in magnolia, and then making a right turn, then a left, then a right turn again proceeded to walk down another stone staircase. The walls that surrounded them now were painted white.

"Elsie, I wonder, is there a color sequence to the areas of the house? It would make sense if there were, it's so big, a person could easily get lost in here."

To Flo's surprise Elsie did not answer. They reached the bottom of the staircase and were faced with a wall, where the white paint had started to peel. There was a doorway to the left and a doorway to the right. Elsie opened the left door and walked into a room. Flo followed, having no idea where she was going. Elsie seemed non-communicative, Flo thought, *I know Mrs Crabtree told me to follow Elsie's lead but Elsie has taken her words in the most literal sense possible.*

Flo realized rather quickly that they had stepped into the laundry room. There were three girls dressed like Flo and Elsie, all engrossed in working with three identical noisy machines that Flo had never seen before. Four sturdy metal legs supported these machines; the body consisted of a huge metal tub with a mangle on top at the open end of the tub. Flo's rational thinking quickly came to the realization the machines were used to wash the laundry. "Wow, electric washing machines! Ma would love one of those," Flo declared.

Elsie was still non-communicative with Flo as she called out to the three girls, "Where is Mrs Bloom?"

None of them replied, as the washing machines were so loud. So, Elsie walked over to the nearest girl and tapped her shoulder to draw her attention. Elsie asked the question once more, "Where is Mrs Bloom?"

The girl pointed straight ahead and did not speak. It was difficult to see what was straight ahead because of the suspended clothes racks filled with white sheets that were blocking the view. Elsie walked towards the space between the suspended clothes racks. Flo followed, absorbing the scent of freshly laundered laundry. She counted the clothes racks as she walked. Two, four, six, eight, ten, twelve, fourteen, sixteen, eighteen, twenty clothes racks all filled with laundry. Flo was amazed by the abundance of laundry.

There were two women at the end of the clothes racks, ironing next to a shiny blue, cast iron stove. One woman was dressed like Elsie and Flo; the other woman wore a dark navy-blue dress with a white pinafore. The two were engrossed in their work. Elsie walked over to the woman with the dark navy-blue dress. "Hello, Mrs Bloom, this is Flo, our new scullery maid." Elsie waved Flo on, to walk up to Mrs Bloom.

Mrs Bloom looked up from ironing, peering over her round spectacles. Once she took focus, a startled look engulfed her expression. She froze for a moment holding the iron in mid-air, and then, as if she was collecting her thoughts, she moved again placing her iron back on the stove amongst many more irons that were being heated. She had soft features and pale blue eyes, but her skin was rather rugose and her silver-grey hair made her look much older than Flo's grandma. The tales of time had certainly made an impression on her face. She looked sad and Flo wondered if a huge hug would make her feel any better. Hugs are sooooooooooo good for the soul she thought, especially Ma's. Flo knew that etiquette would not permit her to do so. She curtsied instead. "Pleased to meet you, Mrs Bloom."

Mrs Bloom raised a smile from her drooping lips. "Nay, girl, ya do not need to curtsy for me."

The other girl who was ironing started to giggle.

"Less of that, Ivy!" Mrs Bloom scoffed. "Save the curtseys for His Grace and family upstairs, Flo." She smiled, "I believe ya have some washing for me, so Mrs Crabtree said. I am not to ask ya any questions as to why your clothes are so dirty. Although I am intrigued, I won't, nor will anybody else in this room." She grimaced at Ivy.

Flo looked down at her bundle of muddied clothes and back up at Elsie. Elsie produced the same dumbfounded look on her face as she did earlier. Mrs Bloom, recognizing this look, could not hold her silence. "Elsie, if ya need to say somethin', then say it. Ya look like you're two sandwiches short of a picnic!" she admonished her.

"We are in a rush, Mrs Bloom. I, I need to light the fire in His Grace's study before he finishes his breakfast and I'm sure he is likely to put his spoon down any time soon. Could I please borrow one of your fire lighting kits? If we have to go to the kitchen, I fear I won't be able to light the fire in time."

Mrs Bloom smiled and nodded yes. "Ehhhhhhh, Ivy, could you pass Elsie the fire basket?"

Ivy bent down near the wood stove, grabbed a basket and walked over to Elsie and gave it to her. "It's all there." Ivy smirked. Flo's gut fluttered inside her, something was not right, but there was no time to analyze.

Mrs Bloom stepped forward to Flo. "I'll take your laundry for now, Flo. We have a procedure that staff normally follows, but your clothes will be ready in a day's time. I'll run through that procedure then. Now be away with ya girls. Ohhhhh and Elsie don't forget to bring that fire kit back where it belongs."

"I won't, Mrs Bloom. Thank you." Elsie turned around and walked very briskly as Flo followed with eagerness.

"At last, I'm finally going upstairs to see the finery, opulence, and grandeur that Chandringham is renowned for," Flo commented. "I have heard many a tale in the village. It's now time to see if those tales are true."

Elsie completely ignored Flo's comments and shouted out whilst climbing the stairs, "Flo, we must make haste to get to the study before His Grace does. Follow me closely and please do not stop to talk to anyone or stare at anything! If we don't light that fire in time, I will be in trouble with Mrs Crabtree."

Gosh, heaven forbid, Flo certainly did not want Elsie to feel the wrath of Mrs Crabtree. She had seen her demon eyes once today, so she made a pact with herself not to stop and stare at all the wonderful antiquities and masterpieces as much as she wanted to. The wrath of Mrs Crabtree fueled her fear for Elsie. She seemed very nervous as it was, with that stunned, cross-eyed stare of hers. Flo felt embarrassed for her, so she would merely glance at the artifacts as they walked through the upper level of Chandringham.

Flo wondered about the color scheme on the walls once again but did not ask Elsie this time. They had climbed up the white-walled staircase, turned right onto the narrow corridor and made a left turn. They were walking now down a light-blue painted corridor. Flo was bubbling with curiosity, there had to be a reason for the different colored walls, but she did not dare ask Elsie the significance for fear of slowing her down. Suddenly her eyes caught sight of a love heart drawn on the wall with the inscription Mary Tav & Bobby Mc. As her fingers touched the writing, she developed a strange feeling, a knowing of her being here previously, although she had never stepped foot in Chandringham before. She no longer made a mental note of whether they turned left and right, instead there was an innate knowing of where they were going. She thought. *How strange*.

Elsie blurted out, "Keep up!" without turning her head around to see if Flo had caught up. She had remained at the same distance, right from when Elsie up and turned out of the laundry. Maybe she was preparing her for what was ahead, Flo thought. They were facing a wooden staircase with spindles and a handrail that were not as steep as both sets of stone staircases, they had just climbed. Flo noticed the corridor had now doubled in size too. The wooden stairs creaked as they made their way up the staircase. Flo could see a large, six-paneled wooden door with a gleaming brass doorknob; it was now only seconds away from being opened. Flo's heart started to beat faster with the sheer excitement of what was beyond the door.

"Oh, Elsie, it has been a morning full of shenanigans so far and I have doubted this moment in time would ever happen. I've been waiting for this very second since I was the age of ten. It has been my dream to work in Chandringham. Ever since I heard my father talk of the grandeur and exuberant architectural adornment of the 'Ole Girl'."

Elsie shrugged her shoulders and tutted, uninterested.

Flo smiled and continued talking. "I'm totally enchanted by Chandringham and its history and somehow I have always felt a strange belonging." She chuckled, "At last I'm now going to walk in the footsteps of the gentry: dukes, duchesses, princes, princesses, queens and kings."

Elsie tutted once more, shaking her head and turning the brass doorknob. The solid wooden door opened. She walked through the doorway. Flo followed, closing the door and opening her mouth with sheer delight at the same time. Her eyes danced across the stunning embellished gold-leaf ceiling with gold and crystal chandeliers. The crystals' refractions lit up the beautiful multitude of rich wooden tones in the herringbone floor in the corridor. Flo realized she was falling behind with her pace, as Elsie seemed to have quickened her stride and was more than fifteen feet ahead of her. So Flo lengthened her stride, accelerated her pace and caught up. Elsie approached a doubled doorway with ornate wooden doors; each door had seven panels. On the large center panel of each door, Flo recognized the intricate carving, with the shield and carved cross separating two lions. Underneath them were the carved words 'Nemo Me Impune Lacessit'. This provoked Flo's curiosity once more. This was not the time or the place to ask Elsie what the words meant but she could not help herself, she needed to know the answer. The question had been burning in her brain since she set eyes on the words.

"What does 'Nemo Me Impune Lacessit' mean, Elsie?" Flo spluttered in her desperation to ask the question.

"Pardon?" scoffed Elsie, looking at Flo in the eyes.

"Do you know what the words 'Nemo Me Impune Lacessit' mean?" She spoke with confidence now.

"I have no idea what ya talkin' about!" She turned and faced the door and although Elsie looked right at the words, 'Nemo Me Impune Lacessit' she was oblivious. Flo was bemused by Elsie and her ignorance as Elsie knocked on the right door twice. There was no answer so she opened it and walked in, Flo followed her footsteps.

"Ya should knock four times really, to give His Grace a chance to reply. However, because I'm in a rush and I know His Grace is in the dining room, that's why I only gave two knocks." Elsie smiled, falsely.

Flo listened to Elsie but her eyes were now preoccupied with the study. "Oh my, I have never seen so many books!" Flo declared.

The three walls were covered from floor to ceiling with carved ornate wooden bookshelves, laden with books. It was almost as if they were jostling to be picked. Flo was so tempted to run her fingers across the closest books and gaze at the titles and authors. There was no time though; Elsie was now nearing the central wall of the study, where a huge white marble fireplace, with two contrasting ebony marble posts stood on either side of the fireplace. Each column was separated by a heavy sculpted white marble ledge, edged in gold leaf. The fireplace commanded supremacy over the room but did not achieve it, due to the sheer volume of books. Above the fireplace, in prime position, hung a large portrait of the captivating duchess. Her perfect bone structure was adorned with creamy silk-sheened skin and crystal blue eyes which seemed to follow every footstep Flo made. In contrast to her eyes were beautiful alluring rose-colored lips; her face was framed by her long, dark lustrous, wavy hair. She sat on a ruby red leather couch holding an open book (in her hands) and appearing to have been pleasantly interrupted from her reading.

"I think the duchess is the most beautiful woman I have ever seen," Flo commented.

"You and the rest of the world alike think that, too," Elsie mocked.

There were two huge ruby red leather couches in front of the fireplace that looked incredibly comfortable. Flo knew it was not her place to sit or even perch her behind on any seats that the nobility or the gentry sat on.

"Ohhhhhhhh fiddlesticks! Nowt' seems to be going reet today!" Elsie blurted out while searching through the basket.

Flo's thoughts were instantly distracted by Elsie's outburst of agitation and she asked apprehensively, "What's a matter, Elsie?"

Searching with haste through the basket once more, Elsie groaned, "There does not seem to be any matches in me basket… Ohhhhhhh, that Ivy Shufflebottom 'It's all there', she said. Note: she's not to be trusted, Flo! She seems to always be doing this sort of thing ta me."

Flo's sixth sense was right about Ivy Shufflebottom.

"Now, where's the nearest box of matches I can lay me hands on?" Asking herself the question, Elsie's face formed her renowned dumbfounded look once more. "Ohhhhhhhhh I'll need to run back downstairs. You stay here, Flo. I'll be quicker that way and if you hear any footsteps, hide."

"Hide?" Flo was unnerved at the thought. "Where?"

"Under His Grace's desk." Elsie made her way towards the door, pointing her finger at the desk. "I'll leave the door open just in case anyone comes."

Chapter Fifteen
The Gemini Complex

Flo stared at a grandiose rosewood desk featuring two outer segments embellished with the two intricate golden rearing lions. The middle of the desk was the largest section. It was decorated with a pronounced gold edged shield and at the center an inlaid gold cross-stood proud. Centered underneath the shield ran a large gold leaf ribbon where the words 'Nemo Me Impune Lacessit' were inscribed.

Flo quickly quashed her thought of curiosity, wanting to know the meaning of 'Nemo Me Impune Lacessit'. Instead, she was overcome by the sheer panic at the very thought of having to hide underneath the duke's desk; it made her feel queasy. Flo needed to think quickly; luckily for her she was really good at it. She walked over to the leather-topped desk and noticed a large, intricately carved wooden box. That bore an uncanny resemblance to her pa's box that held his pipe, tobacco and lighter. Her hand paused over the box; she was now in deep hesitation, unnerved by her consciousness of prying into the duke's belongings. The very thought of hiding underneath the desk was much more daunting and the consequences of His Grace peering down at her while she was crouched on all fours in a compromising position, horrified her. Flo opened the box with care; her eyes lit up with delight, as she located a lighter with her glance. In haste, she grabbed the lighter and tested it for a flame. To her relief the lighter worked. She darted over to the fireplace and lit the pre-assembled fire, then blew on the mini flames to start the fire. "Ohhhhhhhh." She sighed with relief. "Now, to get out of here." Flo dashed to the desk and placed the lighter back in the box, in the exact position where she found it. Just as she was closing the lid, she heard voices, one of a well-spoken man and one of a man with a German accent, their footsteps drew closer. Flo's expression was one of sheer alarm. She pulled the ruby red leather chair away from the desk, it glided with ease as the castors took the chair a little further away from the desk than anticipated. Flo looked rather white-faced with sheer terror in her eyes. The very thought of not being able to pull the chair back in time consumed her, and her body froze for a few seconds. "Oh, dear Lord," she whispered, crouching down on all fours, as she grabbed the chair and crawled backward underneath the grandiose desk as far as she could.

The voices were very prevalent in the room. The words were distinctly pronounced, but muffled to Flo, as she was unable to concentrate on the conversation. She could only hear her heart pound. Her thoughts turned to focus on her pa's words: 'Flossy, stop worrying your pretty little head, sometimes the best thing you can do is not to think, not wonder, not obsess. I can hear the cogs in your brain clicking right now they're working that hard. So, just breathe, and have faith that everything will work out for the best'.

There was silence in the room as the door was shut. The sound of footsteps moved towards the couches that were set close to the fire. The men sat opposite each other as Flo breathed a sigh of relief.

"There is no easy way to say this, but I need to know — are there any signs of life?"

"I have just examined Her Grace and there is not one heartbeat between the two."

There was a long pause and a gasp of desolation from the duke.

Flo was stunned by the conversation and held back her gasp.

"Oh, God in heaven why…? Why in God's name does He see fit to punish me?"

There was a long pause of silence and Flo could only hear the crackling of the fire.

"Is Alexandra's life at risk if we continue to wait for the babies?"

"Ja, I will need to operate immediately or otherwise her life is in imminent danger."

"Imminent danger… imminent danger?"

"Ja."

"I could lose her, too?"

"Ja."

He spoke with delirium. "My life did not begin until I met her. She's my sunshine and rain. I live and breathe through her, 'imminent danger'. Why are you talking to me now and not operating?"

"You know why and ja, imminent danger, Your Grace, the preeclampsia is controlled for the very present but the monster within can erupt like thunder, strike like lightning and seize Her Grace's life any moment… Especially now."

There was a long pause of silence, then movement off the couch followed immediately by the sound of footsteps which moved closer to the desk. Flo was frightened; her eyes closed as she prayed with all her heart and soul for the footsteps to turn back. The footsteps stopped in their track.

Flo was sure by now that His Grace could hear the sound of her heart, it was pounding that loud. The sound of footsteps made their way back towards the couch once again.

"Dr Goodman."

"Ja."

"Alexandra knows of only life?"

"Ja, as we've agreed not to tell Her Grace." The Germanic man's voice spoke with deep sincerity.

There was movement off the couch and footsteps started to pace up and down on the herringbone oak floor once again. This time they did not venture towards the desk, to Flo's relief.

"Then we must advance with the Gemini Complex although I'm not sure how."

"With respect, Your Grace, you do realize what is expected and what's at stake here?"

The pacing stopped.

"I have read and understood what The Order asks of me and we have previously discussed this matter at length… Yes, I do know what's at stake! Fate leaves me no option now."

"With respect, Your Grace, you have two options."

"There is no option, Goodman, not when I am faced with my wife's grieving eyes and a lifetime full of sadness. I also need to protect the primogeniture. I have a chance to make this nightmare all but a dream. What would you do if you were in my shoes?"

"There would be no question in this matter for me, ethics are a forbidden word when it comes to life."

"I'll sign the agreement and uphold all requirements, no matter what."

"Excellent, Your Grace, just as long as you know we do not know what the outcome is at this moment?"

"Outcome?"

"Ja."

"Do you mind expanding on that one word?"

"Will it make a difference if I do, Your Grace?"

"Probably not, there is a need now. Just as there was with Father's need."

"Well then I do not think it will do any good if I disclose in-depth what could happen, but what I can say is these babies will become advanced humans physically and mentally."

"Just as long as they are healthy, that's all I ask, Goodman."

"Ohhhhh, they are very healthy," he spoke wryly.

"Well, Goodman, you must know I will do anything to save my wife's life and forever uphold her happiness, to save her from the grief that awaits no matter what it takes. I, in turn, will deal with my own grief."

Once again Flo heard movement off the couch. She braced herself. Each footstep drew closer to her. Flo's mouth suddenly ran dry; she closed her eyes tight as if to wish the footsteps away. It did not work, they became louder as her eyes opened and her veins suddenly ran cold. She started to tremble; realizing this, she stilled herself. The blood now drained from her face, she remained cold, looking lifeless, like a statue poised forevermore. The footsteps were now at the foot of the desk. Flo could hear the sound of a drawer opening and a document being lifted, then the drawer gently shut. Silence followed for a short time. Then the ruby red chair smoothly started to roll away from the desk. All was frozen in Flo's body, there seemed to be no sign of life as the frail body stilled. A pair of brown leather Oxford shoes aligned with the opening of the desk and the ruby-red, leather chair was filled. The castors of the chair gently rolled towards the desk, where the brown Oxford leather shoes were all but inches away from Flo's nimble fingers.

"So how do we move on from here?" the duke's voice defined now.

"I have taken foresight with this very matter, knowing that you possess an open mind of the Gemini Complex. I have informed The Order and taken the liberty of ordering release at Algen two days ago. The timing here is of grave concern."

There was a noise of rustling papers.

"Concern?"

"Ja, Your Grace."

A long pause of thought prevailed. Flo's heart regained its normal pace, as she now awaited the words to be spoken. Yet the room was silent and all that could be heard was the crackling of the fire. Just then there was a knock at the door. Still, no one spoke. Another knock followed and no words were spoken again. The silence of the room was overshadowed by the power of thought.

Flo could hear the doorknob turn, followed immediately by the sound of the door opening, footsteps followed posthaste. The footsteps came to a sudden stop.

Flo could hear Elsie's voice. "Ohhhhhhh, er sor... sorry, Ya Grace, I did not hear your reply, so I did not think ya were in here."

"That is because I did not reply, Elsie."

Flo could picture Elsie's face now with her dumbfounded look.

"Sorry, ya Grace."

"Elsie, four knocks are required before entering a room, then if there is no answer you may enter."

"Yes, ya Grace."

"Now why did you enter this room?"

"I was just coming ta..." Elsie paused, distracted by her thoughts.

"To what?" the duke scoffed.

"To light the fire."

"But it's already lit!" the duke mocked.

"Yes, I can see that now, ya Grace. I... I must of got me wires crossed. Sorry for interrupting."

"Very well." He dismissed her.

There was a pause and Flo thought maybe Elsie was curtsying, footsteps followed and the sound of the door being shut.

"So, getting back to the word 'concern'."

"Ja, Your Grace, we do not want to arouse suspicion here, in any way. Anyone directly involved has already been sworn to secrecy."

"Directly involved?"

"Ja, with the medical procedure. We are light years ahead here. These babies will be exceptional human beings."

"Of course, I see."

"With due respect, Your Grace, you will need to have all your staff sworn to secrecy too. We are not sure what awaits us in the future."

"Yes, yes, I understand."

The castors of the chair rolled back slightly and Flo could hear a drawer opening. From the opening of the desk, she could see the duke holding a quill in his right hand and stabbing his left forefinger with the tip of the quill. Flo flinched as the duke then squeezed his forefinger producing a pod of blood. The castors of the chair rolled towards the desk and Flo heard the faint sound of scribbling followed by the turning of pages and repeated by the faint sound of scribbling once again. The same drawer was entered a second time, but this time there was something hard that clattered on the desk and the sound of the large carved wooden box creaked as it opened. A lighter was struck and Flo now smelt the distinctive scent of wax. The stillness in the room resigned itself to the sound of dripping wax, followed by a resonating thud. Flo flinched as she placed her right hand on her chest.

"There you have it, Goodman, in blood."

"Thank you, Your Grace."

"No, it's a huge thank you to you, Goodman, and The Order."

The castors of the chair rotated backwards once again and Flo sighed with relief as the brown leather Oxford shoes slid away from her dainty hands.

"I am only too thankful to be given this opportunity, to right this huge wrong."

The ruby leather chair moved further away. The chair stilled and the sound of footsteps faded towards the couch. There was movement from the couch, imminently followed by, "I will call for the ambulance immediately and have the operating theatre ready and waiting for Alexandra's arrival."

"You must promise me that you will not leave Alexandra's side until all is well."

"I can't promise that, but have faith, all will be well, Your Grace. We are dealing with a lightning bolt here. Timing is of the essence. I will do all that I can to save Her Grace's life. That you can count on."

The sound of footsteps moved towards the door, the doorknob was turned and the oak door creaked open. There was a sudden gasp of desolation followed by the drowning noise of silence.

Chapter Sixteen
A Spider with Clogs on

Flo stilled, totally absorbed in her thoughts; she no longer felt her hunched body, her bones and taut muscles. She was engulfed with raw emotion. Her body and mind were completely one constricted mass. She no longer acknowledged any sound the study made. She was oblivious to the footsteps entering the room and the stoking of the fire.

Her thoughts were totally absorbed with sentiment for the duke and duchess. How torrid life could be, no matter who governed supremely. Her sky-blue eyes darkened underneath the shadow of the desk and now resembled the color of a deep dark blue ocean. Tears welled in her eyes, they were released as she closed her eyes and prayed. She muttered, "Dear Lord, please, please give the duchess strength to live and do not let that bolt of lightning strike her. The duke needs her so, so much. So please, please let her live a healthy life."

Simultaneously, as Flo prayed, the footsteps on the oak floor became louder. She was oblivious as the ruby red chair slid back on its castors. Flo uttered, "Please, please." Suddenly she became aware that she was not alone as she spoke her last, "Please."

The opening of the desk became shadowed, and the brightness within her closed eyes became dark. In turn the darkness caused Flo to open her eyes; immediately they became wide open with the incredulousness of the situation she found herself in.

Flo recognized the shadowed, crouched portly figure. She could feel the burning sensation of the demon eyes that were glaring down at her, although she could not see them. "What on earth are you doing down there, Florence?" Mrs Crabtree scoffed.

"H-h-hiding," Flo spluttered.

"Hiding? What on earth are you hiding from?"

"Errrrrrr," Flo expressed sheer puzzlement.

Demeaningly spoken, "Errr what? Go on, spit it out, girl!"

"A spider."

"A spider?" Mrs Crabtree ridiculed.

"Yes, Mrs Crabtree, a huge spider."

She blurted out sardonically, "Oh and I suppose this spider had clogs on?"

Flo looked rather puzzled by the remark but decided to reflect a moment longer. She then decided that no answer was the best answer.

"Do you think I was born yesterday, lass?"

"No, Mrs Crabtree. I have arachnophobia!"

"Arachnophobia? You, a farm girl? Arachnophobia!" she jeered.

"Yes, Mrs Crabtree."

She spoke sympathetically, "Ohhhhhh, good Lord!" Mrs Crabtree straightened up her body and rolled the ruby red leather chair away from the desk a little more. She proceeded to look around the floor. "Well, there's no spider here." She then bent down on all fours, level with Flo, looking straight at her, no longer blocking the light from the window. This time Flo could see her kind eyes. "There are no spiders in this country that can hurt you, Florence, so come on out." She held her right hand out. "Let's get you out of here before His Grace comes in the room."

Flo's eyes responded to Mrs Crabtree's words, particularly, 'before His Grace comes in the room', followed by a rather startled look on her face for a brief moment.

Mrs Crabtree sensed there was something not quite right, but as she only had a fleeting glimpse of the startled look on Flo's face, she did not feel the need to question her further, although instinct was telling her the duke had already been in the room, judging by Flo's reaction.

Flo crawled out from underneath the desk and clasped Mrs Crabtree's hand.

"Now then, Florence, I'm pretty sure that you should be pulling me up, not me pulling you up. I have the old bones and remember you have the young bones."

Flo beamed a smile of relief that the tone of the conversation had turned to lightheartedness. She stood up, still holding Mrs Crabtree's hand and with one sudden firm yank, pulled Mrs Crabtree up.

"And to think you're scared of spiders!" Mrs Crabtree smiled wryly at Flo while dusting herself down. It was then that Flo knew there would be further questions and her beaming smile diminished. "So, Florence, where on earth is Elsie? Did she run away from the spider too?"

"No, Mrs Crabtree. Elsie had to run and get another lighter."

"But the fire is lit and we use matches to light the fire?"

"I can explain."

"Do!" Mrs Crabtree jibed.

"Elsie was showing me how she lights the fire. The lighter struck, I mean the match struck a flame but looked like it did not light the fire properly. So Elsie had used her last match. She told me to wait here while she went for more. She'd be quicker without me."

"And?" spoken sardonically.

"So while she was gone, I blew on where she had struck the match within the kindling hoping that I could invoke a flame. It worked!"

"Why do I think there is more to this story than meets the eye?" Mrs Crabtree scoffed.

Flo looked rather dumbfounded, on purpose, to prevent Mrs Crabtree from questioning her further. "I'm not sure why, Mrs Crabtree."

"So why were you hiding under His Grace's desk?"

"Because of the spider, it was hiding in the wood, in the fire."

Mrs Crabtree's glare spoke only of unbelieving humiliation to Flo but instead of intimidating her, it only spurred Flo on to think quickly and sound convincing, to eradicate any more questioning.

"When the spider ran from the fire, it seemed to chase me. It appeared to know I was scared of it, I'm sure. Wherever I moved it seemed to follow. I am sure it was angry at me."

Mrs Crabtree now crossed her arms, her glare still evermore intense.

"I moved towards the door and it came after me. So, I turned and thought about hitting it hard with a book. I reached for one; the nearest was called Robert The Bruce King of Scots. Meanwhile, the spider cut me off from reaching the door. I remembered how Robert the Bruce studied the spider trying to make a web. The spider failed five attempts to make his web, and then on the sixth attempt, he succeeded. So, Robert was inspired by the spider, battled a sixth time with Edward II and won Scotland back. Well, that changed my mind."

Mrs Crabtree dwelled a little

"It has every right to live, as it's one of God's creatures, too. So, there was no other direction left for me to run, so I ran towards the window and hid behind the desk hoping that the spider would not like the light from the window therefore it would not follow me. It did not but I was too scared to come out, just in case it was still lurking."

Mrs Crabtree's eyes softened. "So where's Elsie all this time, while you were being stalked by a spider?"

"I'm not sure, maybe she had difficulty in finding a box of matches?"

Mrs Crabtree unfolded her arms and placed her right forefinger on her lips, while she pondered with her thought. "Ahhhhh matches, they do seem rather scarce of late. We need lighters. I shall have a word with Mr Ferguson, his footmen seem to be slacking!"

Chapter Seventeen
The Switch

Two loud knocks at the door startled Flo, but Mrs Crabtree did not flinch; instead, she replied to the sound with a poignant, "Enter."

Elsie opened the door and peered around it before entering the room. She appeared rather shocked at seeing Mrs Crabtree and her dumbfounded look started to metamorphosize on her face.

Flo blurted out in haste. "Did you find a box of matches?"

"Errrrrr, yes. What a job I had, it's bedlam out there."

"Bedlam?" Mrs Crabtree spoke with irony in her voice.

"Yes, Mrs Crabtree, it's bedlam out there." Her dumbfounded look now vanished. "You would think the world was coming to an end and we have only just won the war!"

Flo had more than an inkling as to why bedlam had descended on Chandringham, however, she was far from having a vacuous mind. The implications of her divulging her knowledge could be devastating and leave deep-rooted scars forevermore.

"Ohhhhhhh, good Lord!" Mrs Crabtree scoffed. "Do you know what has caused the bedlam?"

"I don't really know, Mrs Crabtree, but Miss Alan, the new duchess's maid seems rather distressed and I am sorry if I'm speaking out of turn 'ere but I don't think she knows if she is on her heels or her arse!"

"Heels or her arse?" Mrs Crabtree yelled.

"Yes, Mrs Crabtree, and she seems to be spinning all servants that talk to her into a muddle. I think it's something to do with Dr Goodman's orders. I think the babies are about to arrive any second."

"Dr Goodman's orders? Babies?" Mrs Crabtree looked startled.

"No, Mrs Crabtree. I'm just, puttin' two and two together." Elsie proceeded to curl her lower lip above her upper lip.

Mrs Crabtree, viewing Elsie's expression, was now becoming a little aggravated and jibed back, "Well this time I think you're right, you've made four instead of persistently making a three.

Elsie's stuttered, "I-I j-just caught the end of what she was saying, that it's Dr Goodman's orders."

"My, you have been very observant." She spoke dubiously but had little time to question her thoughts. Realizing the implications of the situation and knowing that time was the essence she blurted out, "Oh good Lord and hail Mary, whatever is the duchess going to think? I must go and sort matters out immediately." Mrs Crabtree turned on her heels and commanded, "Right, girls, come with me, just in case you're needed."

Flo and Elsie looked at each other with blank expressions.

"Today, girls," she urged.

Flo and Elsie followed Mrs Crabtree in haste. Turning left out of the doorway and continuing along the corridor, Flo was far too caught up with the feeling of anxiety to notice all the splendor. Instead, she felt helpless, captured by emptiness. That was unwarranted and she could not explain for she had no right to feel a loss she did not own and worst of all a loss that had not happened but was imminent. She was powerless and now dazed by her concern. The corridor opened into a palatial hall, which mirrored the corridor with its stunning embellished gold leaf ceiling and golden crystal chandeliers. The crystals' refractions lit up the beautiful multitude of rich wooden tones in the herringbone floor, on a far greater scale. Flo's expression did not change all the while. The daze of concern did not allow her to acknowledge the beauty of the Great Hall. Mrs Crabtree turned right into the Grand Entrance Hall with its black and white checkered marble stone floor and huge masterpieces that engulfed the walls and ceiling. Flo did not notice them. The three now ascended the huge opulent limestone staircase with gold leaf curvaceous newel posts, intricate balustrade, and handrails. Mrs Crabtree was on a mission and her pace seemed to quicken every step she took. She did not need any handrail to steady her; her foot placement on the stairs was firm and precise as she took center stage of the staircase. Unlike the two young girls who followed, gripping onto the handrails parallel to each other. They moved in unison like the head of an arrow, poised for target as they climbed the stairs. Mrs Crabtree's authoritative pace affirmed to Flo the necessity of timing and that it could make all the difference to whether Her Grace lived or died. Flo was going to do all that was expected of her and more if need be. Just as they reached the middle of the stairs, the Great Entrance Hall was invaded by two ambulance men, dressed in dark-navy uniforms bearing a stretcher, followed by four nurses, three dressed in red capes and white pinafores with a red cross on the bib. The fourth nurse was dressed in a navy cape and white pinafore.

Mrs Crabtree stopped in her tracks, turned and faced the retinue of medical staff, looking rather alarmed. She quickly put her thoughts together regarding Miss Alan's disarray and Dr Goodman's orders although she did not know what those orders were. No one had the common sense to inform her. So before the nurse with the navy cape had the chance to open her mouth and voice the question for directions Mrs Crabtree bellowed, "Are you here for Her Grace, Sister Crouse?"

"Ja," said the nurse in the navy cape.

The bellow had diminished and she spoke as if there was something obstructing her speech, like a lump in her throat. "Well, you had better follow me." Flo too, felt the same dispiriting lump that now awakened her daze.

The medical team wasted no time. Before Flo knew it, they were hot on her and Elsie's heels. When Mrs Crabtree turned left up the corridor, Flo noticed the rich, colorful carpet that she walked upon, wainscoted oak-paneled walls, lustrous silken-papered walls with many portraits of the ugly-looking gentry.

Mrs Crabtree knocked twice on the door of the duchess's bedroom and, not waiting for a reply, entered the room. Flo and Elsie followed as they were hustled along by the medical team. Flo instantly deduced that the tall, dark, wavy-haired man with striking chiseled facial features must be the duke. He was holding the duchess's right hand and stroking it gently with his other. Miss Alan stood next to a rather decorative oriental table. She was a petite woman with dark brown hair and green eyes and was occupied with folding a nightdress and placing it into a case. Dr Goodman, Flo presumed, was the tall, slight, pale-white-skinned, freshly barbered, white-haired man, who was listening to Her Grace's stomach with a stethoscope. Flo thought this strange, considering Dr Goodman had said there was not one heartbeat between the two. In fact, Dr Goodman himself looked rather strange, his red eyes seemed to move in opposite directions as he glanced upwards at the medical entourage and then at Flo, despite him wearing spectacles. All of this made Flo feel a little queasy, for she had never seen eye movement like this before or a man so pale. He must have a glass eye she deduced and as soon as she found a reason for the strangeness, the queasiness dissipated. Dr Goodman smiled and then his eyes returned back to the task at hand. All in the room stood silent, awaiting his word. An eternity seemed to lapse in the interim. The duchess's crystal-blue eyes slowly opened, gazing around the room. Her gaze stopped at Flo and all eyes in the room turned to look at Flo except for Dr Goodman's and Elsie's.

The duchess whimpered, "Mary, Mary, it's so nice to see you again; it's been so long." She then held her left hand out to Flo, beckoning her to come close.

Flo was hesitant. She had no idea what to make of the situation; somehow the duchess had mistaken her for a girl called Mary, her eyes were wide open and mouth agape.

"Mary, come, come hold my hand." She spoke deliriously, her skin paling by the moment.

Mrs Crabtree intervened, "Go on, Mary." She spoke softly but with poignant eyes.

Flo, unquestioning, walked up to the duchess with uneasy steps, full of uncertainty, yet she held out her hand all the while. Once she reached her destination the duchess slightly clasped Flo's hand and uttered the words, "I am so glad you're here, Mary. It's been soooooo long."

All in the room focused on the strange behavior. Dr Goodman's eyes saddened immediately. "We need to operate right now," he jeered.

"Right now? Here?" the duke cried out suddenly, looking rather horrified at the words he had just heard.

"Right now! We have no time for the journey to the hospital. If I don't operate now, we are going to lose Her Grace and the twins."

The duke toughened up his alarmed gaze. He had to stay strong and his expression now reflected that of his hardened exterior. "Yes, of course."

"Sister Crouse, I'll need the prepared operating kit, right now and light!"

Sister Crouse was a tall buxom woman, with a rather large nose and glaring brown eyes that were exaggerated by her black-rimmed, circular, goggle-looking spectacles.

"Ja, Dr Goodman, I have it in hand." She held out a black case and extended it away from her body for Dr Goodman to see. "I will set up straight away." She proceeded to move a tall side table close to where Dr Goodman stood, while balancing the reading light that was on the table.

"Good! Nurse Hermans and Janssen, prepare the bed." He spoke brusquely as time was the essence and the time was diminishing with every second. Both nurses were slim and almost identical looking with platinum blonde hair and similar pretty facial features. Each nodded and commenced turning down the bed covers.

"I'll need to scrub up, Mrs Crabtree."

"There's fresh water in the jug by the basin, Dr Goodman. Elsie and I will bring more water. Flo, you stay where you are needed, beside Her Grace. Miss Alan, we will need lots of towels."

Flo was now totally overwhelmed by the whirlwind of fate she now found herself in.

"Nurse Smets, you will need to be ready for the babies," said Dr Goodman.

She nodded yes and replied with, "Ja, Dr Goodman." Her beady eyes swept the bedroom. She proceeded to walk toward a double set of doors, opened them and walked into an adjoining room. She had barely disappeared through the doorway when she re-appeared again. "Jens and Thomas, I will need you in here." The ambulance men eagerly walked towards Nurse Smets. They all disappeared into the adjoining room.

Sister Crouse was now set up with the operating equipment. Miss Alan found more towels and placed them on the decorative oriental table. Dr Goodman peeled back his shirtsleeves, washed his forearms and hands. "Sister Crouse, can you administer the chloroform inhaler?"

"Ja." She took out a rather odd-looking piece of apparatus from the black bag.

The duke looked horrified at the contraption. Flo, on the other hand, scrutinized the inhaler with its three cylindrical glass vessels, one placed inside each other with what looked to be like a telephone dial holding all the glass vessels in place. The central cylinder contained coils of blotting paper placed in the lower two-thirds of it. Attached to the cylinder was a dark brown, rubber tube with a brown rubber mask on the end of it.

Sister Crouse made her way over to the duke's side of the bed; she too could see the horror on the duke's face. She spoke softly, "This is so the duchess does not feel any pain."

The duke's expression of horror mellowed.

"Would you like to hold the mask, on Her Grace's face, while I adjust the inhaler?"

He replied with unease, "Yes, I will feel I am being useful."

Sister Crouse handed the duke the mask and he instinctively placed it over the airways of the duchess. Sister Crouse opened the inspiratory valve on the mask so that the duchess would inhale the vapor of chloroform. The duchess's dainty hand released its grip on Flo's hand. Flo was about to move when the duke spoke. "Please stay, you have a calming effect on my wife. When she wakes I would like her to see you."

Flo nodded, acknowledging the duke's wishes. She wondered why the duchess thought her name was Mary. Flo was pretty sure it was Mary who had the calming effect.

Sister Crouse turned another valve on the mask. "Please, could you hold the glass vessel of the inhaler upright, Your Grace while I check Her Grace's blood pressure?" She then placed the glass vessel in the duke's right hand. Before releasing her grip, she asked, "Do you have a firm hold?"

The duke replied with a reassuring voice, "Yes."

She then released her grip from the inhaler and placed the earpieces of the stethoscope in each ear. She pulled out of her dress pocket a black cuff with two separate rubber tubes attached to it. One of the tubes was attached to a small black ball and the other one attached to what looked like a thermometer on a wooden stand. It was placed upright on the bedside table. She attached a black cuff around the middle third of the left upper arm of the duchess. Sister Crouse then proceeded to pump the ball, which inflated the black cuff. She watched the mercury fall on the manometer, while listening to the artery just below the cuff with her stethoscope. "The duchess is now stabilized, Dr Goodman." She closed the valves on the mask. "Your Grace, you can release the mask now."

The duke slowly pulled the inhaler and mask away and placed it on the pillow beside the duchess and stroked her hair.

Dr Goodman reacted to Sister Crouse's word with, "Glove me, Nurse Janssen." Both hands were outstretched as Nurse Janssen placed the white rubber gloves on Dr Goodman hands. He then turned towards the duchess whose stomach was now exposed. "Swab me, Nurse Hermans."

She passed a large pair of tweezers, which held an amber-colored iodine swab into Dr Goodman's right hand. He wiped the swab over the entire exposed area on skin of the stomach, turning the pale pink skin into a vibrant amber shade. He passed the tweezers back to Nurse Hermans, who had the scalpel ready for his clasp. Dr Goodman's surgeon's headlight shone brightly on her stomach as he made several incisions and pulled back the skin either side, as water gushed out of the opening. Flo turned her head at the sight. Her stomach turned and a sickly urge to vomit engulfed her. Her cheeks inflated then deflated as she fought the urge, closing her eyes in hope that no one in the room was looking at her reaction.

Nurse Smets stood next to Dr Goodman. He delved inside the opening and pulled out a newborn baby. There was a sense of overwhelming joy in the room as Dr Goodman handed Nurse Smets the baby. She placed the baby in a white towel while Dr Goodman cut the umbilical cord; he then delved inside the stomach for the second baby.

Nurse Smets made no attempt to clear the newborn's face of blood. The baby looked lifeless. The overwhelming sense of joy quickly turned to a vexed state of gloom. The duke responded to her cold action with a cry of help. "Please, clear the airways so that the baby can breathe."

Nurse Smets just walked into the adjoining room. A tap was heard and then a cry from the newborn. Relief flourished on the duke's face and the warmth of joy engulfed the room once again. Flo could remember her ma saying, 'A new life being brought into the world brings a truly remarkable feeling of glowing happiness, a gracious being and a blessed moment in time that forever stays within one's soul.' She wasn't feeling her mother's words and knew why.

Dr Goodman pulled out the second newborn. This time he placed the baby into the arms of Nurse Janssen who was ready and waiting with a towel in hand. The atmosphere in the room was still not truly glowing with happiness. Dr Goodman cut the umbilical cord while Nurse Janssen wiped the newborn with a white towel and walked into the adjoining room. Flo had plucked up the courage once more to gaze at Dr Goodman's operation. Another tap was heard from the adjoining room and once more a cry from a newborn baby was heard again. Jubilation was sensed around the room. Dr Goodman then produced a large placenta with two umbilical cords attached. He held it in his hands and smiled as if the gruesome sight was a trophy. "Congratulations, Your Grace. You have male and female monozygotic-sesquizygotic twins. This is very, very rare."

Flo felt rather overwhelmed at the sight of blood and confused with the huge event that had just unfolded right before her eyes. It all seemed rather surreal, in contrast to the conversation she had overheard just an hour ago. Also, how could a male and female be identical? Plus, she had no idea what the word sesquizygotic meant, but she surmised it had something to do with there being a boy and girl.

The duke's expression was one of trepidation more than elation, even though he had just become a father for the third time.

Mrs Crabtree and Elsie entered the room with jugs of fresh water. Elsie took one look at the huge, bloody placenta Dr Goodman held as a trophy and horror struck her face. Her mouth dropped wide open, her eyes rolled, as the color from her skin depleted into a whiter shade of pale. Simultaneously her body withered and dropped to the floor, followed by the jug of water crashing on the herringbone oak floor, before anyone could react.

Dr Goodman gave a nonchalant shrug and sarcastically uttered, "Timing couldn't be better." He placed the placenta in a large glass bowl that sat on the table next to him. He turned and commenced stitching the uterus back into place.

"Oh, good Lord!" Mrs Crabtree cried out. "Miss Alan, please take my jug of water, whilst I tend to Elsie." Miss Alan stood steadfast all the while and was now rather dazed with the births she had just witnessed. So much so that she did not react to Mrs Crabtree's cry for help.

"Miss Alan… waakkkee uupppp!" she spoke with a commanding tone.

Miss Alan fluttered her eyelashes, seemingly to awaken her wits and walked up to Mrs Crabtree, tiptoeing around the broken pieces of china as she drew close to the hazardous zone. Her dainty feet paused as she stopped and took the jug and then navigated back around the broken china to the safe haven of the oriental table. She placed it on the table as if it was a trophy of some sort.

Mrs Crabtree, in turn, nodded her head and tutted with disapproval. "After you have finished your dancing, you'll need to clean this mess up!" Miss Alan looked rather stunned at Mrs Crabtree's reaction.

In turn, Mrs Crabtree gently lifted Elsie's head and proceeded to tap her cheeks. "Elsie, Elsie, Elsie, can you hear me?"

Elsie's eyes slowly opened and she murmured the words, "Yes, Mrs Crabtree, I'm sorry."

"Miss Alan, can you please help me lift her to her feet? I fear she will cut herself on the porcelain shards if she stays here much longer."

"Yes, Mrs Crabtree," Miss Alan sneered, as her feet once again navigated the pieces of broken china and the slick water that covered the floor.

"Please feel free to sit Elsie on the chaise lounge, Mrs Crabtree, until she comes to her senses," the duke said.

"Thank you, Your Grace, that will be a great help." Mrs Crabtree spoke with candor.

"Miss Alan, if you support Elsie's right arm and I the left, we can lift on the count of three and move her over to the chaise lounge."

Miss Alan nodded in agreement.

"One, two." Then with a huge huff, "Three!" (Mrs Crabtree instructed.)

Elsie now stood on her feet although supported by Miss Alan and Mrs Crabtree. They dragged Elsie to the chaise lounge. Meanwhile, Dr Goodman made haste with stitching the uterus. It was almost completed. When Sister Crouse checked the blood pressure of the duchess once again.

The duchess's eyes slowly opened blinking as they did so, until her stare stilled and she focused on the pleated silk above the four-poster bed.

The duke watching the duchess closely, generated an expression of uncertainty, his lips parting slightly on the brink of alarm and his stare intense.

The duchess turned her head slightly and gazed at the duke. Her voice was soft and very faint. "Am I in heaven with Mary?" Her eyes closed, then blinked open several times. "Where's Mary?"

The duke's stare instantly depleted and turned to a softening gaze. "Mary is right by your side, darling," he consoled.

"Ohhhhhhh good." She slowly closed her eyes.

The duke's calm demeanor dissipated the very second the duchess closed her eyes, it transpired into one of sheer fraught. "Can she feel the pain?"

Sister Crouse explained, "Nein, very occasionally this happens. Her Grace can feel no pain and she is now dreaming peacefully, deep in REM. Look at her beautiful eyelashes fluttering."

The duke and Flo gazed at the duchess, concerned.

Elsie became alert and able to sit up on the chaise lounge, unsupported. With her eyes wide open, she sniveled, "Ohhhhhhh sorry, I don't know what came over me."

Mrs Crabtree looked Elsie steadfast in the eye with a puzzled look on her face. "Don't you know? Are you able to focus?"

"I think so," she murmured.

"Right, how many fingers am I holding up?" Mrs Crabtree held up four fingers on her right hand and three on her left hand.

"Four, five six seven… seven." Elsie lit up with enthusiasm.

Mrs Crabtree smiled with delight. "Right you are then!"

Elsie turned her body towards the direction of where Dr Goodman was working in order to lever herself off the chaise lounge.

"Careful, dear," murmured Miss Alan.

Directly in Elsie's line of sight sat the bloody placenta in the glass bowl. She raised her body in an upward motion and focused on the bloody placenta at the same time. Her body started to wither once more.

"Ohhhhhhhhhhh, I feel funny all of a sudden." Her body then flopped back down on the chaise lounge.

"My goodness, not again!" Mrs Crabtree's apathy seemed to drain from her face. She supported Elsie's neck once more and tapped her face gently. "Elsie, Elsie, Elsie, can you hear me?"

This time Elsie stilled for a while before she reacted by opening her eyes slowly. Still incoherent she muttered the words, "Sorry," rolled her amber-blazed brown eyes and then closed them.

Mrs Crabtree's eyes widened with despair. "What am I to do with her? She can't see the placenta again, or we will never move her off this chaise lounge, or for that matter out of Her Grace's room."

"Nurse Hermans." Dr Goodman looked up at Nurse Hermans. "Can you discard the placenta, please?"

The duke's expression turned to one of intrigue. He seemed provoked. "Goodman, what will happen to the placenta?" he asked with an abrasive tone.

Dr Goodman's eyes were focused on his stitching, unflinched by the duke's reaction. "Well, in ancient times the placenta was eaten by the mother. It's thought that it is packed with nutrients, which is just what a new mother needs to recover from childbirth; it also helps with the breastfeeding and milk production. However, with the pre-eclampsia, I cannot trust that this will be the case, it could be toxic." He looked up at the duke for his reaction with compassion in his eyes. "So, what would you like to do with it?"

A tear welled within the duke's left eye. Mrs Crabtree looked at Flo, intrigued. Flo knew full well in her heart why the duke had a tear in his eye, her heart pained at the thought that he may be grieving.

"I would like to bury it." He spoke with a soft stern voice.

"Well, bury it you shall," Dr Goodman replied with deep feeling in his voice. He paused for a moment and gazed at Nurse Hermans. "Please cover the bowl for now so that Elsie can become upwardly mobile. She's a rather dizzy girl, Mrs Crabtree, to say the least." He then gazed at Mrs Crabtree, furrowing his white eyebrows. Mrs Crabtree reacted in turn, shrugged her shoulders and developed a surprised expression on her face as if she had an afterthought.

"Ja," piped up Nurse Hermans. She strutted over to the oriental table, crushing some broken china underfoot as she walked, grabbed a white towel and flicked it in the air, at the same time just missing Mrs Crabtree's nose.

Mrs Crabtree did not blink, nor flinch, instead, she composed herself. Firstly, she breathed in, with a deep breath and smiled, as if to inhale in the good and on a long exhale out, she made an O shape with her lips as if to exhale out all that was bad. She knew this was neither the time nor the place to react to a nurse that had little prudence and was a folly to her profession. Nurse Herman's reaction provoked Mrs Crabtree's intuition though. She raised her eyebrows in momentary thought, then quickly distracted herself with the task in hand. "Miss Alan, could you please clean up the broken china and the spilt water before an oblivious person hurts herself and slips and falls."

"What about Elsie?" Miss Alan queried.

"I can deal with Elsie, Miss Alan." Mrs Crabtree's voice was firm in reassurance.

"Yes, Mrs Crabtree. I'll go and fetch a mop, bucket, dustpan and broom, immediately." An embarrassed expression appeared on Miss Alan's face as she carefully glided across the floor avoiding the crushed china.

Meanwhile, Mrs Crabtree tapped Elsie lightly on the face. "Elsie, Elsie, can you hear me? Elsie?"

Elsie stirred and flickered her eyes. "Ohhhhh, sooooooo sorry, Mrs Crabtree, I have never been good at the sight of blood."

"You don't say? Can you focus?" (Rolling her eyes at the revisited scenario.)

Elsie pitifully spoke, "Yes. Can I be excused from this room?"

"You certainly can, as long as you look nowhere else other than the direction of the doorway. Can you do that?" Mrs Crabtree scoffed.

Elsie softly replied, "I can," with an embarrassed look on her face.

"Here." Mrs Crabtree held out her hand. "I'll help you up."

Elsie steadied herself with Mrs Crabtree's hand and lifted her body off the chaise lounge. Her eyes focused on nothing but the door ahead, as she took her second step, she crushed a china shard under her foot. Her body flinched in doing so.

"Ohhhh goodness, watch out for the broken china and for that matter the slick floor." Mrs Crabtree spoke in despair.

Elsie headed for the door and opened it. All in the room seemed to breathe one huge sigh of relief. Apart from Dr Goodman who was skillfully busy stitching as the door closed.

Barely twenty seconds went by and there was a knock on the bedroom door. All in the room gasped and were taken aback by the knock, apart from the duchess, who was asleep and Dr Goodman who seemed to be very much in his own world, displaying an apathetic expression on his face.

The duke scoffed, "Surely not, she's interrupted matters more than enough this morning!"

Mrs Crabtree acknowledged the duke's dismay with a sigh. "I'll go to the door, Your Grace."

The duke nodded with a stern look on his face. Mrs Crabtree tottered over to the door and braced herself before opening it. She took a deep breath in and clasped hard on the brass doorknob as she twisted her wrist and jerked the door open. Relief engulfed her vocal cords as the words flowed from her lips. "Oh, am I glad to see you. We all thought Elsie had come back for a third glance at the placenta."

Miss Alan's eyes looked rather astonished but the sudden realization that Mrs Crabtree was glad to see her brought delight in the form of a smile.

"Mop, bucket, dustpan and broom in hand, Mrs Crabtree!" She gestured, raising all with both hands to her shoulder level.

"Wonderful, all will be cleared in no time then. I'll take the mop and bucket while you clean up the broken china, Miss Allan." Mrs Crabtree gently grabbed the mop and bucket, with a smile in tow. The two briskly set to work.

Chapter Eighteen
It's a Miracle

There was a sense of calm and joy that resonated throughout the room. Sister Crouse once more placed the black cuff around the middle third of the left upper arm of the duchess. She inflated the cuff by squeezing the black rubber ball. The duchess's arms stiffened suddenly, her hands became outstretched in synchronized movement, in response to the squeezing of the black cuff. Sister Crouse quickly placed her stethoscope just below the black cuff and listened to her artery as she watched the mercury on the manometer. "Blood pressure is high. 140 over 90!" she shrieked.

Dr Goodman ceased the stitching immediately. His eyes opened wider looking rather annoyed at the inconvenience. "Don't look so shocked, Sister Crouse, the duchess is having a postpartum seizure, all part and parcel of the throes of giving birth where preeclampsia preexisted. For the unlucky few don't you know?" The needle and thread slid out of his bloody gloved hand and he proclaimed. "However, this is bad timing!"

Sister Crouse uncuffed the duchess's arm in a quick and concise manner. The duchess's entire body now stiffened as her muscles contracted, and her back and neck arched. The duke's expression was now consumed with despair; all who stood around the room mirrored his expression on their faces, apart from Dr Goodman. Mrs Crabtree dropped the mop she had clasped so hard in her hand with the sheer shock of seeing her beloved duchess in such a contorted position.

"Please, Goodman, do something!" the duke pleaded.

The duchess screamed out, "Ahhhhhhh!" as her vocal cords contracted.

All in the room were now silenced by the paralyzing sound and sight, portraying their alarming despair, although not a word was spoken.

The duchess's muscles started to twitch simultaneously, each muscle spasmodically working her slender frame; each twitch forcing a stronger motion. Her body violently burst into a conjunction of rapid, violent jerking that rhythmically vibrated. She rebounded uncontrollably, pounding the mattress, the sight was unnerving to the calmest temperament.

"Do something, Goodman, please! There must be something you can do?" the duke shouted with horror.

"I can't, Your Grace." He stared back with despair in his eyes. "We must wait for the seizure to pass."

The duke stared at Dr Goodman, with disbelief. He frantically yelled, "What about her tongue, could she swallow it?"

"It's not physically possible for Her Grace to do that," piped up Sister Crouse.

"The seizure should pass within the next minute, maybe sooner," intervened Dr Goodman.

The duchess's body seemed to hit the mattress harder with every contraction her body made. All in the room were helpless onlookers, cringing with every thump her head, hands, and feet made.

Flo shut her eyes with her despair and placed the palms of her hands together, bowed her head and prayed underneath her breath. "Please, Lord, let the suffering stop, please Lord, let the suffering stop, please, Lord, let the suffering stop..." Tears rolled down her cheeks.

Miss Alan's eyes were closed too, fraught with nervousness and distress.

The raw emotion filled the room. Tears of distress were now contagious and there was not a dry eye in the room apart from Dr Goodman's.

The seizure continued to punish all the distraught, who could only stand by helplessly as the thrashing of the frail body picked up strength. Blood started to dribble from the right side of the duchess's mouth.

The duke glared into Dr Goodman's eyes with sheer horror. Dr Goodman replied, "Her Grace has most likely bit her tongue."

Flo opened her eyes to view for herself, as she felt an inner sense of calm, a beacon of light inside her. It glowed from within, as she focused her calmness on the duchess and placed her left hand around her left hand, although the duchess's hand was fully outstretched and rigid at the time of Flo's touch. The calm touch flowed through her body, instantaneously freeing the duchess's tortured body from the grasp of the seizure. Her frail body no longer thrashed but stilled, it looked limp and lifeless.

"Ahhhhhhhhhh." The duke gasped in relief with one breath. He stared down at her lifeless body. Then with another gasp, "Ahhhhhhhhh, Alexandra, Alexandra, please don't go!" He gently cupped her right hand with both of his hands as tears welled in his deep blue eyes.

There was an unwelcome stillness in the room; all seemed consumed, immersed momentarily by its depth. Dr Goodman surfaced first. "Sister Crouse, blood pressure please."

Sister Crouse nodded her head and blinked her eyes. She took a long deep breath and placed the cuff around the duchess's arm. Dr Goodman peered over his spectacles, waiting eagerly on Sister Crouse's words.

"It's normal!" she blurted out, smiling with her words.

"Ahhhhhhhhh good, I can resume stitching, just a few more to go," he announced.

"Swob me, Nurse Hermans."

"Ja, Dr Goodman." Nurse Hermans passed a large pair of tweezers, which held an amber-colored iodine swab. He wiped the swab over the bloodied area of stitched skin and then passed back the tweezers to Nurse Hermans.

Normality spanned in the room once more as Mrs Crabtree and Miss Alan swept up the last few shards of china off the floor. The duke stroked his wife's forehead with a gaze of relief. Sister Crouse uncuffed the duchess and proceeded to pack the manometer away as Dr Goodman washed his hands. Flo felt like she should now move, there was no reason as to why she was still standing next to the duchess. Although the very thought of her taking one step away from where she was standing made her evermore uncomfortable. She had been told to stay by the duchess's side and she would do so until told otherwise.

The duke's voice tremored as he spoke. "So, Goodman, will Alexandra survive this?"

"She has done, miraculously." He paused momentarily his eyes dazed, as he collected his thoughts and looked at Flo. "But at what cost, we will not know imminently. We will need to keep a close eye on Her Grace, all the while. Her Grace has won the battle but not the war."

The duke held a cold long stare into nothingness while his thoughts encaptured his mind. His expression saddened, mirroring his thoughts.

"I will need to check on your newborns, Your Grace, please deal with the now. Time will unveil what we are all to receive but for now we deal with the present. Her Grace is strong." He smiled victoriously. "She has just proven that there are not many that survive a bolt of lightning! It's a miracle."

The duke seemed to mull over Dr Goodman's words, as Dr Goodman made his way through the double doors in the room, Nurse Hermans followed and closed the door behind her.

Sister Crouse straightened up the bedding, while Mrs Crabtree passed the mop and bucket to Miss Alan and picked up the broom and bucket full of china shards. "Will that be all, Your Grace?"

"Yes, for now, Mrs Crabtree, I will call if I'm in need of anything."

Mrs Crabtree smiled and then poignantly spoke. "Very well, Your Grace. Florence, you may leave Her Grace's side now. I'm sure the duke and duchess will want to be alone."

The duke seemed unresponsive to the words as he gazed at the duchess. Flo nodded and gently placed the duchess's right hand down on the bed. In doing so she invoked the consciousness within the duchess. Her lilac blue eyes began to gently flutter open.

"How are you feeling, my precious?" declaring his feelings of concern in his voice while bestowing heartfelt love in his eyes.

Her eyebrows furrowed as she thought. "My head feels a little fuzzy," she uttered, smiled and turned her head to see Flo standing next to the bed. "Ahhhh, Mary, I thought you were all but a dream, but you're actually here." The duchess smiled warmly at Flo.

Flo smiled nervously, understanding the duchess's state of delirium but not knowing what to make of the situation she had found herself in.

"It's good to have you home again, Mary." She turned her head towards the duke, her eyes glazed now. "Charlie, where are our babies?"

The duke smiled. "They're in my room, whilst you rest. Dr Goodman is in there too, examining our newborn baby boy and girl, making sure they're healthy." His smile dissipated. "Alexi, you need to rest. You've been through quite an ordeal." The duke bent and gently kissed the duchess on her forehead and stroked her hair. "Now rest, you need it."

Her eyes widened. "I can't rest... not until I have seen our babies, Charlie, I need to bond with them, then I will rest." Her insistence was followed by an endearing smile. The duke released a sigh of despair. "Ahhhhhhhh, why are you being so onerous?"

She softly spoke. "Because it's my prerogative." She smiled and closed her eyes at the same time, exuding her inner happiness.

"Sister Crouse, would you inform Dr Goodman that the duchess and I now want to see our babies?"

"Ja, Your Grace." She scuttled around the bed.

"Flo, now's a good time!" Mrs Crabtree scoffed.

"You mean Mary, surely Mrs Crabtree? Do you remember our conversation?" the duke mocked.

"Yes, Your Grace, I am sorry, I mean Mary!"

Sister Crouse left the room through the double doors.

"Mary, now would be a good time!" Mrs Crabtree's voice was ever more insistent.

"No," the duchess uttered. "I want Mary to stay," the duchess still a little delirious, commented, "Why are you dressed like that?"

Flo, now more dumbfounded than ever, wondered if Elsie had been treated the same way, on her first day. Maybe that's why she developed such a weird, funny facial expression she thought. Flo was tempted to express her dumbfoundedness, it may make her feel better short term but it would certainly make the whole situation worse.

The duke asserted himself. "Thank you for your help, Mrs Crabtree and Miss Alan, you may leave the room."

"Yes, Your Grace. Please call if you need anything." Mrs Crabtree smiled as she turned on her heels and ushered Miss Allan out the door.

The silence in the room became a welcomed state of mind for all. Flo no longer thought, for her thoughts were too tangled in her mind to make sense. She was dazed by her encounter.

The duke walked over to Flo and placed both hands on her shoulders. Somehow Flo's heart slowed pace and she became relaxed.

"Mary, your life will change from this day forward. You are going to feel greatness and witness greatness, you do not know it, but you are a gift to the world," the duke smiled. "This greatness will constantly amaze you. However, you must never discuss what you witness with anyone else other than Dr Goodman, your tutors, your kind and me. Can you do that?"

Flo paused for a short while. There were so many questions she had but dared not ask one. "Yes, I can do that."

"Good because you have been chosen a long time ago and it's now time you knew the truth." His smile dissipated as his expression transformed, he glared now with all seriousness.

"It's a great honor to be bestowed on such a young woman... it's your calling, Mary." A smile emerged on his lips. "All will become clear in time."

Chapter Nineteen
Who am I?

Sister Crouse walked into the bedroom with a beaming smile on her face, cradling a baby wrapped in a cream crocheted blanket edged in blue and lined in white cotton. She stopped walking and paused close to the bed. "I am very proud to present you with your baby boy, Your Grace!" She dutifully handed over the baby to the duke whose expression was stern and his facial muscles seemed unrelenting to break into a smile as he held the newborn in his arms.

The duchess watched with scrutiny. "Charlie, what's wrong?"

Dr Goodman walked back into the room, cherishing a bundle of joy in his arms, wrapped in a cream-crocheted blanket with pink edging and lined in white cotton. He seemed to glide over to the duchess's bedside. "You have a beautiful baby girl." The duchess became distracted and overcome with joy at the sight of her other newborn child. Dr Goodman lowered his arms for the duchess to see.

"Ohhhhhhh, Charlie she's so beautiful." She held her arms out, gesturing to Dr Goodman. "Can I hold her?"

"Yes." He smiled as he placed the baby in the duchess's arms.

She looked down adoringly at her baby: "I am amazed at her beauty. There is not one wrinkle on her face. Charlie, look." She paused for a while as the duke sat on the bed next to the duchess cradling his son. "Bless, her eyes are wide open. She's so alert, mirroring my every smile."

"She looks just like her beautiful mother." The duke smiled "As for this little man, I am not sure who he looks like."

The duchess peered to see her baby boy; the duke in response lowered the baby's head.

"Bless, he certainly seems very alert too, however, he's frowning," she jested.

"Try smiling at him," Dr Goodman suggested.

The duke placed his pinky finger in the clasp of the baby's hand, gently moving his hand up and down with the slightest of movement. The duke began to smile. "He's a strong little man. There is certainly a strength to his grip."

The duchess peered over to see the baby's face. "Ohhhhh, Charlie, he's smiling too. Such clever babies, for newborns."

"They certainly are!" intervened Dr Goodman. "Your Grace, you need to rest. The babies are adorable and seem to be in good health. I will need to keep a close eye on them for a while though, solely for precautionary measures only."

The duchess looked at the duke with a saddened face. "I wanted Harry to meet his new sister and brother."

"When you have built up a little more strength, my darling. He's two years old, unpredictable and highly energetic. He could split your stitches open with one eager jump to hug you, rest for now."

"Mary, please take our beautiful daughter, Diana."

Flo did not question or pause, instead, she smiled, stepped forward and gently lifted baby Diana out of the duchess's arms. It was all very natural to her; she'd been holding babies ever since she could remember.

Dr Goodman commented, "So you have named your beautiful baby girl Diana, the name of the Roman Goddess of the Moon and hunting. Do you have a name for your son?"

The duke and duchess smiled, but Dr Goodman did not give them time to answer. "Perhaps, Apollo the god of sun and light? The god of prophecy, after all, he was the twin of Diana!" He turned to his thoughts.

The duke looked deep in thought at Dr Goodman's name suggestion.

"Ohhhhhh, as fitting as the name seems, Dr Goodman, the name's really not considered an aristocratic name, is it darling?"

The duke was still in deep thought.

"Darling?" the duchess rasped.

The duke gently shook his head as if to rid his thoughts. "Yes, darling."

"I'll give you the honor," she announced with delight.

'The honor?" he questioned.

"Yes, the honor of announcing, Theodore our son's name," the duchess chuckled. "Ohhhhhhhh dear, I spoke his name." She chuckled louder this time, and the laughter was contagious within the room.

"Theodore means god's gift," Flo chirped above the laughter.

Smiles were now prevalent on all present in the room.

"Yes, Mary, it does." (The duchess now piqued by her thoughts.)

"Sister Crouse, could you take Theodore?" said the duke.

"Ja, Your Grace." She stepped forward and gently took hold of the baby from the duke.

Well, darling, for the final time, you need to rest," the duke jested.

"Yes, my body is telling me that too." The duchess placed an outstretched hand to her mouth and yawned.

The duke leant down and kissed the duchess's lips. "Thank you," he whispered in her ear. The duchess gulped and seemed fixated within her thoughts for a moment in time. She smiled, a smile of relief.

"Come, Mary, follow me!" Sister Crouse commanded.

Flo followed without question, although her head was full of questions. Mary, who is Mary? Why are they now calling me Mary? Should she now call herself Mary? Life would become awfully confusing if she didn't. What will Ma and Pa say? The duke said all would become clear. How long before all becomes clear? It's her calling. Somehow, she had always felt different and been treated differently at school by her teacher. Her inbuilt intuitive awareness to sense the unexpected had failed her this time; she never saw this coming. She must have faith to keep her buoyant even in the most turbulent waters of life. A voice inside her was telling her to, *Relax and float with the tide*. Her father's voice was loud and clear in her head. She looked down at the beautiful baby she was holding and smiled with faith in her eyes; her smiling eyes were mirrored back at her and Flo felt an incredible warmth and attachment. She never wanted that feeling to leave her.

Flo had followed Sister Crouse into the duke's bedroom; it was palatial and masculine. She could see two cots on castors placed in the middle of the bedroom. One painted in a baby blue color and the other a light pink; both were made from wicker. Each cot was topped with a canopy crown of two gold rearing lions, with the shield and carved cross on it separating the lions. Underneath the lions were the carved words

'Nemo Me Impune Lacessit', which perked Flo's curiosity. The cots looked rather misplaced with the royal blue, cream and rich dark oak colors of the room.

"You may place Diana in her cot," Sister Crouse suggested.

Flo gently put baby Diana in her cot and touched her gently on her cheek with her forefinger. The lustrous cream silk and white lace draped from the canopy crown, dimmed the brightness of the light in the cot as baby Diana focused on Flo's eyes. Her eyes danced in unison with Flo's as she mimicked Flo's facial expressions of O's and Ah's.

"Gosh, she is incredibly alert for a newborn!" Flo remarked.

There was no reaction from Sister Crouse, so Flo thought better about asking her the burning question she had, which so far remained unanswered, what was the meaning of 'Nemo Me Impune Lacessit?'

Sister Crouse cut into Flo's thoughts. "I will need to make some formula for the babies. Could you show me where the kitchen is, Mary? It's been two years since I've been here."

"It's my first day working here, I think I know but could be wrong. You could call for service by pulling on the cord that's by His Grace's bed?"

Sister Crouse looked at Flo with pure puzzlement on her face. "I can pull the cord if you want me to." Flo said.

"Ja."

No sooner had Sister Crouse settled Theodore into his cot, there was a knock at the door, followed by a second knock. "Ja, enter," Sister Crouse replied.

The brass doorknob turned and the large oak door opened revealing a handsome but obscure-looking man, dressed in a black morning suit with decorative gilt buttons, white shirt, with a long black tie tucked into his waistcoat. His angular facial features and dark brown eyes made Flo feel somewhat uneasy. His stare at her was rather intense, his eyes darkened and his skin seemed to pale with every second of his stare. Flo's stomach started to churn. It looked like he was staring at a ghost but Flo was no ghost.

He turned his attention to Sister Crouse. "Keane at your service, ma'am." He spoke with disdain in his voice.

"I would like you to show me where the kitchen is," Sister Crouse cuttingly responded, suggesting that she had duly noted Keane's contemptuous attitude.

Keane turned his attention back to Flo with a glare of recognition and a hostile stare.

"Right, follow me." He sauntered out of the room.

"Mary, stay with the babies."

"Gladly," Flo replied.

Just at that moment the duke opened the left double oak door from the adjoining bedroom and walked into the bedroom with Dr Goodman. "I will just need to finalize today's examination of the babies, Your Grace."

"Right, Goodman."

"Are you coming or what?" Keane scoffed as he entered the room once more. His hostile expression turned to one of dismay when he saw the duke standing in the room. "Oh, sorry, Your Grace, I did not know you were present."

The duke raised his eyebrows. "Clearly!" he declared. "Keane, you need to learn that one gives respect to earn respect."

Keane coweringly, replied, "Yes, Your Grace."

"Could you please send Mr Ferguson up to see me?"

"Yes, Your Grace, right away." Keane looked at Sister Crouse. "I do believe you want to know where the kitchen is?"

"Ja." Sister Crouse sighed in mockery.

"Follow me then, ladies."

Flo looked at Sister Crouse in hesitation.

"Mary, you can now come too," said Sister Crouse assuring Flo, as she picked up a small brown leather case from a side table.

Keane walked out of the room, Sister Crouse and Flo followed. They turned left down the corridor with the rich colorful carpet underfoot, wainscoted oak paneled walls, lustrous silken-papered walls with portraits of the gentry. The ugly looking characters looked just the same and the portraits of many beautiful women suddenly paled into insignificance as Flo needed to put a spurt on to catch up to Sister Crouse who closely followed Keane. They descended the huge opulent limestone staircase with its gold leaf curvaceous newel posts, intricately carved English baroque balustrade and handrails. Keane increased his pace centered down the staircase and was now making headway on Sister Crouse and Flo. They held onto the handrail every step down the staircase. Flo noticed another butler heading towards the stairs, an older more distinguished man, dressed in similar attire as Keane.

"Mr Ferguson," Keane bellowed from the middle of the staircase.

A tall man with freshly barbered dark grey hair looked up and replied with a sharp tone, "I'm not in the garden, Keane, just merely at the foot of the staircase. No need to shout."

Keane met Mr Ferguson at the bottom of the staircase. "Mr Ferguson, the duke would like to see you. He can be found in his bedroom."

"I was just on my way up," acknowledged Mr Ferguson passing Keane and ascending the staircase.

Flo now altered her path on the staircase to make way for Mr Ferguson. She stared down at a pair of kind blue eyes, staring right back at her. All she could do was smile back, upon her recognition.

Flo quickly turned her attention to Keane who was now tapping his foot on the black and white checkered marble stone floor, while folding his arms. His foot tapping echoed in the entrance hall, amplifying his arrogant attitude. "Come on, ladies." He sighed. "We don't have all day!"

Sister Crouse did not utter a word, but the expression on her face was enough. She looked like she had swallowed something nasty, as she closed her eyes. She was discouraged with Keane and his lack of empathy. Flo had distaste in her mouth too, but it did not manifest her agitation or alter her expression. She just smiled politely at Keane as she reached the bottom of the staircase.

"My, my, aren't you the polite one?" Keane leered at Flo completely invading her personal space, waiting for her to react.

Flo did not flinch; her focus was on Sister Crouse whose brown eyes dilated with belligerence. "If I should stand here für another second, so help me Gott! I will not be responsible for my actions!" She slashed the atmosphere with her tongue.

Keane replied, "Right, off we go!" he chirped, puckering his lips and stepping right. He walked towards an opening and then turned right into the Great Hall, embellished with a gold leaf ceiling with golden crystal chandeliers. Entering the Great Hall for the second time and no longer entranced by her thoughts of concern, Flo was now able to appreciate the sheer luster of opulence and grandeur of the Great Hall. It implicitly warranted Flo's full attention. She marveled in the splendor, her head swaying in wonderment at her thoughts. How wonderful it must feel to dance in this huge opulent hall! In her mind she could vision herself dancing here.

Flo's marveling gestures had not gone unnoticed by Keane as he turned his head to look at her walking. "Ahhhhhhh, entranced by it all, are you?" he smirked.

Flo's marveling expression dissipated at an instance.

Keane turned his head again and stopped walking. "Whilst you are privileged to live here, Mary, you must remember you are not one of the privileged. May I remind you, that's a servant's uniform you are wearing!"

"I'st das so!" Sister Crouse scoffed, her German becoming ever more present within her voice.

"Yes!" Keane sneered. "Even if you are a lookalike!" He stared at Flo with disdain.

"Wir werden sehen (we will see)!" Sister Crouse mocked back.

Flo's thoughts rocketed into orbit within her head, 'look-a-like'. It was obvious she looked like Mary but where was Mary? Her thoughts began to escalate now, firing her neural signals throughout her brain, the bombardment of thought pained her to think. She could feel herself pale; at this point, she knew she needed to focus on one thing only, her breathing. Nothing more; she took a deep breath in.

Keane sniffed the air with disapproval. "Wir werden sehen. Errrr, care to say that in English, Sister Crouse? After all, tomorrow will be the mark of the end of the war. The eleventh day of the eleventh hour!"

"Nein," she mocked.

"I'll take that as a no then!" Keane laughed mockingly back at Sister Crouse. "I think it's time you found your own way to the kitchen. We only speak English here. Nein begreifen (No comprehend)!" he taunted, and turned back in the direction from which they came.

"Dummkopf (fool)," Sister Crouse muttered under her breath. She smiled at Flo. "Now let's see if I can remember the way," Sister Crouse said looking a little puzzled, holding her right forefinger to her lips.

"I know the way to the servants' staircase." Flo smiled, looking rather pleased with herself.

"I will follow you then."

Flo smiled and took the lead through the Great Hall, turned right, then left, passing the duke's study and four oak doors; she had no idea what was behind them.

"The servants' entrance," Flo gladly announced as she pointed to the door. Flo opened the door to the oak stairwell.

"Now then let's see if I can remember. I've been in that many stately homes it gets rather confusing. Now, there is a color code here." Sister Crouse thought for a minute, placing her forefinger on her lips. "Well, we will need to go down the stairs for me to get my bearings."

They both started to descend the staircase. (Sister Crouse thought out loud as they went.) "White for the kitchen and laundry... I remember that, now. Only one is in the left wing and the other the right, I think?" (Sister Crouse was questioning her thoughts.)

Flo chirped, "I am sure the kitchen is to the right side of the blue corridor, as the left white area contains the laundry."

"Ahhhhhh I can see the blue corridor now!"

"Do you know why there's a color code?" Flo asked.

Sister Crouse laughed. "No, although the colors of the corridors mimic the color spectrum." She laughed again. "It must be so that people like us don't get lost, I imagine."

Flo laughed too.

"There's a doorway to the right, that could be the kitchen entrance. I can see what looks to be a white wall the closer we are getting."

"Jaaaaa!" Sister Crouse beamed. "We are here, I can smell the baking. Ja." She stopped and sniffed the air first, then took a deep breath in savoring the scent, then exhaled. "Mmmmm, smells good, apple and cinnamon strudel!"

"Yes," Flo replied, not thinking about her words, she didn't even know what apple and cinnamon strudel was. Her olfactory senses had stunned her thoughts momentarily. Now all she could think about was apple cinnamon pie. Her mouth watered as her thoughts devoured a piece of pie with its buttery short crust pastry, succulent sweet-tart apples, and juicy flavorful cinnamon sauce. "Mmmmm, smells just like Ma's apple cinnamon pie." Flo had started to drool a little, down the left side of her lip. She reacted quickly and wiped it away with the back of her hand.

Sister Crouse retorted, "Well, we had better make Diana and Theodor's formula before we're both totally overcome by our taste senses."

They entered a huge, noisy kitchen with many maids occupied with their daily duties. The first thing Flo really noticed was the heat from two huge cast-iron range cookers, which stood opposite each other. Each was inset into a large chimney with huge sandstone mantles. Separating them in the center of the kitchen were three extensive bulky wooden tables. A plump lady with rosy cheeks to match her red hair, dressed in a grey dress, white pinafore, and a white mop cap shouted above the noise of the kitchen clatter. "Rose, is that stuffing ready for the pheasants?"

"Yes, Mrs Thorpe," shouted a skinny girl wearing a beige dress, white pinafore, and mop cap. "I'm stuffing them, Mrs Thorpe," she shouted.

"Stop, I need ta taste it first! Violet, has that kettle done boiling? Only, there will be nowt' left of the water for me pot of tea," Mrs Thorpe scorned.

"Yes, it's ready, Mrs Thorpe. Shall I pour the water?" said Violet.

"Ohhhhh no, just take it off the burner!" she bellowed. "Nobody touches me teapot, but me. It's been in me family for donkey's years! Bone China, 'tis." Mrs Thorpe picked up her much-loved teapot from the middle table and admired it while walking over to the pheasants, close to where Flo and Sister Crouse stood. "Reet, give us a taste then!" She opened her mouth to taste as Rose placed a spoonful of stuffing in her mouth, munching on her thoughts. She looked Rose in the eyes and scoffed, "More lemon juice!" Her concentration became distracted as she turned to see Sister Crouse and then Flo. Her eyes widened in disbelief at what she was seeing, jerking her head back, stilling her body, her skin paled, her jaw dropped open as she lost her grip of the much-loved teapot. It descended and impacted the hard-worn floor in an instant. The entire kitchen became silenced by one huge clatter, followed by the rebound of china. Mrs Thorpe stared at Flo along with all the kitchen staff.

Sister Crouse quickly diffused the silence. "What a shame. I had a lot of nice cups of tea from your teapot."

Mrs Thorpe looked down at her teapot and shook her head. "Life… life happens." She smiled firstly then frowned and looked up at Sister Crouse who opened her arms. "Come here and give me a huge hug. You look as if you need one."

"Ohhhhhhhhhh, I do at that." She walked to Sister Crouse and shouted, "Violet, clear me mess up, please. Everyone else get back to work, the show's over!"

"Yes, Mrs Thorpe." Violet scurried for the broom and shovel; the clattering in the kitchen began once again.

Sister Crouse and Mrs Thorpe embraced each other.

"Ohhhhhhh it's wonderful to see you, old friend," Mrs Thorpe declared.

"You too!" Sister Crouse affirmed.

Mrs Thorpe stepped back and cupped each hand on Sister Crouse's shoulders. "I wasn't sure if I would ever see you again, with the war and that."

"Ohhhhhhh, it will take more than a war to keep me away from your apple strudel." Sister Crouse smiled.

Mrs Thorpe smiled too, but her smile was short lived. 'So who's this?" She nodded her head in the direction of Flo.

"Well, she is my new helper."

"Helper dressed as housemaid?" Mrs Thorpe questioned.

"It is only temporary until I find her something more suitable.

Mrs Thorpe replied with a questioning look on her face. "Well does she have a name?"

"Mary. Her name is Mary," Sister Crouse proclaimed.

"Mary, Mary's her name? Ohhhhhhh, I think I'm having an acute feeling of déjà vu. I feel a little weird all of a sudden!" Mrs Thorpe took a seat at the table. "I don't understand this at all."

Elsie ran into the kitchen, stood behind Flo and Sister Crouse and blurted out "So, you're hidin' in here?" Not a soul paid any attention to her. So she tapped Flo on her shoulder and shouted, "Mrs Crabtree needs to see you, Flo. Now!"

Flo turned and looked Elsie in the eye, but before she had time to answer Sister Crouse interrupted. "Nein, there is nobody here called Flo." Sister Crouse looked intensely at Elsie.

Elsie looked confused. "Yes, there is, she is stood right next to ya."

"The woman stood right next to me is called Mary, not Flo, you are mistaken."

Elsie produced her dumbfounded look on her face.

"Elsie don't be pulling a face like ya doin', cos one day you might get stuck with it!" Mrs Thorpe scoffed. "Now be off with ya."

Elsie quickly straightened out her face. "Yes, Mrs Thorpe," she muttered, turned and headed out of the kitchen.

Sister Crouse placed her bag on the table and took out two decorated boxes, labeled: 'The Alexandra Feeding Bottle'. She placed them on the table and opened each box. "Mary, we will need to sterilize these bottles with the caps, tubes and teats." Flo had seen the oval-shaped glass bottles before and knew how to sterilize them in boiling hot water.

Mrs Thorpe smiled with glee. "Ohhhhhhh this would mean, the baby has arrived?"

"They have. Both very healthy," said Sister Crouse.

Mrs Thorpe looked slightly puzzled. "Both?"

"A boy and a girl, but don't mention anything!" Sister Crouse shrugged her shoulders in excitement. "I-I should imagine the duke will want to announce it just as he did when little Harry was born."

Mrs Thorpe patted the end of her nose with her forefinger and smiled. "Mum's the word," she uttered. "Although I'm sure everyone knows by now. I'm usually the last one to be told anything around here." She smiled amusingly. "Well, you will need a couple of me copper pans."

"Ja, a large one and a medium one, please," Sister Crouse confirmed.

"Violet, pass Sister Crouse two of me best pans: a large and a medium one."

In the background, Flo took the two copper pans from Violet and placed the medium-sized pan on the stove, then filled the large pan up with water and placed it on the stove to boil.

Sister Crouse sat down at the table with Mrs Thorpe. "Am I right in thinking Her Grace is not breastfeeding the babies?" Mrs Thorpe asked with a concerned look.

"Unfortunately, she can't, she's not strong enough. We very nearly lost her," Sister Crouse said and gulped with shock.

Mrs Thorpe's eyes glazed over with Sister Crouse's words. "Ohhhhhh, dear Lord, nearly lost her?"

Sister Crouse nodded.

"Will she fully recover?" Mrs Thorpe's eyes narrowed.

"We do not know if…"

"If what?" Mrs Thorpe mocked with worry and eagerness.

"If Her Grace will ever fully recover. She was extremely lucky to survive and at the same time, unlucky enough having preeclampsia and a postpartum seizure. They may well have caused permanent damage to her vital organs. Only time will tell." Sister Crouse looked rather grim-faced.

"Ohhhh, she'll be in my prayers daily, Sister." Mrs Thorpe placed the palms of her hands together.

Flo took two bottles, connectors, tubes and teats from the table, as Sister Crouse looked stunned with her thoughts, momentarily. She quickly came to her senses when she realized that Flo was sterilizing the bottles.

"Mary, do you know how to sterilize the bottles?"

"Yes, Sister Crouse, I've been doing it for me ma, for donkey's years.

"Good, well tell me how you do it?"

"Well, I am going to wash the bottles, completely submerge all parts into the water, bring the water to a boil and leave the bottles to soak for ten minutes." Flo smiled proudly.

"Ja that is good, Mary. Do you have a watch?"

"I do, Sister Crouse." Flo pulled back her left sleeve to show that her watch was clearly visible. It looked rather large for her wrist, with its thick leather strap that had clearly seen better days. All the same though, Flo gazed at the watch and smiled. "It was my brother's watch, Archibald's."

Rose interrupted the conversation by delivering a pot of tea, three cups and saucers, a bowl of sugar and a jug of milk, on a tray.

"Ohhhhh, you read my mind, I am so parched!" Mrs Thorpe chirped.

"Thank you, Rose," Sister Crouse acknowledged.

"There's a cup for you too, Mary," Rose declared.

"Thank you, Rose." They smiled at each other; as they did Flo could feel a warmth in her heart which helped ease her mind with her thoughts of Archibald's death.

"I'll be mother," Mrs Thorpe declared as she poured the tea.

"So, Mary, when the bottles are ready, we will need more boiled water for the formula, enough for the two bottles." She opened her bag, with a glass jar full of a cream-colored powder. "We will need eight teaspoons of formula per eight fluid ounces of water. Ja."

"Yes, Sister Crouse." Flo looked puzzled. "I have never heard of baby's formula before."

"It is a special formula Dr Goodman has developed especially for the twins, so that they develop into very healthy children," Nurse Crouse twittered.

Sister Crouse and Mrs Thorpe were now seated at the table sipping their tea. Flo sipped her tea too but stood while she periodically checked on the boiling water and bottles. Just as Flo was taking her second sip of tea, Mrs Crabtree walked into the kitchen. At first sight Mrs Crabtree seemed almost demon-like, flaring her nostrils, with her eyes wide and full of anger. In her fright, Flo's gulp of tea instantaneously caused her to momentarily choke. In order to relieve the feeling, a spate of coughing and spluttering followed until she could gain her breath back.

Mrs Crabtree tapped Flo on the back several times. Flo made one final cough to clear her airways. "Thank you, Mrs Crabtree, I think it must have gone down the wrong way."

Mrs Crabtree smiled. "Well, ladies, how dare you start afternoon tea without inviting me!" She smiled condescendingly at Sister Crouse and Mrs Thorpe, placing both hands on her hips.

The two women looked a little lost for words. "I'm just kidding, ladies." Her frown turned into a wry smile. "Mary, I need to talk to you… alone!" The smile instantly dissipated from Mrs Crabtree's face. Flo looked at the bottles on the stove. "I am sure Sister Crouse is more than capable of finishing the job; ohhh and bring your tea if you want to. Rose, I will have my afternoon tea in my office."

"It'll be with you shortly, Mrs Crabtree."

"Follow me, Mary." Mrs Crabtree walked towards a different doorway to which Sister Crouse and Mary entered the kitchen.

Flo followed with cup and saucer in hand. Her nerves somehow seemed to have deserted her, for some unknown reason she remained calm. She could feel her feet within her shoes, flexing and relaxing as each shoe touched the wooden floor. The corridor they were walking in was quite wide due to large alcoves that run along the side of it. However, the color white remained the same. Mrs Crabtree entered the second doorway, Flo followed her, her cup now started to rattle on her saucer, as her nerves woke.

"There's no need to be nervous, Flo." Mrs Crabtree took the cup and saucer out of Flo's hand and placed them on her desk.

Flo was relieved, she could now listen to Mrs Crabtree instead of being distracted with the rattling of the cup on the saucer and her wanting to make it stop.

"Now, notice I called you Flo."

Flo nodded yes.

"That will be the very last time I call you Flo. You are from this day forward known as Mary."

Flo's mouth opened as she verged on asking a question.

"I will not be answering any questions, because I do not know the answers. I just know that you are now known as Mary."

Footsteps down the corridor could be heard. Mrs Crabtree closed her door so that it was ajar and stared at Mary. "Some people are born great in this world, Mary. Some people achieve greatness and some have greatness thrust upon 'em!"

Mary gulped.

"You are the latter. However, in time, I feel it in my heart that you will achieve greatness too, all of which you can call your own!"

Mary smiled at such a thought.

"Your life will not be the same from this day forward. You are no longer a servant member of the household but a family member. Thus, you shall now be treated like that. It's His Grace's wish."

Outside the doorway, Rose's voice could be heard. "Keane, have you knocked?"

Keane did not answer, instead, he stood right next to the door in stillness, listening.

Rose stood there for a little while longer, out of sheer politeness. Now realizing that Keane was not going to answer anytime soon, unless she orchestrated an answer, she blurted out. "Well, I'll take that as a no, then! Could you please knock? Only I 'ave got me 'ands full." She looked down at the tea tray and scorned the words, "With this tray."

Keane looked sternly at Rose, with arrogance; eventually he knocked on the door, did not wait for a reply, but bit his lower lip as he walked away.

"Enter," scoffed Mrs Crabtree.

Rose pushed open the door with the tea tray in hand.

"Have you been standing outside long?"

"No, Mrs Crabtree, but Keane was standing by the door, listening and walked away as soon as I came along. Shall I put the tray on your desk?"

"Yes Rose, thank you. That will be all, please shut the door on your way out, just in case Keane decides to return. I'll need to see Mr Ferguson about his unruliness."

Rose placed the tray on the large meticulously tidy mahogany desk, looked up at Mrs Crabtree and smiled and turned her smile towards Mary. She then walked out of the room and closed the door shut.

"It is shrewd not to seek a secret, Mary, and honest not to divulge one. I know only of what I have been told and I am doing what His Grace asks of me. You need to do the same. Will you promise me that you will, too?"

Mary paused for a short time. "Yes… yes, I will, Mrs Crabtree."

"Good! Well, we need get you out of those clothes and into something more fitting. Follow me, Lady Mary Tavistock." Mrs Crabtree smiled.

Chapter Twenty
Common Sense is Intellect dressed in Working Man's Clothes

Mary followed Mrs Crabtree, although her body was in motion, she wrapped herself within her thoughts and the hundred questions she had burning inside her. Questions she could not ask about Lady Mary Tavistock. How does she detach from herself, from her existence, of her free will, self-awareness, her soul, when all she has ever known and been is the being of Flo? The person she knows so well… What self-sacrifices will she need to make to become Lady Mary Tavistock? Does she deceive her moral judgment, consciousness and for that matter her own spirit? Does she have a choice? No. Her thoughts were making her body nauseous with her questions; her mouth dry and a dizzy feeling began to overwhelm her.

They had now reached the Grand Entrance Hall with a black and white checkered marble stone floor, where huge masterpieces engulfed the walls and ceiling. Mary was oblivious to all that surrounded her, trapped with being and no longer in touch with herself. Had she already begun to lose Flo? The two climbed up the huge opulent limestone staircase with gold leaf curvaceous newel posts, intricate balustrade, and handrails. Mary followed Mrs Crabtree straight up the center of the staircase, where Flo had previously steadied her pace and stride, she no longer did. Her mind set on the here and now as she took her fifth step up the staircase. She misplaced her right foot on the corner of the tread, her left foot no longer steadied her slender body. She completely lost her footing. "Eweeeeeeee," she screeched as her body took flight for a very short time but long enough for her to grab the handrail and steady her footing. Although her heart was pounding with the fear of falling, she realized that her reflex was all Flo. Flo saved her from the fall. The way forward was for Flo and Lady Mary Tavistock to coexist. She could not erase who she was or alter who she was to become.

Mrs Crabtree turned to see Mary clinging onto the handrail. "Are you all right?" Mary took a deep breath and placed her right hand over her heart. "Ohhhhhh, I thought I was going to take a tumble."

"Well to be sure you do not make that mistake again, always make sure you have one foot firmly fixed in the center of the staircase before you transfer your weight. This carpet is silk spun, which makes it rather slippery. I've seen many of the gentries fall puddin arse over heels, completely exposing full sight of their bloomers on this very staircase." Mrs Crabtree stared into space for a moment as if she was viewing each memorable fall. She smiled in a sardonic way. Aware now of her unbefitting smile she turned her eyes to Mary. "Ahhhhh, the little things make life memorable." She smiled irreverently. "Are you ready to continue, Lady Mary?"

"Yes, Mrs Crabtree."

"Good, then we will proceed." She turned and continued up the stairs.

Mary followed making her way to the center of the staircase slowly but surely, concentrating on each footstep, as if it was the first time she had ever climbed a stairway.

Mrs Crabtree looked down upon Mary once she reached the top. "Grace will find you in time, Lady Mary." She turned and did not wait for a reply.

By the time Mary reached the top, Mrs Crabtree was already standing in front of an open doorway at the far end of the darkened corridor. So Mary quickened her pace, as she approached Mrs Crabtree standing in a beam of light. It illuminated her face as she smiled, beckoning her into the room. "This is your room, Lady Mary."

Mary slowly walked into the bedroom, as if she was treading on seashells, cautiously bearing her weight with each step she took, Her mouth aghast and her eyes wide open with amazement.

Mrs Crabtree followed Mary in the room, closely watching her reaction. "It's important to breathe, Lady Mary."

"Yeesssss." Mary took a deep breath in and slowly exhaled. "This is my room." She gasped with her eyes wide open. "Really, my room?"

"Indeed, it's your room." Mrs Crabtree smiled a bittersweet smile.

"The colors remind me of my favorite flower, the forget-me-not. Oh, there's one carved on the oak headboard, just like my bed at home, except this bed is much, much larger." Mary's eyes danced around the room. "I have dreamt of this room, many times with the cream wainscoting, pale blue walls, a humongous bed dressed with a cream and yellow jacquard canopy with its blue silk eiderdown and cream silk sheets." She walked over to the white marble fireplace, bent her body and reached out her hand, running her delicate fingers over the face of a carved cherub sitting on scrolled acanthus leaves at the base of the fireplace, facing its twin. "They symbolize divine abode and presence. Did you know that?"

Mrs Crabtree just nodded yes with her head.

Mary paused for a while before standing. Her gaze moved to the woman's face, in the center of the mantlepiece surrounded by carved marble roses that glistened. "She must be their mother."

Mrs Crabtree took a deep gulp and tears welled in her eyes. "It's my favorite room in the whole of Chandringham. The room seems to possess a spirit all of its own."

Mary felt a warm sense, albeit peculiar rushing through her body; there was an innate sense of righteousness, a being that she had never felt before. Maybe the duke's words, "It's your calling, Mary," would make sense sometime soon.

"Right, I must familiarize you with the room. Although I feel that somehow you have been here before. Only God knows how!" Mrs Crabtree took a good long stare at Mary. "I'll need to get you out of those servant clothes and dressed for dinner with His Grace and Dr Goodman."

"Dinner with His Grace!" Mary turned a lighter shade of pale.

"Don't worry, Mary, clothes may disguise a fool but his or her voice will give them away. You have nothing to concern your pretty head with. You have common sense and common sense is an intellect dressed in working clothes; you will just be changing your clothes, that's all."

Mary smiled as she thought about Mrs Crabtree's wise words. Her lower lip started to curl very slightly. She quickly retracted her lip as the very thought of Mrs Crabtree not possessing a sense of humor crossed her mind, it would be unfair to jest about Elsie. However, Mrs Crabtree caught sight of Mary's lip motion with her quick eyes. She decided to ease the moment. So she copied Elsie's dumbfounded look.

Mary stared for a moment, seeing but not quite believing what her eyes were viewing. Yes, Mrs Crabtree certainly had a sense of humor, she thought. "I was just about to—"

Mrs Crabtree finished Mary's words. "Pull a face like Elsie."

"Yes, do you think it will help me?"

Mrs Crabtree laughed. "Try it and see!" she encouraged Mary staring into her eyes.

So Mary curled her lower lip onto her upper lip and moved her blue eyes close together so that they almost looked cross-eyed. She quickly retracted the facial expression. "Ohhhhhhh it's uncomfortable and did not help ease my thoughts in the slightest."

Mrs Crabtree began to chuckle, which soon turned into a deep chortle, provoking Mary into laughter. Their bodies in turn convulsed each laughing at the other and seemingly completely out of control in the fit of reverberating laughter, both losing balance. Mrs Crabtree first, gasping for breath and collapsing in a yellow silk jacquard chaise longue. Mary, in turn, stumbled over to the bed clasping her stomach as she fell back on top of the blue silken eiderdown.

Mrs Crabtree caught her breath. "Ahhhhhhhh, laughter is soooooooo good for the soul and this moment has been a long time coming, bless even if it is at Elsie's expense."

Mary steadied her breath, still clasping her stomach. "It makes light out of darkness and heals the body and our very soul. I love to laugh."

"Me too." Mrs Crabtree beamed with her smile. "Right, Lady Mary, you need to bathe and then I'll dress you. You now need to keep up with your appearance and dress impeccably at all times, it's very important you do so. I'll be teaching you all I can." Mary was enthralled with the notion of dressing in fine dresses and gowns.

"Follow me, Lady Mary." Mrs Crabtree walked towards a mirrored door embellished with an ornate carved wooden doorframe, its crested, central, scrolled, carved M, was surrounded by leaves and grapes within an entwined vine. It was a work of art. She turned and smiled at Mary before grasping at the crystal doorknob.

"I feel like I am dreaming… am I?" Mary's eyes were mesmerized.

Mrs Crabtree did not react as she opened the door and stepped inside. Mary followed, gazing at a young woman's dream come true: there were rails of gowns, dresses in every color mentionable, shelves of shoes, hats, bags, two tallboy chests stood side by side. Her eyes turned to the beautiful adorned carved dressing table and opulent mirror with a very similar design to that of the framework of the doorway.

Mary's fingers ran along and around the forget-me-not embroidered cushion on the stool. It was centrally placed in the middle of the dressing table. Her eyes quickly caught a glance of a photograph of two horses and their riders. She focused in on the two women riders, and then Mary picked up the photo. "She's very beautiful." Mary paused momentarily. "Her Grace." Her mouth dropped open in shock at what her eyes were telling her when she studied the other younger woman rider. "The other woman... she could be me!" She looked at Mrs Crabtree with questionable eyes.

"That's because it is you, Mary."

"But how can that be, Mrs Crabtree?"

"I'm not in the habit of telling lies, so ask no questions and you shall be told no lies." Her eyes were set with a stern glare.

Mary did not dare ask her questions instead a fog of questions filled her thoughts while her body was motioned fulfilling Mrs Crabtree's requests. As she bathed and dressed, her thoughts tainted her positive thinking and she was finding it hard to grasp the very present. She had paid little attention to the finery of the bathroom and it's free-flowing water or Mrs Crabtree's suggestions of choice of the forget-me-not blue silk evening gown. She merely just nodded her approval.

Eventually Mrs Crabtree silenced Mary's thoughts with an abrupt brushing of her long, curly, golden-blonde hair. "Are you paying attention, Lady Mary?"

Mary glanced at the photograph once more as she sat at the dressing table staring at the other Mary. "Yes, I am with you now," she sighed.

"Good, because you need to watch how I'm dressing your hair. It's important that you are well-groomed at all times because you're a lady now and where you are going, you may not have the help you need!"

They both stared at each other, but there was no ill will between the two but an allegiance.

"It's important to always have beautiful hair. You have it, it just needs to be tamed a little. How do you wash your hair normally?" Mrs Crabtree busily set to work with rolling Mary's hair and clipping the rolls with bobby pins.

"I whisk an egg, with a little water and lather it into my damp hair and scalp. Miss Dawson my teacher says it's the best way to clean hair. It cleanses the scalp and also works as a tonic, strengthening the hair follicles and cuticles."

Mrs Crabtree began to talk whilst gripping a bobby pin in between her teeth. "You have had an excellent teacher but you're also very clever. We have had excellent school reports at Chandringham."

Mary smiled but was a little dumbstruck by Mrs Crabtree's words. She couldn't help but question Mrs Crabtree's words. "Excellent reports?"

"Yes, we always have school reports on our up-and-coming staff. However, His Grace took a special interest in you, now we know why." Mrs Crabtree raised her eyebrows.

Mary was more puzzled than ever. "Why?"

"Because of who you were to become." She smiled sincerely.

Mary stared into space, trying to make sense of Mrs Crabtree's words. "Was I always meant to become Mary?"

Mrs Crabtree ignored Mary's question and changed the direction of the conversation. "You have perfect skin. Did Miss Dawson teach you how to keep your skin looking that way?"

"Yes, she did!"

"Well, surely it's not that much of a secret?" Mrs Crabtree scoffed.

"If you don't mind me saying so, there are many secrets surrounding me but my skin routine is not one of them. I use cold cream and a warm damp cloth to cleanse my skin, then rinse in cold water and rose water to refresh it. Miss Dawson said, when I get to her age I'll need to moisturize too, with vanishing cream." Mary smiled. "To banish any wrinkles that may be lurking under my skin." She became bashful; speaking such words so much so the apples of her cheeks were pronounced and rosy.

"Well, that may well be. I started a little late because the vanishing cream did not banish my wrinkles." Mrs Crabtree looked po-faced and then broke out in a laugh, making her crow's feet around her eyes even more pronounced.

Mary laughed with her, trying to stay as still as she could while Mrs Crabtree put the finishing touches to her hair.

"Now, I must say, you are incredibly beautiful. Your beauty should never be ignored, Lady Mary, not by anyone, nor by you, for one day you may find yourself without it." She turned and stared Mary in the eyes. "Always know that you are beautiful inside and out and hold on to that beauty deep within your heart and it will never do you any wrong." Mrs Crabtree's eyes glazed "Now you're all ready for dinner, once you have put your gloves on." She passed Mary a long pair of white satin gloves. Mary started to place one glove on her hand.

"Follow me, Lady Mary, the duke awaits you." She walked briskly out of the dressing room and into the bedroom, Mary following closely behind. Mrs Crabtree turned her head slightly as they walked down the corridor. "Do you know your dinner table etiquette?" she asked, turning her head quickly back in the direction she was walking in.

"I believe I do, I practiced table etiquette with Miss Dawson at school. I place my napkin on my lap firstly then work my way through the cutlery from the outside to the inside."

"Yes, that's right, Lady Mary."

They reached the staircase; Mrs Crabtree took the central position and descended several steps before she realized Lady Mary had not taken one step. She stopped in her tracks and turned facing Mary. "Remember what I told you?"

"Yes, I place one foot firmly fixed in the center of the stairs before I transfer my weight. I conquered that but now I need to lift up my dress slightly, balance myself and look elegant at the same time. This means not looking at where I'm treading. Oh, I do fear I am going to become a tumbling puddin arse." Mary took a deep gulp and lifted up her dress slightly and stood in an upright position, gracefully making her way down the staircase. Mrs Crabtree turned and descended the staircase smiling proudly. Her smile soon dissipated once her eyes viewed Keane waiting at the bottom, watching their every move.

He no longer could contain himself as Mrs Crabtree reached him. He leant over and sniffed the air before whispering in Mrs Crabtree's ear,

"She scrubs up really well that Flo... you almost had me convinced she was Lady Mary. Oh where, oh where has Lady Mary gone?" Keane lifted his head, sniffed the air once more and walked away from Mrs Crabtree.

In turn her eyes became ablaze with fury. "Keane, you will do well to remember that some secrets are so blistering, it takes another fire to put them out. Now, I suggest if you do not want to get burnt, never broach this subject again." She smiled sternly. "You have been warned!"

He rolled his eyes in disapproval then turned to face Mrs Crabtree, smiling falsely. "His Grace has sent me to tell Lady Mary that dinner will be served very shortly."

"Well, tell Lady Mary, not me!" Mrs Crabtree mocked.

Keane took a deep breath in, exhaled his disgust and looked Lady Mary in the eye. "Dinner will be served shortly in the dining room, the family dining room that is. His Grace is waiting."

"Thank you, Keane. I can find my own way there. That will be all."

"Very well, Lady Mary." Keane bowed his head ever so slightly then proceeded up the staircase.

"Do you know where the family dining room is?" Mrs Crabtree mocked with sincerity.

"No, but I could not stand him being so close to me. He has such a contemptuous attitude and has been nasty to me thus so far." Mary smiled.

"Well, I had better show you. We can't keep His Grace waiting too long. Follow me, Lady Mary." Mrs Crabtree walked spritely towards the Great Hall.

Mary suddenly felt very nervous. All the while she had been encaptured by the surrealism of the events that had unfolded within the day, as she became Lady Mary. She had tried to convince herself that it may all be but a dream; like many she encountered before and woke from. Would she wake momentarily? Mary's footsteps and Mrs Crabtree's were ever present as they echoed in the Great Hall; this was no dream.

Mrs Crabtree passed through the doors at the end of the Great Hall and approached another set of doors; she turned and looked at Mary, viewing her nervousness. "Do not be afraid, Mary, you have a great head on your shoulders to handle yourself and a great heart to handle others."

She cupped both hands around Mary's shoulders. "All will be good in your life, I am sure."

"Thank you." Mary stared back at Mrs Crabtree with glazed grateful eyes.

"Now, there is no need to knock, they're expecting you."

Chapter Twenty-One
Cinnamon Apple Pie

Mary took a deep breath in placing her hand on the doorknob and twisting it, as she breathed out, she opened the door. "I believe you have been expecting me, Your Grace." Mary curtsied.

The duke stood still for a while staring at Mary, his blue eyes fixated, entranced within his own thoughts. Mary stilled too, wondering what to make of the duke's uncomfortable glare. She did not notice the beauty and opulence of the dining room. All she could do was stare back in trepidation.

Dr Goodman intervened between the motionless staring of the two. "Please be seated, Lady Mary, it is customary for ladies to be seated before gentlemen." He pulled a chair out from underneath the table and stood by it, gesturing for Mary to sit.

Mary gladly walked over to the chair and sat down. "Thank you, Dr Goodman."

All the while the duke watched Mary's every move. "Remarkable, absolutely remarkable." He stared for a moment longer, before he walked up to the dining table and took his place at the head of the table and was seated by a footman. "Thank you, Gigglesworth."

Gigglesworth, my goodness, what a giggle would be worth right now, Mary thought.

"Wine, Your Grace?" asked Mr Ferguson

"Yes, it's very much needed tonight, Ferguson."

Dr Goodman sat opposite Mary as Mr Ferguson began to pour the wine.

"I must apologize for my awkwardness just then, Mary. You rendered me speechless."

"I was in turn speechless, Your Grace."

"Please, Mary, call me Charlie, there is no need to be formal, I've always been Charlie to you," he smiled.

Mr Ferguson finished pouring the three glasses of wine, as Gigglesworth served the appetizer, starting with Mary. He bent down and placed a dish at her left-hand side. "Mackerel, Lady Mary?"

"Yes, please," she replied, waiting for Gigglesworth to serve. The dish was laid at her side and Mary began to wonder if she should help herself.

The duke noticed Mary's hesitance. "Help yourself, dear heart, you must have worked up quite an appetite today."

Mary's appetite had disappeared along with her identity as Flo but to be polite she took a fish and sat staring at it while Gigglesworth served the duke and Dr Goodman, and Mr Ferguson poured the water to all.

"That will be all for now, Ferguson. I'll call you when we are ready for the main meal."

Mr Ferguson replied, "Very well, Your Grace." He, in turn, nodded to Gigglesworth and they both left the room.

"May we bow our heads and give thanks for the arrival of the healthy babies and for our food?" The duke bowed his head. Dr Goodman followed and Mary lowered her head a little more. There was a moment of silence, then the duke took his napkin and commenced eating. Dr Goodman followed and in turn Mary tried to eat some of her mackerel but began to choke. She started to cough, covering her mouth with her napkin in hand. The duke offered her a glass of water. She quickly gulped it down and gasped.

"Better now?" the duke asked with a concerned expression.

Mary nodded her head. "Yes, I am sorry, I'm struggling with my appetite."

"It has been a very eventful day for you; well, it has for us all," said the duke.

Dr Goodman shook his head in agreement with the duke's words.

"Mary, when I told you that you were going to witness greatness and feel greatness earlier, I meant every word I spoke. Fate, prophecy and a little collaborating have deemed that you are now, Lady Mary Tavistock. Your pa and ma knew you were not their blood daughter, as my father and mother knew my sister was not theirs. You were both separated at birth." The duke took a deep breath expecting some form of reaction from Mary.

Mary did not flinch at the duke's words; all she could do was sit and listen.

"It was easier to keep your anonymity that way, so you could both remain safe. You are identical to your sister and therefore, separating the two of you made matters easier so that we could protect you both and the bloodline. It's important now that you carry on through life as Mary, as your sister can no longer be Mary, even though I know, Flo is very much alive in you. This is your calling." The duke paused once more.

The words of the duke were hard to digest and only made little sense, but she felt a deep sense of hurt, knowing her parents knew all the while that she was not their blood child and never told her. Mary's tears started to well, as a wave of untold sadness struck her heart with an incredible innate sense of not belonging. Loss and grief engulfed her mind, albeit, aware that her tears were about to fall, she fought the compulsion to cry.

"Please, eradicate all your questions from your mind and tongue, for your own safety. The less you know at this moment in time, the safer you will be. Your life could depend on this. You need to focus on the here and now." The duke placed his hand on Mary's.

Dr Goodman looked on with compassion in his good eye. "Tomorrow, Mary, I will be taking you to Portu Satis Tuto, where there will be others like you, and many that will protect you. You will be safe there. Your training will commence and in time many of your questions will be answered."

She gulped with apprehension. "Are there people wanting to harm me?"

"Yes, Mary, it is our belief." The duke clutched her hand, and then released his grip, in an effort to emancipate Mary's dread.

Her expression remained the same: one of shock and horror. "Wouldn't I have been best just keeping my anonymity? And who is wanting to harm me?"

Dr Goodman answered, "I am afraid the answer is very complex. It is impossible for me to give you an answer, right now."

Her expression changed to one of utter confusion.

"Mary, you need to rid your mind of these questions. All you need to think of right now is apple cinnamon pie," the duke jested. "The here and now."

Mary had a look of disbelief as if she had not been sitting at the table hearing the words spoken, she could hardly grasp the conversation that had just occurred. Now it seemed that the duke was making a mockery of her safety... *Apple cinnamon pie. What kind of brainwashing was this?* she asked herself.

"Would you like a piece? Mrs Thorpe made one especially for Alexandra, it's her favorite. Mmmmmmm, I think we should skip the main course and eat dessert," the duke smiled.

Dr Goodman piped up, "Sister Crouse has led me to believe it's one of your favorite foods to eat, too!"

"Yes, Ma's apple and cinnamon pie... except she is not my Ma, is she?"

"Your ma will always be your ma, as your pa will always be your pa. Time and your heart cannot change what the past provided for you. However, it is very important now that you honor your new identity." The duke clasped Mary's hand. "Your own happiness lies only in knowing who you truly are and making peace with it."

Mary's eyes widened. "But I have no idea who I am any more."

Dr Goodman piped up with deep sincerity within his voice, "It's very important you comprehend His Grace's words, for they are very wise words."

"Thank you for your wise words, Your Grace, but if you do not mind me saying so, I feel very overwhelmed with the words spoken and I cannot possibly eat a morsel of apple cinnamon pie. All I feel inside of me is a huge sadness in my heart and a feeling of not belonging. I have no idea of who I am or why I have been put on this blessed earth." Mary tried to hold back her tears but they flowed, regardless. Her lips trembled in the defeat of her efforts to stop her tears from falling. "I, I would like to be excused." She did not wait for a reply, but backed up her chair and made a run for the door and opened it with great haste. Gigglesworth stood startled in the doorway as Mary nearly jumped out of her skin with initial shock in her perplexed state of mind.

"Ohhhhhh, sorry," she whispered and ran past Gigglesworth, his startled look remained frozen, eyes like saucers, mouth aghast and fingers outstretched.

Mary ran into the Great Hall, tears falling uncontrollably, her lips trembling, delaying her every want and need to wail as her footsteps echoed. She did not notice another set of footsteps as her tearful gaze obstructed her vision.

Keane walked directly towards Mary. He could see that she was hindered by her thoughts and tears the closer he got. Knowing he was now directly in the line of collision, he did nothing to avoid it. The inevitable happened and the two bumped together. Mary stood in shock, motionless and unreactive, her tears still falling.

"Better look where you are going, Flo." Keane looked Mary in the eyes, with envy in his soul. He snarled the words, "What's a matter, did the duke not like your dress?"

"No," Mary muttered.

Keane yielded yet another blow with his spoken tongue of wrath. "Must have been your hair then. Oh, it's such a hard life being you!"

Mary stared at Keane for a moment with the look of sheer bewilderment. She had no mind to argue and decided to retreat by running away from him.

Keane shouted with sarcasm, "Careful now, I would not want you to fall!" He laughed loudly in jest at his own words, just so Mary could hear his echoing arrogance.

Mary made haste as she reached the Great Entrance Hall. Her tears started to dissipate slightly with Keane's intervention. Somehow his wrath had intervened with Mary's self-pity. Her footsteps echoed all the more as her shoes met with the marble checkered floor. She reached the huge opulent staircase with its slippy stair treads. She did not flinch with the thought of falling as she took stride in the center of the staircase. In no time at all, she reached the top of the stairs as Mr Ferguson stood there watching her every move.

Mary was breathless. "Oh, Mr... Mr Ferguson, I'm sorry I did not see you there." Her tears were prevalent on her face.

"I could see so, Lady Mary." Sincerity weighed deep within his voice. "You know, when you're feeling raw with adversity, know there is always someone else worse off than you." He smiled with his good intentions.

Mary managed a smile too. "How's Her Grace doing?"

"Well, she was well enough to enjoy her apple cinnamon pie." He looked down at the tray in his hands, at an almost empty plate of apple pie.

"Do you think I could see Her Grace, Mr Ferguson?"

"She is sleeping now. It would be better to see her tomorrow. Are you retiring for the night, Lady Mary?"

"Yes."

"I'll call for Mrs Crabtree then." He looked pensive.

"I would rather you not call, if you don't mind."

"Very well, Lady Mary, sleep well." He sauntered down the staircase.

Mary observed him for a little while, no longer feeling the need to run. She wandered to her room, gazing at the portraits hanging on the walls of the corridor. She closed the door behind her and breathed a sigh of relief. The room felt very cozy with the open fire burning brightly and the soft glow of the bedside lights. She slid off her shoes and gloves and sprawled right out on the humongous bed, face first into the blue silk eiderdown. Her dress blended perfectly with the silken forget-me-not blue eiderdown. Her eyelids dropped as she turned her head and before long, she fell asleep, fully dressed.

Hours went by before she woke to the sound of neighing horses and the wheels of a cart on the gravel driveway. Her eyelids flickered and her immediate thought was with her father. "Pa, pa!" Mary turned off each bedside lamp so that she could see outside. She walked in haste to the front window and gazed down on a stationary cart. Two men placed two small coffins on the cart. A third man walked towards the front of the cart with a flashlight in his hand and as he did so he peered upwards at Mary as if he sensed her being there.

"The duke," gasped Mary. Her joyous expression disappeared to one of fraught and intrigue.

The duke turned his flashlight upwards towards Mary's window. Her immediate reflex was to step back behind the curtain as the light hit the window. She stood statuesque until the light dimmed, peering around

148

the curtain to watch the cart leave with the three men. She stared until she could no longer see the cart in the moonlight. Mary moved slowly, deep in thought, to the dressing room and took off her dress, leaving her white, cotton, lace, bloomers and camisole top on. She was once more, drawn to the picture, perched on the dressing table. She picked it up and studied it.

"Where are you?" Mary murmured, willing the picture to talk back at her. She eventually placed the picture back down on the dressing table and switched the dressing room light off. She walked into a darkened bedroom, lit only by the moonlight now and fire and peeled back the eiderdown and settled into bed. "I need to sleep." Her eyes studied the moonlight for a while, before she fell into a deep sleep.

Chapter Twenty-Two
Where Has Flo Gone?

"Wakey, wakey rise and shine." Mrs Crabtree briskly peeled back the bedclothes and eiderdown from Mary's bed. Mary was lying down on her stomach, her face crushed against the cream cotton pillow with her mouth open, drooling ever so slightly, her hair tousled and snarled.

"My goodness! Looks like you had a rough night."

Mary stirred patting the bed, to validate her thoughts. "Oh, it's not a dream," Mary murmured.

"No, it certainly is not. Elsie tends to the fire, not your thoughts," Mrs Crabtree scoffed.

Elsie stood staring at Mary, producing her dumbfounded look.

"Elsie! Snap out of it, I mean today not tomorrow," Mrs Crabtree scorned.

Elsie shook her head in disbelief but any more of Mrs Crabtree's wrath was far to imposing for her to ponder with her thoughts any longer. She transfigured her face to normality then continued to make the fire.

Mrs Crabtree took a rather large sigh and continued to say, "Now, Lady Mary, I've got my work cut out with you today."

Mary sat upright in bed and a large clump of her hair fell down over her face. Mrs Crabtree pushed the hair away from Mary's face. "Oh deary, deary me, how come you wore your underwear to bed?" she whispered as she placed the hair behind Mary's ear.

Mary shrugged her shoulders.

"We are under the gun today!" Mrs Crabtree jested.

"Under the gun?" Mary gulped as she recalled the words of the duke in her head. *The least you know at this moment in time, the safer you will be, your life could depend on this.*

"Yes, under great pressure with time. We have a lot to do and little time to achieve it. I need to get you looking respectable and packed for Portu Satis Tuto. His Grace requires your presence for breakfast and we all have a meeting in the Great Entrance Hall at ten minutes to eleven. So, if you don't mind, Lady Mary, can you get moving?"

Elsie turned and stared once more at Mary as she elevated herself off the bed.

"That means you too, Elsie," Mrs Crabtree mocked.

Elsie looked down with a thoughtful expression on her face as she continued her task of lighting the fire.

Mrs Crabtree ushered Mary to the dressing room. "Now into the bathroom, Lady Mary, whilst I start your packing."

Mrs Crabtree took a set of white cotton lace underwear from an ornate, cream, tallboy. "You'll be needing these." She smiled as she handed the perfectly folded underwear to Mary.

"Yes, thank you, Mrs Crabtree." Mary thought to herself, did she intend for me to bathe or body wash?

Mrs Crabtree amplified her voice. "Just a body wash will do, Lady Mary. We don't want your skin to dry out."

Mary gazed into the mirror and pinned her hair up, off her face and commenced brushing her teeth with the bathroom door ajar. Mary could hear a faint conversation with Elsie and Mrs Crabtree.

"Em… Mrs Crabtree, I've finished making the fire, is there anything you need me to do before I carry on with me normal duties?"

"No, that will be all for now, Elsie," she replied curtly.

'Oh." Elsie lingered for a while as Mrs Crabtree continued to pack.

"Is there anything else, Elsie?" She directed her question as if it was a yielding knife, cutting the air between the two, trying to deter Elsie's curiosity.

Elsie, far from being the brightest person of class did not take heed. "Well, I-I was wonderin' what has happened to Flo? Only I've not seen her since yesterday… since Her Grace called her Mary. It's uncanny how Flo looks like Lady Mary and now it seems Lady Mary is back from being dead and acting a little weird."

Mrs Crabtree took a large sigh before answering. "The only real mistakes we make in life, Elsie, are ones from which we learn nothing. Now, I'm going to point out to you, loud and clear, when you sign a secrecy agreement, you agree to not divulge any secrets. So, I'm adhering to the secrecy agreement, you need to learn from that and do the same." Her pupils dilated with her stern look.

Elsie gulped as if to swallow the rest of her thoughts. "Yes, Mrs Crabtree," she whispered and looked down. "I'll be getting' on with me work now." Elsie walked out of the dressing room.

Mrs Crabtree rolled her eyes in relief as Mary walked out of the bathroom looking concerned. "Don't ask," Mrs Crabtree replied before Mary had spoken a word. She placed her hands on her hips and looked a little pensive. "Now, I will need to concoct a story as to where Flo is so that other staff do not get any ideas." She placed her forefinger on her lips.

Mary took a deep breath before obstructing Mrs Crabtree's thoughts. "How are you going to explain Mary is not dead? Keane already knows I am Flo," she sputtered.

"Seeing is believing, Mary, and yes Keane is trouble, but he will not say a word to others. He knows which side his bread is buttered on." She pursed her lips together. "Mr Ferguson has his eye on him." She paused for thought momentarily, her expression turned to one of concern, and then she shook her head as if to disagree with her concern, her mind now concentrating on the here and now. "Now for the task in hand, your packing! Can you manage to dress your own hair, as I showed you yesterday?"

"Yes, Miss Dawson has shown me many times how to dress my hair in many styles including the way you dressed my hair yesterday." Mary eagerly sat down at the dressing table and set to work on her hair, briskly undoing the hairpins, brushing her hair, sectioning and folding her hair into an up-do. Mrs Crabtree smiled and continued to pack and not before long the two had completed their tasks.

"How does my up-do look?" Mary asked with a smile.

Mrs Crabtree inspected Mary's hair, as Mary turned a full three hundred and sixty degrees. "Yes, that's very good, for a pretend novice. I hope it can withstand the journey you have ahead of you." She looked a little reflective momentarily. "Now, I have packed all your essentials and your nightwear. Please note the difference between your nightwear and underwear!" Mrs Crabtree smirked.

"Yes," Mary replied and smiled nervously.

"I've packed underwear, just in case that's why you're looking nervous." She pointed to the case. "Day clothes, riding attire, the odd evening dress, shoes, boots, hosiery, hats and gloves. You'll need a warm dress and coat today, it is rather chilly and there is snow in the air." Mrs Crabtree took a look at the coats and pulled one from the rail. It was a heavy woolen, teal-colored coat with a navy-blue rollover collar that elongated into a point in the center of the back. The turn-back cuffs accented the collar with navy blue ornamental braid. In contrast to the teal-colored coat, she chose a navy dress with a sailor style collar embellished in white lace with two separate skirts of varying lengths.

"Now put these on." Mrs Crabtree passed Mary a pair of navy-blue stockings. Mary gently rolled the first stocking and placed it over her foot and unrolled the stocking eagerly past her right ankle, calf, and knee until she reached her upper thigh. Mrs Crabtree simultaneously rolled the other stocking ready for Mary so that Mary could continue the same sequence with the opposite foot. In an instant Mary was fully dressed. She gazed at herself in the mirrored door. "It's hard to believe this is me. I feel incredibly distant from myself." Mary's fingertips stroked her lace collar.

Mrs Crabtree's eyes narrowed as she produced a stern look. "A word of advice, your life will be forever changing, dear. Sometimes you need to go with the flow of life. Don't think that holding on to who you once were will make you strong. It's the letting go that will give you that strength." Mrs Crabtree stared at Mary directly in the eyes. "Now you're expected in the dining room and I will need to check on Her Grace and have a word in Mr Ferguson's ear."

The two walked out of the bedroom and down the corridor, Mrs Crabtree leading the way, stopping outside the duchess's bedroom door. "Could I take a peep?" Mary hunched her shoulders in hesitance of Mrs Crabtree's answer.

"Later, His Grace is expecting you," she scoffed.

Mary did not reply; she continued down the corridor while Mrs Crabtree entered the duchess's room. A petite woman with dark brown hair walked towards Mary as she reached the balcony to the staircase.

"Good morning, Lady Mary," Miss Alan chirped. "Good morning, Miss Alan, did Her Grace have a comfortable night?"

"Yes, she slept like a baby. Speaking of babies, there was no filling the babies last night, I believe. Poor Sister Crouse and Nurse Janssen did not get a wink of sleep."

"Are they sleeping now?"

Miss Alan smiled. "Yes, I believe they all are."

"Oh good, I must get on." Mary chirped.

Chapter Twenty-Three
'Theory of Recollection'

Mary walked down the staircase, primed with pride as she took each step. Just like clockwork Keane was poised waiting at the bottom of the staircase, cocksure with arrogance as he stared Mary in the eyes.

"I was just coming to get you," Keane snarled.

"Really?" Mary questioned sardonically.

Keane curled his upper right lip before answering. "Yes, you're keeping the duke waiting! Unlike you, he has a busy schedule." He stooped towards Mary and whispered, "A word of advice, Miss High and Mighty, you stand on hallowed ground here, don't take that for granted!" Keane clicked his heels and walked away.

Mary was stunned once more by his words and looked rather befuddled.

Keane turned his head to show the right side of his face so that Mary could hear him. "Better get a move on!" He turned his head back in the direction he was walking. Mary continued to walk to the dining room all the while puzzled by Keane's words, *Hallowed ground*. The doors were open, so she proceeded to walk in.

"Ah, Mary, I trust you had a good night's sleep?" the duke inquired.

She replied softly, "Yes, I did, thank you."

"Please help yourself to breakfast." The duke pointed to a separate table full of different types of bread, toast, eggs, bacon, a huge bowl of porridge, a jug of orange juice and a fresh pot of tea.

Just as Mary scanned the delights, Dr Goodman walked into the dining room. "Nothing to worry about, Your Grace, we will just need to increase the consistency of the formula. Diana and Theodore certainly have an appetite."

The duke looked concerned.

Dr Goodman acknowledged his concern firstly by raising a rather bushy silver-haired eyebrow over his false eye. "Sister Crouse knows exactly what to do. The babies are in excellent hands, Your Grace." He smiled.

The duke paused for thought momentarily and smiled too, before he bit into a piece of toast.

Dr Goodman focused on Mary as he walked towards the breakfast table. "Mary, we have a long tiresome journey ahead of us, so please eat some food today. You are going to need all the strength you can get."

Mary turned towards Dr Goodman with her plate in hand. "I'm rather hungry today, Dr Goodman." She looked down at her plate. "See?" Her plate was full with two eggs, three rashers of bacon, tomatoes and two pieces of toast.

"That's a pleasant sight to see and it looks delicious, I think I'll have the same." He continued to help himself.

Mary approached the dining table with her plate as Mr Ferguson stood by watching. "Would you like a glass of orange juice, Lady Mary? It will help you with your digestion."

Mary smiled with the knowledge. "Yes, please, Mr Ferguson."

"Would you like a glass of orange juice too, Dr Goodman?"

"Yes, Ferguson, that would be herrlich."

Mr Ferguson looked a little puzzled by the spoken word herrlich. Mary sensed his non-perception of the word.

"Splendid," Mary blurted out.

The duke and Dr Goodman smiled at Mary as if to beckon an explanation as Mr Ferguson was looking befuddled now.

"Herrlich means splendid in German," Mary informed Mr Ferguson.

Mr Ferguson smiled. "Thank you for being informative, Lady Mary, I would have never known." He placed two glasses of orange juice on the dining table, one to the right of Mary and one to the right of Dr Goodman. His smile now dissipated and a stern look transpired. "Is there anything else I can get you, Your Grace, before I leave?"

"That will be all for now, Ferguson, thank you." He pursed his lips together. "Oh, Ferguson, all the staff will need to sign the secrecy agreement, before the ceremony at eleven a.m. today."

"Yes, Your Grace, I have it in hand, it's almost completed." Mr Ferguson turned around and proceeded to walk out of the room.

Mary conjugated her thoughts as if the words 'secrecy agreement' were a perplexing algebra question. She sipped her orange juice deep in thought.

"Are you all packed, Mary?" Dr Goodman continued to munch on a piece of toast.

Mary blinked her eyes to suppress her thoughts and concentrate on her answer. "Yes, I am. I have Mrs Crabtree to thank for her keen eye and efficiency. If it was left to me, I'd still be deciding what to take, with the abundance of choice and the not knowing where, 'Portu Satis Tuto' is." Mary paused for thought. "Does that mean 'Safe Haven' in Latin, Dr Goodman?

"Yes, Mary, it does."

Mary stared into space, momentarily. "It's weird because I have no recollection of how I know that."

Dr Goodman looked intrigued. "Have you heard of Plato?"

"Yes, he's a famous Greek philosopher who laid the foundations for Western philosophy, science and mathematics."

Dr Goodman smiled in jubilation. "Yes, he did and he was also cited as one of the founders of Western religion, spirituality and particularly Christianity.

The duke piped up, "Have you ever heard of his 'Theory of Recollection', Mary?"

An intrigued look emerged on her face. "No."

The duke looked at Dr Goodman. "I think I will let you explain this one, Goodman?"

Dr Goodman nodded. "Well, Plato concedes that, in some sense, inquiry is impossible. What appears to be learning something new is really recollecting something already known."

Mary looked a little befuddled.

He proceeded. "According to Plato this is implausible for many kinds of inquiry in relation to empirical questions such as: Who is at the door? Does that glass jar contain water or white vinegar? So in these cases there is a standard procedure in finding out the answers to the questions. One can indeed come to know something that one did not previously know. However, there are also non-empirical questions too, where there may not be a recognized method or a standard procedure for getting answers. These answers are more intuitive. Plato's theory denotes we already have within our souls the answers to such questions."

Mary felt incredible warmth within her body as she pondered over Dr Goodman's words.

Passion seeped through Dr Goodman's voice. "Everyone has intuitive feelings, an inner connection, and some feel that connection more than most. It is our belief, Mary, that you have a deeper connection with your soul much more than most, it's a gift you were born with." He smiled. "Now that's enough food for thought for now, you really do need to eat up, we have a long journey ahead of us."

Mary looked down at her plate, she'd hardly eaten a morsel of food out of sheer politeness and her intent for listening. She was extremely hungry and focused on eating along with the duke and Dr Goodman. Mary had to invoke her self-control and fight the urge to mop up the egg yolk on her plate with her piece of toast, as that would not conform to the rules of etiquette. She could see her schoolteacher frowning at her. It was not long before everyone at the table placed their used cutlery on top of their plates in an almost simultaneous fashion.

The duke stood first. "I really must get on; I trust I will see you both in the Great Entrance Hall for the ceremony at eleven a.m. today?"

Dr Goodman answered for Mary and himself. "Yes, indeed you will, and shortly after we must leave to catch the Green Knight Express at eleven forty-five."

Mary gulped as she felt nervousness in the very pit of her stomach with the thought of leaving Chandringham so suddenly, having only just arrived and her innate attachment barely quenched. Mary piped up, "I would very much like to see Her Grace and the twins before I leave, if that is at all possible?"

"Yes, indeed, I am just on my way up."

"Me too," Dr Goodman announced.

The duke smiled. "Well, we will all go together then."

They left the dining room and made haste, walking through the Great Hall.

Elsie walked towards them with a feather duster in hand. She talked with a cheery smile. "Good morning, Your Grace, Lady Mary and Dr Goodman."

The duke replied first. "Good morning," as he passed her.

Dr Goodman nodded. "Guten morgen," as he passed Elsie.

Mary smiled. "Good morning, Elsie."

Elsie stared Mary in the eyes, her cheery smile drooped and her eyes stared with stern intent. Her look sent a loud and clear message to Mary, one of animosity. She'd seen that look before, one of which reminded her of Keane. It seems that Elsie had not heeded Mrs Crabtree's words. The three now reached the Great Entrance Hall and just like clockwork Keane appeared.

The duke stopped at the foot of the stairs. "Ah, Keane, could you arrange for Wigglesworth to have the car ready at eleven fifteen today for Lady Mary and Dr Goodman? Oh, and I still want him to attend the ceremony at eleven a.m."

"Yes, Your Grace, I will tell him straight away." Keane smiled as he turned towards the main entrance. Mary glanced at Keane as he passed. His eyes deceived his smile. Mary detached herself from her unnerved feeling Keane wanted her to feel, as she ascended the stairs. She transferred her thoughts with the lighthearted notion of Gigglesworth and Wigglesworth, (smiling from the inside out). Mr Ferguson must have had a good chuckle to himself with those ambiguous surnames and Mrs Crabtree for that matter, too. Her notion then turned to a stupendous thought, what if they were twins and Gigglesworth and Wigglesworth were their first names. They approached the duchess's room. The duke paused before he opened the door. Mary's glowing smile captured his thought. "I am intrigued, do tell me of your amusement."

"I know I should not be amused but I'm amused by the names Wigglesworth and Gigglesworth," Mary confessed.

The duke laughed as he opened the door to the duchess's room. "Ah yes, Alexi and I were rather amused too, truth be known."

The duchess was sat up in bed, supported by many pillows, gently touching her lower stomach area over the cream silk eiderdown. "Well, what's so funny? I could do with a good laugh." She paused for thought. "Although I am not sure I should."

Dr Goodman failed to see the hilarity as the duke glanced in his direction, he gestured a nonchalant expression.

"Mary and I were laughing when we shouldn't be."

"Are you going to tell me?"

The duke walked up to the duchess and kissed her on her lips then whispered the names "Wigglesworth and Gigglesworth," as their noses touched.

She giggled with pleasure. "Oh, darling, you are such a hoot!"

Mary, the duke and duchess all looked at each other and broke out in a bout of laughter. The more they laughed the more pompous looking Dr Goodman's face became. His skin became paler than pale. His red eyes rolled in opposite directions, and his creases became visible on his forehead, his eyes narrowed revealing a scar on the eyelid of his glass eye, which extended to his right temple. His face became amusing to the three and they were unable to stop their deep-rooted belly laughter.

Dr Goodman pushed his lips together, with disapproval. "You will bust your stitches, Your Grace, if you carry on laughing. Please stop! Laughter is not so good for your soul right now." He gazed at the duchess with concern. "Right, I am going to take a look at Diana and Theodore. I am sure I will have a better chance of intelligent conversation with day old newborns than I have in here." Dr Goodman walked through the double doors to the duke's room.

The duchess uttered with a fractured giggle, "Really, I must stop, he's right." She placed her hand on her lower abdomen over the eiderdown and calmed herself. "Oh, it was certainly wonderful to laugh!" Her Grace smiled.

By now the duke and Mary's laugh had subsided too.

"Did you write your speech, darling?" the duchess asked.

"Yes, I did, with difficulty and heart wrenching thoughts." He formed a somber look as his eyes glazed.

"Would you read it to me later?" She reached out her slender hand and stroked the duke's cheek with deep sincerity in her heart and love in her eyes.

The duke stroked the duchess's hand. "Yes," he whispered. "My darling, I need to dress into my uniform, I will see you shortly." He placed a light kiss on her lips and smiled before turning and walking through the double doorway.

"Ah, Mary, I believe you are leaving us yet again?" she frowned. "Come and hold my hand." She held her hand out to Mary. "I do enjoy the inner peace you bring me. There's a calmness within you that calms my very soul. Did you know?"

Mary clasped the duchess's hand gently. "I did not know until yesterday."

"Charlie tells me you're leaving again. How long will you be gone for this time?" She smiled but there was sadness in her eyes.

Mary hesitated with her answer, wondering why the duchess has mentioned twice that she was leaving in a space of a minute and unsure what to say. "I'm unsure how long. I know the duke wants me to bond with Diana and Theodore, so hopefully it's not too long."

"The duke, he's always been Charlie to you?" She looked concerned.

Mary thought quickly. "Did I say the duke? Ohhhhhhhh, I did not sleep well and I'm over thinking matters."

"Well, you know over thinking is not good. Resolving to mend the hereafter does not resolve to mend now. It's the now that's important." She smiled endearingly at Mary as Mary contemplated her words.

"Talking of the now, why don't you do some baby bonding? As much as I love you being by my side, I feel rather tired."

Mary intuitively kissed her on the forehead and patted the duchess's hand.

Alexandra whispered the words, "I love you."

Mary had a pang of sudden guilt, one that struck her heartstrings. "I love you too."

"Promise you will write, this time?"

Mary smiled, but had concern in the pit of her stomach with her thought. How could she promise to write, when her handwriting would be different to the Mary that once was? "I will try."

The duchess smiled and closed her eyes. Mary gently placed her hand on the bed, smiled, then walked quietly out of the room through the double doors to the adjoining room. Sister Crouse and Nurse Hermans sat on a royal blue jacquard couch at the far end of the bedroom, bottle-feeding the twins. Each sat upright, almost back-to-back, resembling two bookends on opposite sides of the couch. Both were engrossed in their enchantment but it seemed quite clear to Mary that the two disliked each other.

Sister Crouse looked up first. "Ah, Mary, you look very pretty today." She smiled and gazed for a short time. "Would you like to feed Diana?"

"Yes, I would love to," Mary declared.

"Nurse Hermans, you can take a break, my help has arrived." Sister Crouse scoffed.

Nurse Hermans scowled at Sister Crouse making it quite clear that she disapproved of her request. Nevertheless, she placed the bottle of milk down on the table and stood with baby Diana in her arms. "I will need to wind her first, otherwise you may well be wearing a cream-colored dress and not a blue one."

Mary responded with politeness, "Yes, of course."

Nurse Hermans gently lifted the baby in an upright position, placing her head above her shoulders and supporting the back of the baby's head with her left hand. She gently rubbed her back in a circle motion and patted baby Diana's back. It was not before long little baby Diana let out one almighty belch.

"There, there, there, you needed that." Nurse Hermans smiled. "I think it's safe to take her now."

Mary nodded in agreement as Nurse Hermans placed baby Diana in her arms. Mary cradled the baby as she walked over to the couch, all the while looking at baby Diana. She marveled, "Such beauty graces her face, I truly have never seen a baby so beautiful. I love the way she smiles."

"Ja, unlike this little chap, although they're identical you can certainly tell he's a boy." Nurse Hermans pondered her own words.

Sister Crouse chirped, "Ah but, he has an impish smile that's why."

Mary continued to feed baby Diana the rest of her bottle. "It's amazing how their little hands know how to clasp the feeding bottles already, don't you think, Sister Crouse?"

"Yes, I agree, it's truly amazing. Life is truly amazing. There's an inner peace that comes with holding innocence. If only that innocence stayed with each and everyone. We would live in a much better world."

Mary smiled with Sister Crouse's words. "We would live in a perfect world, without war, hostility, crime and the futile loss of life."

Mr Ferguson suddenly appeared within the room. "Excuse me, ladies." He proceeded to open the duke's mirrored dressing room door and closed it without making any fuss.

Nurse Hermans waddled out of the room as Mary walked over to Sister Crouse and peered down at baby Theodore. "I believe you had a rather busy night feeding these little babies?"

Sister Crouse rolled her eyes. "We did, every hour on the hour! It's sleep time for Nurse Hermans and I. I must admit I am getting rather tired." She yawned as she put the feeding bottle down and winded little Theodore.

Mary scanned the bed; it had barely been slept in.

"The duke slept in the duchess's room most of the night, occasionally trying to pacify the twins." Sister Crouse barely spoke her words before yawning once more as little Theodore belched.

"I think it's sleep time for you too, once we settle these little angels. Do you mind if I hold Theodore for a little while?" Mary asked.

"Not at all, Lady Mary, he's fresh out of wind."

Mary placed baby Diana in the hands of Sister Crouse, then picked baby Theodore up from Sister Crouse's lap. She gazed into little Theodore's eyes. "Is it true that all babies are born with blue eyes?"

"Ja, all Caucasian babies are born with dark blue eyes. Their true eye color may not reveal itself for a few months." Sister Crouse looked intrigued.

Mary looked a little dumbfounded. "I can't help notice the twins have captivating crystal blue eyes they are far from dark blue. It certainly would be a shame, should their eye 'color change." Mary smiled as she placed her forefinger next to Theodore's tiny hand, in a matter of seconds he wrapped his fingers around Mary's finger and clutched it. "You're adorable, yes you are." Her smile glowed back at her from little Theo, his eyes danced mimicking Mary's eye movement. "I think you are a very handsome little chap, yes I do. You don't look impish one bit!" Mary turned her smile on Sister Crouse.

She gestured a smile back. "We will see about that. You know time reveals all and little boys are renowned for being mischievous and playful."

Mr Ferguson suddenly appeared from the duke's dressing room. "Excuse me, ladies." He proceeded to walk through the bedroom. The duke followed him looking incredibly handsome dressed in his army captain's uniform. Six medals were displayed with pride, over his heart across his left chest. Mary wondered how he had gotten them. What pain and suffering he had witnessed or what act of valor did he render? She did not ask her questions, as the time did not seem right. Maybe one day soon when the timing was right, she would, she thought.

Mr Ferguson walked straight out the bedroom door as the duke walked over to Mary and gazed down at baby Theodore. "He has quite an impish look about him, don't you think, Mary?"

Mary looked astonished and looked at Sister Crouse. "I don't see it, all I see is a handsome little chap." She smiled. "Have you and Sister Crouse been in cahoots with each other?"

The duke smiled wryly. "Now that would be telling." He placed his forefinger on his nose momentarily and looked at Sister Crouse and smiled from cheek to cheek. There was suddenly seriousness in his eyes as he turned and faced Mary, his smile dissipated.

Mary felt a heart wrenching sadness suddenly as she connected with the moment in time. Time that she no longer had left.

"It's almost time to go?" she softly whispered.

"Yes," he whispered back.

"I'll just wrap a swaddle around Theodore, if that's all right, Your Grace?"

"Yes indeed. Just as long as you are in the Great Entrance Hall before eleven a.m. Oh, and Mary, please call me Charlie, it's important that you do." He proceeded to walk through the door Mr Ferguson had left open.

Mary walked to Theodore's cot and picked up a square cotton sheet and placed it flat on the bed in a rhombus shape, folding the top corner of the blanket with her right hand while holding baby Theodore into her chest with her left hand. She gently placed him in the center of the blanket so his head just lay over the edge of the folded area of the blanket. He was now tired and content as she laid his left arm by the side of his tiny body. She gently swaddled baby Theodore in a soft cotton muslin cream blanket, tucked it underneath him and placed him in his wicker baby blue cot. Mary's eyes caught sight of the canopy top shaped like a crown with two centered gold rearing lions, with the shield and carved cross separating them. Underneath the lions were the carved words, 'Nemo Me Impune Lacessit'. Surely, she should now know the meaning behind these words? After all, she was now a Tavistock.

She kissed baby Theodore on his cheek and whispered the words, "See you shortly, little handsome chap." His crystal blue eyes were now closed, as she laid him down against a rolled-up blanket and placed the cream and blue crocheted blanket on top and tucked it into the mattress. She walked over to Sister Crouse and kissed baby Diana gently on the cheek.

"I will miss you all dearly but I am hoping it will not be long before I return." She looked at Sister Crouse with skepticism. "Have you been to Portu Satis Tuto?"

"Ja, Mary, do not be worried, it's a beautiful place, it's also known as Castle of the Spirits. You will know why when you live there. It's full of wonderful people like you and I. However, there's also a darkness there, don't be drawn into it."

"Don't be drawn into it?" Mary uttered.

"Ja. Don't dwell on my words, just remember them. Now, it's time for you to go!" Sister Crouse placed Diana gently in her cot. "Here," she gestured to hug Mary holding both arms out wide. Mary wrapped both of her arms around Sister Crouse. "Ach, hugs feel sooooo good." She rubbed and gently patted Mary on the back. Mary felt an encompassing warmth throughout her body, a warmth she wanted to remain ever-present.

Sister Crouse released her arms. "I will see you shortly."

Reluctantly, Mary released her hug too. As she pulled away her heart felt a strange sadness, but the warmth from the hug still resonated through her body. "Goodbye for now." Mary smiled with hope that all would be good and turned and did not look back.

Chapter Twenty-Four
On the Eleventh Hour of the Eleventh Day of the Eleventh Month, Forevermore

Dr Goodman and a nurse were deep in their German conversation, moving their arms quite erratically at the end of the corridor. The closer Mary got, she could see the nurse was Nurse Hermans.

"Warum (why), warum?" she shouted and stared at Mary with disdain as she walked past her.

Mary looked down and uttered the words, "I will see you downstairs, Dr Goodman."

"I will be there shortly," he replied. "Ende der Diskussion." He turned and followed Mary down the staircase.

The Great Entrance Hall was filled with all members of staff lined up on either side of the Hall. Mary could see some familiar faces such as Miss Alan, Elsie, Mrs Thorpe, Rose, Violet, Mrs Bloom, Ivy, Gigglesworth and Jim the gatekeeper. However, there were many more she didn't recognize. Their clothes seemed to match the black and white marble checkered tiled floor, Mary thought. Mr Ferguson and Mrs Crabtree were standing at the foot of the staircase on opposite sides. Mrs Crabtree gestured by pointing her forefinger for Mary to stand on the next stair tread, next to her. Dr Goodman stood opposite Mary. They both turned and faced upwards on the staircase as everyone in the Great Entrance Hall looked above and beyond Mary at the duke who now took center stage.

"Mr Ferguson, has every member of staff signed the Chandringham secrecy document?"

"Yes, they have, Your Grace. I have the agreement right here." He raised a black leather folder in his hands for the duke to see.

"Good, I shall proceed then." The duke raised his head and voice so that all persons present in the Great Entrance Hall could hear him.

"We are all gathered here to witness a great moment in time, the end of fighting on the Western Front. On the eleventh hour of the eleventh day of the eleventh month, from today and this day forward, it will mark a victorious significant moment in time in our lives, our children's lives and also their children's lives. It will become an historic moment in time, for us and all our allies with the defeat of the German army and the signing of the Armistice agreement.

"This victory has come at great cost to all of us and loss of lives to many of our brave loved ones, who fought with valor and gave the greatest sacrifice that man could ever make, so that we can stand here today, free. Free from fear, free to work as we please, free to walk our lands and free to enjoy peace and for that we are truly thankful and bow our heads with heartfelt gratitude and reflection."

Everyone in the Great Entrance Hall bowed their heads. The huge nine feet walnut carved grandfather clock chimed eleven times as the clock read eleven o'clock each chime echoed within the hall. All stood still, as a solemn mood engulfed the room, each and everyone, deep in their own realm of thought. Mary's thought brought her deep sorrow; her pain was expressed as a lonesome tear welled in her right eye. The tear overflowed and gently trickled down her cheek, her thoughts fixed on the moment her ma opened the first letter from the war office. She had felt the loss of Richard the very day he had fallen at the Battle of the Somme. However, because of her persistent hopefulness and her endearing heart, she refused to allow her intuitive certainty to persuade her otherwise. Her ma stood in shock after reading the war office letter; no words were spoken, as the letter dropped to the floor. Pa stared at Mary with his piercing blue eyes. She picked the letter up and reluctantly read it out loud as her pa gestured her to do so.

Dear Sir and Madam,
It is my painful duty to inform you that a report this day has been received from the war office notifying us of the death of:
(No.) 16989 (Rank) Corporal
(Name) Richard Ned Dwyer (Regiment) Royal Fusiliers

which occurred at Beaumont-Hamel on the 13th of November 1916, and I am to express to you, sympathy and regret of the Army Colonel at your loss.

The cause of death: Killed in Action.

If any articles of private property left by the deceased are found, you will be notified. Time will probably elapse before their receipt and when they are received, they cannot be disposed of until authority is received from the War Office.

Application regarding the disposal of any such effects or of any amount that may eventually be found to the late soldier's estate should be addressed to 'The Secretary, War Office, London SW1 and marked outside 'Effects'.

I am Sir and Madam,

Your obedient Servant

D.K.A. Stapleton

OFFICER IN CHARGE

INFANTRY RECORDS DISTRICT 6

Mary looked down at her wrist and gently stroked her fingers over a watch. As she did, there was a strong sense of inner connection within her heart to Richard. His Waltham brown, leather strap wristwatch with luminous dials had been worn with pride the very day his heart had stopped beating. However, his watch continued ticking. There was a deep analogy present in the ticking watch; it was all the family had left of him. Pa made a symbolic gesture and had insisted that she kept it as long as she would wear it and keep the watch ticking at all times, keeping Richard's spirit alive.

Her mind turned to Archibald; she had never felt his loss innately, although the telegram came almost a year after Richard's death. Her instinctive perception told her he was still alive. He had always had luck on his side. Richard would talk of Archibald falling in pig shit and yet emerging, smelling of roses. She smiled at the thought and at a deep knowing inside that someday she would see her brother again.

The duke interrupted the silence in the Great Entrance Hall. "We now will celebrate the ending of the war and a new beginning. I have two new beginnings to announce on behalf of the duchess and myself: the births of my son and daughter, Theodore and Diana. May we celebrate their lives and good health in the Great Hall. I do believe Mrs Thorpe and her staff have been very busy preparing the celebration buffet." The duke looked directly at Mrs Thorpe. In turn, Mrs Thorpe smiled and shrugged her shoulders in a nonchalant way.

The duke continued. "If you would all like to make your way through to the Great Hall, we can all commence with the celebrations." The staff started to filter through to the Great Hall, Mrs Crabtree, Mr Ferguson and Wigglesworth remained in position.

Dr Goodman looked pensive. "We really must be going now, if we are to catch the Green Knight."

"Yes, of course," replied the duke as he turned to look at Wigglesworth.

"The car is all ready to go, Your Grace." Wigglesworth smiled with enthusiasm.

"We should get your coat, Lady Mary," Mrs Crabtree suggested.

"Yes." Mary turned and walked up the staircase, followed by Mrs Crabtree; not one word was muttered, the two, deep in their own thoughts. Mary opened the door to her bedroom, and stood waiting for Mrs Crabtree to walk through.

"Now where is the etiquette in that?" Mrs Crabtree scoffed.

"I feel you have more of a right than I do to go through the doorway first." Mary smiled insistently, bowing and beckoning Mrs Crabtree by waving her arm.

Mrs Crabtree rolled her eyes and walked into the bedroom. "I have only walked through the doorway first, because you have a train to catch and dithering about much longer will leave the train long gone before you even step foot onto the platform at the station." She smiled. "But thank you for your consideration." She walked over to the bed, where a navy-blue felt, flapper-style hat embellished with a thick teal ribbon and a pair of matching leather gloves sat on a heavy woolen teal-colored coat, that lay on the forget-me-not blue silk eiderdown. She picked up the pair of navy-blue gloves and passed them to Mary who in turn slipped them on her hands. Mrs Crabtree held Mary's coat up so that she easily slid her arms through the sleeves. She buttoned up the frog fastening on the navy-blue ornamental braids and adjusted the rollover collar so that the pointed center fell perfectly down the middle of Mary's back. "Now for your hat." She placed it on Mary's head, adjusting her hair slightly so that one of her golden curls fell loosely onto her face. "Perfect." She pouted her lips and smiled as she stood back and admired Mary. "Oh, I've packed your passport in your bag with some tinted lip balm, powder, mints, comb, spare hairpins and a lemon squeezer." She handed Mary a clutch bag from a nearby chair. "Time to go, dear heart."

"Why will I need a lemon squeezer?" Mary questioned.

"I really hope you don't need it but just in case there is a need, you have it to use and please use it, if your life is in danger. I know you can use this handgun well. It's loaded and ready."

Mary, full of apprehension, knew she must follow through with her destiny. "I need to do something first, before I go, I hope you do not mind." She threw her arms around Mrs Crabtree and hugged her for dear life.

Mrs Crabtree was aghast. "Careful, you will squeeze what life I have in me, out of me." All the same, Mrs Crabtree equally gave Mary a huge hug and patted her on the back. "You'll be seeing me before you know it. Now, you need to make haste!"

Mary walked to the bedroom door and waited for Mrs Crabtree, lifting her head high with an insistent attitude.

"Oh, my word, this is poppycock." She smiled as she walked past.

Mary followed behind her. Mrs Crabtree passed the duke's bedroom and then the duchess's bedroom. In turn, Mary stopped in the middle of both doors, with a want to go inside to say goodbye to the twins and the duchess.

Mrs Crabtree stopped immediately but did not turn her head. She mocked, "You are going to give Dr Goodman a heart attack, if you dither about much longer. He's poignantly charged when it comes to timekeeping." She turned her head. "You will do well to remember that!" She scorned, turned her head, and continued walking at a fast pace.

Mary felt pensive inside at the thought that she had upset Mrs Crabtree with her dithering. The two descended the staircase while the duke and Dr Goodman looked on. Dr Goodman was now wearing his dark brown bowler hat and double-breasted brown and cream tweed overcoat, clutching a briefcase.

"We must go immediately!" he scoffed.

Mary reached the bottom of the staircase and looked at Mrs Crabtree who had a very vacant look on her face, so Mary decided not to hug her instead she turned to the duke. "Goodbye, Your Grace."

The duke stepped forward, hugged her and whispered in her ear, "Call me Charlie, please."

"Goodbye, Charlie." *Gosh,* she thought, *how will I ever get used to calling His Grace Charlie?* They released their embrace.

Dr Goodman cleared his throat loudly, to usher matters along. He turned and walked towards the huge, double-diamond, glass paneled doors, where Keane stood waiting and opening the left-hand door. As Mary walked towards the doors, he grinned with disdain in his eyes. She did not flinch as she had previously done; instead, she smiled at him as she walked by. Outside, Wigglesworth stood proudly by the side of a beautiful, cream-colored car, glistening in the sunshine, dressed in his chauffeur's uniform looking rather dapper, holding the passenger door open. Dr Goodman proceeded to enter and sat down as Mary beamed with delight at the sight of the stunning car, her eyes skimming every detail, aware that time was of the essence. She spryly stepped into the car and was seated. She had not seen many cars in her life, let alone ridden in one so beautiful. Wigglesworth closed the door, walked around the front of the car to the driver's side and entered the car, started the engine, then closed the door.

"What a beautiful car!" Mary declared.

"Yes, indeed." Dr Goodman smiled as he glanced around the interior. He then waved at the duke and Mrs Crabtree, who waved back. Mary smiled and waved goodbye too. She was pleased to see Mrs Crabtree smiling. Mary stared out of the window gazing at the scenery surrounding Chandringham.

"She's a Rolls Royce Silver Ghost, commissioned by the duke." He laughed drolly; it almost could be mistaken for a cough.

Mary was a little bewildered with Dr Goodman's laugh; she turned to look at him. "I hope you do not mind me asking, but why did you laugh?"

"Well, she was commissioned by the duke with the duchess's specifications."

"Ah, I see." Mary smiled to herself.

Dr Goodman rolled his eyes. "The duke wanted a blue Silver Ghost but the duchess was most insistent on cream exterior and beige upholstery. As you can see."

"I can," Mary acknowledged. "I wonder why this beautiful car was named the Silver Ghost, there has to be a story attached, it sounds so mystical."

Dr Goodman tilted his hat. "There is. Well, originally the car was first named the 40/50. However, when the automobile was painted silver, coupled together with an extraordinary stealthiness traveling at a top speed of eighty miles per hour, the title Silver Ghost was taken up by the press and all 40/50s became Silver Ghosts." Dr Goodman grinned with delight.

"Ohhh, I thought there would be more of a story to the name." Mary looked rather disappointed.

"Ja, there is," Dr Goodman said with enthusiasm.

"The statue on the front of the car looks very symbolic. Is there a story to that too?" Mary asked.

Dr Goodman smiled. "It's called the Spirit of Ecstasy, it has a story of love and passion attached to it."

Mary looked intrigued; her blue eyes glimmered with delight. "Do tell me, please!" She stared at Dr Goodman, with need-to-know eyes.

"Well, John Walter Edward Douglas-Scott-Montagu, Second Baron Montagu of Beaulieu was the pioneer for the automobile movement. He's editor for the 'Car Illustrated' magazine. He fell in love with his secretary, Eleanor; they had a secret love affair for more than a decade. The duke and I both knew, as we are close friends. It was a secret because he was already married and Eleanor came from an impoverished background.

"Like me," Mary commented.

"You no longer come from an impoverished background." He rolled his good eye.

"Despite her background, he loved her dearly. He commissioned his friend Sykes, to sculpt a statue, who I think loved her too. He set to work on sculpting the cast; a personal mascot for the bonnet of the 1910 Silver Ghost. Sykes chose Eleanor for his model of course. He originally sculptured her statue with her gown fluttering in the wind, resembling an angel, placing one finger against her lips to symbolize John and Eleanor's secret love affair. Sykes called it the 'Whisper', As much as John Walter loved the figurine, it would not bode well should Lady Cecil Victoria Constance Kerr find out. He then sculpted the 'Spirit of Ecstasy' that was far more fitting and captured Eleanor's beauty and elegance." He paused for a short time, seemingly entranced by his memory. "She was a beautiful woman."

Mary interrupted. "She was?"

"Yes, she was. Sadly, the war took Eleanor; she died when a U-boat torpedoed the SS Persia on the 30th of December 1915.

Mary looked saddened. "Why was Eleanor aboard the SS Persia?"

"She was accompanying Lord Montagu, who had been directed to assume command in India."

"Did Lord Montagu die too?" Mary inquisitively asked.

"A huge part of him did that day. He was saved, found several days later, adrift on a raft and has never been the same man since, so I'm told."

The two both gazed out the window. Mary could see the train station drawing closer, her eyes fixated on the sign 'Chandringham', although her thoughts were taken with the story she had just heard. The Silver Ghost pulled alongside the Chandringham Station sign.

Chapter Twenty-Five
The Order

Wigglesworth stepped out of the Silver Ghost, and opened the passenger door and stretched his hand into the car for Lady Mary to grasp.

She took his hand as he led her out of the car. "Thank you, Wigglesworth." She smiled with gratitude.

Wigglesworth held out his hand for Dr Goodman to grasp in turn. Dr Goodman patted Wigglesworth's hand away. "Paaaa, I can manage, Wigglesworth," he scorned.

Wigglesworth smiled, looking Mary in the eye, jesting. She responded, smiling too, holding back her laughter she felt within herself, as Dr Goodman stepped out of the car with a subdued look on his face.

"I'll get the baggage, shall I?" Wigglesworth did not wait for a reply, but continued to walk around the back of the Silver Ghost. The car door was left open where Dr Goodman expected Wigglesworth to close it. Mary closed the door behind Dr Goodman, knowing full well there may well be repercussions to her action by the look on Dr Goodman's face.

"Come, Lady Mary, we need to catch the train." Dr Goodman took hold of Mary's right hand as they walked side by side in a hurried fashion with the sound of the steam train's whistle drawing close.

"Please do not forget you are Lady Mary Tavistock. You do not close or open doors when there are paid personnel or men present. You are gentry and destined for high status. Do I make myself clear?"

"Yes, perfectly clear." Mary smiled to herself as they walked onto the platform. The train blew its whistle once more as it rolled into the station, releasing the steam from its chimney and engulfing all who waited on the platform in a fog of excitement. All Mary could see was a flash of red and green, and the gold words 'The Green Knight' as the train rolled past grinding to a halt. A further influx of steam was released by its pistons. All Mary could do was stand and wait for the smoke and steam to dissipate with the rest of the passengers waiting on the platform.

She took time to enjoy the fog, smiled, tilted her head back, took a deep breath and exhaled the vapors of steam. In complete contrast Dr Goodman stood beside her with his handkerchief covering his mouth and nose, coughing and spluttering. Wigglesworth joined them with a suitcase in each hand and two small suitcases under each arm. The steam started to dissipate and Mary could now see the number one on the door of the carriage. She was rather tempted to open it, as Dr Goodman still continued to cough and Wigglesworth had his hands full. However, a sudden wave of innate intensity distracted her and her hands were stilled. Wigglesworth placed all the cases on the ground and opened the door. Instead of stepping into the carriage Mary stood motionless, trapped within her thoughts. She turned her head and looked down the platform, the steam and smoke were still rather prevalent.

"Lady Mary, will you please step into the carriage," Dr Goodman scoffed as he coughed and spluttered more into his handkerchief. "Or must I die of smoke inhalation first?"

Mary listened to every word, but she still stood deep in thought, staring in the same direction.

"Lady Mary!" Dr Goodman mocked.

"S-sorry, Dr Goodman, please step on before me. I have this strange feeling I need to let go of, but can't until the fog disperses."

Dr Goodman nodded his head muttering, "Ich, ich, ich," as he stepped onto the carriage.

Wigglesworth followed but stared in the same direction Mary was fixated on as the sound of other carriage doors opening and closing could be heard. Still there was no clarity to Mary's stare; suddenly the fog of steam and smoke dissipated enough for Mary to see other passengers moving towards the exit of the station. Her hopeful eyes scanned each person on the platform.

Dr Goodman popped his head out of the doorway, handkerchief in hand covering his mouth. "Lady Mary, will you please step in the carriage? The train will be leaving shortly and you need to be on it!"

Mary's was torn between her innate sense and time; suddenly she could see Archibald walking towards her, twitching while he limped along the platform. He looked totally disconnected and a former shadow of himself within Mary's eyes.

Mary couldn't help but run towards her brother shouting, "Archie, Archie, Archibald!" She placed both hands on his shoulders, and somehow, she felt a strong sense of carnage, as if she was stood on the battlefield herself viewing the gore of war at her feet. Three dead bodies laid on sodden ground; all around her was one immense bloodbath. The gloom of decimated soldiers seemed to vibrate from his body. She blinked to rid her vision and stood silent before responding to the here and now. "You're alive!"

He did not react, not one word. His eyes held a blank darkness and were stilled in contrast to his body, rhythmically twitching down his left side.

Mary willed his twitching to stop with her mind. It stopped.

Mary whispered into his ear. "It's Flo, Archie, do you remember me?" Her eyes started to well at the sight of her life-loving brother, who always played the clown. The thought that he may well be acting crossed her mind and as much as she willed him to come alive to his former glory, he just stood there staring into space.

"I am sorry if I'm speaking out of turn, Lady Mary, but you really need to board the train." Wigglesworth now could see the tears in Mary's eyes as he viewed Archibald, with a keen eye. "Poor guy. He has shellshock, do you know him?"

Mary removed her right hand from Archie's shoulder and wiped a tear from her left eye and placed it back on his shoulder. "Yes."

The train conductor's voice could be heard as he walked past them. "Last call for boarding!"

Wigglesworth looked concerned. "Is there something I can do, Lady Mary?"

"Yes, could you please take him to Rosewood Farm?"

"Aye, I'll get him there safe and sound, don't you worry." Wigglesworth linked into Archibald forcing Mary to remove her hands from Archibald's shoulders.

The engine of the train sounded as more steam and smoke were released from the chimney and pistons of the train.

"I must go." Mary turned and ran back to the carriage where Dr Goodman was eagerly waiting, poking his head out of the door opening.

She could see him shaking his head and the closer she got she could hear his displeasure.

"Ich, ich, ich. I do hope this will not be a regular occurrence!" he mocked as Mary stepped into the carriage.

"I'm sorry,' She muttered as she was seated, wiping the tears from her eyes.

"Why are you crying?" Dr Goodman's annoyance immediately turned to concern.

"That was my brother." She paused for thought as the train chugged in motion.

Mary looked disorientated. "Well, I always thought he was my brother."

Dr Goodman opened his mouth as if to speak but changed his mind and nodded his head.

"Pa, Ma and I thought he was killed in action, so the telegram told us so, at Passchendaele. They grieved for him; I did not feel his passing as I did with my older brother Richard. I had felt his loss deeply." Her eyes welled once more. "Now… now it looks like Ma and Pa will be grieving all over again. When I looked into Archie's eyes, I could see no signs of life but darkness, a darkness I have not seen before. Pa would say, 'Lights are on but nobody's home', Ohhhh and his body was still shuddering as if it's still on the battlefield." She stared out of the window, the train was at full speed clicking rhythmically in motion.

"He has shellshock." Dr Goodman frowned.

Mary turned her head to look at Dr Goodman. "Yes, that's what Wigglesworth said. Will he recover?"

"I don't believe he will ever fully recover, but in time there will be life in his eyes again." Dr Goodman paused for thought. "He needs a lot of psychological and physiological help to do that though."

Mary looked dumbfounded. "Why isn't he in hospital receiving help now?"

"I should imagine the hospitals are maxed to their full capacity and Archie has nothing broken structurally, he still has all working limbs and can see, although he clearly is broken inside." He paused for thought, staring out of the window, watching the greenery pass by. "I will make sure he has all the help he needs, Mary, once we get to Portu Satis Tuto. I will send word to the duke and Sister Crouse."

"Thank you so much, Dr Goodman, your words bring great relief to me as they will also to Ma and Pa. Just knowing he will have all the help he needs means the world to me."

"Mary, I need to be clear once more, you can only speak to me or the duke regarding your attachment to Ma, Pa and Archie. No one else should ever know your secret. If anyone found out, other than the people that already know, well there would be so many questions it could leave The Order a little vulnerable." Dr Goodman stared at Mary intently.

In turn Mary stared right back, intrigued. "The Order."

"Ja, Mary." He paused. "Now, what I am about to tell you must remain secret. Do you swear to God, Mary, it will?"

She spoke with sincerity. "Yes, I swear to God it will."

"Good because there is no easy way to tell you this, however you need to know about 'The Great Order', alias 'The Order'." He paused for a moment while a man in a cream suit stopped and stared into their carriage looking at Mary, momentarily, he then walked by. Dr Goodman uttered, "Most peculiar," looking pensive for a short while narrowing his good eye, he then continued. "The Order is the most ancient sect in this world, amongst many of our duties, it's our duty to protect a sacred bloodline and preserve the bloodline, and mother earth herself. We are a totalitarian collective." He waited for Mary to process his words.

Mary thought, as she gazed at Dr Goodman, although her vision hazed, with a puzzled expression on her face. "Totalitarian, I'm not sure what you mean?"

"Well, the collective of The Order has the ability to write history, influence global political power, control industries, monopolize world trade and banks. We are the guardians of the world." He paused so that Mary could digest his words. "You are a descendant from an ancient sacred bloodline, Mary."

Mary churned over her thoughts. "An ancient sacred bloodline... I don't understand?"

"You will, soon enough," he replied.

Mary mulled over her thoughts a little while longer and then piped up. "Why didn't The Order stop the War, if the collective are so powerful?"

Dr Goodman smiled. "Good question, Mary, sometimes war is a necessary evil, it's a controller of the world's population. This war was designed and premeditated. Right throughout history there have been monarchs that have gotten greedy with wanting more, by extending their empires. The devious Kaiser Wilhelm II is a perfect example. Firstly, he gives a blank cheque to support Austria's invasion of Serbia. Shortly after Franz Ferdinand, Archduke of Austria and Hungary was assassinated with his wife, by a paid Serbian nationalist. I wonder who paid the assassin, Gavrilo Princip? He conveniently died in jail the same year without a full trial."

Mary gasped, "Are you saying devious Kaiser Wilhelm II had the Archduke assassinated?"

Dr Goodman smiled. "Kaiser Wilhelm knew full well that the Austrian-Hungarian Empire would fall weak and vulnerable after the death of the Archduke. He would become the Austrian-Hungarian people's savior. He was presented with a perfect opportunity to articulate more military strength with the Austrian-Hungarian Empire to enlarge the German Empire. So, he flexed his muscles, provoking Britain into war. He literally turned on his first cousins, King George V and Tsar Nicholas II. They all knew each other very well, Queen Victoria saw to that, but when she died small feuds turned into war, the Kaiser initiating all by showing his strength, invading France, Belgium and Russia. I have always thought very little of the saying 'blood is thicker than water'. He paused for thought and gazed out of the window. "Especially where royalty is concerned, history has taught us that."

Mary piped up, "What about The Order? What is their perspective on the saying blood is thicker than water, if they are protecting an ancient sacred bloodline?"

Dr Goodman's eyes widened. "The Order takes your bloodline very seriously. Like I said before, The Order takes every precaution to preserve your bloodline. Just look how we concealed your identity. Your family is well dispersed throughout the world. Many not even knowing they belong to the bloodline. This is solely done to protect the bloodline.

The Order knows only too well how easy it is to assassinate an entire family. The Tsar and his family are a perfect example."

Mary gasped and mulled over her thoughts. "Are there many like me?"

"Many like you, well, not as many as we would like, but most definitely there is an unknowing bloodline, until their time comes and they are called for just as you have been. Some may never know, but all the same we keep an eye on them."

Mary looked more puzzled with each answer of Dr Goodman's. "Why have I been called? Is it because something dreadful has happened to the real Mary?"

Dr Goodman laughed and coughed for some time, all the while Mary wanted to pat his back but refrained from doing so as she knew now it was Dr Goodman's everyday laugh.

He coughed out the words, "Because you are needed, you have strong abilities."

"Needed now because the real Mary is not alive?" Mary questioned.

Dr Goodman looked pensive. "I do not want to discuss the other Mary, as far as I am concerned you are the real Mary."

Mary snapped, "I'm needed for what?"

"Ahhhhhhhh, all will be revealed in time, that's enough in-depth discussion for now." He smiled and sniffed the air in the carriage. "Can you smell the food?"

Mary sniffed the air. "Mmmmm, smells like Ma's Sunday roast, except it's Monday and Ma would not have cooked the roast I can smell."

"Are you hungry, Mary?"

"Yes, I'm rather famished."

"Well, we had better make our way to the dining carriage, by the smell of it, it must be the next carriage." He stood and made his way to the glass-paneled door and slid it open for Mary to walk through. "After you, Lady Mary, just follow your nose and remember what I have said." He smiled wryly to reinforce his words.

Mary stood and uttered the words, "I will." She mulled over her thoughts as she made her way to the dining area. As Dr Goodman answered her questions, her questions multiplied, more and more she realized how little she knew. She had always had an innate feeling of not belonging. She looked very different from her siblings, Ma and Pa. No one in her entire family had blonde hair, or curly hair, for that matter. Village folk had jested in the past to her ma on several occasions, 'Who fathered her? The milkman'. Ma had just shrugged her shoulders, laughed, and walked away, all the while knowing what she knew.

Chapter Twenty-Six
The Man in the Cream Suit Won't Stop Staring

Mary's thoughts were being interrupted by the splendor of the cozy dining carriage accompanied by a waiter greeting them at the door. He slid the glass paneled door open for Mary to step into the carriage. "Your usual table, Lady Mary?" the waiter asked.

Mary turned and looked at Dr Goodman who nodded.

"Yes," she nervously replied and waited for the waiter to lead her to the table.

He made his way to the central table on the right side of the dining area and pulled out a red velvet chair, his white gloved hand gesturing for her to take a seat.

She glanced at the waiter's name, which was embroidered on his white jacket in gold thread to match his epaulets as she sat down. "Thank you, Rashford."

Dr Goodman sat opposite Mary and smiled; he then stared at the man dressed in the cream suit, sat in the corner of the dining carriage, staring back.

"Would Lady Mary like her usual drink?" the waiter asked dutifully.

An uncomfortable feeling resonated in Mary's mind, as she churned over the question. What would Mary's usual drink be? At a guess it would most probably be tea, she reasoned with herself and announced, "Yes, please."

Rashford turned to Dr Goodman. "What would you like to drink sir?"

"I will have a ginger beer, Rashford."

Rashford nodded his head and Mary cringed the moment Rashford's back was turned.

Dr Goodman reacted to Mary's cringing. "All you need to remember is to be yourself, so what if your usual drink has changed, it will be the new usual." He smiled. "If you are in doubt as what to do, pause for thought and let someone else answer for you, if need be, you'll be surprised how eager people are to voice their thoughts, when you have no voice of your own."

Mary mused over Dr Goodman's words. To take time to think would certainly help, and would ease the inner panic she had just felt. However, her intrinsic way of thinking could confuse matters more, especially now with her newfound life and all the questions she had no answers to. Pa had told her many times, 'Thinking too much could create problems that were not there in the first place'. She needed to take heed of his wise words.

Rashford now returned with the drinks. He placed a teapot on the table with a white and gold bone china cup and saucer. "Your dandelion tea and honey, Lady Mary, warmed, just as you like it." He then continued to place a small saucer and a jar of honey with a honey spoon on the table.

Mary smiled all the while intrigued. "Thank you."

Rashford then served Dr Goodman. "Your ginger beer, sir."

"Thank you, Rashford."

Rashford smiled as he dropped the silver tray at his side. "Would you like to order, Lady Mary? Our specialty today is lobster bisque to start then a main meal of roasted chicken with Asiago polenta, truffle mushrooms, croquette potatoes and crème brûlée for dessert."

"Mmmmmm, that sounds delicious, Rashford." Mary's mouth watered at his description.

Dr Goodman pursed his lips, mimicking eating. "I very much want the specialty today, too."

"Very well, would you like any wine with your meal?" asked Rashford.

Dr Goodman answered, "Yes, whatever you suggest, Rashford, I'm counting on you to pick the perfect accompaniment; a quenching, crisp, fresh, light, invigorating white wine will do nicely."

Rashford announced, "Yes, sir. I have just the wine, it's a white Bordeaux from Château Haut Brion."

Dr Goodman pursed his lips once more. "Wonderful!" he declared.

Mary poured her tea, as she did so a clear, gold liquid formed in her cup. She had never seen gold-colored tea before, or for that matter had honey with her tea.

Rashford looked on and could see Mary's apprehension. "It's dandelion tea, Lady Mary, lightly infused, just as you like it."

"Yes, thank you, Rashford."

"I'll be back shortly." He smiled flashing his pearly white teeth and left the table, looking back occasionally at Lady Mary while he walked to the back of the carriage.

Mary twirled the honey dipper in the honey pot. "There must be an art to using the honey dipper. I'm afraid I'll drip honey all over this white tablecloth," she commented.

Dr Goodman looked on sipping his ginger beer. "There certainly is." He gently took the honey dipper from her delicate fingers. "Firstly, one needs to collect the honey in the ridges, by gently swirling the dipper around in the pot."

Mary looked at Dr Goodman as he twirled the dipper.

"Once the ridges have encaptured the honey, the excess honey needs to drain back in the honey pot, so more twirling of the dipper is needed slightly above the honey pot in a horizontal position."

Mary licked her lips.

"Once the drips stop, the honey dipper can be placed over your tea cup, and turned to a perpendicular position so the honey drips into your cup." He smiled. "I think you can take the dipper from here."

Mary gently took the dipper as Dr Goodman released his two-fingered clasp. "Thank you."

"You are very welcome."

The last drip of the honey fell in Mary's cup and she gently placed the dipper back in the honey pot, and then stirred her tea with a teaspoon. "It's quite a ritual, I hope the honey has not been sacrificed."

The two laughed out loud for a short time. Then Mary stared at her cup. "Well, are you going to take a sip?" Dr Goodman scoffed.

Mary smiled and sipped the tea gently swirling it around in her mouth. "Yuck! It's horrid," she declared and laughed a little more. "I'm joking I could really get to like this."

Dr Goodman smiled wryly as Rashford returned with a tray in hand. "Your lobster bisque, Lady Mary." He placed a white china soup coupe on a saucer in front of Mary and centered the rolled butter curls and two bread buns in the middle of the table.

Mary breathed in the air around her, closing her eyes and savoring the scent. "Mmmm the aroma of freshly cooked bread, it entices one to become hungry." She opened her eyes. "Thank you, Rashford."

Rashford gazed with appreciation at Lady Mary momentarily and then placed a white china soup coupe of lobster bisque in front of Dr Goodman. "Your lobster bisque, sir. Would you like a glass of iced water, Lady Mary?"

"Yes please, "she answered.

Rashford looked at Dr Goodman. "And you, sir, would you like a glass of iced water?"

Dr Goodman replied with a curt tone in his voice, "Ja."

Mary picked up her gold rose curled napkin from her side plate as Rashford walked away. "It's a shame to spoil this work of art." She rotated the napkin in her hand.

Dr Goodman pulled the ring from his napkin and flicked it out. "Ja, but needs must." He then placed the napkin on his lap. "Your bisque and my bisque will become cold, if you stare at that napkin shaped as a rose much longer!"

He clearly seemed agitated for some reason and Mary had no idea why.

She unwrapped her napkin gently and placed it on her lap, then picked up her soup spoon and began to sip her soup. Dr Goodman looked on and started eating once Mary had placed the first spoonful of soup in her mouth.

Rashford once more was ever present at the table, poured the iced water, firstly in Mary's glass then in Dr Goodman's glass; not one word was spoken. He dutifully left the table as the two consumed the lobster bisque and bread. All the while Mary mulled over her thoughts as to why Dr Goodman was agitated.

Mary broke the silence after eating her last piece of bread, fighting with all her will not to mop the last dregs of soup up. "I'm sorry if I forget the rules of etiquette. I have never lived by them until yesterday."

Dr Goodman looked Mary in the eyes. "I know, Mary, but it's really important that you don't. You very much need to keep up appearances. Lady Mary would have not smelt the aroma of bread or stared at the artistry of the napkin."

"I understand what you are saying, Dr Goodman, and I will try harder. Although it's very hard not to be Flo, because Flo is all I have ever been until yesterday."

Dr Goodman rolled his eye. "Try!" he scoffed.

Rashford returned with a bottle of wine placed in a silver wine-cooling bucket. He set down the bucket at the center of the table and uncorked the wine. He then poured a small amount of wine in Dr Goodman's glass. "Your white Bordeaux from Château Haut Brion, sir."

Dr Goodman picked up his wine glass and smelt the bouquet. He gently swirled his wine around in the glass and finally took a sip, then swirled it around once more in his mouth, while Mary and Rashford eagerly waited for a decision.

Dr Goodman eventually swallowed the wine and pursed his lips in appreciation. "Ja, this will do."

Rashford bowed his head in acknowledgement and poured out two glasses of wine. He then collected the used plates, coupes and cutlery.

All the while Mary had a puzzled look on her face; once Rashford had turned his back she confronted Dr Goodman with her thoughts, in a curt tone. "Dr Goodman can you explain to me, why it is so wrong for me to openly smell the scent of freshly baked bread and marvel at the artistry of a napkin, whilst you can take all the time in the world to smell the bouquet of wine, play with the wine in your glass and then once again in your mouth? This does not seem at all fair!"

Dr Goodman smirked. "Etiquette!" He then placed his forefinger in the air to silence Mary as he could see Rashford returning with their main course.

Rashford returned with a tray in hand. "Your roasted chicken with Asiago polenta and truffle mushrooms with croquette potatoes, Lady Mary."

He placed the plate of culinary delight in front of Mary then the second plate in front of Dr Goodman. "Would there be anything else, Lady Mary?"

Mary looked at Dr Goodman before replying. He stared back at her nonchalantly. "No, that will be all for now, Rashford, thank you."

Mary's words were bubbling and bursting in her mouth as soon as Rashford nodded, turned and walked away. She blurted the words out. "That is not fair! Why can't a lady openly express her joyous thoughts?"

"Because life is not fair and it's seen as hauteur for a lady to openly express and share her thoughts in company or while servants are nearby."

Mary took a large sigh and rolled her eyes. "That would mean I would never get to talk then!"

Dr Goodman sympathetically replied, "There is always a right time, Mary, to express your thoughts with people that care about what you think, you just need to work out who that is and when it's appropriate. Now, eat your food please, before it goes cold."

Mary curtly replied, "I thought you cared," as she picked up her knife and fork and started to eat her food, staring at Dr Goodman intermittently with fury in her eyes. He observed her for a short time watching the fury mellow with each mouthful of food she ate before he started to eat his meal too.

Not before long their plates were empty and Rashford appeared once more. "Would you like your crème brûlée now, Lady Mary?"

Mary looked at Dr Goodman for the answer, as she was now unsure how to answer, although the voice in her head was saying, *yes*.

Dr Goodman answered. "Yes, Rashford, that would be wonderful." Rashford collected the empty plates and turned and walked away.

Dr Goodman raised his eyebrow. "Would you like the crème brûlée now?"

"Yes, I'm curious as to what it tastes like." Mary paused and a perplexed look appeared on her face. "I was also unsure of whether it was etiquettely appropriate for me to answer."

"Mary, you are an intelligent young woman, I know you know it was right for you to answer then. We have a long journey ahead of us still and I need you to be compliant, it's imperative you are." He paused for thought and pursed his lips, stared back at the man in the cream suit who passed their coach window; he did not drop his stare until the man looked away. "I am here to help you and protect you, it may not seem that way, but all the same, that is what I am doing."

The words 'imperative and compliant' resonated like an alarm bell in Mary's head. Compliant! Such an authoritarian word to use, it made her feel rather uneasy. She really must take heed of his words and become less expressive which would be so hard for her to do. Her mind drifted with thoughts to what happened to the original Lady Mary, did she become noncompliant? If so, what had happened to her? She feared to ask Dr Goodman the question, as the consequences to asking may well instill far more fear than she was feeling inside her right now and maybe in time the truth would reveal itself.

Rashford returned with two crème brûlées and placed one in front of Lady Mary and the other in front of Dr Goodman. "Is there anything else I can get you, Lady Mary, Dr Goodman?"

Mary smiled. "That will be all for me. Thank you, Rashford."

"I would like an Irish coffee to wash the crème brûlée down, Rashford, not too much sugar please."

"Yes, Dr Goodman, I'll be right back." Rashford smiled and walked away.

Mary glanced at Dr Goodman, as she picked up her spoon and started eating. She paused for a moment in time. "Mmmm, this is delicious. The crème brûlée melts in one's mouth whilst at the same time bursts of vanilla flavor coupled with explosions of caramel tantalize one's taste buds."

Dr Goodman just smiled in agreement and enjoyed watching Mary eat her crème brûlée; it seemed with every mouthful her face lit up a little brighter.

He picked up his spoon and dug into the crème brûlée, "It is good?" Dr Goodman agreed.

Mary answered by looking up, her eyes shining with her entire facial expression basking in glee!

He grinned and commenced eating the rest of the crème brûlée. Rashford returned with a glass of Irish coffee. He placed it to the right of Dr Goodman. "Your Irish coffee, sir. Will there be anything else?"

Dr Goodman finished eating his last mouthful of crème brûlée and savored the flavor before answering Rashford. "Mmmm, that will be all, thank you!"

Rashford nodded with acknowledgement and proceeded to walk away, occasionally glancing back at Lady Mary.

"He does not seem to be able to keep his eyes off you, Mary. Nor does the man in the cream suit with a funny looking haircut."

Mary glanced at the man in the corner, and then stared back at Dr Goodman. "I noticed your dismay before. Did I draw attention to myself? Should I be worried?" Mary uttered.

"No, they're probably just admiring your beauty."

"Beauty." Mary jested. "Gosh, I have never been associated with the word beauty before."

"Well, you are a very beautiful young woman."

Mary's cheeks started to blush with embarrassment. She had always found compliments pretty hard to digest, never feeling worthy of the words spoken even when they came from an honest heart. She looked down at the mouthful of crème brûlée she left in her bowl and proceeded to eat it.

Dr Goodman sipped on his Irish coffee and observed Mary until she'd finished eating, placing her spoon on the saucer, next to her empty bowl. Mary looked up, glanced at Dr Goodman and then looked out the window at a sign outside with the name Maidstone.

"Well, we had better retire to our coach and rest for the latter end of the journey. It will not be long before we reach Dover." Dr Goodman walked over to Mary's chair and proceeded to pull out her chair as she stood to her feet.

"Thank you." She smiled politely and walked to the sliding door where Rashford was waiting eagerly.

"I hope everything was to your liking, Lady Mary?" He opened the sliding door of the carriage.

"Yes, Rashford, it most certainly was." Mary smiled and walked through the doorway followed by Dr Goodman.

Meanwhile the train slowed and ran to a holt, causing the carriage to jerk. Mary maintained her composure but Dr Goodman stumbled a little causing him to step ahead of Mary.

"Ah that was aptly timed," he said and slid the door open for Mary.

Mary smiled, stepped into their coach and was seated. Dr Goodman followed and sat opposite her. They both looked out of the window gazing at the other passengers in the station and listening to the carriage doors opening and closing. Mary's eyes started to close as the train started to move and not before long, she fell asleep.

Dr Goodman observed Mary and pulled out of his jacket pocket a small Smith & Wesson snub nose revolver. He loaded six bullets in the cylinder, closed it and waited for the man in the cream suit to return.

Chapter Twenty-Seven
Forget-Me-Not

Mary woke to a gentle tapping on her left shoulder, her eyes squinting at the light in the carriage as she slowly became alert to her surroundings and her eyes focused in on the present.

"Mary, we have arrived at Dover Harbour Station. We need to move quickly to Granville Dock, where Captain Powell is waiting for us," Dr Goodman said sharply.

"Captain Powell, who is Captain Powell?" Mary looked a little perplexed, as she rubbed her left eye.

"He's the captain of the Forget-Me-Not. He's waiting for us so we can sail to Calais." Dr Goodman held Mary's coat open.

Mary placed both arms in her coat. "Thank you!" She then eagerly fastened her coat and placed her hat and gloves on.

Dr Goodman was already wearing his winter clothing, he proceeded to take the luggage down from the luggage rack and pulled a muscle in his back as he twisted with Mary's last case. He cried out with pain. "Autsch, ich fiddlesticks." Dropping the case to the floor he reached for the lower region of his back.

"Is there anything I can do to help, Dr Goodman?"

"I wish you could miraculously make this pain go away, but failing that could you please take care of your own luggage, that way the pain will ease in time?"

"Yes of course!" Mary placed her outstretched hands on the lower region of Dr Goodman's back and slowed her breathing; a warm light pulsed though her body and transferred heat to Dr Goodman's back. He felt instant relief and smiled with appreciation.

Mary picked up her suitcases and balanced her posture.

"Mary there should be a porter waiting for us on the platform of the station, please open the door and check outside."

Mary placed both cases back down on the floor and opened the door and looked out of the doorway to see if there was a porter. She could see the man in the cream suit standing by waiting for someone. "There is no sign of any porter, Dr Goodman. If we're not going to keep Captain Powell waiting, we really must make haste. I can carry my cases. I'm really stronger than I look." She smiled with her words.

"Well, this certainly goes against the rules of etiquette but we really do not have a choice. I am not sure how well you have fixed my back," he said apprehensively as he peered out of the window at the man wearing the cream suit.

Mary placed her purse over her left hand and proceeded to pick up each case so that her body remained balanced and stepped out of the carriage followed by Dr Goodman. The station seemed to be rather eerie and dimly lit as the remaining steam from the pistons of the train dissipated into the darkness of the night. Mary spotted a lonesome sailor waiting in the shadow of the gaslight, leaning against the station wall smoking a pipe. He turned his gaze towards Mary and Dr Goodman, nodded his head and tilted his cap to acknowledge them. He then sauntered towards them placing his pipe in his pocket and introduced himself.

"Lady Mary Tavistock and Dr Goodman I presume?" He did not wait for a reply. "I am Able Seaman Scholes, Ma'am, at your service. Captain Powell has sent me to escort you to the Forget-Me-Not." He smiled and looked down at Mary's cases then looked up at Dr Goodman and frowned a little at him. "Could I carry your cases, Lady Mary?"

"Yes, thank you Able Seaman Scholes that would be very helpful." Mary smiled with relief and gladly handed both suitcases to the strapping young sailor smartly dressed in his uniform proudly displaying his embroidered badges. Two red badges at the top of his left sleeve were displayed, one shaped in an S wrapped around an anchor. The other badge underneath, showed two red stripes. Mary noticed on the bottom of his left sleeve a red embroidered abbreviation RNVR and on his top right sleeve an embroidered badge of a gun with a star centered above the gun and a P centered below the gun. Mary was not really sure about the meaning behind the badges apart from knowing RNVR was the abbreviation for the Royal Navy Volunteer Reserves. Not wanting to appear unknowledgeable, just in case she should know, she did not ask about the badges she did not recognize. However, the Flo inside of her very much wanted to know and certainly would have asked.

"Please follow me, we have a short walk to the harbor." Scholes proceeded to walk towards a staircase at the end of the station, turning his head in the direction of Mary. "It's a wee bit chilly tonight with the cold and damp air."

Mary nodded in agreement as he turned his head forward and ascended the wrought iron staircase. The clatter of his footsteps could be heard as Mary followed; she felt the sea breeze on her face and smelt the fresh salty air. They all walked in single file along the wrought iron bridge to cross the railway lines. As Scholes descended the staircase Mary could see a vast view of the open harbor filled with many lights reflecting and glistening on the sea; as the nearing full moon cast its light too. She'd never seen so many ships and vessels in one contained area and was so overwhelmed at the sight she had to stop and stare.

Dr Goodman stood right by her side; he too absorbed the view. "Rule Britannia rules the waves, the moon is certainly shining down on her fleet tonight."

Scholes reached the bottom of the wrought iron staircase and stopped in his tracks realizing the sound of footsteps behind him had stopped. He turned and faced Mary and Dr Goodman. Scholes raised his voice so that he could be heard above the howl of the wind. "Aye, it's extremely impressive or daunting, whichever way you want to look at it, ma'am."

Mary smiled "I would say extremely impressive, Able Seaman Scholes." The wind carried Mary's voice.

Dr Goodman pursed his lips. "We really must get going, Lady Mary, Captain Powell will be waiting."

Scholes butted in now bellowing above the wind. "If you don't mind me saying, sir, the captain will not be sailing until first light so there is no rush, ya can take your merry old time. However, he'd like to see you and Lady Mary as soon as you board the Forget-Me-Not."

Dr Goodman looked at Mary bewildered and shouted out to Scholes, "But why are we not sailing tonight?"

"It's far too dangerous to sail in the dark, as there are still many mines out there in the open water that need clearing, sir." Able Seaman Scholes looked away and smirked at Dr Goodman's naivety.

Dr Goodman frowned at the reply. "Well, I had not accounted for this time-lapse in my plans." His frown deepened as he pursed his lips and clutched his chin in humiliation.

Mary looked at Dr Goodman with concern in her eyes as she shivered with the cold. "Surely, it's best that we are safe, Dr Goodman, than to stick to a schedule that will endanger our lives and worst still, we will not arrive at all?"

Dr Goodman shrugged his shoulders. "Well, I had not accounted for this time-lapse in my plans." His frown deepened as he pursed his lips. "You speak wisely, Mary. I will need to send a message to Captain Cassidy so we do not miss our flight. We had better get on board the Forget-Me-Not before you catch a chill."

Mary smiled with relief and continued walking down the stairs as Dr Goodman followed.

The three walked side by side along the dock passing the first trawler called the Wild Rose. It was full of celebratory life on board, with the sound of whistling and rhythmic drumming of hands forming a beat, followed by harmonicas and voices singing in tune. The three stood still and listened to the jubilant voices.

"Pack up your troubles in your old kit bag
and, smile, smile, smile.
Don't let your joy and laughter hear the snag
Smile boys, that's the style
What's the use of worrying
It never was worthwhile
So, pack up your troubles in your old kit bag
and smile, smile, smile."

A voice shouted out on the trawler, "Raise your mugs to King George V in triumph!" All men on board raised their mugs and spoke the words, "Long Live the King." The clashing of metal mugs could be heard as Able Seaman Scholes proceeded to walk to the next trawler.

Dr Goodman whispered in Mary's ear. "I bet they are not drinking tea."

194

Mary smiled. "Rum, would be my first guess."

Dr Goodman raised his eyebrows in acknowledgment.

The two followed Scholes. As they did Mary could see the words Forget-Me-Not near the bow of the trawler. She stilled her stride for a moment, staring at the words as if spellbound. "Lady Mary, this is our trawler!" Scholes yelled.

Mary acknowledged with a, "Yes… the Forget-Me-Not."

Scholes stepped aboard the trawler and placed Mary's cases down on the deck. He held his hand out for Mary to grab. "It's just a step-down, Lady Mary."

Mary steadied herself by holding Scholes's hand. "Thank you."

"Captain Powell is waiting for you, ma'am, in his cabin, I'll show you the way."

Dr Goodman tried to grasp hold of Scholes's hand to help him steady his footing on entering the deck but just as he was about to grab his hand Scholes retracted his hand, leaving Dr Goodman clambering on deck with a bewildered look on his face.

Two sailors watching just stared in amazement, one shouted out, "There's a step there, Doc!"

Dr Goodman picked up his doctor's bag from the deck and scoffed at the sailors. "Better to be a witty fool than a foolish wit." He then proceeded to follow Mary as both sailors looked at each other and shrugged their shoulders.

There was a somber feeling on the deck of the Forget-Me-Not, no celebratory singing, and no merriment. All that could be heard was a faint haunting sound of a harmonica playing, 'Keep the Home Fires Burning', as Mary walked further along the deck.

She couldn't help but ask, "Why is no one celebrating on the Forget-Me Not, Able Seaman Scholes?"

He turned to face her; she could see a tear in his eye, her heart panged in reaction with the thought of dread at his next spoken words.

"Ma'am, we suffered a loss today, all through the war, not one man has been injured on the captain's watch and the day the war ends we lose one of our chief gunners. His DSC 1917 semi-automatic jammed and as it did the outgoing bullet misfired causing Chief Gunner Siddall to hit a pin on the mine. He stood while everyone else took cover." He looked flummoxed. "I'll never know why?"

Mary's eyes widened with hopelessness. "He died today?"

"Yes, ma'am." He looked down and continued to walk along the narrow deck passing two doors, the first door had a plate marked D.C.T, the second one had a plate marked officer and the third one had a plate marked captain. He placed Mary's cases down on the deck at the side of the doorway and knocked on the wooden door.

A voice from inside could be heard. "Enter."

Scholes entered the captain's cabin and saluted with his right hand. "Lady Mary and Dr Goodman, Captain."

Mary entered the cabin, as a tall burly man stood under the cabin light. The casting shadows emphasized a told story within the scars of his face, albeit his sufferance hidden behind his eye patch. His weathered olive-toned skin contrasted his salt and peppered-colored hair. Although Mary thought it was strange that his mustache was dark brown which seemingly matched the color of his right eye.

"At ease boy-o." He tipped his captain's hat at Mary. "Captain Powell at your service, Lady Mary."

Scholes stood at ease as Dr Goodman entered the cabin.

"Ahhh, Dr Goodman, you're back for more misery?"

"Unfortunately, Captain Powell, I am. I hope the sea will be good to us tomorrow!"

Captain Powell chuckled.

Dr Goodman clamored for his words. "Ohhhh n-no, are we in for a r-r-rough voyage?"

"I'm afraid so, the whitecaps will be abundant." Captain Powell tapped Dr Goodman on the shoulder. "I'll make a sailor out of you yet!"

A wave of sheer terror transformed Dr Goodman's expression, as he gulped in anticipation of crossing of the English Channel.

"And are you a seafaring lady, Lady Mary?" Captain Powell asked.

Mary stood silent as her thoughts were rushing through her mind at deliberating the smartest answer to the question. She had never crossed the sea before and had no idea how she would react or for that matter how her twin had previously fared on open water. "The sea has always behaved herself, Captain Powell on my previous crossings, so I'm unsure how I will react if the sea raises her fury. Hopefully, I will not be deluged with adversity." Her inner conscience smiled with her answer, but she frowned at the very thought of sufferance.

"Ad-vid ah thoog wibod-eyth ah gwibod-eyth doy-theen-eb." Captain Powell smiled.

Mary looked dumbfounded. "I'm sorry but I do not speak Welsh."

"Would you care to translate, Dr Goodman?" Captain Powell mocked.

"Well, as you have spoken these words many times over the years, yes." Dr Goodman pursed his lips. "Adversity brings knowledge and knowledge brings wisdom. Yet, I'm here once again with the knowledge of a rough voyage that will have very unpleasant side effects on me."

"I guess you still need to wisen up then!" Captain Powell chuckled and tapped Dr Goodman on the shoulder once more. "Well, we had all better get an early night, we will all need our sleep as we leave for Calais at first light." He pursed his lips to assimilate Dr Goodman's expressions.

"Gute nacht (Good night)." Dr Goodman pooh-poohed, he was not impressed by Captain Powell's mocking, turned on his heels and walked straight out of the captain's cabin.

Mary had a stern look on her face, looking Captain Powell in his eye.

"I'm sorry, Lady Mary, but the trawler is going to be tossed around tomorrow like a mouse in the clutches of a cat, it's not going to be pretty. You would think by now that Dr Goodman would give up his seafaring days and just fly."

"I do not think Dr Goodman has a choice in the matter, Captain Powell, there are many that rely on him. It's unfair for you to jest at his inadequacy to travel the sea, which is why he's a doctor and not a sailor. Could you please show me to my cabin?" Mary smiled jubilantly and thought Mrs Crabtree would have been rather proud of her.

"If you do not mind me saying so, we should never lose sight of our sense of humor, it's our bandage when life cuts deep." Captain Powell smiled wryly. "Scholes will show you to your cabin, ma'am."

Mary's smile quickly dissipated as she reflected on Captain Powell's wise words and the death of Chief Gunner Siddall.

Able Seaman Scholes saluted Captain Powell. "Captain. Would you like to follow me, Lady Mary?"

"Yes, certainly." Mary nodded her head at Captain Powell. "Captain."

She turned and followed Scholes who had her cases in his hands. He walked several steps, turned left and stopped outside the cabin with the nameplate D.C.T. "This is your cabin, Lady Mary." He placed the cases down on the deck and opened the door.

Mary stepped forward and walked into a slightly larger cabin than the captain's. There was a statement of grandeur although it was small, with its cream-colored shiplap, a long narrow bed dressed in a royal blue silk eiderdown with gold pillows. An oak wardrobe with one carved rearing lion facing a rearing unicorn, made Mary think this could not be the duke's cabin, but the initials D.C.T. matched the duke's, so she would need to pry a little further. On the opposite wall, a large carved oak dresser/desk stood in all its glory, above the desk an intricate brass mermaid chandelier hung, which lit up the entire room. Underneath the desk, an oak swivel chair without casters stood. Scholes set Mary's cases down in the corner of the cabin opposite the wardrobe facing a gold leafed dressing mirror.

"Your bathroom is next door, ma'am, along with the captain, Dr Goodman, and the officers."

Mary looked a little baffled as she uttered the word "Officers?"

"Yes, ma'am."

"Well, that should be rather interesting. Does the duke use this trawler often, Able Seaman Scholes?"

He looked puzzled. "The duke, ma'am? There's no duke that travels on this trawler."

"Well, why are the duke's initials on the door?"

"Because D.C.T are the initials of the owner of the trawler, ma'am, and I wasn't aware he was a duke."

"Do you know who he is?"

"Yes, ma'am, he should be boarding later, that's if he hasn't already."

Mary looked puzzled. "But where will he sleep?"

"In one of the officer's cabins. Now, Lady Mary, breakfast will be served at six a.m. In the officers' mess or galley or I could bring you breakfast in your cabin, whichever you prefer?"

"Where will Dr Goodman eat?"

"I doubt if he will eat, ma'am, after the captain's warning of a rough crossing."

Mary thought for a moment before answering. "I see, well I would very much like to meet some of the crew. Perhaps cheer them up a bit, so I'll visit the galley and eat in the officers' mess. How does that sound?"

Scholes smiled. "They would appreciate that, ma'am. Goodnight and sleep well, Lady Mary." He turned and walked out of the cabin and closed the door behind him.

The warm comforting light in the cabin made Mary feel rather tired so she quickly unpacked her nightdress, nightgown, hairbrush, toiletry bag, and towel. She then made her way to the washroom, next door, and knocked on the door with politeness.

Mary could hear a voice within the bathroom. "Just one moment!" Dr Goodman hollered.

Mary smiled and walked a few more steps so that she could see past the large funnel blocking her view. As she cast her eyes on a lonely, eerie, dimly lit poop deck, she could feel somebody's glare. So she scanned the deck but there was nobody to be seen. In acknowledgment, a chill ran right down her spine causing her to shiver with the feeling. In the distance, she could still hear the celebrations on the Wild Rose. Numbed by her thoughts, she did not hear Dr Goodman leaving the bathroom; she jumped with shock as Dr Goodman placed his hand on her shoulder.

"Sorry, I didn't mean to make you jump, Lady Mary."

"Ohhh, I am relieved to see you, I thought for one minute you were the person I was thinking of and yet I never knew him. So how could that be so?"

"Chief Gunner Siddall," Dr Goodman suggested.

"Yes. Although he passed on today, I very much still feel a presence."

Dr Goodman smiled. "Goodnight, Lady Mary, lock your door and sleep well."

"Goodnight, Dr Goodman, sleep well too."

Dr Goodman sauntered back to his cabin as Mary quickly stepped into the cream shiplap bathroom. Still hankered by her feeling, she quickly brushed her teeth, washed her hands and face and rushed back to her cabin, locking the door behind her. She undressed and put on her nightdress, peeled back the eiderdown, switched the light off and jumped in bed wrapping her body within the eiderdown. All the while the eerie feeling clutched at her very soul. Footsteps stopped right outside her cabin door. She covered her head with the eiderdown, willing the footsteps to walk away, her body stilled by unease as she waited. Eventually, she wondered whether she heard footsteps in the first place as she lay still for some time listening to the sounds on the trawler and the water that surrounded her, until eventually her eyes closed and she fell asleep.

Chapter Twenty-Eight
Premonitions

The warm gentle morning light peered through the porthole of the cabin as Mary's eyes flickered with the variance of light, arousing her to wake. She fought with the here and now as her sleeping mind once more became transfixed, where the scent of a woody, earthy, conifer fruity odor and dark damp air surrounded her. Mary was stood at the edge of a cliff staring down into a dark abyss. She raised her head to look up at the moonlit starry sky. "May God be with me," she uttered in the here and now.

There was a rat-a-tat-tat on her door; her eyes blinked and finally stilled into a stare as they focused on the shiplap. Her brain tried to define the noise, as to where she was, not quite acknowledging the sound at the door or for that matter the man peering in through the porthole. Her sea blue eyes suddenly opened wide, alert now, as she bolted up in bed, her long strawberry blonde hair tousled by her night's sleep, fell around her heart-shaped face. She turned her body and placed her pale feet on the cold deck. There was another rat-a-tat-tat on her door. She grabbed her white lace nightgown from a chair and wrapped it around her body while peering through the porthole at the right-hand side of the door. To her surprise she couldn't see anybody, then suddenly her eyes met with a striking set of light green eyes with a blue circle around the pupils. She was startled at the first glance but the more curious she became the longer the two stared; the longer the two gazed the more drawn to each other the two became. The stranger was mesmerized but Mary gave in and collected her thoughts as she could feel the trawler moving. She opened the cabin door slightly, filled with trepidation, peering around the door as if it was her shield.

Her eyes fixated on a tall, young man with short ash blond hair. His facial features looked like they had been chiseled by Auguste Rodin, with sculptured lips by Michelangelo. His sun-kissed skin and masculine physique gave Mary butterflies in her stomach. She was totally entranced and could not help but study the young man further as his biceps bulged under the sleeves of a cream, cable-knit, turtleneck sweater. His quadriceps flexed within his navy-blue pants as he picked up a tray of food off the deck. She felt quite overtaken by what her eyes were making her body feel. A curl fell onto her face and into her mouth all the while it was wide open, aghast captivated by his awesomeness. She dragged her hair from her dry mouth and managed to mumble the word, "Yes?" Although she did not have any idea why she was saying yes.

"Mary, it's Darius."

"Darius?" she questioned as her thoughts started to rush through her head on how she needed to react, as she had never met this magnificent specimen of a man before, but her intuition told her, her twin had. She concluded very quickly the best thing to do was to act dumb for that is all she could be at this moment in time.

"Darius?"

"Yes, Darius Caelum Titmuss," he said looking all starry-eyed.

Mary's inner conscience exclaimed, *As if that makes a difference, and how could anyone ever forget this Adonis!* "I'm sorry I still do not remember you."

Darius's expression turned to one of concern and sadness. "Ahhh, Dr Goodman warned me that you might have memory loss."

Mary looked ever more confused as she fought the urge with herself to pull an expression like Elsie. "Memory loss?"

Darius laughed loudly, but nervously. "Don't you remember, dear heart; you took quite a tumble." He stared at Mary willing her to remember. "Lierre Sombre."

"Dark Ivy?" She pursed her lips in thought.

"Yes, your horse, you fell badly, I thought you were a goner, dear heart." He looked pensive, saddened by his thoughts.

"Well, I'm very much alive, so please do not feel so sad." Mary looked at the tray. "Oh dear, have I missed breakfast?"

"Yes, Dr Goodman thought it better you sleep in, rather than mix with the crew, so Cook made you a bowl of fresh blackcurrant porridge with honey and a pot of tea."

Mary looked disappointed with herself. "Oh poppycock, I was rather looking forward to meeting the crew, I thought I'd be able to cheer them up a little after what happened yesterday."

Darius looked down at the tray. "Yes, it was shocking for me too, I'll never know why he just stood there. You'd better eat up, dear heart, before your breakfast gets cold." He then stared at Mary for a reaction. "Can I come in?"

Mary opened the door just enough for Darius to step into the cabin and closed the door as Darius placed the tray on the desk and poured a cup of tea for Mary. "It's not quite the dandelion tea you're used to, but it's wet and warm." He placed a white china cup in her hand. "Drink up, dear beam."

Mary sipped her tea a few times as Darius watched on. She then pursed her lips, before speaking, "Were you watching me last night?"

"No, I did not arrive on board until the early hours of the morning. I was in London." He looked pensive.

"I had an innate feeling that someone was watching me but I couldn't see anyone in the light or shadows." She stared into his eyes. "The weird eerie feeling stayed with me until I fell asleep."

"Ahhhhh, the heebie-jeebies got the better of you?" he chuckled.

Mary chuckled too. "They did. Well, I hope the porridge tastes better than the tea, Mrs Thorpe would say this tea would not be fit for dishwater."

Darius chuckled but thought deeply.

She placed her cup back in Darius's hand, pulled her arms through each sleeve of her nightgown and sat down. She stared at the nicely decorated porridge, sprinkled with blackcurrants and a large swirl of honey. She placed a serviette on her knee and started to eat, munching on a few mouthfuls. "Well, this is delicious, I'm glad to say."

Darius smiled. "Good, we wouldn't want you hungry. Now, are you still a good shot?"

Mary was taken aback by the question and almost choked on a mouthful of porridge, coughing to clear her airways.

Darius politely tapped Mary on the back. "Sorry, I didn't mean to distress you."

Mary regained her composure with the knowledge that she could shoot and shoot well. She had learned from an early age, being the only sister to four brothers on a working farm. It had made her into a tomboy at heart so much so she had won many village-shooting competitions. "I am all good now." She placed her right hand over her heart. "It must have gone down the wrong way… and yes I am still a good shot."

"Good because we will need you. Siddall was our best shot and we're now a man down; the mines are plentiful out there," he grimaced.

"Oh my, are you being serious, Darius?"

"I am completely and utterly serious, we need every good shot on deck."

Mary stared at Darius, awaiting his serious expression to change but it didn't. "I do not have my gun!" Her eyes now wide like saucers.

"Well, we have a gun you can use."

Mary gulped. "Chief Gunner Siddall's?"

Darius cupped Mary's chin with his hand, his touch encapsulated a vision for Mary of a rifle and dirt being placed into an open channel situated next to the firing bolt of the rifle. A puzzled look appeared on her face. *Why did I just see what she saw?* It made no sense.

Darius looked concerned. "No, that gun jammed yesterday and it could jam again… I would not risk your life for anything, Mary, even if it meant giving up mine." He smiled with sincerity and kissed her softly on the forehead. "Now eat up, because we will need to get some target practice in quickly. There's a set of suitable clothing in my wardrobe, you'll need to wear them. It's going to get rather wet out there and I sincerely doubt that you have the correct attire."

Mary smiled; she could envisage Mrs Crabtree rolling her eyes with his comment.

Darius placed Mary's cup on the desk and walked to the door, opened it, then turned and grinned at Mary. "Toodle loo for now."

He did not wait for a reply. As the door closed Mary continued to eat her porridge quickly, and then placed her spoon in the bowl with some of the uneaten porridge. Undressing as she walked over to the wardrobe opening the door in haste, there was a pair of navy pants, a cream cable-knit sweater, a yellow set of wax waterproofs and sou'wester hung, awaiting Mary's hand. She quickly got dressed uttering the words to herself, "Well this is rather undignified but needs must, Dr Goodman." As she placed her arms into the sleeves of the jacket, she glanced in the mirror. Her tousled curls hung around her face as she gently pulled the rest of her hair back and rolled it into an untidy chignon. (Her thoughts very much abandoned her as she opened the door not knowing what to expect.) The hostile cold wind immediately greeted her like a smack in the face. It peeled her eyes wide open by its constant force of cold sea air surrounding her, biting at her rosy cheeks, her mouth wide open with the shock of it all. It took a short while for her to acclimatize and to find her footing with the momentum of the trawler. She could hear her name being called, "Marrry, Marrrrry, Marrrrry." She was unable to focus on where the voice was coming from with the distortion in the wind. She looked to her right and then to her left. No one was in the immediate vicinity. "Marrrrry, Marrrrry," the voice called again. She looked up to see Dr Goodman sat down on the roof of her cabin clinging to the corner pole of the railing. His legs dangled over the edge of the deck. His grey face grimaced.

Mary shouted above the wind, "Dr Goodman, you do not look well. Do you want me to help you down?"

Dr Goodman dithered with his words, "Th-h-is i-s-s th-e-e b-b-e-s-tt p-l-l-l-a-c-e ffo-r-r m-me. Yo-ou ne-ed to-o g-o-o ba-a-ck in-n-nside, it's to-o da-n-n-gerous o-o-ut he-ere."

Mary looked down; she could hear Darius calling her name. "Mary, Mary I'm down on the poop deck!"

She looked pensive for a moment before replying and looking up. "I'm a good shot, and they need me, Dr Goodman." She looked away immediately and walked down the steps and opened the door to the poop deck leaving Dr Goodman barely able to nod his head with disapproval.

Mary stepped onto the deck sheltered from the wind, standing between a chimney and the boxed entrance that she had just stepped out of. Darius greeted Mary with a big smile on his face and placed a rifle in her hands. She was very much intrigued by the rifle as she scanned it. "My goodness, it's twice the size of Smiley."

"Smiley?" Darius questioned.

A sharp twinge of panic set into Mary's inner sanctum momentarily; she quickly recovered with a reply, "Yes, my SMLE."

"I thought you called your rifle Bertha." Darius shrugged his shoulders.

Mary chose to ignore Darius not really knowing what to say. "Well, are you going to show me how this works?"

"Yes, of course, this is a DSC 1918 semi-automatic. It's a long stroke, gas piston, fixed barrel."

Before Darius could explain any further Mary interrupted. "Sorry to interrupt but how do I load the gun? Does it have much recoil and what are my distances on the line sight?" She smiled instantly.

He stepped behind her and gently pushed his body in close to her, cradling his hands around hers as they held the gun together. He pulled back the bolt to the bullet ejection port. "The ejection port will open automatically, that's when you know you have run out of bullets."

Mary cast her mind back to the vision of the rifle being tampered with. "There's no open channel next to the ejection port on this rifle, was there one on Chief Gunner Siddall's rifle?"

"Yes." He then placed her hand on the magazine cover. "Now pull the magazine cover down and slip your clip of five bullets into the chamber."

"Oh," She said. Her thoughts were still with Chief Gunner Siddall's rifle and her recent vision as Darius touched her chin. Did Darius deliberately place dirt into an open channel of the DSC 1917, with the intention to jam the rifle?

Darius raised his voice. "Pull down on the magazine cover. You need to concentrate, Mary!"

Mary narrowed her eyes and pulled down the magazine cover as Darius handed her a clip of five bullets from his pocket. He caressed her hand as he placed the clip into her hand and inhaled the scent of her hair. Mary paused for thought for a split second in order to calm her inner sanctum; her heart began to beat faster. She exhaled to rid her mind of what she was feeling in order to regain control of her physicality. Her fumbling fingers placed the clip of bullets into the chamber. "Have I placed the clip in correctly?" she questioned.

"Yes." Darius then placed Mary's hand back on the magazine cover. "Now, push your hand back up and all will click into place."

Mary pushed the magazine cover back against the body of the rifle. Darius whispered into Mary's ear, as he did so his breath tickled her ear. "We're fully loaded." He pulled back the safety catch. Her eyes rolled but not with delight. "Now for your line of sight, there are three settings. The battle sight zero is already set with the sight folded all the way forward. Now for shooting at very long range stand the sight up at ninety degrees."

Mary composed herself and pulled the sight up at ninety degrees, then pulled the rifle into the crease of her right shoulder and looked down the sight. "Is the safety on?"

He smiled and whispered, "Yes," as he leant forward and kissed the back of her head.

She cringed at herself. "Sorry, I saw what you did but my feelings overtook my thoughts for that split second." She took a deep breath in and exhaled out. *Now, focus on the task in hand, Mary, so the sight is set at a very long range.* She frowned.

"If you want to shoot between four hundred yards and eight hundred yards you pull the sight back towards you, Mary".

Mary pulled the sight back until it clicked onto the barrel of the gun and looked down the sight. "So I could shoot way past the trawler, from here?"

"Way past the trawler, Mary." Darius attempted to kiss the back of Mary's head again, but she stepped forward and turned to face him, leaving him kissing the air.

She smiled wryly. "I'm impressed and can't wait to shoot it. Now is there much recoil?"

"It's not too bad, just make sure you're composed before you take the next shot." He stared at Mary with assurance in his eyes.

"Well, I guess I'm ready for my target practice," she smiled flashing her white teeth.

Darius's expression did not mirror Mary's although he gave a fleeting smile. "We had better get a move on, dear heart, before the mines are released by the Wild Rose, she's towing her sweep wires now. Watch your footing it's bad out there." Darius wrapped his hand around her waist. "We are going to make our way to the stern."

The two made their way onto the starboard side of the open deck and were instantly greeted by a powerful northwest wind that seemed intent on forcing the two over to the port side. (Away from the sea spray caused by the waves thrashing against the side of the trawler.) Darius's guiding hand helped Mary to steady her footing as she fought the wind with determination and balance as the trawler stabilized after greeting a huge wave.

Through Mary's squinting eyes she could see an old man, bald and scrawny in stature, waiting to meet them at the stern; in his hands, he held two life jackets. As they approached, he shouted. "Life jackets, Master Titmuss, don't ya ever learn?" He sardonically snarled, flashing his pickle stabbing front tooth.

Mary wondered how he could possibly chew with just one front tooth within his whole mouth, and a rather brown nasty looking tooth at that. She was also baffled at how he had managed to stay on board the trawler with his skeletal frame. His dark brown googly eyes looked extremely angry, in contrast to his grey face; he looked like he had met death, and death had turned him away.

Darius shouted above the roar of the ocean. "Thank you, Boatswain Black. Where's yours?" He bestowed a one-armed hug around his shoulder, still clutching at Mary's waist with his right hand.

Boatswain Black chuckled, "Get away with ya, I don't do hugs. I don't do life jackets either. If I fell into the deep, I'd be spat right back out." He shrugged his shoulder to detach Darius's arm. "Life jackets on." He handed Darius and Mary a life jacket and took the rifles from Darius.

They both slid their arms through the life jackets and tied the ties at the front of the jackets.

Boatswain Black watched the two and handed Mary her riffle. "Rite, now that ya both ready, I'll chuck the sixteen-inch orange glass buoys in the deep." He then turned and started to throw five large buoys overboard, one by one as if there was someone catching them within the sea.

Darius placed his hand around Mary's waist, leant his head down so that his mouth was close to her ear. "The object here is to hit the buoy at the bottom so that the buoy will sink. If the buoy shatters in mid-air, then you would have failed, dear heart, for if it was a mine, it may well have blown up the Forget-Me-Not." He smiled sardonically.

Mary looked transfixed at the buoys as their bounces turn into bobs, upon the wake of the trawler. "So no pressure, then." She gulped but did not stop to think as she took the safety catch off. She steadied her position, pulled the rifle into the crease of her right arm, and dropped her cheek close to the rifle, aimed, and fired. The tin projectile cut through the foaming iced air and hit the buoy with unwavering force, blasting and shattering at the same time. "This is harder than it looks!" Mary yelled.

Darius looked a little alarmed. "Since when have you shot with your right hand? You might want to shoot with your left, you're a much better shot that way."

Mary knowing full well she had never shot with her left-hand thought quickly. "To shoot on my left side now does not feel right, I'm much happier on my right side after my fall." She concentrated on her breathing and aimed once again so that the rifle and she became one, deepening her breathing so that she could release the trigger without faltering once she saw her precision. She released the trigger and eagerly watched the bullet, knowing that this time she would sink the buoy.

"You missed!" Darius shouted. "I really think you need to change to your left."

Boatswain Black interrupted Darius, blurting his words out. "Watch that far left buoy, it's sinking. There ain't nothin' wrong with Miss Mary's right side!"

Mary knowing now full well, innately, physically and externally when to pull the trigger, fired three more bullets. She smiled with satisfaction as the last casement flew out of the ejection port.

The three watched as the remaining buoys sank in the deep blue turbulent sea.

Darius wrapped his arms around Mary to congratulate her "Well done, dear beam!"

Boatswain Black looked intensely at Mary. "Aye, Miss Mary, t'at were some good shootin', but ya must know what ya dealin' with here. These sea mines have immeasurable psychological value, ta't will rip ya mind apart if ya let them; there is something so incredibly frightening when ya opponent is a mindless automatic machine. Ya know it's there and it is not gonna make a mistake." He spat out some chewed tobacco into the sea and turned back to face Mary with menacing eyes. "Na if you do, it may well kill ya and everyone else on this trawler!"

Mary looked horrified while absorbing every word from Boatswain Black's tongue and somehow, she wished he had never said the words he had just spoken, as now she felt fearful of her target.

"So, Miss Mary, don't let any thoughts get in the way of ya good marksmanship and we'll all live ta see tomorrow." Boatswain Black smiled as he looked down and pulled out of his pocket a small tin. He opened the lid and pinched some of the light brown powder, placing the lid back on the tin with his pinched fingers. Just as he sniffed the snuff, gunshots could be heard from the forecastle deck. He jumped at the sound and missed his nose and lost his snuff. "God darn, couldn't they have waited a moment longer!" he growled. Now determined and unfazed by the gunshots he opened the lid of the tin once more and pinched a small amount of snuff and closed the lid almost simultaneously. He then placed his crusty hard skin, dirty nailed pinched fingers towards Mary. "Ya want some, Missy? It'll keep ya alert." He smiled, flashing his only tooth.

Mary was rather stunned by his gesture as his fingers were almost touching her nose, with a quick reaction she pulled her nose away.

Darius curtly replied, "Lady Mary doesn't need to be any more alert than she is already." He, in turn, pulled Boatswain Black's fingers towards his nose and sniffed the snuff himself. Gunshots could be heard the whole time. Darius inhaled deeply and exhaled as Boatswain Black took a pinch of snuff for the third time. His eagerness to inhale the snuff stopped him from closing the lid of the snuffbox. Just as he was about to sniff there was a huge deafening boom to the port side of the trawler. He jumped, as did Mary and Darius with shock. His snuff from the box became airborne as if synchronized with a huge projectile of water erupting from the sea. It towered over the trawler and became greater in size as it climbed. All three followed the climb having to move their heads up to follow the height.

Mary gasped at the spectacular sight; her mouth and eyes were wide open as she viewed the breathtaking vision, all the while breathing in the airborne snuff. The three instantly began to cough and sneeze, all eyes teary from the irritation from ingesting the unwanted snuff. The explosion of water projected to a narrowing climax and swooped downwards towards the trawler as if it were a serpent diving back into the sea, leaving a mighty backwash, showering the trawler and all who were on deck. The shower was very much welcomed by the three as they stood with their heads held high, eyes wide open as the sea-spray cascaded down onto them. It bought much relief as it washed their snuff ridden faces.

Mary smiled at the thrill. "Wow, that was spectacular, energizing, invigorating and refreshing all rolled into one."

Boatswain Black flashed his pickle stabber. "Ya don't need a wash now, Missy." He stared at her with dripping wet hair.

Gunfire could be heard once again from the forecastle deck, this time from the starboard side of the trawler.

Darius looked anxious. "There's not usually another one so soon. We had better make our way to the forecastle deck just in case there is a cluster of mines."

They made their way to the front of the trawler in a speedy fashion, not needing to fight the wind so much now, passing the navigation bridge where Captain Powell stood tall in wheelhouse like a king watching out on his realm. Boatswain Black saluted the captain as they passed; he, in turn, saluted Boatswain Black back. Mary could now see six sailor gunners firing off the starboard side of the forecastle deck with intent determination. There were many other sailors standing on deck watching the constant stream of tin projectiles. Somehow the bullets did not seem to be penetrating the mechanical monster as it drifted closer to the Forget-Me-Not.

"Are you ready, Mary? Remember, try not to hit a pin, but slowly penetrate the mine at the base so it sinks." Darius handed Mary her rifle, ammunition clips and grabbed his rifle from Boatswain Black.

The two made their way to the starboard side edge of the deck. Darius shouted, "Do you see it, Mary?"

Mary focused on the sphere-shaped steel-clad warrior armed with its detonators of destruction, jouncing on the ocean waves, navigating its way closer to the Forget-Me-Not with each passing wave. Mary timed her breathing. She answered, "Yes," as she exhaled, then inhaled and braced herself to pull the trigger. There was a huge explosion, this time there was no watching with the thrill of the spectacular, everyone on deck automatically responded by taking cover. Darius shielded Mary from the blast, wrapping his body around her curled body resembling the shape of a half-sphere. Her mind was gripped by the thought of Chief Gunner Siddall. "Why did Chief Gunner Siddall just stand there, when the automatic response is to take cover?"

Darius replied with his mouth close to her ear. "Shock, maybe, that his gun jammed, or maybe he was trying to unjam his gun. I don't know, Mary, we all took cover."

Mary twitched with a nerve surge, as her mind focused on Darius's words 'I was in London' and in doing so she developed an uncomfortable feeling. Why was he lying about the time he boarded the trawler? She was immediately distracted from her thoughts by a great splatter of water hitting the deck bringing with it lots of mackerel flip-flopping around her.

Darius stood and held out his hand for Mary to hold. She ignored his gesture, instead she marveled at all the mackerel and stood up by herself. "Thank you for shielding me."

Darius rubbed the base of his back and smiled drolly.

"Did you get hit by a fish?" said Mary trying to look concerned.

"Yes, by two."

Boatswain Black eagerly picked up the mackerel around them and placed them in a bucket. "Suppa's sorted." (Grinning, flashing his pickle stabber he continued to pick up the fish along with several other crew members on the forecastle deck.)

Captain Powell now made his presence known by tapping Darius on the back. "It's good to see the age of chivalry is not dead, however, I don't think being on this deck is any place for a lady, Master Darius, regardless of how good her aim is."

Before Darius could answer, Mary curtly replied. "I am sure I can be of some help here, Captain Powell. It's not Darius's choice, it's my choice to help and by the looks of what has just happened you need all the help you can get." She smiled insistently.

Captain Powell looked rather perplexed. "Well, all right, you had better know how to tell when and where a mine will emerge." He cupped

Mary's shoulder and lead her up the forecastle deck, then to the bow (Mary stood, armed with her gun in hand as Captain Powell pointed directly in front of him at the Wild Rose). "Now, the Wild Rose is towing two lines of wire, can you see them?"

Mary scanned each line, in the dark grey-blue sea, the whitecaps occasionally rearing from the depths. "Yes, they both have flags attached to their ends."

"Well, each line of wire has cutters attached to them on an otter that forces the cutting wire to extend outboard from the trawler."

Mary looked rather perplexed. "Otters?"

Captain Powell amused at Mary's reaction produced a cheeky grin. "Yes, Mary, but not the furry kind you're used to seeing. Nawr, attached to the otters by another line of wire is a float pennant with a flag attached to it. Nawr, when you see the flag submerge the sweep cables are taking the strain, a mine is being cut as the flag submerges. So when a flag emerges so will a mine on the same line. Then it's time to aim and fire." He smiled with apprehension. "Nawr, are you quite sure about this?"

Mary curtly replied, "Yes, as soon as a flag submerges, I need to prepare to fire and as the flag emerges so will a mine, I then take aim and fire." She looked rather pleased with herself and smiled with certainty at Captain Powell.

He mocked, "Yes, Lady Mary, however, it's easier said than done when your opponent is a deadly mindless automatic machine, and it will not make a mistake but if you do it could kill you and everyone on this trawler."

Mary stared at Captain Powell while absorbing his words. "Yes, Captain Powell, Boatswain Black spoke similar words which unnerved me immensely. If my thoughts are wrapped up with your words and Boatswain Black's I'm not going to be able to aim on target, but if I concentrate on the task at hand then my rifle and I become one, just as my father taught me. I know I can destroy those deadly mindless automatic machines."

Captain Powell cupped Mary's shoulder. "Well, we had better move away from the firing line." He laughed mockingly at himself and said, "Just in case... I'm not sure how much my gunners like me."

They walked down the deck and Mary took her position amongst the gunners on the portside of the trawler, while Captain Powell made his way back to the wheelhouse. Darius headed over to Mary, as six gunners on either side of the trawler and Mary watched the sea ahead with eagle eye intent. They all waited for their opportunity to sink an ironclad warrior with their poignantly placed guns.

Darius leant in towards Mary so that his lips were almost touching her ear as he spoke. "The waves are mesmerizing, don't you think?"

Mary's stared transfixed on the floats and their flags bobbing up and down on the waves. The sea around them now shimmered with the reflection of the sun. "Yes," she replied, "It's really quite relaxing... if one lets their mind drift that way." Her focus became distorted. The deeper her stare, she developed a very mellowed out feeling; the feeling transformed into a relaxed smile. Time seemed endless as Mary viewed the floats, slipping in and out of concentration, entranced by the waves.

Behind Mary two sailors appeared, one with a flute and the other with a mandolin; the flutist began to play. The sound mellow at first, a wavering melody infused with the sound of the waves, hypnotized Mary further into relaxation. Then life wafted into action as the mandolin player started to strum and pluck his strings. Mary and Darius turned to look at the two talented musicians.

Darius smiled. "It's Captain Powell's way of easing the gunners' minds. He says patience is needed. To become patient, one needs a peaceful mind without becoming disturbed or agitated so that the mind can calmly deal with any situation once it arrives."

Mary took a moment to think about the words Darius had just spoken, while gazing at the floats on the open sea. "He's a wise man Captain Powell."

No sooner had she spoken her words the portside flag on the float began to submerge. The gunners took aim waiting for an ironclad warrior to emerge. Mary waited for the flag to totally emerge before raising her rifle, knowing she needed all the strength in her arms to steady her rifle. As the flag emerged so did the Iron Clad Warrior. Mary took aim at the bottom of the sphere and steadied her breathing; on inhaling she pulled her trigger and exhaled after the bullet had gone. She continued until the mine began to sink.

Darius rejoiced as the mine's head disappeared underneath the waves. "Now that's how to sink a deadly mindless automatic machine. Well done, dear heart!" He couldn't help himself and planted a lip-smacking kiss on Mary's lips. She was totally shocked with saucer-like eyes and stared at him with her mouth wide open, not knowing whether to celebrate the moment of triumph or slap Darius for his forwardness.

A sailor close by congratulated Mary with a "Well done, Missy."

"Thank you." She smiled with glee, her eyes scanning the sea once again. As she did so the starboard side float sank with its flag.

Boatswain Black shouted, "Mine about starboard!"

The gunners and Darius took aim, however Mary waited until she could see the mine emerge. She lifted her gun and took aim, concentrating on her breathing, the rhythm of the waves and the movement of the trawler. She became one with her rifle. Mary pulled the trigger and released the poignantly placed steel projectiles into the bottom of the sphere. Her furrowed expression of deep concentration transformed into a smile as the mine sank. She could hear the gunners' jovial cheers with the victory.

Able Seaman Scholes appeared and placed his hand out to shake Mary's. "Well done, Lady Mary, I've never seen a woman shoot better than any of these gunners before or Master Darius, for that matter."

Darius placed his hand around Mary's shoulder and smiled at Scholes. "She's one fantabulous shot!"

"Captain Powell will be most impressed; he will not want you to disembark the Forget-Me-Not." Able Seaman Scholes saluted Darius and Mary then continued walking down the forecastle deck.

Mary's eyes were still scanning the sea all the while. In the background, she could see land on the horizon. "I can see Calais."

Darius looked out to the horizon. "Oh yes."

Mary smiled as she stared at Calais. "I no longer feel danger."

Darius grinned at Mary's naivety. "Your senses, dear heart, could be deceiving you, there are mines that have been strategically placed around the vicinity of the port."

Mary nodded. "Warfare tactics."

"Yes, to cut off supplies. We need to keep our wits about us." Darius placed his hand around Mary's waist as he scanned the sea ahead.

Mary still felt rather uncomfortable with Darius's affection and her intuitive thoughts, so she unhooked his hand and placed it on top of his rifle. "Why did you do that?" he asked.

Mary stared straight into Darius's eyes. "Because I'm not used to being treated this way. It makes me uneasy and I will not be able to concentrate on the task in hand." She turned her head and stared back out to sea.

The mandolin player began to play Bach, Sonata Number 2 in A minor. As they approached the port of Calais the two stood with their rifles placed on the deck in the middle of their bodies, resting their hands on the barrel, not uttering a word to each other, all the way into the port.

"Your perception was strangely right, Mary, we were out of danger," Darius commented.

"Yes," Mary replied. "Strangely I was right." She smiled, amused at herself. "I had better get ready to disembark." She handed Darius her rifle and started to walk towards her cabin.

Darius floundered for his words "D-d-dress warmly, Mary, we'll be flying shortly and it's very cold up there with the gods."

Mary stopped in her tracks and turned back and looked at Darius. "Flying?"

"Yes!"

Mary scanned her thoughts on her attire and couldn't envisage a suitable outfit for flying, that Mrs Crabtree would have packed. "Will my clothes that I am wearing now be warm enough?"

Darius laughed. "Yes, Mary, but we'll need to change your waterproofs."

Mary knowing now not to change made her way back to her cabin. She saluted Captain Powell as she passed the wheelhouse, then made her way up the steps where Dr Goodman was standing by her cabin.

Mary smiled. "Ahhh, Dr Goodman, you are looking less green than you did before but rather tired all the same if you don't mind me saying so. Is there anything I can get you?"

He grimaced. "You can get me off this trawler, as soon as possible, Mary. My seafaring legs are just about to give way. It will take me some time to adjust to land."

Mary looked confused. "I thought you were flying?"

Dr Goodman looked disappointed. "Ohhhhhhh, do not remind me right now?"

Mary laughed. "I'll take that as a yes then." She opened the door to her cabin and pulled off her fallen sou'wester, jacket and boots, and placed them back in the wardrobe. She then turned to face herself in the mirror and adjusted her chignon and smiled once it was done. She packed away her nightwear, coat and dress, slipped her shoes on and tidied up her bed, then left the cabin where Dr Goodman awaited her with his bag in hand.

"I'm ready for the next adventure." She smiled gleefully.

He brandished a scowl. "What do you think you look like?"

A veil of shock replaced Mary's happy face and her disdain was vocalized. "A woman about to board an airplane! Darius told me it would be rather cold, so if you don't mind, I'd rather not freeze for vanity and change after we land?"

Dr Goodman scowled. "Very well."

Able Seaman Scholes appeared. "Captain Powell has sent me to collect your cases, Lady Mary."

Mary smiled. "Yes of course."

The three made their way to exit the trawler where Darius and Captain Powell awaited them.

Captain Powell held out his hand for Dr Goodman to shake. "It's good to see a little bit of 'color in those cheeks of yours, Doc." He shook Dr Goodman's hand. "Until next time, the pleasure, as usual, was all mine."

Dr Goodman rather embarrassed at his behavior nodded politely.

Captain Powell placed his hand out to shake Mary's, as she grasped hold of his hand; he lifted her hand and kissed it. "It's been a pleasure having you on board, Lady Mary, you have truly lifted mine and the crew's spirits. Any time you want to go mine hunting, I'll be happy to take you," he laughed jovially.

Mary chuckled with him; Captain Powell developed a serious expression. "Nawr, are you sure you don't want to stay on board? We could use your marksman skills, they are certainly second to none."

Dr Goodman piped up, "I'm afraid that is out of the question, Lady Mary is needed elsewhere." He grinned falsely at Captain Powell and linked Mary's arm and lead her off the trawler.

Chapter Twenty-Nine
Numb Bum

Able Seaman Scholes placed Mary's cases and food hamper in the back of an Albion military truck while the diesel engine on the truck ran loudly. The driver stepped out of his seat to greet Darius from the doorless truck. He placed a man hug around Darius. "It's good to see you, Toots."

Darius, in turn, patted him on the back. "You too, although you look exhausted."

Dr Goodman butted in, "That's what a man looks like, when he's helped win the war!"

Darius gave Dr Goodman a fleeting glance and patted Bobby on the back once more. "It's certainly good to be on the winning side of the war." He unhooked his grip and turned to face Mary and Dr Goodman.

Mary was in conversation with Able Seaman Scholes. "Your cases have been secured on the truck, Lady Mary, and Dr Goodman's." Scholes saluted. "I wish you a safe journey, ma'am, Dr Goodman, Master Titmus."

Mary uttered, "Thank you, and you too."

Dr Goodman nodded his appreciation and Darius just ignored him. Scholes turned on his heels and walked back towards the Forget-Me-Not.

Darius shouted above the diesel engine, "Mary, you remember Baron MacFarlane, don't you?"

Mary studied the tall thin man with grey skin and bloodshot sunken eyes, exhausted from his battles of the war. His angular facial features reminded her somewhat of her father's but his kind blue eyes and boyish looks somehow drew her in; how she wished she had known him. She knew very well that she had never met this tall dark stranger but by the words Darius just spoke, her twin had. She quickly decided she had no option but to tell the truth. "I am afraid I do not." She turned to face Dr Goodman with a questioning look.

Dr Goodman belittled Darius with his reply. "Do not worry, Mary, in time your memory will recover, I am sure of it." He scowled at Darius and then smiled. "Well, we had better make our way to the airfield, Bobby, Lady Mary and myself will ride up front. Darius, you can ride in das (the) back."

Darius did not question as he clambered onto the back of the open truck and sat on a side bench, while Mary, Bobby, and Dr Goodman sat together at the front of the truck as the truck started moving.

Dr Goodman smiled at Mary and chuckled. "It's a little different, ja, to the comfort of the Silver Ghost."

Mary smiled and thought about her father's cart. *It's luxury compared to his bone-shaking, life-threatening cart*, but she did not repeat her thoughts. "Do tell, Dr Goodman, are there any intriguing stories about the Albion truck company?"

He looked thoughtful for a moment. "Unfortunately, no… although I do believe each truck could tell a story about this dreadful war we have just had." He tutted. "If only they could talk."

Bobby laughed. "Do you want me to fly straight to Portu Satis Tuto, Dr Goodman?"

"Nein (no)!" He looked saddened. "I would like to go to Bertangles near Amiens. I want to pay my respect."

Bobby's mood became somber, he then uttered, "Manfred."

"Ja," Dr Goodman replied.

Bobby developed a concerned look. "You do know I had nothing to do with his Fokker being shot down, don't you?"

Doctor Goodman patted Bobby's knee. "Ja, but even if you had I would not have blamed you, it's unfortunate you were on opposite sides." He smiled while in thought. "How many planes did Manfred shoot down?"

Bobby thought a little before answering. "Well, they have accredited Manfred with eighty, but I'm sure it was much more than that. I'll never understand why he pursued the Canadian Wilfrid Reid, alias Wop May at such a low altitude, he broke all his rules and must have known he was open to enemy ground fire."

Dr Goodman tutted once more. "He was saving his cousin Wolfram, I believe." He tutted once again. "I don't think his thought process was the same after his brain injury. I told him no more flying or it could be the death of him."

All the while Mary was listening to the conversation and processing the information.

Dr Goodman squinted his eyes. "Did you know the Canadian pilot that shot him down?"

Bobby smiled. "Yes, I have flown with him several times, he's a good man Captain Roy Brown. Although there is controversy as to who fired the one fatal bullet as it penetrated Manfred's body from the right armpit and resurfaced next to his left nipple. Brown's attack was from behind on the left and from above. Plus, if he had shot him down it would have been at close range and his Vickers machine gun would have shredded Manfred's insides; he could not have pursued Wop as he did and land his Fokker DR 1 in one piece. Then speak his last word."

Dr Goodman stared out at the passing scenery, then turned to face Bobby. "Kaputt."

Dr Goodman looked thoughtful. "So you think he was shot down by the Australians on the ground?"

"Yes, by another Vickers machine gun but from long distance, as the 303 bullet was found in his jacket." Bobby sighed as he pulled the truck by the airfield. "He most probably never lost a dogfight."

Dr Goodman sighed. "He knew Prussia would lose the war and knew of the plan Fokker made for him, he was well aware of that, somehow it's as if he had a death wish."

By now Mary had managed to put the pieces of Dr Goodman and Bobby's conversation together and her curiosity got the better of her. "I do need to ask after listening all the while, are you both talking about the Red Baron, Manfred Von Richthofen?"

Dr Goodman still showed his sadness in his eyes. "Yes, Mary."

Mary decided not to question any further as she deemed asking any more questions would upset Dr Goodman and be in poor taste. So she placed her slender hand on top of his and clutched his hand for a short time, smiling sympathetically before she stepped out of the truck.

Darius was standing in front of Mary as she stood upright from exiting the truck. "Are you hungry, Mary?" he asked as he munched on a chicken drumstick. "Only, Able Seaman Scholes left a hamper packed full with delicious food."

Mary had not thought about food until now and immediately felt hungry. "Yes, I am rather hungry."

Dr Goodman was now standing next to Mary. "How about you, Dr Goodman, could you eat right now?" Mary asked.

"Ja, I am famished, where is the food, Darius?"

"It's on the back of the truck, Dr Goodman, I've eaten my share." Darius smiled with chicken stuck to his teeth. "Bobby, have you eaten?"

"Yes." Bobby rubbed his stomach "Hachis Parmentier."

"Ah, two layers of heaven," Darius laughed. "Well, we should execute our pre-flight checklist." He walked to the back of the truck, where Mary and Dr Goodman were looking at the delights in the food hamper.

Darius whipped in his hand and took a green apple, before Mary or Dr Goodman had chance to take any food out of the hamper. He bit the apple and as he did so he pointed to the Scotch eggs.

Dr Goodman tapped Darius's hand. "I thought you said you had eaten your share?"

Darius pulled away his hand. "I was only pointing to the Scotch eggs, to tell you to try them, they're delicious."

Dr Goodman tutted. "Don't you have a pre-flight procedure to carry out?"

Darius answered with a sarcastic salute and walked over to Bobby with Mary's cases in hand. Mary looked a little puzzled. "You don't seem to like Darius much at all, why?"

"He lacks thoughtfulness and I have my suspicions, Mary; I do not like my thoughts and no matter how I try to eradicate them they still tussock back, like weeds in a flower bed."

Mary listened and contemplated his answer whilst biting into a Scotch egg. Dr Goodman took the lid off a jar of lemonade and handed it to Mary and then proceeded to eat a Scotch egg too. He finished munching his last bite. "He's right about them, they're delicious." He then helped himself to three sandwiches, two pieces of fruitcake and an apple. "Mary, is that all you are going to eat, just one Scotch egg and one sandwich?"

"Yes, Dr Goodman, I'm excited about flying."

"Ahhh yes, flying I dislike it more than sailing." He contemplated and then produced, a sickly look by inflating his cheeks as he looked at the airplanes on the flight field. He closed the lid of the hamper and buckled the straps.

Mary gazed out onto the flat velvet green of the flight field where there were numerous allied planes lined up with wooden blocks placed at their wheels. Darius and Bobby were having two separate discussions with two men dressed in grey overalls, as they continued with their pre-flight checks.

Mary looked down at the wicker food hamper Dr Goodman was carrying. Dr Goodman glanced at the hamper and then at Mary. "Yes, Mary, I know, I shouldn't insist taking this hamper, but I will be rather ravenous later." He inflated his cheeks once more and swallowed.

"I did not say a word," Mary jested.

"No, you didn't." He smiled his wry smile. "Well, we had better get ready to fly and make our way to the pilot's room. We will need our flight wear, it gets icy cold up there with God and the chill caused by the prop wash."

Mary looked dumbfounded as they walked to the pilot's ready room. "Propwash?" she blurted out. "What do you mean?"

"It's a very, very cold mass of air caused by the propeller, Mary."

They walked into the pilot's ready room, which looked very much like a classroom, with rows of chairs. There was a huge map where the chalkboard would normally be, at the front of the room. At the rear of the classroom, a large square table had a huge map on it. The walls were filled with leather aviator jackets and pants, Mary could barely see the painted light green, cladded walls, as there were that many hooks full of aviation clothing. She could smell the aroma of stale smoke mixed with the scent of leather and stale sweat.

Darius and Bobby were now present in the room and made their way over to the aviation attire and collected their jackets, pants, gloves, scarves, and boots.

Bobby placed his attire on a table then looked Mary up and down. "I think our small jacket and pants will still drown you, but it's the best I can do."

Meanwhile, Dr Goodman scanned the aviation attire and helped himself to the least worn jacket and pants in his size.

Bobby handed Mary a jacket and a pair of pants, sheepskin boots, aviation leather gloves, scarf, aviator helmet, and goggles. She placed them down on the table nearest to her.

Bobby picked up the scarf and wrapped it around her neck gently, and tied it into an aviator knot and smiled with kind eyes. "There that will help keep you warm."

He started to dress; Mary watched him for a little while and then dressed too. Her leather pants were far too large but the braces attached would help her to keep them up. She wrapped the sheepskin lined leather-flying jacket around her body and tried to buckle the belt; there was no notch small enough for her waist so she decided to knot the belt instead. She took off her shoes and placed a pair of sheepskin lined leather boots on. She chuckled to herself, as she could just see Mrs Crabtree looking right at her with her hands on her hips, tutting with disgust. She then placed her sheepskin lined aviator helmet on her head and squashed her chignon. Her strawberry blonde hair stuck out from the sides and back of the helmet. She secured her goggles over the top of her helmet. (Then picked up the peculiar pair of gloves, which looked like malformed sheepskin lined leather gauntlets with a separate space for her thumbs, forefingers and her three other fingers fitting snug together.) Mary placed the gauntlets on her hands and noticed two eyes drawn on the beige leather forefinger of the left gauntlet. As she looked up she could see Darius, Bobby and Dr Goodman staring at her.

"All set." Bobby smiled.

Mary couldn't help herself and placed her left hand out and pulled her forefinger and thumb together at the tips, to make her glove come alive with eyes and a mouth. She separated her finger and thumb and smiled with a, "Yes."

Dr Goodman smiled and picked up his hamper and cases. All four made their way out to the airplanes.

Dr Goodman placed his cases and wicker hamper down on the grass as soon as they reached the two airplanes. "Which one are we flying in, Darius? I need my cases on board."

Darius looked a little baffled. "The left Brisfit, but I am flying with Lady Mary." He looked at Mary. "I already have Lady Mary's cases on board."

Dr Goodman tutted, "I am afraid to say you have me as your passenger, Lady Mary will be flying with Bobby."

Darius looked dumbfounded. "Why?"

Dr Goodman smirked, "Because I want it that way."

Darius shrugged his shoulders and nimbly climbed in the cockpit in response.

Bobby picked up Dr Goodman's cases. "I'll transport your cases, Dr Goodman."

Dr Goodman replied, "Danke (Thank you)." He then struggled a little as he climbed into the passenger seat of the Brisfit, muttering, "Ich-ich-ich."

Bobby placed Dr Goodman's cases safely in the hold, shut the hold door of the aircraft, and smiled at Mary. He held his hand out for Mary to grab, as she climbed into her seat. She replied with a, "Thank you," as she beamed with excitement.

"You're very, very welcome." He pointed to a control stick in front of Mary. "Please don't touch this control and the Vickers machine gun behind you, or you could well be flying solo." He smiled wryly.

She looked back at the deathly machine gun and frowned as Bobby leant forward and placed the safety straps around Mary. "Buckle up, so that you're comfortable and snug with the straps."

Mary nodded her head and Bobby turned then hopped into his cockpit seat.

Darius started his engine and signaled to the ground crew, with a thumbs up. Bobby started his engine. It was surprisingly quiet, however, the wind buffet caused by the propeller was quite unexpected for Mary as she gasped with shock for a short time and then placed her goggles over her eyes for protection, as did the three men.

"Bobby shouted to Darius, "They'll need a ten-minute warm up first." Darius signaled with a thumbs up.

(By the time Bobby called for, "Chocks away.")

Mary's buttocks hurt through sitting on a vibrating wooden seat; this was not going to be a comfortable ride and it very much reminded her of Pa's bone-shaking cart.

Two men in green overalls pulled the wooden blocks from the Brisfit wheels. Bobby opened the radiator shutters and they throttled up to taxi to the runway. Darius followed behind. Unfortunately, there was some distance to taxi to the airfield strip and the journey getting there was quite rough. Mary's buttocks were numb now so she turned to look at Dr Goodman to see his facial expression as both airplanes were now level. His twisted expression showed his pain, and in a way, she was somewhat pleased to not be experiencing the pain alone.

Chapter Thirty
Red Baron

Bobby and Darius held the Brisfits back at the threshold of the strip, as they scanned the air for aircraft on approach. No other airplanes were in the circuit, so Bobby and Darius were safe to take off. Bobby then gave Darius the thumbs up and gave the Bristol full throttle. They rolled down the flight strip at a seemingly fast pace, so much so that Mary clutched the sides of the cockpit, as the airfield became blurred and the blue sky became more prevalent; the horizon disappeared and the Brisfits became airborne. Mary forgot about her buttock pain instantly, the exhilaration and freedom flooded her with happiness. In reaction to this, she stretched both arms outright as if they were her wings. They climbed to two thousand feet and Bobby leveled his stick and turned to look at Mary who was still engaged with her reaction.

She shouted, "It's wonderful!" Then smiled with glee.

Bobby, not being able to hear, lip-read her words and smiled as he turned his head back to concentrate on the task in hand. He signaled to Darius with his right hand to veer right then turned the Brisfit and Darius followed. As they did so, both Brisfits were engulfed for a short time in a mist of cloud and Mary could feel the saturation on her face so she wiped it and her goggles with the back of her glove. She was very much relieved to see and feel the clarity of the air once more as the mist dissipated. They flew for some time in the crisp cold blue sky. Mary plucked up the courage to look over the edge of the Brisfit. Her heart wrenched at the sight of dismal skeletons of the buildings below desecrated by explosions of destructive fury while black dots on the ground milled around aimlessly amongst the craters and carnage. War had certainly wreaked havoc and it seemed that people did not know where to start picking up the pieces. Eventually, everything began to look incredibly small masking the effects of war. The fields appeared to look well-manicured with the hedge groves and trees. Bobby signaled to descend and Darius reacted with a thumbs up, rolled his Brisfit upside down aggressively and inverted the airplane, descending rapidly. All Mary could think about at that split second was poor Dr Goodman. His expression of dread and inflated cheeks as Darius rolled the Brisfit upside down; left nothing to the imagination. She hoped that Dr Goodman would somehow keep his Scotch eggs, three sandwiches and two pieces of fruit cake, down in his stomach where it belonged.

Bobby turned to look at Mary and shouted, "Are you ready?"

She eagerly replied, "Yes."

Bobby rolled the Brisfit upside down; the sensation disorientated Mary for a very short time, until her brain accessed her optical information. Now she could see a variance of green and yellow fields, amber, umber, vibrant reds, and green trees below with a river that looked as if it was made out of glass reflecting the blue sky.

Bobby pulled back on his stick, performed a half loop and leveled out the Brisfit.

They still needed to catch up with Darius as he was now well below them and had performed two, Split-S's to their one maneuver. Bobby turned to look at Mary and shouted, "Again?"

This time Mary just produced a thumbs up, as she was not so happy about becoming disoriented. Bobby rolled the Brisfit upside down once again and this time there was no disorientation for her, to much relief. It seemed that somehow her brain had instantly adapted to the maneuver. Bobby pulled back on his stick and performed a half loop and leveled out the Brisfit. They were still way above Darius, so Bobby performed one more Split-S maneuver, which now brought their Brisfit in close with Darius. Mary could see Dr Goodman's expression was one of sheer terror.

Bobby signaled for Darius to land with a thumbs down, in reply Darius nodded. They landed in a field and surprisingly to Mary, it was a rather smooth landing. Darius landed close to Bobby's plane and jumped out of the Brisfit with eagerness to get to Mary first and help her out of the cockpit. Dr Goodman sat in his seat trying to contain his want to vomit, with his cheeks enlarged. Unfortunately, he couldn't contain himself any longer and a projectile of vomit was airborne from the edge of Brisfit.

Mary ignored Darius's hand and hopped out of the Brisfit and made her way over to Dr Goodman to see if she could help him somehow.

Bobby looked disgusted with Darius. "Why snap roll into a Split-S maneuver when you know very well Doc Goodman has a tetchy stomach?"

"Because I wanted to teach him a lesson." Darius smiled with contempt.

"In what?" Bobby frowned.

"In how to avoid nauseousness." He laughed.

"By not flying with you?" Bobby poignantly asked in one breath. "That's not funny."

"That would be a matter of opinion, dear fellow." Darius shrugged his shoulders. "So why have we landed here, in the middle of nowhere?" He scanned the open field with a nearby church and trees.

"We are in Bertangles near Amiens to pay our respects, to Manfred." Bobby looked saddened.

Darius had the look of disdain in his eyes. "I don't know why you're so sad, he would have killed you if the opportunity arose."

"I am not so sure about that, he had his opportunities and so did I." Bobby smiled and patted Darius on the back. "Well, we had better go and see how much damage you have done to the Doc."

Bobby walked over to Dr Goodman and Mary as Darius stood still contemplating.

"Ahhh, Doc. Goodman, how are you feeling?" Bobby's sincerity transferred into his expression.

"I feel a little better now, I've rid the turbulence inside me. Are we close to Manfred?" Dr Goodman managed a smile.

"Yes," Bobby pointed to a church belfry. "He's just past the church. Are you good to go?"

"Ja." Dr Goodman held out his hand for Bobby to help him out of the cockpit. Bobby pulled, and his feet touched the ground. Dr Goodman shook his legs and rubbed his buttocks. "Someone needs to improve on the comfort of those seats." Dr Goodman frowned. "I'll be lucky if I have any buttock muscles left, by the time we get to Portu Satis Tuto." Mary smiled, she knew only too well how Dr Goodman was feeling.

"What do you say, Mary?" Dr Goodman asked as the three walked through the field to the church.

"I totally agree, sitting on a hard wooden seat with a vibrating mechanism is incredibly painful and numbing." Mary very much wanted to rub her buttocks better, but instead suffered the sensation all for the cause of etiquette. She looked back at Darius; he was oblivious to her stare. She turned to see that Bobby and Dr Goodman were well ahead of her now as she strolled behind them. Mary could hear the songbirds singing as the sun shone on her face. A very peaceful feeling within her grew; a calm she truly had never felt before, a light within her. She wanted to bask in the feeling for as long as she could and deliberately took her time following Bobby and Dr Goodman, although keeping them in sight all the while.

Eventually, she caught up to them as they stood under a vibrant red Acer tree which cascaded down on the grave. The three looked down at the two wreaths dressing Manfred's grave. There was a polished wooden cross with an engraved stone plate in the center. On closer inspection, she could see the cross was made from parts of propellers.

Mary looked down at the wreaths, in the center of one, read, 'To Our Gallant Worthy Foe', the other read, 'To Our Friend and Enemy Ace of Aces'.

The gravestone read:
KOMMAND DES JAGDEGSCHW JG1
MANFRED FREIHERR VON RICHTHOFEN
DER ROTE BARON
(1892-1918)
ACE OF ACES

Mary couldn't help herself; her eyes became teary with an overwhelming sense of sadness. Although she herself celebrated the fall of the Red Baron's reign of terror with her ma and pa, she now found herself crying at his grave.

Bobby placed his arm around Mary to comfort her, while consoling Dr Goodman with his words, "We gave him a funeral with full military honors and I managed to rescue a part of his propeller from the Diggers and used it for marking his grave with the remains of a Camel propeller to create the cross."

Dr Goodman smiled although he had tears in his eyes. "That's a wonderful symbolic gesture, to have marked his grave with the propellers of two most famed fighter airplanes of the war his DR1 and one off a Camel. He would have liked that." He sighed with deep endearing sadness. "He knew he was going to die that day, I am sure of it. His mother told me he had dreadful toothache and that he would not go to the dentist. (When she asked him why?) He told her, what was the point." Dr Goodman stepped forward and placed his hand on the top of the propeller made cross. "You were one of Germany's greatest tacticians, why-oh-why did you break your own rules, dear friend?"

There was a deadly silence as the songbirds became silent and Mary felt an innate sense of danger and a compelling feeling of a great presence all at once. A bright red hawk swooped down from the Acer tree with its talons outstretched with deadly intent in the direction of Dr Goodman. It pounced on a coiled viper within striking distance of Dr Goodman's legs, snatched the snake close to its head and flew away with its spirited red majestic wings outstretched into the blue, towards the sunbeams. The three stood amazed, aghast for some time without one word being spoken. All the while an intense warm feeling touched Mary's very soul. The songbirds started to sing once more sensing the danger had passed.

Dr Goodman finally closed his mouth. "Well, that was momentous, I will remember this happening for the rest of my life. I felt he somehow touched my heart with a very warm thrall."

Bobby looked at Mary with questioning eyes as he squeezed her shoulder lightly with the palm of his hand.

Mary swallowed. "I felt it too and I will never forget this."

Dr Goodman smiled. "Well, we had better make our way to Rennes-le-Château."

Bobby looked shocked at Dr Goodman. "Rennes-le-Château?"

"Ja," Dr Goodman answered nonchalantly.

Bobby still in a state of shock with Dr Goodman's remark scoffed. "That's almost six hundred miles away and will take us five hours. We'll need to fuel up twice."

"Ja, is there a problem?"

"No, Dr Goodman, I'll just need to make appropriate arrangements. There's an air base close to here, where we can fuel the Brisfits and I can message ahead of time to make sure the fuel is ready and waiting for the second stop." Bobby smiled but he looked weary.

"It's of great importance to Mary, Bobby." Dr Goodman stared at Bobby insistently.

Mary was totally intrigued by Dr Goodman's words. "Great importance?"

Dr Goodman answered with sincerity, "Yes, Mary."

She had never heard of Rennes-le-Château, why would it be of great importance to her? She did not ask why, since she did not want to seem like a fool in front of Bobby, for she should surely know why Rennes-le-Château held great importance to her.

Bobby still standing with one arm wrapped around Mary squeezed her shoulder and declared, "Well if it's of great importance to Mary, I had better get her there." He then eased his arm off her shoulder and they walked back to the Brisfits.

Darius was lying down in the grass looking up at the sky, chewing on a blade of straw. Bobby blocked the light from the sun and cast a shadow as he looked down at him. Darius stopped chewing and glared at Bobby. "Ah did you converse with the Great One."

Bobby smiled and Mary now peered over Darius and answered, "We certainly did."

Dr Goodman peered over him too. "Time to fly once more, Darius."

Bobby placed his hand out to help him up. He grabbed his hand and pulled himself up. "Thanks, old boy."

Bobby tutted. "Less of the old, old boy and go easy on Dr Goodman this time, will you?"

They both chuckled as they all walked back to the Britsfits.

Chapter Thirty-One
The Dead Stick Landing

The Brisfits had refueled and taken to the air once more but all the while Mary was deep in thought, the here and now, the spectacular aeronautical scenery was being out won by many multitudes of collective thoughts of the duke's words in the library, "What would you do if you were in my shoes?"

Dr Goodman answered poignantly. "There would be no question in this matter for me, ethics are a forbidden word when it comes to life. Anyone directly involved has already been sworn to secrecy."

The duke questioning, "Directly involved?"

"Ja, with the medical procedure, we are light years ahead, here."

"Of course, I see."

Mary questioned what Dr Goodman meant by, 'We are light years ahead here,' and what medical procedure would warrant sworn secrecy? There was more to it than just swapping the babies, would she ever find out?

Her thoughts turned to the way the duke smiled and his words, "Mary, your life will change from this day forward, you are going to feel greatness and witness greatness. This greatness will constantly amaze you."

What did he mean by feel greatness and witness greatness? She always had unexplained dreams, as surely most people did, but do most people have dreams that come true? She had never questioned why her dreams became significant reality. Her thought now shifted to a conversation with Mrs Crabtree when she first physically stepped foot into Lady Mary's room. She dwelt on her words and retraced her steps. "I have dreamt of this room, many times with its cream wainscoting, pale blue walls, the humongous bed dressed with a cream and yellow jacquard canopy, blue silk eiderdown, and a large forget-me-not flower centered in the middle of the headboard." She walked over to the white marble fireplace, bent her body and reached out her hand running her delicate fingers over the face of a carved cherub sitting on scrolled acanthus leaves at the base of the fireplace, facing its twin. "They symbolize divine abode and presence; did you know that?" Mary asked.

Mrs Crabtree had just nodded yes with her head.

She paused for a while before standing. Her gaze moved to the woman's face, in the center of the fireplace surrounded by carved marble roses that glistened. "She must be their mother."

Her thoughts shift once again to the conversation she had with the duke and Dr Goodman as they landed, refueled and took to the air once again.

"Portu Satis Tuto." Mary paused for thought. "Does that mean 'A Safe Haven' in Latin, Dr Goodman?"

"Yes, Mary, it does."

Mary stared into space momentarily. "It's weird because I have no recollection of how I know that."

Dr Goodman looked intrigued. "Have you heard of Plato?"

"Yes, he's a famous Greek philosopher who laid the foundations for Western philosophy, science, and mathematics."

Dr Goodman smiled in jubilation. "Yes, he did and he was also cited as one of the founders of Western religion, spirituality and particularly Christianity."

The duke piped up, "Have you ever heard of his, 'Theory of Recollection', Mary?"

An intriguing look emerged on her face. "No."

The duke looked at Dr Goodman. "I think I will let you explain this one, Goodman?"

Dr Goodman nodded. "Well, Plato concedes that in some sense, inquiry is impossible. What appears to be learning something new is really recollecting something already known."

Mary looked a little befuddled.

He proceeded. "According to Plato, this is implausible for many kinds of inquiry in relation to empirical questions such as: who is at the door? Does that glass jar contain water or white vinegar? So in these cases, there is a standard procedure in finding out the answers to the questions. So one can indeed come to know something one did not previously know, but there are also non-empirical questions too, there may not be a recognized method or a standard procedure for getting answers. These answers are more intuitive. Plato's theory is that we already have within our souls the answers to such questions."

Mary felt an incredible warmth within her body as she pondered over Dr Goodman's words once again as she did the first time.

She recalled Dr Goodman's passion as it seeped through in his voice. "Everyone has intuitive feelings, an inner connection, some feel that connection more than most. It is our belief, Mary, that you have a deeper connection with your soul more than most, it's a gift you were born with," he smiled.

Why couldn't she now answer all her own questions if Plato's theory was right, she thought, *if I already have within my soul the answers to my questions?*

Her mind turned to her recurring dream of deep dark serene water bubbling ever so slightly, giving nothing away of the fraught, torrid, battle that lay beneath. The battle to live was purely one-sided as the aggressor played with his prey, pulling the body deep down every time the slender body drew close to the surface. The woman's clenched fists thrashed for dear life against a predator, her eyes wide and mouth shut, she pushed past reaching for the surface then gulped as much air as she could, before being dragged down by her long locks. (Her strength drained as she gulped the water, a state of delirious calm set in, as her mouth filled with water finding any pathway it could.) Was this the way she was going to die? Mary coughed to rid her thought.

She had burning questions. What happened to the real Mary? According to Darius, he thought she was a goner when she fell off her horse. Was this the way she died? Dr Goodman had said she could not be Mary any more but had not told her why. If she was dead this would explain why, or did Darius do something perverse to cause the riding accident?

Her mind flashed back to when Darius cupped her chin with his hand, and his touch encapsulated a vision for Mary of a rifle being sabotaged by dirt being placed into an open channel, situated next to the firing bolt of the barrel of the gun, where the name Siddall was engraved.

"Why would Darius deliberately jam Chief Gunner Siddall's gun? Was he lying about being in London too?" She spoke out loud, unknown to Bobby.

Her mind switched to the present, she could no longer ignore the pain she was feeling within her buttocks; the numbness had come and gone several times in the duration of the flights. She could no longer hone in on depleting the pain with her thoughts, somehow, she needed to physically move her legs up and down to alleviate the pressure and pain, at the same time avoiding any controls in the cockpit. She skillfully scissored her legs up and down in between the pedals and stick. It helped but it wasn't enough. She then placed her padded gloved hands flat underneath her buttocks, so that they would cushion the vibration of the wooden seat. Mary marveled at the overwhelming beauty of the contrasting sunset sky, ladened with monochrome cumulus clouds at the base of mother nature's artistry, furrowed by a vibrant scarlet orange bleeding pathway to the heart of the spectacular, the sun. The rays of orange beamed across an all-new horizon where color met monochrome. The huge vivid tangerine orange stratocumulus clouds engulfed the small umber clouds. Somehow amongst all the orange, reds, yellows and sepia clouds, a vibrant blue sky became their background. Mother nature may well have had some help from God with this spectacular; it was a masterpiece which had a time limit.

Mary was completely oblivious to Bobby waving at her. He finally distracted her from the beauty that surrounds them. "We are approaching Rennes-le-Château." He smiled.

Mary read his lips and nodded to confirm she had understood him.

He turned to check his flight path then looked at Darius who was flying level and gave him the thumbs down. Mary could see Dr Goodman's expression of excruciating pain as he turned to look at her before the Brisfit quickly turned. His expression was transformed into one of sheer horror, his eyes wide open and mouth aghast as Darius rolled the Brisfit upside down. He inverted the Brisfit and they disappeared from Mary's view. Bobby turned to look at Mary. "Ready?" he mouthed.

"Yes," she mouthed back.

He turned the Brisfit upside down, inverted, pulled back on his stick, and performed a half loop and leveled out the Brisfit. They were still way above Darius, so Bobby performed one more Split-S maneuver, which now brought their Brisfit in close with Darius. He then performed another Split-S maneuver and was once again out of Mary's sight. All of a sudden, their engine cut out, there was an instantaneous difference in the wind buffet sound and no vibrating seat. Mary knew there was something instantly wrong, as the Brisfit now became a glider and drifted ever so slowly in the evening sky.

Bobby did not turn to look at Mary, as she now placed both arms out straight as if they were her wings. She wasn't afraid, as many would be. There was an inner calmness within her as they descended to the ground, the view of landmass now became greater within her eyes.

Bobby gently turned the Brisfit to the right for landing and leveled the airplane, turning the malfunctioning Brisfit once more, this time to a greater degree, so much so that Mary decided to clasp the sides of her cockpit. Bobby leveled the Brisfit as they were now aggressively losing altitude. The buildings, fields, and trees no longer looked like they belonged in toy town, instead, a small village appeared with tree-lined roads surrounded by farmed fields. Bobby aimed the Brisfit towards a huge field where Darius had already landed. The landscape passed so fast now, as the Brisfit touched down smoothly and rolled to a stop. Bobby tried to start the prop so that they could motor over to where Darius and Dr Goodman were standing, but he was unsuccessful, the engine did not even sputter.

The Brisfit came to a steady halt, and Bobby turned to face Mary. "Are you all right, Mary?" His concerned voice was a little shaky.

"Yes, that was quite the landing, I really felt like I was flying with angels and eagles," Mary replied with a spirited voice.

Bobby smiled with relief in knowing that Mary had not been scared by her experience and recovered from his shaky voice of worry. "I'm sure the angels had a hand in our safe landing."

Mary looked a little puzzled and inquired, "So I take it you had not planned to land like that?"

Bobby exclaimed, "No, Mary, I did not! I would never dead stick land unless it was necessary, and it was necessary." He climbed out of his cockpit and peered at the fuel gauge in Mary's cockpit. He then helped Mary out of her cockpit, as Mary placed her two feet on the ground, Darius and Dr Goodman were standing at their Brisfit.

Darius had a perplexed and disappointed grin on his face at Mary's first glance. His grin quickly turned into a false smile, in contrast to Dr Goodman's expression who still had the look of shock on his face.

"Showing off, old boy, were you?" Darius scoffed as he tapped Bobby's back with his hand.

Dr Goodman dribbled out the words, "Whatever possessed you, you both could have died!"

Bobby looked saddened at Dr Goodman's dismay. "I didn't have a choice in the matter, we ran out of fuel." He stared at Darius with skepticism in his eyes. "It seems that somehow we were given an insufficient supply of fuel." Deepening his stare of suspicion, he asked, "I think I know the answer to my question but I need to ask it all the same. Did you need to dead stick land, Darius?"

Darius looked perplexed. "No, no I did not."

"Well, what seemed like a full tank of fuel was not!" Bobby exclaimed.

Mary looked at Darius with doubt in her eyes. How very strange she thought to herself but did not say anything.

Darius patted Bobby on his back, with a sincere smile and said, "Well you have both landed safely and soundly. I'm sure there is a simple explanation as to why the Brisfit ran out of fuel, sooner than it should. I have an eighth of fuel left in my tank. Your Brisfit will need a thorough going over before we take to the air again. So I'll make sure she gets the attention she needs. I left it to you last time." Darius shrugged his shoulders and jested, "And look what happened."

Dr Goodman quickly scoffed, "He left you in charge of making sure the Brisfits were fueled correctly last time and look what happened? Bobby, if you want something doing, do it yourself!" He turned and looked at Darius with disdain in his eyes. Then scorned him with one word, "IDIOT." He smiled at Mary. "Come, Mary, I need to show you why we have come here."

Mary nodded as she took her helmet off and shook her strawberry-blonde hair free as she followed Dr Goodman.

Darius narrowed his eyes as he stared at Mary and Dr Goodman walking together through a freshly cut striped golden hay field with the largest sunset full moon he'd ever seen.

Bobby all the while was watching Darius, watching Mary and Dr Goodman. "I thought you loved her, but that's not what I see in your eyes."

Darius pursed his lips. "I do but she doesn't love me and the disdain in my eyes is not for Mary, it's for Dr Goodman, he's a German after all."

Bobby jested in a German accent. "Now, now, remember we are all on the same side and always will be!" He chuckled.

Darius's frown turned into a smile. "Now you don't need to stoop that low to make me smile." He looked around Rennes-le-Château and could see Mary and Dr Goodman walking up the long winding road. "Just pointing me in the direction of the nearest air base will do."

Bobby sighed "We are at least a mile away, it's the southeast road, we had better get a move on."

Chapter Thirty-Two
I am Just a Farm Girl

Dr Goodman stopped three steps from the top of the twisting stone staircase, huffing, and puffing. Mary waited as he caught his breath. She looked up to see a pretty little middle-aged woman with olive-toned skin, and brown eyes that seem to be draped in a veil of sadness; she was dressed in black with her hair tied back in a chignon. The woman placed her hands on her hips at the top and piped out with sincerity, "Only three more steps to go, Dr Goodman, and relief will infuse your body."

Dr Goodman looked up and smiled. "Ahhhh, Marianna, do you promise me that will be the case?"

She smiled but her eyes were still saddened. "Yes, I do, because I do it every day and it happens to me." She then held her arms out to embrace Dr Goodman.

He smiled and continued to climb the last three steps, as he reached the top and held his arms out and embraced Marianna.

She patted him on the back. "What took you so long? I was beginning to think you would never arrive." Her voice was shaky and nervous. "There have been far too many murders of late that are making me fearful. Ade warned me to be on my guard with the three murders of Priest Belvis, Bishop Rolland and Priest Tournebouix, before his suspicious death. I am sure he was murdered, poisoned in some way and I'm unable to do anything. The police are totally uninterested." She paused and tears welled in her eyes. "I had thought something awful had happened to you and I would not see you again." She broke her embrace and looked at Mary.

Dr Goodman looked at Marianna looking at Mary with questioning eyes. He replied, "You are perfectly safe. I am certain of that and we were delayed, crossing the English Channel."

Mary was still standing on the third step down from the top step, not really knowing what to make of Marianna's welcome. All that was clear was that the two were fond of each other.

Marianna's tears started to roll down her cheeks and the veil of sadness was no longer prevalent as she stared at Mary. "Is this Mary?" She smiled as her tears still flowed. "Dr Goodman."

"Ja, this is she." Dr Goodman held out his hand to beckon Mary up the last three steps.

"Ade waited a long time for this moment, it's incredibly sad he's not here." Marianna now held her hand out to Mary as she climbed the last three steps.

She placed her hand in Mary's, then kneeled and kissed her hand. (Mary all the while not sure what to make of the situation stood as an incredible warm light caressed her very soul.)

Mary placed her free hand on Marianna's shoulder and uttered, "Please, please stand, there is no need to kneel for me."

Marianna looked up and smiled, as Dr Goodman held out his hand for Marianna to grab and in turn, helped her to her feet.

Marianna smiled. "Thank you."

"You're welcome." Dr Goodman clasped his hands with a clap and then rubbed each hand back and forth. "Now, is there a light in the Church of Magdalene?"

"Oh, ohhh, Dr Goodman, there is only light in the Church of Magdalene." Marianna smiled in jest. "Come this way." She beckoned Dr Goodman and Mary towards the church door.

The church was small but ostentatious, with the doorway covered by a porch. The gable edge had gold leaf embellished forget-me-nots with an ornate link, linking each flower. At the end of each gable, two white doves sat, looking like they were watching all who entered the church. Within the porch, there was a statue of Jesus Christ surrounded by four vases of large forget-me-not flowers and a line of Latin writing.

Mary stood gazing up studying the words for a while. Dr Goodman spoke softly, "Can you translate the words, Mary?"

Mary smiled and studied the Latin words as a strange sense of knowing overwhelmed her. She pursed her lips before speaking. "THUS, MEA DOMUS TERRIBILLIS EST LOCUS ISTE DRATIONIS

VOCABITUR. My house shall be terrifying called the home of prayer." Mary looked skeptical with her translation, but she then translated the words up above the first line. "This is a place of awe, this is God's house, the gate of heaven."

Dr Goodman smiled. "You did exceptionally well Mary."

Mary looked confused. "I am confused with my first translation, I'm unsure if I have translated it right? Why would the house of prayer be terrifying?"

Dr Goodman smiled and just nodded his head.

Mary looked puzzled. "How was I able to translate the words, when I've never learned Latin?"

Dr Goodman smiled. "This home of prayer has triggered your memory, just as I thought it would... Plato's theory!"

Marianna smiled too with appreciation. "Ade thought long and hard over those words. This house of prayer is only terrifying to those who do not want the truth to be known and have sinned for many, many years." She reflected on her words for a short while, before talking once more. "Ade often preached from the Bible (Genesis, The Revelation, Chapter 4, Verse 2). 'The time will come when men will not put up with sound doctrine instead to suit their own desires they will gather around them a great number of teachers to say what their itchy ears want to hear, they will turn their ears away from the truth and turn aside to myth'." Marianna reflected somewhat more as did Dr Goodman and Mary. Eventually, Marianna spoke. "Come," as she opened the right ornate carved wooden door and Dr Goodman and Mary followed her inside the church. Marianna dipped her fingertips of her right hand in the holy water and touched her forehead with her four fingers and whispered the words, "In Nomine Patris..." She moved her hand to her chest... "et Filii..." Touched the front left shoulder with four fingers "...et Spiritus..." then touched the front right shoulder with her four fingers with the right hand and spoke the words, "Sancti." She placed her hands in the prayer position with an "Amen."

Mary looked rather perplexed at the devil holding up the holy water stoup. "Isn't it very unusual to have a devil in the church? Or perhaps he's not the devil, he could be the bad God; the wrathful God."

Dr Goodman looked intrigued. "Why did you say he could be the bad God?"

"I'm not sure, I guess it's because Saturn is the bad God. He's the God of death and destruction. Mary furrowed her eyebrows, and then spoke the words, "How unusual."

Marianna replied, "Yes, there are many unusual adornments here but then the Church of Saint Mary Magdalene is very unusual and very special. Ade liked Jean Gisard's sculpture and thought it was fitting for the devil to be weighed down carrying the holy water stoup." Her eyes narrowed. "Not all is what it seems when you look close enough."

Mary piped up, "Does the devil symbolize the men that turned their ears away from the truth and are now being weighed down by Holy presence?"

Marianna nodded her head with a yes and smiled. "I also liked the idea of the four angels above the water stoup making the sign of the cross and Ade implemented that for me." She smiled as she viewed the candlelit church and walked down the church aisle. Mary couldn't help notice the black and white checkered marble floor, it reminded her of the floor in the Great Entrance Hall at Chandringham. In fact, the theatrics of the church very much reminded her of Chandringham. Dr Goodman dipped his thumb and index finger in the holy water and made the sign of the cross on his forehead, then on his lips and then on his chest. Mary did the same and the two followed Marianna down the church aisle.

Mary was drawn to the altar, where two large brightly lit, free-standing triangular shaped candle arbors stood each side of the altar. Dr Goodman and Marianna turned their heads and watched Mary kneel at the base of the altar where there was a sculpture of a beautiful woman kneeling immersed into a painting with all her fingers crossed and a skull touching her knee.

"This is Mary Magdalene, isn't it?" Mary asked.

"Yes," Marianna replied candidly.

Mary knelt and ran her delicate fingers over the woman's face. "Is it a coincidence that her facial features are exactly the same as the woman in the center of the marble fireplace in my bedroom at Chandringham? She was looking down at the two cherubs, except here she's gazing up at the statue of Mary holding baby Jesus, looking at Joseph holding a statue of another baby Jesus."

Tears welled in Marianna's eyes.

In contrast, Dr Goodman smiled. "No, it's not a coincidence, Mary, except it's not Joseph holding the baby, it's Jesus. It's time you knew part of your being, one that can't be explained by Plato's Theory." He held his hand out to beckon Mary to come to him.

Marianna turned to the right of the altar and walked towards a decorative carved oak confessional booth. It reminded her somewhat of a miniature castle with its crenellations.

Marianna did not enter the confessional booth but walked to the corner of it and placed her hand on the center of where there once was a cross, that time had marked on the wooden panel. It opened up, transforming itself into a door. Marianna walked through. "Come quickly," she beckoned with her hand.

Dr Goodman walked quickly through the doorway, as did Mary. Marianna then closed the door behind them. Mary followed Dr Goodman down a candlelit stone stairwell. It looked far, far older than the servants' staircase at Chandringham. They reached the bottom of the staircase, where they were faced with a stone wall. Mary looked totally bewildered but Dr Goodman knew exactly what he was doing as he walked to the right edge of the wall. He measured seven-foot steps and marked the front of his foot with a small stone. He then turned to Mary and looked at her with commanding eyes. "Please step back, Mary."

Mary instantly stepped back onto the first step. Dr Goodman grabbed a handful of yellow earth from the left-hand corner of the wall; he stepped to where he had marked the center, and threw the yellow earth on the wall. He repeated his actions two times more; grabbed a large candle from the candle arbor and placed the flame on the area of the wall where the yellow dust stuck. The dust began to ignite and burnt into a bright blue light, where the symbol of a unicursal hexagram was revealed with a forget-me-not flower appearing right in the center of the hexagram.

Dr Goodman stared at Mary looking at the spectacular, and smiled.

Mary gasped, she could barely grasp her words; tears began to well in her eyes with a deep intrinsic knowing. "It's… it's beautiful. I've seen this flame many times in my dreams and never knew what to make of it."

They watched the flame die. Mary placed her hand in line with the bottom petal of the forget-me-not, her fingers lingered over the center petal. She turned to look at Dr Goodman. "Will it be hot?"

He replied, "Warm, Mary, there is only warmth here."

Mary pressed her hand on the wall, as she did so the middle section of the wall slowly began to sink into the ground leaving an opening the size of a doorway.

Dr Goodman passed Mary his candle and then took another from the candle arbor. He smiled. "After you, Mary."

Mary cautiously walked through the doorway; she could instantly smell a woody, earthy, conifer fruity scent, which made her feel warm and relaxed. Dr Goodman walked ahead of her and lit a torch on the left of the cave. A huge flame was activated immediately, he then lit the torch on the right of the cave. Mary could see three bodies loosely wrapped in cream linen with huge bows loosely tied around their necks, waist, and knees. In between each central bow someone had placed a bouquet of freshly cut flowers. The right body had a bouquet of roses and the other bodies had bouquets of wildflowers with an abundant number of forget-me-nots. Each body lay on a large stone, draped with a white flag, and one central red cross with four smaller red crosses on each side.

Mary piped up, "They look like they're holding flowers the way the bows are draped around their bodies." She looked at Dr Goodman with questioning eyes. "Who are they?"

Dr Goodman looked at Mary with serious intent. "I think you know, Mary, in your heart of hearts... Do you remember reading Walter Bagehot's words of 1865: The English Constitution, where he asserted the relevance of the dignified and the efficient?"

Mary looked transfixed. "Yes, Mrs Thorpe made sure I knew Bagehot's words very well," she replied. "The dignified are monarchs, they are answerable to god: Dignified ones 'impress the many'. They are leaders, a figurehead in Bagehot's words: 'To be consulted, to encourage and to warn'. The efficient are answerable to the monarch and the people: they are the government, they look after the way things work and are actually done, they govern the many; so we have god, the dignified, the efficient and the people."

Dr Goodman smiled in agreement. "Very good, except Bagehot did not mention two other vital abstractions, one of which concerns you and the other me. Bagehot did not mention the Divine and the Influential. The Influential being The Great Order the guardians, defenders, protectors and the keepers of the world."

Mary marveled at the three bodies in their shrouds as tears started to well in her eyes. "They're divine, aren't they?"

Dr Goodman kneeled. "Yes, they're the Holy Grail." He then bowed his head and kissed Mary's hand. He looked up with tears in his eyes. "Just as you are, Mary."

Mary placed her right hand on his shoulder. "Please do not kneel for me, Dr Goodman, you know I'm really just a farm girl."

He looked up at Mary. "You have always been more than a farm girl, Mary, you must have always known that. You have Perfecti divine Holy Blood running through your veins, a direct lineage to Jesus and God. I am a mere servant albeit an influential one at that, but you, you have the capacity to see like no other, know like no other and heal like no other. The natural power you possess inside is immense." Dr Goodman stood up. "In time you will learn how to channel your gift and do a lot of good in this world. There are others like you, that will help you, Mary, you're not on your own. However, it is very, very important that you do not reveal who you actually are to anyone, other than to your own bloodline."

Mary looked rather puzzled. "Why and how will I know my own bloodline?"

He smiled. "In time you will instinctively know, you have those instincts now but they need honing." He looked saddened. "Why, it's important for you not reveal who you actually are, if you do, your life will be in danger. There are many that have gone to great lengths to eliminate your bloodline already. They burnt almost an entire religious creed of Cathars and many gospels which confirmed your ancestor's bloodline in the 12th and 13th century. However, The Order has gone to great lengths to protect and preserve the very existence of your bloodline. Sadly in 1244 we almost broke our vow and only managed to save and rescue two of your ancestors from Montségur; unfortunately, the rest of the Divine and many Cathars were burnt alive." He placed his fingertips on the foot of the body. "When the time is right, the world shall know... slowly but surely."

"There are people that would kill me?" Mary gasped.

"Yes, in a blink of an eye... because your very existence denotes the truth in human form, rather than embracing the love of the Holy Bloodline, they would rather eliminate it. Your bloodline is problematic to them, to say the least; heresy is their word for your existence. How would they ever right their wrongs?"

Mary's eyebrows furrowed in despair. "Eliminate it?"

"Yes, they have been trying, but we have always managed to stay one step ahead since the French Inquisition of the twelfth century." He held out his hand.

"What about The Order?" Mary blurted out. Does everyone know in The Order?"

"No... not everyone in The Order knows, there are good and bad people within the ranks. There are many that cannot be trusted. You are sacred, only the fellowship of the Cabal know, and Marianna."

"Who are the Cabal?" Mary asked

"The Inner Sanctum of The Order, the heart and head of the body of The Order. You have no enemies within the fellowship of the Cabal at this moment in time." Dr Goodman smiled. "Come, it's time to meet your kin."

Chapter Thirty-Three
Sabotage

Mary woke to bright sunshine and the sound of voices downstairs. As she began to focus and look around the room, she realized that she had never slept in the room before. However, it bore a resemblance to her bedroom at Rosewood Farm with its plain magnolia painted walls, yet there were several differences. Her bedroom did not have a black onyx fireplace with a huge crucifix above it, or a mirrored wooden wardrobe. However, the single wooden bed was the same as the one she had slept in at her ma's and pa's the only difference was two large white cats that were curled up at the foot of her bed. Maybe that's why she had slept so well or for that matter, the traveling had made her incredibly tired or that the last three days had been incredibly emotional. She had never thought so hard about who she was prior to the last three days. Although yesterday revealed an empowering truth, she still felt a loss. *I had better embrace who I am today*, she thought.

She looked up at the carved burr walnut headboard and ran her fingertips along the grooves of the centrally placed forget-me-not. She had always thought her bed was rather ornate compared to everyone else's beds in the family, but never questioned why. She patted the two cats as they purred away.

Marianna walked into the room and gazed at her for a brief moment before talking. "Good morning, Mary, did you have a good sleep?"

Mary smiled as she took her hands away from the cats. "Yes… yes, I did, it's all due to this bed, I'm sure. I have one just like it at home."

Marianna curtly replied, "I know, dear, this bed was Ade's. He made sure all the forget-me-nots slept well, he had yours made for you." She smiled. "Now, breakfast is ready. We are all in the dining room, waiting for you, dear. Limoux and Maurina your breakfast is ready, too."

The two cats jumped down from the bed and walked out of the doorway. Mary looked mystified for a moment and pondered on questioning Marianna about all the forget-me-nots. She decided not to, with the scent of breakfast and her hunger getting the better of her. So she replied with, "Mmmmmm I can smell it, I'll be down shortly."

"Very well, just follow your nose and the noise and you will find us." Marianna smiled, turned and walked away. Mary quickly undressed out of her white lace nightdress and slipped on her navy-blue pants and a white cotton lace shirt, brushed her long curly strawberry blonde hair and tied it up into a chignon. She slipped her shoes on while walking to the door and made her way down the steep stone spiral staircase following the scent of freshly baked bread and noise. As she reached the bottom step, she could hear Bobby and Darius talking loudly, cajoling each other. She followed the sound and walked into a bright, quaint dining room.

The conversation stopped between the two instantly, as Mary walked into the room. "Good morning, sleepy head, looks like you have gotten your beauty sleep," Darius chirped.

"I did, surprisingly." Mary smiled. "Good morning to you all. Please do not let me interrupt your conversation, it was sounding quite interesting."

Bobby smiled at Mary, as she was seated and then frowned at Darius. "So, the question is, who would crimp the fuel line, so that the fuel gauge would read an inaccurate reading?"

Bobby looked at Darius intensely. "Not me... I don't know. If you remember correctly, I had just arrived and flew the Brisfit that I was told to fly. You were the one that had the Brisfits prepared for flight. I don't know why Dr Goodman thinks I had the time to oversee the fueling of the Brisfits as he implied yesterday."

Dr Goodman did not react to Darius's comment, he continued gazing out of the window.

Bobby scoffed, "I'm not suggesting for one minute that you had anything to do with my Brisfit being tampered with." He looked shocked and perplexed at Darius. "Who told you to fly that Brisfit? And why would you jump to that conclusion so quick?"

Darius smirked sarcastically. "McNeil told me to. Do you trust him?"

"Yes, he's been with the flying corps from the beginning of the war." Bobby looked puzzled.

Darius sighed deeply, "And why, well maybe because you seem to be insinuating that I had something to do with it."

Dr Goodman still sat silent, an onlooker to the conversation, as Darius and Bobby discussed when and how the Brisfit fuel line had been tampered with. He then decided to become active in the conversation. "One question for you, Bobby, McNeil would know if anyone else worked on the Brisfit, wouldn't he?"

Bobby's eyes widen as he replied, "Yes he should know."

Dr Goodman raised his eyebrows whilst speaking. "Well, you need to ask McNeil a few straightforward questions and I am sure you will find the perpetrator. Then you can deal with him."

Bobby smiled at Mary and then frowned at Darius. "So, the question is are you going to be flying the faulty Brisfit?"

"If I have to, yes… I will, although I'm nowhere near as good as you are at deadstick landings." Darius looked at Dr Goodman and sneered. "Dr Goodman could be in for a bumpy landing." He then began to laugh.

Marianna piped up, "Would you like any more croissants and la religieuse? I know how much you like that two-tiered little cake. It baffles me why it's otherwise known as the 'Nun'; it doesn't look like a nun to me, or perhaps you would join Mary and have some eggs and bacon with freshly baked bread, Dr Goodman."

Dr Goodman puffed his cheeks and sighed at the thought of a bumpy landing and replied, "I am really quite full, Marianna. Thank you."

Marianna placed a large serving of eggs and bacon in front of Mary and then poured her a cup of tea. She scanned the table to make sure that Mary had everything she needed. "Ohhhh, I'll just get the honey pot." She walked out of the dining room in a hurry before Mary had time to react.

Bobby smiled as he watched Mary enjoying her breakfast. He then looked at Darius. "Well, it's settled then, you get the faulty Brisfit." He stood up from his chair. "We had better make haste then and get these Brisfits ready for Geneva."

Marianna walked into the dining room with the honey pot just as Darius stood from his chair.

Bobby made his way over to Marianna and kissed her on each cheek before she had time to put the honey pot on the table. Limoux hissed at Bobby.

Marianna commented, "He doesn't seem to like you."

"Perhaps he senses I don't like him. Thank you for your hospitality once more, Marianna. Au revoir for now." Bobby stood aside whilst Darius stepped in and kissed Marianna on both cheeks.

"Thank you. I hope to see you again, one day in the near future." Darius smiled in a strange and menacing way, which unnerved Marianna a little. He bent down and patted the long white-haired cat. No one else in the room saw his expression. Mary was preoccupied with eating, Dr Goodman was staring out of the window looking at the morning glory, fighting the urge to ask Marianna for a piece of la religieuse and Bobby turned to walk out of the room.

Marianna curtly replied. "Au revoir," and stared at Darius vexed.

Darius smiled with a sardonic gesture and blurted out, "Mary, is your case packed?"

Mary jumped a little as she finished chewing and replied, "Yes, yes, it is."

Darius scoffed, "Good," as he walked out of the room.

Mary, Marianna, and Dr Goodman looked at each other puzzled by Darius's sudden outburst. Dr Goodman nodded his head and tutted. "Ich, ich, he has a lot to learn."

Marianna frowned, "There is something bad inside of him and it truly scares me. Yet you must trust him for him to be here, Dr Goodman?"

Mary looked at Marianna with agreeable eyes, then at Dr Goodman with questioning eyes. Dr Goodman shrugged his shoulders. "The trust is out of my hands, for I do not. However, the powers that be, say differently."

Mary looked dumbfounded and the word, "Who?" slipped out from her mouth.

Dr Goodman's eyes widened. "You are going to find out sooner or later. He's the Grand Master's illegitimate son. I believe he's not quite found himself yet and he still has a long way to go with his indoctrination." His eyes narrowed. "I am afraid the war has messed with his mind further."

Mary looked ever more puzzled. "The Grandmaster?" she whispered.

Marianna piped up, "Of The Order."

Mary looked perplexed.

Dr Goodman smiled. "Remember our conversation yesterday, also when we were talking on the train and while you were under the duke's desk, Mary?"

Mary's eyes widened and all of a sudden, she became dry mouthed and her thoughts started to flood her brain so much so that she began to feel intoxicated, her brain fog rolled in, as if it were a mechanism to stop her thinking any more than she should. She uttered the words, "Under the desk. Yes, I remember every discussion we had and you talking to the duke."

Dr Goodman stood and walked over to Mary and patted her shoulder. "Don't be alarmed, Mary, we are here to take care of you. Remember what I said last night?"

Mary barely spluttered the word, "Y-yes."

He released his hand from her shoulder. "Good, now, drink your tea as we will need to make haste. We are a day late as it is."

Mary looked at her teacup for a short while and decided to add more honey, thinking somehow, the sweet would help her to deal with the shock her body was feeling. She sipped her tea and the sickly feeling became more apparent, as her thoughts started to swamp her brain. Her physical motions now were merely secondary to the thoughts that engaged her brain. She went through the motions of thanking Marianna for her hospitality but missed the feeling of Marianna's embrace. She did not see her endearing gaze and tearful eyes or heard the words she softly spoke. "I hope to see you again, dear Mary, someday soon."

She deprived herself of the serenity of the sun-kissed morning glory with the adorned blue sky, early morning scent of freshly cut hayfields and the songbirds singing with merriment on her walk back to the Brisfits with Dr Goodman. Dr Goodman did not say much either, knowing that Mary needed time to process her thoughts and feelings. All the while though, he felt endeared to witness such splendor.

The two were now standing by the Brisfits and awaited instructions from Bobby and Darius who were in deep conversation with a tall man wearing khaki coveralls. Finally, it seemed that the three realized the presence of Dr Goodman and Mary when Dr Goodman coughed loudly. Bobby instantly uttered the words, "Je Vous remercie (Thank you)," to the man as he stared at Mary. He could see she was preoccupied with her thoughts and so he walked over to her and offered her his hand. "Mary you'll need a hand and a leg up into the Brisfit."

Mary clasped Bobby's hand, still very much deep in thought as they walked over to the right Brisfit, while everyone else watched on.

"Better fasten your jacket, Mary, it's cold up there with the gods," he jested and smiled.

The word gods woke Mary's consciousness momentarily as she looked into Bobby's eyes and noted his concern, she then started to wrap her flying jacket around her body. (While Bobby gently tied her scarf into an aviator's knot.)

He stood back. "You'll be good to go once you're wearing your gloves, goggles and aviator's hat, they're in your cockpit." He helped Mary into the Brisfit with a leg up and steadied her with his hand as she climbed into the Brisfit.

She was completely oblivious to the Brisfits taking off and at Dr Goodman's many expressions of discomfort that had previously made her chuckle. She missed seeing Bobby's occasional smiles, waving and pointing at the breathtaking sights below, so much so he had stopped turning around. The blue-sky journey, the here and now was hampered by a deluge of thoughts and feelings she'd rather not feel. The incredulous sickly feeling was still prevalent within her. She had never been more terrified in all her life, even when she had to cling on to her pa's cart for dear life, or when she knelt under the duke's desk, listening into a conversation she had no desire to listen to; a conversation that was highly secretive, one that caused the duke to shed his own blood. Yet all the time Dr Goodman knew she was kneeling underneath the desk. How? Did the duke know she was kneeling underneath the desk too? Did Dr Goodman want her to know the secrets of the twins, or for that matter the duke? Could it be, the twins have the same bloodline as hers? Is she a changeling too? Maybe she was placed at birth in the same way; another baby died so she could take their place. She wondered who the twins' real parents were, who her real parents are? Would she ever meet them, were they still alive? How awful would it be to have your baby or babies taken away from you? Surely The Order would not do that? Would she ever be able to have babies and raise them herself, or would they be taken from her? Her thoughts reverted to the danger of her revilement. How much danger was she really in? The Order had gone to incredible lengths to conceal her true identity, an identity she was still not sure about herself. How did she know how to read and translate Latin all of a sudden when she was unable to translate NEMO ME IMPUNE LACESSIT, two days ago? The Latin words may well have triggered déjà vu, coupled with Plato's theory of recollection could well be an explanation. She dwelled on the words of Dr Goodman, 'We already have within our souls the answers'. She processed the words NEMO ME IMPUNE LACESSIT, once again, she had not thought much about the words until now and now she finally knew their meaning. 'No one provokes me with impunity'. Mary mulled over the meaning of the words and their implications. They induced a certain sense of calmness with the thought of her being protected by The Order, no matter how calculated they were.

Her thoughts drifted to the three bodies. They looked incredibly peaceful in a well-kept shrine. All the while Dr Goodman did not give the bodies any names, his words: 'I think you know Mary, in your heart of hearts...' confirmed her thoughts. In her heart she thought it had to be Mary Magdalene, holding the roses and her children, holding the forget-me-nots (were they twins?). As Dr Goodman confirmed they were the Holy Grail and now she was. Did she feel different by knowing her bloodline? Yes, yes, she did, she felt spiritually elevated so much so it brought tears of joy to her eyes once more. She wondered why she had not had an overly religious upbringing, her father was an agnostic; seeing would make him believe and he had never seen anything to make him believe in God. He had often said there was far too much suffering in the world for God to exist. Her mother was a Christian though, and she would go to church whenever she had a chance. She would take Flo (Mary) with her. There was never any reference to Jesus having children. Why would the church keep silent about something so sacred?

A sudden thought niggled her. Why the congregation and her mother did not pray with their hands together? Instead, they cupped their hands in their laps. Yet in school she was taught to place her hands together like the rest of the children. At the time she thought that children and adults prayed differently, but there was more to it than meets the eye.

Her thoughts then switched to Marianna's words, 'Ade thought long and hard over those words'. [This house of prayer is only terrifying to those who do not want the truth to be known and have sinned for many, many years.] Ade often preached from the Bible (Revelation Chapter 4. Verse 2).

'The time will come when men will not put up with sound doctrine, instead to suit their own desires. They will gather around them a great number of teachers to say what their itchy ears want to hear, they will turn their ears away from the truth and turn aside to myth.'

Marianna's expression of reflection very much reminded her of her mother's words she spoke out loud. 'Oh, what a tangled web we weave, when first we practice to deceive'.

"Pardon, Mary." As Bobby spoke, he alerted Mary to his presence.

Mary could not help but repeat the words, still partly entranced by her thoughts. "Oh, what a tangled web we weave, when first we practice to deceive."

Bobby smiled. "Walter Scott, I do believe?"

Mary looked a little confused for a short time, just realizing they had landed. She soon came to her senses and muttered, "Marmion, A Tale of Flodden Field."

"Yes, Mary." He quoted the rest of the poem.

"Oh, what a tangled web we weave

When first we practice to deceive!

A Palmer too! — no wonder why

I felt rebuked beneath his eye;

I might have known there was but one

Whose look could quell Lord Marmion."

Bobby grinned. "You quell the disturbance in me, Mary, for a long, long time I have not felt peace, but now I truly feel a peacefulness in your presence, I thank you for that." He handed Mary his hand. "We just need to refuel. Do you need the powder room?"

Mary clasped Bobby's hand and replied, "Yes." She looked around the airfield as she stepped out from the cockpit and scanned to see Darius had landed, then instantly felt reality bite in the form of buttock pain, as she began to walk. Her expression showed her sudden shock of pain and all Mary could do was rub her behind to alleviate the pain.

Darius looked on and couldn't help himself. "Would you like me to give you a helping hand there?"

Mary scoffed. "No! I would not! I can manage on my own thank you," as she followed Bobby.

Darius turned to look at Dr Goodman as he rubbed his rear too. "You're on your own, Doc," he mocked and followed Mary and Bobby into a large domed hut, camouflaged with grass on its exterior. The interior was rather bizarre-looking with a Camel airplane taking center stage. A side stage was set with a lounge bar, dining room, and kitchen, all dressed with crystal chandeliers.

"How was the landing, Dr Goodman, not too bumpy I hope?" Bobby asked with sincerity in his eyes.

"Gut, considering." He turned and smiled amusingly at Darius.

Mary made her way to the W.C. which was surprisingly opulent with its cream and grey flecked marble floors, brass fittings, and a French chic vanity with carved wooden detail of roses on the doors. This was no military air base she thought, as she looked at herself in the ornate carved wooden mirror, her tousled curls were now abundant. She stared into the mirror for some time and asked, "Who are you?"

The person staring back at her was motionless. Her pupils dilated as she was feeling an inner disconnection she had never felt before, a feeling she most certainly needed to oust from her mind. She stared into her eyes deeply then suddenly closed her eyes and reopened them, smiled as her reflection smiled back at her. "Don't be a fool, I have known me all my life and nothing will change the inner me, no matter what." She dried her hands quickly and walked out to see Dr Goodman and Bobby deep in conversation. Darius was nowhere to be seen.

"Ah, Mary, are you ready for another, exhilarating, gluteus pounding, aggravating coccygodynia ride?" Dr Goodman mocked.

Mary smirked as she could just picture Dr Goodman's expression of pain. "If it's exhilarating, yes! However, I think I have had quite enough of the pain experience." She looked at six loose cushions on a small sage green jacquard print sofa. "Do you think they would miss two cushions?"

Dr Goodman raised his right eyebrow and quickly took two cushions off the sofa, grinned, and jested, "That's better, now there is some room to sit."

Bobby's dimples in his cheeks began to show, amused by Dr Goodman's stealthiness as the three walked out to the airfield.

Darius was in deep conversation with one of the mechanics, as Bobby arrived with Mary and Dr Goodman.

"Has the fuel line been replaced?" Bobby inquired.

Darius grinned, but the aircraft mechanic replied, "Oui Baron MacFarlane, she will not be giving any false readings now. The crimping of the fuel line was done deliberately, there is no question about that."

"That's not good to hear, Cantona, but good to know the problem has been fixed," said Bobby.

Cantona sneered, "Fixed! The fuel line has only been fixed, however, the perpetrator is still out there. They need to be found and brought to justice. You could have died." Cantona stared at Bobby, while he reflected on his words.

Darius tapped Bobby on the shoulder. "Too much thought is not good. They are fueled and ready to fly, old bean. Take your pick, which Brisfit do you want to fly?"

"We'll take Betty alias Lefty," Bobby smirked. "Merci, Cantona."

Cantona nodded as Bobby turned and helped Mary into the Brisfit. Dr Goodman clambered in the rear cockpit unaided with his cushion in hand as Darius watched and smirked.

The two Brisfits were airborne and made their way through the clear blue sky, with two happy passengers, both having comfortable posteriors. Mary viewed the scenery, gazing at the seemingly manicured trees and multi-colored fields. Soon the scenery seemed to blend into one, as her mind began to wander back to Bobby and Cantona's conversation.

Cantona implied the fuel line had only been fixed. Yet the perpetrator was still out there. He or she needed to be found and brought to justice. Bobby and Mary could have died. It was only Bobby's skill that had kept them both alive.

Did someone want to kill Bobby, or did someone already want to kill her? Knowing what she now knew, she could well be a target for an assassin. How long would it take to crimp a fuel line? Could the man in the cream suit crimp the line? Who knew she had direct lineage to the holy bloodline? She had no idea, but for sure The Order must know and she surely must take solace with that. Her mind drifted back to the church of St Mary Magdalene and the two babies, one baby was held by Jesus and one held by Mary. They must be twins she thought. She retrogressed further to her eyes catching a glance of a photograph of the two horses and their riders. She focused on the faces of the two women riders, as she picked up the photo. "She's very beautiful." Mary paused momentarily, "Her Grace." Her mouth dropped open in shock of what her eyes told her, as she studied the other younger woman rider. "The other woman... she could be me!" She looked at Mrs Crabtree with questionable eyes.

"That's because it is you, Mary."

"But how can that be, Mrs Crabtree?"

"I'm not in the habit of telling lies, so ask no questions and you shall be told no lies." Her eyes set with a stern glare.

What really happened to the original Mary, did an assassin murder her? If so then she was in real danger, for they were identical twins. Her heart began to pound faster; she could feel every beat as her blood pumped rapidly around her body. She began to perspire and her head began to feel woozy so much so she began to lose the here and now. Her eyelashes fluttered as her eyes fought the urge to close. All she could hear was her pa echoing, "Just breathe, Flossy, just breathe... Breathe."

She closed her eyes and breathed deeply, exhaling slowly, slowly she began to slow her heartbeat, transfixed on her words now. "Brrreeeathe," inhaling and exhaling, "breeeeeathe," inhaling and exhaling, "breathe," inhaling and exhaling, "breeeeeath," as the beat of her heart slowed down, "breeeeaathe."

Chapter Thirty-Four
Portu Satis Tuto

Mary's eyes opened and she automatically became transfixed by the turquoise blue lake, beguiled by its beauty as it shone like a huge gemstone beneath the afternoon sun. The surrounding trees were uneven, each tree sculptured by Mother Nature's hand, defined in its own unique way, were dwarfed by the ice-capped peaks. She had never seen such contrasting beauty. There were no signs of devastation here. The evil hand of war had spared this haven, she thought.

The Brisfits descended towards a green band, which ran along the lake where a huge sandstone castle stood defined by its own glory, complementing its surrounding with its numerous turquoise roofs and irregular turrets. Mary's eyes were drawn to one of the large roofs, in particular where the ridge of the roof was covered with a gold pattern of zigzags running either side of the ridge. In between each zigzag, gold and bronze roses and forget-me-nots were aligned, each one interwoven, within the zigzag. She deduced from recent events that she would be seeing a lot of this part of the castle. This is where she would learn to channel her gift and hone in on her innate instincts. 'All would become clear' according to Dr Goodman. She smiled to herself as the Brisfit touched down.

The Brisfits taxied up to the castle, which towered above them, standing in its majestic finery. As Mary hopped out of the Brisfit with Bobby's helping hand she could not help but look up at the looming gargoyles. "They look rather menacing, don't they?" Bobby commented as he gazed up. "King Clotaire ll had them mounted to the walls to ward off evil spirits."

"Clotaire ll?" Mary asked inquisitively.

"He was the only Merovingian King to practice monogamy, he built this castle in memory of his wife Haldetrude."

Mary was even more confused now and her awkwardness showed with her furrowing eyebrows, expressed momentarily. Luckily, to save Mary from embarrassment Bobby was still staring at the menacing stone creatures above. By now Dr Goodman and Darius had joined them and were looking up as well.

"Ahhhh the dragons of Portu Satis Tuto, we are home at last." Dr Goodman sighed with relief. "It's good to breathe the alpine Swiss air."

Darius chirped in, "There's now't like a good ole welcoming committee!"

Dr Goodman stared at Darius for a short while, puzzled, while Darius stared ahead looking at a bald, lean man dressed in black, neither short nor tall, walking towards them.

"Ahhh… you mean Kean?" Dr Goodman derived.

The very mention of the name sent a chill down Mary's spine, *surely not,* she thought.

As Keane drew closer, she could see he had the same cold eyes as Mr Ferguson's under butler, except these eyes portrayed a stern calmness instead of repugnant loathing. However, he was not clean-shaven and looked a little older.

Keane held out his hand as he stood in front of Dr Goodman. "Nice ta see ya, Doc, it's been a while."

"Too long," replied Dr Goodman with a jovial spirit.

"I see you have brought back these two hoodlums." Kean laughed at his own wit, as he shook Bobby's hand and hugged him. He released his hug and placed his hands on Bobby's shoulders. "It looks like the war swallowed ya up, had a chew and spat ya back out!"

Bobby nodded his head. "It certainly feels like it, Master Keane."

Kean patted Bobby on the back. "Well, it's good to see ya in one piece." He shook Darius's hand and tapped him on the back. "And you look unscathed but we all know appearances can be deceptive!" Darius rolled his eyes in reply.

He stepped back from Darius and looked at Mary. "Na don't you look a sight for sore eyes, Lady Mary. If only Mrs Crabtree could see ya now!" Keane jested.

Mary stood silently looking rather bedraggled, still wearing her flying jacket two sizes too big, and her mass of strawberry blonde curls tousled unruly around her face. She was pretty sure he was not complimenting her but decided to smile all the same.

"Na that smile, makes all the difference, even Aphrodite would be jealous." Keane looked at Dr Goodman for permission. Dr Goodman nodded and Keane opened his arms wide. "Give us a hug then!"

As Keane hugged Mary very tightly, an uncomfortable feeling engulfed her momentarily. 'Was this due to her having no idea who Keane was or was it her intuition that this man had a wicked side?' she thought.

Mary's innate sense was right, Keane most certainly had a wicked side to him. Keane was a natural born killer with a conscience, he only killed with impunity, the late Duke of Tavistock had recognized his killer instincts on many hunting trips. Keane had saved his life once, from being taken by a Bengal tiger. It had pounced upon the duke and had begun to maul him. Keane heroically pounced on the tiger and broke its neck with his bare hands. The duke thereafter made Keane a wealthy man and introduced him to the Order and Masters of Silat. Silat being a deadly ancient martial art, created by watching the movements of animals, then exploiting their weakness and the weakness of the enemy. The duke thought Silat would be most fitting for Keane, given his ability to kill a tiger.

Keane released his hug much to Mary's relief. "Well, we had better get you inside and settled in." Keane placed his arm around Mary's shoulder and started walking towards the huge double wooden doors of Portu Satis Tuto. He placed his head close to Mary's. "Na don't worry about not knowing who is who, Mary, I'll help by reintroducing ya with a few words of advice to the who's who. We will soon have ya memory back."

They reached a pair of large wooden arched doors, decorated with many carved family crests. Her eyes scanned the crests: two stags, two dragons, a lion and a dragon, two eagles, a lion and unicorn, two unicorns and a dragon, an eagle and a unicorn and a dragon and a unicorn. Her eyes stopped scanning as she found the two rearing lions in the middle of the door. Mary's eyes smiled, and then frowned as she noticed there was no motto. As she looked closer, she could see other family crests did not have a motto either. Her eyes motioned upwards above the huge wooden doors to a stone archway where the words, Nemo Me Impune Lacessit was inscribed.

Keane stared at the doors too, "Impressive, eh?"

Mary marveled as the word, "Yes," rolled off her tongue.

Keane looked back at Dr Goodman, frowned and shrugged his shoulders.

Dr Goodman pointed to his head and silently spoke the words, 'Her head.'

Keane nodded in agreement as Bobby and Darius looked on with concern.

Keane jested, "Well better not stand here all day or else we'll be takin root." He knocked on the right double door, on the crest of two unicorns and the door began to open all by itself.

Mary started to gasp with amazement but stopped herself the very second her mouth began to open. They walked in through the doorway and were greeted by two huge bronze resting lions, facing a large pond with a gold rearing unicorn centered in the pond. On the perimeter of the pond, large stone statues of two eagles, three horses, two dragons, two cobras, two stags, two bears stood opposite sides of each other with beautiful stone benches intermingled between the segregated creatures. All stone creatures faced inwards, looking at the unicorn.

Mary walked towards the large pond and gazed in the water; there was an abundance of large gold, orange and white koi carp swimming gracefully. She looked a little deeper and saw a young teenage boy swimming underneath the fish. She was totally absorbed by the boy's gracefulness, watching him for some time waiting for him to emerge from the pond to catch his breath, but he didn't. All the while she was oblivious to the younger boy, dressed in a black gee, artfully practicing his katas around a statue of a bear.

Keane shouted over to the boy, "Otto, how long has Ole been submerged now?"

Otto immediately stopped and bowed at Keane, then took a look at his watch. He poignantly replied, "Over ten minutes, Master Keane."

Keane smirked. "Did you lose track of time?"

"No, Master Keane, Ole told me he wanted to break his record of eight minutes. He has beat that now by two minutes." Otto smiled.

Keane shook his head. "Well, it's time he came out, wanna get him?"

Otto nodded his head and took off his jacket then ran and dived into the pond in Ole's direction.

Mary was astonished, as she looked at Bobby, Darius, and Dr Goodman to see their reaction... there was none. It was as if they were oblivious to the conversation, Keane had just had. She then began to be self-conscious of her expression and closed her mouth. (*How could a boy stay submerged underwater for more than ten minutes without any breathing apparatus?*)

Dr Goodman answered Mary's question without her actually asking it. "Somehow Ole and Otto can breathe through their skin." He chuckled rather elated. "With a little help from God and science. Just like an amphibian, except they are not." He smiled and then mocked, "Now you were looking at the ornate stone benches placed around the pond."

Mary beguiled by Dr Goodman's words, for the second time in her life thought, *Can he read my mind?*

He nodded his head in answer to her question. *Surely not*, she thought raising her eyebrows.

Dr Goodman smiled. "I surely can, how do you think I knew you were hiding under the duke's desk?" he replied to her thought. "Please, Mary, which bench do you sit on?"

Mary started to walk closer towards the stone benches, although her mind was somewhat preoccupied by Dr Goodman being able to read her mind and Otto and Ole getting out of the pond. They paid no attention to her as they scuttled away as quick as they could, away from Keane's prying eyes. Her thoughts turned back to the benches. She could see the benches were all different, some had huge talons as legs, paws, miniature stone elephants, horse heads, prowling tigers as legs. Some had backrests with one central flower in it, a rose, forget-me-not, sunflower, orchid, tulip, and others were too far away to make out which flowers were centered.

Dr Goodman piped up, "Do you remember where you sit, Mary?"

All eyes were on Mary as she scanned the benches and stone creatures. Her eyes were drawn to the largest stone bench placed at the head of the pond where two spectacular winged angels stood on either side of the bench. Mary could see the angel closest to her was carrying a wreath of roses in her hands as she lovingly gazed down upon them. She then noticed a huge sun on her chest, within the sun a crescent moon and star were overlaid. Unable to make out what the other angel was carrying, Mary walked over to the other side of the bench, running her fingers across the center of the backrest. (Where a filigree cross cut out from a large stone shield took center stage.) Intermingled within the stone filigree oriental dragons loomed down on top of the shield. In the center of the dragons eight smaller shields, stood on top of each other. Mary recognized the eight shields of eight religions. The Dharmachakra symbol for Buddhism, the Baha'i nine-pointed star, Omkara symbol for Hinduism, the Khanda symbol for Sikhism, Torii the symbol for Shintoism, Taijitu for Taoism, the Ahimsa symbol for Jainism. Her eyes were then transfixed on a sign she had never seen before.

She quickly moved her gaze as she walked over to the other side ofthe bench, to see the other angel and what she was carrying in her hands. A head of a larger-than-life daffodil was clasped in her right hand and cupped in her left hand a stem with many different flowers. Mary ran her fingers gently over the orchid, lotus flower, tulip, and an oversized forget-me-not.

"I'm very much drawn to this bench." She looked up and stared at the angel's chest where there was a sun that extended from breast to breast and overlaid in the center of the sun was the Star of David. "But I'm unsure why?" She stood on the bench and placed her dainty fingers on the Star of David. Her jovial expression changed to a saddened and confused one.

Dr Goodman's look of concern was reflected in his softly spoken voice. "What is it, Mary? What do you see?"

Mary uttered her words, "I see mass piles of used shoes in some kind of warehouse. It's dimly lit, sepia-toned. I see hair, mass piles of cut hair in the same warehouse, they too are sepia-toned. I see many people amazed walking about looking upwards at the snow; they are all wearing summer clothing though. A woman twirls around with her arms outstretched; she stops as she realizes the snow is not snow. A repugnant look transforms her joyful face as she rubs the snow in between her forefinger and thumb." Mary gasped, "It's not snow, it's ash... human ashes."

Her eyes were drawn back to the unidentified symbol. She walked back over to it and touched it with her fingertips, skimming the crevices. "What does this sign mean?"

Keane piped up, "Wellbeing, long life, good fortune, good luck, prosperity. It's a symbol that's been used by the Mayan tribe of South America, Navajo of North America, Acon of Africa, the Greeks, Hindus, Jainist, and Buddhist."

Mary's rosy cheeks depleted of color; her eyes widened as she gasped. She could barely speak, "It's not... I see it's connected to atrocious cruelties." Her eyes started to close, although she fought to stay conscious. (Her mouth became wide open, inhaling and exhaling as if she was trying to breathe.) She trickled out the words, "I-t's h-h-heinous." She slowly started to lose consciousness totally overcome by her vision, gasping as if she was taking her last breaths. She folded like a discarded stuffed Steiff doll and fell into Keane's strong arms.

Bobby, Darius, and Keane looked very concerned. Dr Goodman nonchalantly replied to their concern, "Mary is having a Precognition Seizure, we had better get her to the basement sanitarium."

Chapter Thirty-Five
Bad Company

Mary's eyes flickered open for a short time; all she could see was a white light, blinding haze. Her eyes shut as once again she lost consciousness, diving deep down into her subconscious.

Dr Goodman looked on perplexed. "So, what are your thoughts, Dr Lostus?"

An exceptionally tall man with dark brown slick back hair stood with an equally perplexed expression on his face. His pupils dilated as he processed his thoughts, his brown eyes almost turning black. "I am not sure what to make of her utterings. They simply do not make sense." He twisted the right side of his handlebar mustache, deep in thought. "Unlike Adolphus Hitler, he's a psychopath with hysterical hallucinations, for that I am quite sure."

Dr Goodman looked totally shocked. "Why is he here, lying next to a divine?"

He stared at Adolphus, a gaunt-looking man with a rather large dark brown untamed handlebar moustache who was lying peacefully on a single wrought iron bed, wrapped in white linen, staring up at the ceiling.

"He thinks he can't see yet his oculus dexter, and his oculus sinister, are perfect."

Dr Goodman butted in, "His right and left eye."

Dr Lostus nodded yes and continued. "He was a dispatch runner who has survived the war against the odds of just 14%… that is low, ja?"

Dr Goodman nodded yes.

Dr Lostus still had his amazed expression. "Compared to 86% of dispatch runners being killed. He truly believes that God has saved him to liberate the German people; he thinks he is divine. He also survived drowning in the freezing cold waters of the River Inn when he was a four-year-old, just a 1% rate of survival at 0.1 degrees. Nurse Shobia thought he may be divine too and she brought him to my attention."

Dr Goodman pondered. "I can see why, but her thinking was wrong."

Dr Lostus looked at Mary as his eyes lit up. "Are you sure Mary is divine?"

Dr Goodman answered abruptly, "Ja, we keep a very close eye on our divines and their oracalistic nature. Mary is very strong and will be an attribute to The Order."

"Really? Only listening to these two, one would think he's going to liberate Germany and she's telling him how to do it!" Dr Lostus chuckled nervously. "Absurd as it sounds."

"Now, that's certainly absurd! How could such a feeble, deadbeat of a man, ever have the drive or power to liberate Germany?" Dr Goodman scoffed. "The Order would never lose track of a divine." He looked down at Adolphus and scanned his body from head to toe; he turned his nose upwards and screwed his eyes up, as if he had a very bad taste in his mouth. "Get him out of here as soon as possible, he does not belong!" He then relaxed his face and smiled as he casts his eyes on Mary. "Now tell me more about Mary's utterings."

Dr Lostus looked perplexed. "She has been uttering lots."

His expression changed into a nonchalant one as he proceeded to start reading from his list. "Akira Ogata, will make German soldiers very, very strong?" Dr Lostus shrugged his shoulders. "That's all she mentioned, not how or why?"

Dr Goodman's eyes narrowed. "Akira Ogata is a very talented pharmacologist at Humboldt University, he's presently synthesized methamphetamine hydrochloride (Crystal Meth), and he's undergoing tests as we speak. If all goes well it could be rather profitable." He smiled in a sadistic way. "Who would not want increased performance mentally and physically? Although there is a downside, it induces non-empathetic side effects, sleep deprivation, hallucinations, and paranoia psychosis in some of the human guinea pigs we tested." Dr Goodman was trapped in his thoughts momentarily, "Continue!" he scoffed.

Dr Lostus nodded yes and then looked back down at his list and shrugged his shoulders. "Now, if I didn't know any different, I'd be thinking..." He hesitated as he looked up at Dr Goodman.

Dr Goodman widened his eyes in anticipation. "You'd be thinking what?" he mocked.

"I'd be thinking that Mary was a psychopath too, with hysterical symptoms just like Adolphus. You can see why with this message. Do you know anything about the Trebo concept of a Death Ray?" Dr Lostus probed.

"Nein… although Trebo was a horrendous medical student of mine in Munich. He's obsessed with rockets. I told him he has the potential to become a great rocketeer and not a doctor of medicine. He has no social graces whatsoever and hands like shovels. His rocket designs are impressive though. The Order is well aware of his talent. Who'd have thought missiles using liquid propellant could have a range of 179 miles? Trebo did; the man is a genius. He must not know that. His appetite for success could have been devastating for the world, if we had not intervened." He giggled. "All would have worked, only for that one small tweak."

Dr Lostus looked intrigued. "All would have worked?"

"Ja," snapped Dr Goodman.

"Do I detect sabotage?" Dr Lostus jovially chastised.

Dr Goodman ignored the comment and continued where he left off, "The outcome of the war could have been catastrophic the day Trebo showed Hermann von Stein his creation. Yes, you detected right, we had no option but to sabotage the rocket."

"Which Von Stein?"

"The Prussian Minister of War, oh course, ich, ich." Dr Goodman coughed and giggled at the same time, "Just that one small tweak… Von Stein was not impressed with Trebo, he chastised him for wasting his time. The outcome couldn't have been better for The Order."

Dr Lostus looked a little puzzled.

"For The Order, we have the technology and will keep it in safe hands. In the meantime, Trebo thinks he has to go back to the drawing board." Dr Goodman smiled and clapped his hands. "Anything else?"

Adolphus jumped in his bed.

Dr Goodman looked down on him. "He really should be moved, is he coherent?"

Dr Lostus nervously answered, "Nein." Then quickly reverted back to Mary's utterings. "Yes, the most disturbing of all, she somehow is very connected to Sachsenhausen." A wave of sadness appeared on Dr Lostus's face.

"Sachsenhausen, my home village, the apple wine country, with its cobbled streets and colorful painted houses." Dr Goodman looked puzzled.

"Yes, Mary has had many utterings about death camps there. She firstly was a child, a Jewish girl called Shoshana, whining for her ma'ama. She complains how her stomach hurts and her need for food. Then the need for water, her mouth is that dry and sore it starts to bleed. She cries out for Aura."

"Aura?" Dr Goodman questioned.

"Yes, I can't make out if she is crying for a friend or if she is heading to the light." He paused for thought. "Do you know what this means?"

"Nein, but I wish did. I am afraid to ask, but what else did Mary utter?" Dr Goodman puckered his lips.

Dr Lostus contemplated.

"What else?" Dr Goodman once more questioned him.

Dr Lostus stared at Dr Goodman with horror, his eyes welled with tears.

"She is me," Dr Goodman uttered.

"Yes, they're making you conduct terrible, terrible endurance experiments on our fellow Jews."

Dr Goodman's jaw dropped open. "They?"

Dr Lostus uttered the word, "Nazis."

Dr Goodman shook his head. "But I have never heard of 'Nazis'." A tear welled in his good eye as it rolled down his cheek.

Dr Lostus uttered the words, "Nazi and Aryanism were spoken together."

Dr Goodman deep in thought did not question he just wrote the words, 'Nazi and Aryanism' down on his notepad. He collected his thoughts. "I am afraid to ask if there is any more, but knowing full well there is, I would like you to continue."

Dr Lostus gasped before he continued, "Maybe you can make sense of the following names? Nima la-Niessuh, Grand Mufti of Jerusalem."

269

"The name Nima la-Niessuh escapes me but Grand Mufti of Jerusalem, that's a position that has just been created by Colonel Storrs. He would have everybody believe that Kamil al-Husayni has been given his rightful position."

Dr Goodman chuckled, "He also has made it known that he is the first military governor of Jerusalem since Pontius Pilate."

Dr Lostus's eyes widened. "Those are pretty large shoes he's filling then, or small ones depending on how a person looks at the situation." He looked entranced for a short while before speaking the words, "Jaaa, the person who was chiefly responsible for the crucifixion of Jesus. Although Matthew's gospel would have us believe that he could not find any reason to condemn Jesus on the accusations of the Jewish authoritarians he then washed his hands of the whole of affair... thwarted by his own cowardice to stand up to what was right. I can't imagine the weight on his shoulders; how could he live with himself?"

Dr Goodman scoffed, "He did not, he killed himself, just 199 miles away from here; Mount Pilatus was named after him. He was, after all, the savior of Mary Magdalene and her twins; without him, we would not have our divine Mary today, they too would have been murdered." He reached down and clasped Mary's left hand with his two hands. "Do proceed."

Dr Lostus looked down at his notes. "David Ben-Gurion?"

Dr Goodman pondered for while, before answering. "I have no idea who he is, but others in the inner circle may have knowledge of whom he is." He wrote down the name.

"Otto Yezorks, werewolves?" Dr Lostus laughed with the absurdity.

"Werewolves." Dr Goodman looked more and more perplexed. "Otto Yezorks is young Otto." His face suddenly lit up momentarily. "Keane has been teaching young Otto and Ole how to study animals and young Otto now thinks he's half boy and half wolf." He chuckled as Dr Lostus looked on not being able to see the funny side.

Dr Goodman looked nonchalantly as he shrugged his shoulders at Dr Lostus. "I really have no idea what the significance could be here. Is there any more?"

"Ja, but once again nothing that makes sense." Dr Lostus looked dumbfounded as he read with awkwardness. "PLO, Hamaz, Hezbollah, Jemaah Islamiyah, Al Khidr, Jihad, and Isis."

Dr Goodman scratched his head. "Well, I can only shed a little light on three of the names. Al Khidr is an immortal prophet, in ancient Islamic legend. He killed a youth out of mercy, he scuttled a boat off some travelers to deny a king of his greed. He is described as God's special servant, a protector, trickster, saint, and mystic, who has been identified with various ancient deities, not only as Al Khidr but as Elijah, Idris, Enoch, and Hermes all seem to be the same person, but with slightly different variations depending on which Holy book you read." He grimaced with wry amusement. "Well, Isis, you know who Isis is?"

Dr Lostus looked intrigued. "Ja… very interesting, I had no idea. I do know who Isis is, she's the goddess of life and magic."

Dr Goodman smiled and continued, "Now as for Jihad, Jihad is an Arabic word which means striving or struggling, typically within a praiseworthy aim; to become a better person fighting one's evil impulses, an effort to moral betterment. In Classical Sharia law though it is most frequently associated with war attributed only to self-defense though." Dr Goodman gently placed Mary's hand back down on the bed. "Is there anything else?"

Dr Lostus looked straight at Dr Goodman and frowned. "No that's all for now."

Dr Goodman raised his right eyebrow, which made his false eye seem huge. "Dr Lostus, what is puzzling you?"

Dr Lostus did not know whether to look relieved or anxious.

Mary's eyes slowly started to open as her consciousness awoke. Dr Goodman looked on awaiting her first words with trepidation and uncertainty. "Tell me what's on your mind Dr Lostus, or will I need to read you?"

Dr Lostus fumbled for his words. "Her, I mean Mary, Mary's messages may well have been obscure, but there were many and she has been out of normal consciousness for forty hours, the longest time I've ever known a divine to be transfixed."

Dr Goodman gently placed two fingers on her carotid artery, then counted the beats and checked his watch.

Dr Lostus looked on with concern, peering at the minute hand as if he too was taking Mary's pulse.

Dr Goodman began to smile as he announced, "She has a resting heart rate of an athlete, I do believe she will be up and around in no time at all, so what is the point you are trying to make?"

Dr Lostus's mouth ran dry and he coughed out of nervousness. "On other occasions when I have encountered Mary, she has been dormant, not one prophesy uttered and her heartbeat raced. It's as if Mary has an altered ego or an identical twin. Plus, she no longer has a birthmark on her left iris. Very peculiar, I must say."

Dr Goodman laughed. "Dr Lostus, you are talking such nonsense. Your first thoughts were that Mary was dormant and then your thoughts turned to her being a psychopath with hysterical hallucinations just like Adolphus Hitler, who still needs to be wheeled out of my sight and out of the castle, and now Mary has an alter ego. If I did not know you any better, I would be questioning your capabilities but since I do, I am putting your inability down to lack of sleep." Dr Goodman stared at Dr Lostus with a piercing look. "Now get Adolphus out of here and get some sleep. The Cabal will want to hear all about your findings tonight."

Chapter Thirty-Six
I Am Not Alone

The deep dark serene water bubbled ever so slightly, giving nothing away of the fraught torrid battle that lay underneath. The battle to live was purely one-sided as the aggressor played with his prey, pulling the body deep down every time the woman's slender body drew close to the surface. Clenched fists thrashed for dear life against the predator, eyes wide and mouth shut, she pushed past him, reaching for the surface; she then gulped as much air as she could, before being dragged down by her long locks. Her strength drained as she gulped the water; a state of delirious calm set in. Her mouth now filled with water as it found any pathway it could. Was this the way she was going to die?

Mary bolted upright in bed gasping for dear life, followed by a long spate of coughing.

Dr Goodman gently tapped her on her back.

She gasped again trying to catch her breath; instead, all she could manage were short gasps.

"Mary, Mary," Dr Goodman shouted. He placed his forefinger on the top of her chin and thumb underneath it, then looked straight into her eyes. "Breathe," he commanded.

With eyes wide-open Mary took one last gasp before her breath reached normality as she realized she was no longer in danger.

"It's only a dream, Mary, just a dream." Dr Goodman reassured her in a calm voice.

Mary's eyes were red and tearful from the fright, her voice trembling. "I-I was being dragged down into deep dark water and no matter how hard I battled I could not emerge. Time and time again, I was dragged back down until I had no more air left in my body, I could literally feel the water enter my passageways and then you woke me. This is a recurring dream I have, and every time I have it, it feels more intense."

"It was all but a dream, Mary, nothing for you to worry about." Dr Goodman took a handkerchief out of his pocket and wiped a tear from her eye. "I have brought Claudia to see you, she's your mentor. She will teach you how to develop your divine powers for the greater good of mankind." He smiled and turned to a beautiful blue-eyed woman with long platinum hair. She stepped forward, her olive skin glowed in the afternoon sunlight, as it filtered through the leaded glass castle window. She was dressed in a white gown with a gold crescent brocade sun around her neck. The dress revealed her shoulders, part of her breastbone and muscle toned arms.

Dr Goodman smiled at Claudia, then looked at Mary. "Claudia, do you think you can have Mary ready for the Inauguration Ball tonight? There are members of the Inner Sanctum that are eager to meet her." He produced a wry smile.

Claudia all the while looked at Mary analyzing her complexities, as she answered in the calmest manner, "Only if Mary is ready, Dr Goodman." She smiled at Mary. In turn Mary smiled back, there was an unspoken bond between the two at first sight.

Dr Goodman, none the wiser, furrowed his eyebrows in dismay, but all the same he accepted Claudia's answer. "Right, I shall leave you both to get acquainted." He looked straight at Claudia but spoke to Mary. "Mary, I hope to see you later. I will be the one wearing the white and black ram's head." He turned around and walked out of the room.

Mary looked totally puzzled. "A white and black ram's head?"

Claudia laughed. "Yes, he's part of the Inner Sanctum, the Fellowship of The Cabal of The Order. They wear their identity heads at the inauguration ceremony with The Cult of The Cabal. Dr Goodman is a white and black ram, he's part of the flock as such but he's the master of the sheep and Master of Ceremony, that's why he will be wearing the ram's head."

Mary pondered a little over Claudia's answer. *Dr Goodman was master of the sheep so why would his head be black and white?* She thought.

Claudia all the while was watching Mary's puzzled expression. "Dr Goodman wears a black and white ram's head because he walks in the light and also in the dark. He's an impartial."

Mary looked even more puzzled.

Claudia smiled. "We are divines. We only wear white on this day and night, as we all walk in the light. All the Purists wear white today, too. Unfortunately, there are many here that walk in the darkness within these walls and they wear black on this day and night to define themselves."

Mary looked perplexed. "The Cult of The Cabal?"

"Yes, and many more, Mary, I know first-hand this might be hard to understand. There are many here that see Lucifer as their god. They think he is the bringer of light; they worship him and walk in the darkness. They are in league with the dark angel. They're deep into the occult and have an insatiable quest for knowledge, the essence of life and secrets of the universe. Their knowledge runs very deep. They have experts in alchemy, masters of all languages including ancient languages, they're adept in astrology, astronomy, physics, chemistry, biology, mathematics, metallurgy, medicine, cartography, botany, steganography, scrying, and so much more." Claudia looked deep in thought for a split second. She turned and stared at Mary. "You cannot trust a dark walker. No matter how sincere they might seem."

Mary's expression turned to one of sheer worriment. "How will I know who the Dark Walkers are tomorrow, if they are only dressed in black today and tonight?"

Claudia looked intensely at Mary, her eyes then softened as she smiled. "Fear not, Mary, you were born with instincts, just like many old wise men and women who have honed in on their instincts over the years. After their knowledge of learning to know and life experience, you have been gifted at birth with an innate supernumerary that far surpasses old men and women. An intuitive powerful perception, a 'sixth sense' that only now you will start to understand. This sixth sense will not deceive you and you will know when you're in the presence of a dark walker, regardless of what disguise they are wearing."

Claudia's words ran deep within Mary's veins and brought solace to her momentary distress. They both smiled in the moment of knowing.

"Now we had better get you changed so you can meet your family of fellow diviners." Claudia held her hand out for Mary to grab, in turn Mary clasped Claudia's hand and placed her feet on the floor.

"Do you feel strong enough to walk? You have been in deep consciousness for forty-eight hours."

Mary looked puzzled once again, but answered all the same. "I feel good but I'm a little thirsty."

Claudia walked over to the bedside table and grabbed the full glass of water and passed it to Mary. "That's good to hear, Mary, drink up and I'll show you where our wing is."

Mary uttered, "Thank you," and drank the water rather quickly, quenching her thirst.

Claudia smiled. "Ready?"

Mary gasped as she took her last gulp of her water. "Yes."

"Good, pop your slippers on and follow me," Claudia cheerfully urged.

Mary placed her slippers on her feet, stood up and looked down at her white lace nightdress. "I do not have my dressing gown."

"No, you don't but you're dressed in white and your nightdress is long and unrevealing, unlike my dress. So, if we walk quick enough no one will notice that you are wearing a nightdress, they will think you're also wearing a white gown too."

Mary smiled in agreement, Claudia turned and walked out of the calming cream decorated room. Mary followed entering a large corridor with a cream and rust-colored marble checkered floor. Its stark white walls, grounded the opulent, huge crystal chandeliers hanging from a high ceiling. On the opposite side of the doorway, they had just left stood a row of seven arched stained-glass windows divided by eight limestone pillars. Mary had no time to gaze at the stained-glass windows or for that matter the intricate stone carvings of the four arched marble pillars that stood right outside the room she had slept in. However, she did notice every pillar had different carvings. One in particular had a falcon's head and body with human legs. Mary stopped and stared at the carving, bemused.

Claudia turned and faced the carving too. "Horus," she chirped. "He's the god of the sky, war and hunting, he is the eye. She smiled. "There are lots of carvings, paintings, sculptures, tapestries and artworks of different kinds within this castle, Mary. All have meaning, some even fortuitous and bleak prophecies. However, I do not want you to think too much now, because of what you have just overcome. You need to replenish your mind's power before you use it again. You're too weak, right now." She frowned a little. "I think we had better make our way up to our quarters by the elevator." Claudia looked ahead at an arched double doorway with two carved wooden doors. One had a decorative carving of a huge forget-me-not on the left door and the right door had a huge carving of a rose. Claudia looked back at Mary and smiled as she pressed the up button on the elevator, in turn Mary smiled back.

Mary couldn't help but ask her question. "Why do the roses and forget-me-nots symbolize us?"

Claudia smiled with appreciation at her question. "Firstly, the forget-me-not symbolizes you. It's your connection to all the deities, even though a divine may not know they are divine. We must not forget. It's a connection we have that will last through time with each other. Next comes fidelity and loyalty in our relationships with others, despite separation and extreme challenges. Remembrance for each other during our partings, it's a true and undying love for each other. We are all forget-me-nots firstly. The rose symbolizes wisdom, maturity, balance, a love for the self as for one another. It symbolizes faith, honor, passion and endurance and all that the forget-me-not symbolizes too."

The elevator arrived and the double wooden carved door slid to the right. The two walked into a rather grand wooden paneled elevator. A huge gold inlaid forget-me-not filigree decoration hung on the left of the control panel.

An old man dressed in a navy-blue and gold brocade uniform slipped his words out. "Whhherrrre to, laaddiess?" He reminded Mary of Jim, the gatekeeper at Chandringham, with his crooked back.

Claudia grinned. "Where do you think, Jim?"

"Ahhhhhh now ya making me guess, Miss Claudia, I'd say to the top floor!" Jim's eyes sparkled with delight when the elevator light flashed on the second floor. "Looks like we will have company and I'm no oracle but I can take a pretty good guess, who that'll be."

Claudia looked mystified and smiled. "Are you channeling, Jim?" She laughed vibrantly.

Jim chuckled, "If only, Miss Claudia. I only know, because he's been riding up and down ins me carriage almost all afternoon. He's been driving me nuts. Talk about persistence!" Jim nodded his head.

"Who, Jim?" Claudia asked calmly. "Do tell?"

"That dirty ole man, you are less than half his age!" Jim nodded his head.

Claudia smirked, "Is he... Well?"

"Well, I can't helps me self, it's Nhoj Feckellore."

"Oh, Jim, he is only seventy-eight years old." She laughed. "He's a mere puppy."

"That's what I mean. You are less than half his age, somthin ain't right about that. I can miss his floor if you want me to?" Jim scoffed. Mary knew something was not quite right and Jim had totally missed Claudia's point.

"He's frail, Jim, and I am only too intrigued as to why he wants to see me. Please stop at the second floor."

Jim shrugged his shoulders. "Just as you ask, Miss Claudia, hold on, Miss Mary."

Mary grabbed the handrail, not really knowing what to expect, as she had never been a passenger in an elevator before. Jim pulled the double doors across the walkway and then pulled across the folding lift gates. He pushed on a lever and drove the lift to the second floor, in an instant. It was so quick that Mary's stomach felt like it landed above her head and was taking its time finding its correct place.

Jim opened the double doors as Mary collected herself. A freshly barbered silver-haired man with angular bone features stepped into the lift. His gaunt features made him look like he had no lips. Although Mary saw he had as his frown turned into a smile the very second, he clapped eyes on Claudia.

He spoke with a crisp and concise American accent; his voice had no frailties regardless of his age. "Ah, Claudia, I've been hoping we would meet at some point today." He stood back and looked Claudia up and down.

Jim piped up, "Do ya want the lift, sir, or shall I come back for ya?"

Nhoj narrowed his eyes at Jim and stepped in the elevator, he then marveled once again at Claudia and glanced at Mary. "You certainly are a sight for sore eyes, my dear."

Jim intervened as he closed the gate. "Which floor do ya want, sir?"

"I'm going wherever Claudia is going."

Jim looked at Claudia and shrugged his shoulders, in notion of 'I told you so'.

Claudia smiled and jested, "Now, Nhoj Feckellore, why were you hoping to meet me at some point today?"

His steel blue eyes sparkled under the elevator light and a wry smile appeared before he spoke. "I wanted to make sure I was your first and last dance tonight."

Claudia stared at Nhoj and sighed with sadness in her eyes. "You know that is not possible, Nhoj, Selrach has the first and second dance, it's always been custom for me to dance with the Grand Master."

Nhoj frowned. "I know but he's weak. He always has a headache and forgets matters of urgency? He'll not last long."

Claudia looked a little glum and then smiled. "If that were the case, I could sympathize with him. However, it's not and I can offer you the third dance or the last dance if you have aced in your philanthropy skills this year. Although I believe Drew has excelled this year, once again."

Nhoj began to open his mouth as the elevator stopped. Before he could talk, Jim sharply announced, "Your floor, Miss Claudia."

Mary's stomach churned a little with the sudden halt of the elevator, but her focus was purely on the conversation.

Nhoj scoffed, "I'll take the third dance, then. See you tonight, deary."

In turn Jim opened the elevator gate and door, while Claudia smiled at Nhoj and stepped out of the elevator. "Thank you, Jim."

Mary stepped out too, and quietly spoke the words, "Thank you too."

They walked down a corridor that simulated the sky. The floor, walls and ceiling were all one masterpiece of a painted sky with stratocumulus clouds underfoot. The large dark rounded masses of cloud made Mary feel like she was walking within the clouds as the stratus snow clouds surround her peripheral vision. She looked up at bright white cirrocumulus clouds and twinkling lights, as they became a mere dapple of white within a heavenly blue sky. At the end of the corridor a golden sun shone, above it, bright white cirrostratus clouds, resembling a halo, in Mary's mind, could be seen.

Mary felt a deep penetrating warmth and had lost her train of thought in asking Claudia about Nhoj acing his philanthropy skills this year.

Claudia opened the masked door, just by the mere touch of her fingertips, pressing in on the middle of the sun. The door swung inwards and Mary followed Claudia.

Before Mary had time to take in the splendor of the room and the people within it, Claudia spoke, "Mary, I would like you to meet your fellow diviners. They are all going to introduce themselves one, by one of their own free will. Please join the circle and join hands."

Mary briefly looked around the circle to find her spot. She was drawn to an open space and an intriguing pair of light brown amber blazed eyes. She reached out and placed her hand into a hand much larger than hers, her skin paled by his honey beige-toned skin. She clasped his hand and smiled. Then she looked to the right side of her and stared into a pair of entrancing, dark brown eyes with indigo circles around each pupil. She then looked down and clasped his hand, her skin once again paled by much darker skin.

Claudia joined the circle of six. She stood opposite Mary and before she joined hands, she addressed the group. "From the very moment we were conceived we were given the source of life. Within this life there is light, a light that shines in the darkness; a light the darkness may never put out. We are diviners full of grace and truth, our eternal spirits walk with our physical form, guiding us, so that we may walk within this world to enlighten others and make good within this world. We have the ability to heal, protect and communicate with each other with our extrasensory perception, Mary; it's within our nature. Just as creatures of the world hibernate, altering their physiological state where their body temperature drops, heart and respiration rates slow drastically to survive months without food and water."

Claudia looked around the circle, before proceeding. "Each one of us here today has the ability to receive an echo of thought from each other no matter where we are in this world." Claudia joined hands, and then continued. "There is darkness in this world, that many love, it runs deep within their veins. They hate the light because of their evil deeds and will not come to the light because they don't want their evil deeds to be judged. However, they have already been judged and will forever walk in the darkness if they refuse to make good. We need to be aware of this and protect ourselves, for the darkness in this world wants to engulf the light. We will now strengthen our eternal light."

Claudia smiled at Mary. "Mary, I need you to listen carefully, now and ask no questions. Will you do that?"

Mary's face was expressionless as she answered, "Yes."

Claudia continued to talk softly and quietly. "All our senses, never function, move, operate as a whole, holistically. When one or the other senses becomes dominant, we give one or the other senses a greater power. Thus, we create an imbalance; within the imbalance there becomes the inability for all the senses to operate. It is possible for all our senses to operate as a whole. Whole senses acting together, fully awakened, so that there is no center from which the senses are moving. There are no limitations. To give the senses their rightful place, we must not suppress any sense we have. So our bodies must become fully relaxed and quiet to open the gateway to fully awaken all senses."

Claudia paused with a serious expression on her face as she peered at Mary. "Are you making sense of my words, Mary?"

Mary answered once again, with a blank expression on her face. "Yes."

Claudia continued, "We as divines must tune ourselves to live a life without any form of control or suppression within our minds. How do we do this, Mary? We now know that all our senses must be fully awakened and equal. The next step is to address time. What is time? What power does it play in our life? There is time by the sun; rising and the setting of the sun. Time by the watch. Time as yesterday, today and tomorrow. Time as something happened in the past, something remembered and shaping of the present and our future. The physical, chronological time and psychological time; I will be, I must, questions answered, unanswered questions, ridicule, guilt, self-pity, plans, thoughts of anger, unwritten lists. We are going to enter a state of mind where time does not exist, where psychological time comes to an end. Where the brain itself can be absolutely quiet, every brain cell in its entirety, absolutely quiet.

The time within the self-consciousness stops, the attachment stops, empty, totally, completely within our self-consciousness. Thought as time stops, measurement stops, control stops, we then leave ourselves open to our extra sensual perception; depthless, endless with no beginning and no end. In this tremendous quality of silence, we then will become one."

Claudia smiled once more at Mary. "Do my words make sense, Mary?"

Mary smiled in reply firstly, then answered a softly spoken, "Yes."

Claudia continued. "Innocence is a brain that has never been harmed. No unhappiness, conflict, sorrow or pain. Is it possible for the brain to be freed from all the mechanics of life and never get old?"

Claudia stared at Mary, but Mary did not answer. Claudia continued. "We stand here today as living proof. We can all be our own healers, Mary. We are all part of God's image, omniscient, generous, loving and eternal, but we are solely entirely responsible for ourselves." Claudia looked at Mary with a serious expression, before continuing. "Mary, it is now time to free your mind and awaken all of your senses so that we can all communicate with you telepathically. One by one each person in this room will introduce themselves, when they are ready. Do not worry if you are not able to hear their voices today. There will always be tomorrow, to find your first extrasensory perception." Claudia smiled. "Now let us begin, by closing our eyes." She paused before she began. "There is no belonging of time here, physical, chronological or psychological. The mind is totally free from unanswered questions, guilt, ridicule, self-pity, plans, thoughts of anger, unwritten lists, watch them all drift away, never to return."

Claudia paused once more before she continued. A deep sense of calm engulfed the room.

"We can now begin to operate all our senses as one whole sense by firstly depleting any imbalance. So that all senses are fully awakened and there is no center from which they are moving or floating. Our bodies now become relaxed and quiet." Claudia paused once more.

She continued, "The brain itself can be absolutely quiet, every brain cell absolutely quiet; time within the self-consciousness stops, attachment stops. Empty, totally, completely within our self-consciousness. Thought as time stops, measurement stops, control stops, we then leave ourselves open."

There was silence within the circle, within the silence, a collective calmness. Each person began to generate a glow, within the white collective light. Mary's eyes were shut but she could see an amber glow forming around the man with light brown, amber blazed eyes. She looked deep into his light brown eyes, as she did so a deep echoing voice encapsulated her thoughts. "Pleased to meet you, Mary, my name is Humayun."

The amber glow faded back into the white light. A red mist soon infused the light and Mary began to see a vision of a young Chinese woman, just a little older than her. Mary's eyes became focused on a pair of brown eyes with red flecks around the pupils. She could hear a soft faint voice. "Welcome, Mary my name is Annachi."

As soon as the voice had spoken, the red glow suddenly diminished back into the white light.

For a while, Mary could only see the white light. She was within her sanctuary. Suddenly the light became a blaze of blue. She found herself staring into a pair of green eyes with blue circles around the pupils. She had stared into these eyes once before. "Darius," she whispered telepathically. Conscious of her thought she suppressed it, keeping her mind quiet. She waited to hear the man's voice but the blue depleted back into the white light.

Pigments of green slowly appeared as the white light glistened, as if to celebrate the arrival of the colour. The white light soon turned to a haze of green as a pair of beautiful blue eyes appeared with green flecks around the pupil became defined. Claudia's voice echoed, "You're doing well, Mary, stay within the calm."

The green haze began to blend back into the white light; pigments of a yellow mist became dominant. Through the haze suddenly appeared a pair of mesmerizing green eyes with yellow-flecked rings around the pupils. A strong stern woman's voice vibrated through the haze. "Welcome, Mary, I am Anna." The mesmerizing eyes stared for a while before dissipating within the yellow haze as it transformed back into the white light. It was not long before pigments of indigo invaded the light and a pair of dark brown eyes transpired with indigo circles around the iris. A confident masculine voice appeared. "It's nice to finally connect with you, Mary. My name is Shaka, spelt SHAKA." The eyes stared for some time and eventually faded back into the white light. Mary's violet aura began to filter through the white light. Her blue eyes with violet rings around her irises appeared in the center of the circle. Her soft voice echoed, "Thank you for helping me and introducing yourselves, Humayun, Annachi, Claudia, Anna, and Shaka, I hope I can stay connected with you all, there is only one name that I did not hear."

Claudia's voice echoed, "That's because it was not spoken. In time you will know. You have surpassed us all on our first enlightenment. Well done, Mary. We all now need you to keep within the innocent state of calm in your mind so that we can all stay connected." She paused and then continued, "Can you do that, Mary?"

Mary replied telepathically, "I will try."

Each individuals' aura glowed in the form of colored spheres, orange, red, blue, green, yellow, indigo and violet grew in size. They began to merge into each other and spiral like a small tornado until they reached the ceiling where they centrally fused together to form a transparent, coloured, glowing sphere, that encapsulated the circle within the circular room.

Mary's eyes were closed but her field of vision wide open within her sixth sense as she stared on in amazement, at the transparent rainbow-colored glowing sphere resembling a bubble of light.

Claudia's voice echoed, "You have been enlightened, Mary. Anytime you are in need of us, this is how you can connect, you can open your eyes now."

Mary opened her eyes to see Claudia standing opposite her; Humayun and Shaka were holding her hand. Annachi still stood connected to the circle but there were two empty spaces next to Claudia. (Where Mary connected with a familiar pair of green eyes with blue circles around the iris; however, he did not introduce himself.) She was pretty certain the pair of green eyes were Darius's. If that was the case, then why did he not introduce himself and why did she not see him in the first place? Her thoughts turned to Anna: she did not see her and what she looked like; although she too had mesmerizing green eyes but with yellow flecks around the iris. She was engulfed by the moment and was told to suppress any dominant sense, hers being her eyesight. She reflected on her ma's words, 'The eyes are the gateway to the soul'. Seeing was believing, the color of one's soul was the same color of one's iris, she thought.

Chapter Thirty-Seven
Prophecy Visions of Art

Mary stood facing her reflection in the mirror staring into her violet glowing sphere, her mind transfixed by the glow, love, and warmth she felt.

Claudia's voice echoed, "You look beautiful, dear Mary."

Mary's physical sight returned as she stared at her human reflection, her eyes captivated by her dress. "I have never worn such a beautiful dress before or a dress without sleeves." She looked down at her cleavage and was thankful that it was covered by the beginning of a flowing asymmetrical train. Mary turned to face Claudia, "This golden embroidered forget-me-not bodice must have taken many hours to sew."

"Indeed," Claudia replied as she adjusted Mary's white silken train, to flow to the floor. "Now, how do you feel?"

Mary beamed. "I feel positively radiant."

"You look radiant, too!" Claudia's smile turned into a somewhat earnest look. "Never let go of how you are feeling, right now. Your light is shining inside and out; make sure you walk in your protective sphere. Do not let anyone penetrate it, for tonight, tonight you will see a world you never knew existed."

Mary's expression became austere. "The Dark Walkers?"

"Yes. Stay within the light and walk only within that light; the light you have been born into, it will always protect you. I will be by your side tonight at some point, physically, but we can always talk anytime, telepathically. Humayun will be here shortly. I have asked him to be your escort tonight, he can protect you, should the case arise and help guide you. Just in case you stray."

"I hope you do not mind me asking, Claudia?"

Claudia smiled and replied, "Ask away."

Mary's concerned expression emulated within her voice. "If The Order protects the divine, then why are we mixing with the Dark Walkers tonight?"

"We are not just mixing with the Dark Walkers tonight, the Impartial will be there too, men and women like Dr Goodman. You see, The Order needs the mixing of Dark Walkers, the Impartial and Divine. All separate minds coalesce to form a single body of scientific thought; just as the earth needs the sun and the moon to flourish. The Order needs the Divine, Impartial and Dark Walkers to flourish. That one thought materializes into many and some may even eventuate into making the world a better place or not as we have just seen with a sacrilegious war."

Mary thought long and hard about Claudia's words and for once in her life, she had no questions. Just as she looked up, Humayun walked into the room, wearing a knee length asymmetrical front fastening white silk jacket with gold brocade trim around the neckline. The closer he got, Mary could see the same embroidered detailing on his jacket was the same embroidered detailing on her dress, of gold forget-me-nots and roses entwined on the left opening side of his jacket, cascading down his left arm. He reminded Mary of a Mongolian Emperor, like the one she had seen in a picture inside a history book, except Humayun was not wearing a turban or pajama white, satin pants; his pants were fitted to his legs. He towered above Mary and looked down on her. However, she was not intimidated whatsoever. His long wavy, dark brown, shoulder length hair, framed his handsome features and his kind beguiling eyes gazed at Mary.

Claudia spoke with a cheerful tone, "You look rather dapper."

Humayun smiled as he looked at Claudia and Mary. "I think we all look rather snazzy." He then clicked his feet together and stuck out his left arm. "Your escort for the night, Lady Mary Tavistock."

Mary linked Humayun's arm and smiled at the same time.

Humayun stuck out his right arm for Claudia to link.

She acknowledged with a coy look and shook her head. "I'll be down shortly, I have a couple of things to do."

Humayun looked a little concerned. "Is there anything I can do?"

Claudia answered with a calm demeanor. "No, you two go, I'll be there soon. Never forget what I told you, Mary."

Mary nodded yes in agreement before answering, "I will not."

The two walked out of the room linking arms.

Humayun asked. "What did Claudia ask you to never forget?"

Mary smiled with elation before answering, "I'm never to let go of how I'm feeling right now. My light is shining inside and out and I must always walk in my protective sphere and not let anyone penetrate it. For tonight I will see a world I never knew existed." She gulped.

The two reached the elevator and Humayun pressed the button, as Mary looked on anxiously.

"Do I detect you are looking apprehensive because you are worried about how to protect your sphere of light?" Humayun asked.

"Yes, and what if I am not strong enough? What will happen if my sphere of light is penetrated?"

Just then Jim opened the lift doors. "Evening ya Highness, Lady Mary. Now, don't tell me which floor ya wanna go to? Let me guess."

Humayun looked amused but Mary's anxious expression had not changed.

Jim commented, "Oh dear, Lady Mary, ya look like you have lost a pound and found a farthing." Jim frowned a little, for Mary's expression had not changed.

Humayun butted in. "So, Jim, which floor are we going to?"

Jim looked intense momentarily then replied with a whimpered tone to his voice. "I don't really know, now."

"That must mean we have changed our minds, Jim, and have decided to walk. Sorry for your inconvenience. Come, Mary, we will take the stairs." Humayun placed his arm around Mary's shoulder while directing her toward the staircase. Jim looked on flummoxed, shrugging his shoulders as he closed the lift doors. Humayun and Mary started to descend the staircase, side by side.

"Your sphere of light can only be penetrated when you step out from the light you walk within. So, now that you have gained your telepathic sense you are now open to listening to other conversations, other than Divine conversations, the Impartial and Dark Walkers. Don't be tempted to listen to their conversations just yet, for doing so, you will be stepping out of the light you are walking within. You need more training before you can do so, so that you can always stay within the light, even when you are listening to a Dark Walker." Humayun stopped walking and looked intensely at Mary, "And should a Dark Walker sense that you are listening they will latch onto you and into our frequency of communication. This could have dire consequences for the Divine if they are undetected. So, Mary, please do not step out of the light to listen into any other conversations, as you will open up a porthole within the divine. Stay within the light and walk only within the light you have been born into. It will always protect you." Humayun paused, gazing at Mary. "Do you feel more confident now, Mary?"

Mary smiled and answered with a stern, "Yes."

(The two walked into a large hall, where there was an artist at work painting a huge mural.) Humayun and Mary stopped to view the painting as the painter sat on a plank attached to wooden scaffolding, engrossed in his creation. He was oblivious to Humayun's and Mary's presence.

"What do you see within Per Krohg's painting?" Humayun asked with intrigue.

Mary stared at the painting for a while before answering in a soft delicate voice, "I see darkness firstly, squalor, war deprivation, hell, an abomination." Mary paused, stopping to think. "The phoenix bird rising brings light, a new day, a new world, but he is not standing above his old ashes as the Ancient Greeks have foretold. He is standing above his old skin. I see deception here, for only amphibians and reptiles shed their skin. All is not what it seems." She paused for thought once again. "Behind the Phoenix, the ghostly figures of Dark Walkers seem to be stepping into a void, yet other Dark Walkers are being freed from their sins as they make their way into the light. Many celebrate within the light, yet the pale horse is being released into the light. I do not understand this as the pale horse is the bringer of death from the Book of Revelation through weapons, hunger, and disease. This symbolizes war to me and more depopulation via disease." Mary had a blank expression. "There is going to be another war, isn't there? This painting depicts sinister happenings. Yet the artist within the painting has not painted on the blank canvas. The flames within the background of the canvas are leading me to believe that this is not his vision, but of the blonde lady's within the light." Mary looked at Humayun. "Is the blonde lady Claudia?"

"Yes." Humayun declared. "Throughout the castle, there are many works of art that depict our visions of the future. Many we will not perceive as good, for as divine, we all seek peace and good. Yet The Order perceives war as good, a cleansing of all that is rotten in the world."

Mary butted in, "But we have just had a war, and the cost was life itself: millions and millions died, many millions were injured, all of which are now tainted by their memories, beautiful buildings blown up, lives torn apart, famine, hunger, deprivation, poverty. Influenza all caused by war and greed. I do not see how war cleanses the world, it's mass murder on mankind... I just see greed." Mary paused for a moment staring into thin-air. "We should not foretell our visions. Then The Order will not know what the future has in store for the world. Unless the Dark Walkers can see the future too?"

Humayun stared into thin-air too. "They cannot. They perceive bad as good, we see their good as evil and the evil we see they perceive as good."

Humayun stared into Mary's blue eyes. "Regardless of not foretelling our visions to The Order, these visions we have will happen anyway. Claudia and I agree that it is best for The Order to know about our visions so that they are aware and know full well of the consequences bestowed throughout the world. If certain endeavors are not intervened with, there could be worse consequences. The Order has the power to change these worldly endeavors and the shape of the future."

Humayun smiled. "We are going to be late for the inauguration ceremony if we continue with this conversation, we had better make haste."

Chapter Thirty-Eight
The Cabal

Humayun and Mary walked through one of three huge archways. Each archway only defined by its backlight color, of red, lilac and sun-kissed white. The thirty-foot ogeed columns with arched tops reminded Mary of Canterbury Cathedral. She had only ever seen photographs of the stunning house of God and marveled at the glorious architecture, with its looming Gothic archways. She had wondered how small she would feel looking up at splendorous sculptured stone. She indeed felt very small in comparison as the two walked in between the two sun-kissed white columns of Portu Satis Tuto.

The segregated red, lilac, and sun-kissed white lights continued in the form of many spheres hanging from the tall vaulted ceiling. Humayun directed Mary to a crescent wooden pew, which was positioned on the right-hand side of a huge circular stage. On the floor in the center of the stage, a huge red cross expanded to an outer edge where it met a continuous circular aqua-blue line of the same thickness as the cross.

Mary had never seen the symbol before. Her curiosity led her to ask Humayun the question, "What does the symbol in the center of the stage mean? I have never seen a cross encased by a circle before now."

Humayun smiled and replied whispering in Mary's left ear, "That's because this sign is nowhere else in the world. It signifies the cross embracing the world."

Mary churned over the answer for a very short moment then proceeded to ask Humayun another question. "I recognize the Pagan Symbols outside the continuous aqua-blue-circle.

On the top 'The God sign', has been placed at the twelve o'clock position. The 'water symbol,' placed at two o'clock.

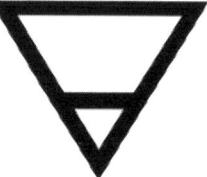

The 'fire symbol,' placed at four o'clock.

The earth symbol placed at seven o'clock.

Then the air symbol placed at ten o'clock.

However, I do not know what the symbol placed at six o'clock means, do you?"

Humayun smiled, flashing his perfect white teeth and commented, "I certainly do, Mary, would you like me to tell you?"

Mary eagerly answered, "Yes."

Humayun whispered once again in Mary's ear. "It's called the Ankh, known by its Latin name, crux ansata, which translates to 'cross with a handle'. It's renowned to be an ancient Egyptian hieroglyph or more ancient, a Neolithic hieroglyph. It means life or living. Over time the Ankh has come to symbolize eternal life and immortality to people from many walks of life. People who wish to show that they have only spiritual beliefs, rather than religious beliefs also choose it. The loop has a couple of common meanings. It represents the three upper chakras, also known as the spiritual chakras, which are associated with the divine. It represents the Godhead, not just the masculine, but God as an all-encompassing divine being. It also represents the female principles or the Goddess, within nature and the divine universe."

Mary reflected on Humayun's words, as she did so her eyes scanned the globe-shaped Gothic auditorium, which now was rather crowded.

Most of the crescent wooden pews had become occupied. A mass of people dressed in black sat on the opposite side to Mary and Humayun. The red globe lights above them seemed to emphasize their evil ramifications. She wondered if they were all Dark Walkers.

Humayun whispered softly in Mary's ear, "Concentrate on the light within you, Mary."

Mary quickly honed in on her inner light as she did so she looked up at the globes of sun-kissed yellow light. Her eyes strayed to a huge bright white chandelier with two triangles suspended, one on top of the other, placed to form the Star of David. Centrally placed below the triangles a crystal oval outline of an eye was suspended. In the middle of the crystal oval outline, hung a crystal globe. Mary had no idea what the chandelier symbolized and didn't feel it was appropriate to ask, as Shaka was now sat on her right side. Instead, she smiled at him and then gazed up to her left at the lilac sphered lights and at the Impartial people who sat under the lilac spheres, occupying the crescent pews. Many men were dressed in grey suits, but some wore suits, which were black on the left side and white on the right side, others wore the white and black on the opposite sides. There were not many women but the ones Mary could see were dressed in black and white dresses.

Mary was quickly distracted by the sound of loud dramatic entrancing music played by an orchestra and sung by a choir. (All to which she could not see. Mary turned to look at Humayun whom had equal delight in his eyes.)

Mary could not help herself as she whispered in his ear, "It's wondrous, I've never heard music like this before. Who is the composer?"

Humayun replied, "Ernest Bloch, it's aptly called the 'Avodath Hakodesh', which means Sacred Service."

As he spoke a beautiful woman dressed in white with a tall white headdress laced with diamonds, pearls and white feathers ascended the stage, with her white-feathered cloak. The headdress intrigued Mary, as it simulated a hawk's head. A small white skull within the middle of the headdress changed to a crystal globe of light as she took her place on the outer edge of the circle where the symbol for water was positioned.

"Who is she?" Mary whispered to Humayun.

"Isis, the goddess of creation and the goddess of destruction. Here comes Cailleach."

An old thin woman with long grey hair that covered her naked body, wearing a headdress of five grey snakes entwined around her head ascended the stage. Her grey toned skin and deep black lined eyes reminded Mary of a picture she had once seen of a crone.

Humayun studied Mary's expression of shock for a short time before he smiled and whispered in her ear, "She is the Goddess of disease, plague, and sorcery."

Mary couldn't help but whisper in Humayun's ear, "She looks like it too."

Just as she said so Cailleach turned her gaze in the direction of Mary. She suddenly felt incredibly uncomfortable, and as she did so a soft eerie voice entered her head. *I caann heeaarr yoouuu.* Mary could feel a cold chill of distress.

Humayun interjected Mary's thought. *Mary, concentrate on the light within you.*

Mary did so, immediately closing her eyes, as Cailleach took her position by the air sign at ten o'clock on the circle. Mary relaxed her mind and thought about nothing else but the glowing light within her and encompassing her. As she felt the light surround her, she opened her eyes. A tall tanned, muscular man with long, golden braided hair stood opposite her for a short time as he took his position. His naked torso had been decorated with white and gold tattoos resembling armor. Across the right side of his forehead were three gold and white diagonal lines. All of them followed through to his right cheek. He looked like a fierce Viking warrior wearing a white kilt Mary thought, as the man stood proud with a large decorated spear in his hand.

Humayun spoke telepathically to Mary. *Mary, this is Lugh, the Sun god of all crafts, the arts, healing, journeys, and prophecy. His skills are without end. His trusted spear is called Sleá Bua, the spear of victory and his horse, Aonbharr can fare over land and sea.*

Mary smiled and thought to herself, *Really.*

Lugh turned, gazed and smiled at Mary.

Humayun telepathically jibed Mary in a light-hearted manner with the word, *Really.*

Lugh's head turned in the direction of the earth sign, as he stood on the ankh sign.

Mary turned her head as well, to see what had distracted Lugh's gaze. A woman with many braids in her long black hair sneered at Lugh with distaste in her eyes. Mary could see the woman's beauty, although one side of her face was almost totally black apart from her rosy red lips. This made her pale skin on the other side of her face look whiter in color. Her huge black and red-feathered collar stood vertically around her neck and head, attached to it was a black cloak that draped around her body, revealing a burgundy dress, which exposed her cleavage.

It was clear to Mary that she despised Lugh, for she had hatred in her eyes as she stared at him.

Humayun did not speak either way, to Mary. Now Mary's curiosity was burning inside of her and getting the better of her. She did not dare speak telepathically, just in case there was a reply from the very woman that spiked her curiosity. So she whispered into Humayun's ear, "Who is she?"

Humayun curtly replied in Mary's ear, "Morrigan, she's a shape-shifting goddess of magic, prophecy, revenge, war, and death. She is known as the Great Queen or Phantom Queen; she often takes the form of a crow. As you can see, she very much dislikes Lugh. The most ironic thing of all is she is neither friend or foe."

Mary uttered once again, "I don't understand that?"

Humayun whispered back, "I know, it took me a long time to understand why, eventually you will too."

Mary did not contemplate Humayun's words as she was drawn to the back of the stage. An exceptionally tall man, dressed in a black morning suit and a long black cloak, wearing a set of huge deer antlers on his head loomed over the stage and scanned the auditorium with his red eyes. His skeletal features and grey-toned skin looked like he had once died and had been brought back to life.

Mary mustered up the courage to ask Humayun yet another burning question of curiosity as she uttered in his ear, "Who is he? He reminds me of Bram Stoker's character, Dracula, with antlers."

Humayun smiled and then whispered in Mary's ear, "I can see why, but this is Gwydion he's God of enchantment, illusion, magic, learning, and music. His orchestra is playing and his choir is singing, right now. He, however, has a very dark side to him. He is the darkest necromancer of all, never trust him."

Mary felt exceptionally uneasy as Gwydion stood on the fire sign at the four o'clock position of the aqua-blue-circle, smiling. Humayun's voice entered Mary's head. *Concentrate on the light within you, Mary.*

Mary closed her eyes once more and focused on the light within and around her. When she opened her eyes, Claudia was standing just below the God sign, smiling at her. Dr Goodman ascended the stage dressed in his half black and half white morning suit, wearing a half black and half white ram's head. He took his position and stood just above the ankh sign with Lugh.

Shortly after Dr Goodman, a bishop of some sort ascended the stage wearing a white chasuble, decorated with three central panels of gold. Each panel had separate embroideries; the top one, a rose, the middle one, a forget-me-not and thistle on the bottom panel. Mary could see the bishop was wearing a white and gold pallium as well as a white and gold stole, each one decorated with embroidered gold crosses of Christianity.

Mary couldn't help but ask another question as she whispered in Humayun's ear. "Isn't a pallium vestment bestowed by the Pope on an archbishop? Giving them metropolitan jurisdiction as a symbol of their participation in papal authority?"

"Yes, and the pallium are also given to some bishops too. Especially this one he's unlike any other bishop. He's the Bishop of Portu Satis Tuto. Bishop Caraman is in a denomination of his own," Humayun replied.

Mary became even more confused, as the bishop was not wearing the traditional miter headdress. Instead, he wore a white embroidered gold taqiyah. Mary studied the bishop further, she could not see all the embroidered signs on his stole, but the ones she could see were the Star of David, the Sikh symbol, and the Khanda, the star and crescent of the Muslim sign. He seemed to be celebrating many religions, Mary thought, as the bishop stood opposite Gwydion, close to Morrigan.

The choir crescendoed, as a man dressed in a black morning suit and an embroidered gold brocade white cloak, with two large black bows placed on his shoulders, walked on to the stage. Placed under his right black bow, hung a red sash that disappeared into the left side of the cloak. The cloak was fastened by gold braided rope with two huge tassels at the end of the rope. Placed around his neck hung a huge livery necklace with a pendant. He clasped his white-gloved hands as he took his position standing on the right of the center side of the cross. Another man stepped onto the stage wearing exactly the same outfit. He looked very much like the man that stood with his hands clasped. (Although, he seemed a little older, with less hair on the top of his head, he was very much overweight and was not wearing white gloves.)

He was holding a white unicorn's head with a golden horn as he took center stage. The choir came to the end of their singing and the orchestra finished playing. A microphone dropped down from the ceiling and stopped in front of him. He lifted his head slightly and looked around the auditorium, and scanned his audience with a smile. He then began his speech with a clear and dominant voice.

"It is with great pleasure and great sadness that I stand here today.

"The Pleasure.

"Well, it's been a pleasure serving The Great Order and acting as Grandmaster.

"My sadness is attributed to my father who should be standing here today." He paused with teary eyes, then collected himself and coughed before commencing his speech.

"The war has been successful, in depopulation and very, very profitable to many of us that are standing here today." Mary shuddered with his words.

He continued, oblivious. "However, we must not become complacent. Even though Cailleach's viral influencer, the Influenza pandemic is wiping out the weak, as I speak. We must remember. We have a Blueprint, to maintain humanity under five hundred million, this was a plan devised by our forefathers and we must adhere to his plan. We still have two more World Wars to go! Why, you might ask? We should now be concentrating on healing the World.

"Well, I put it to you now! It will not be long before Darwin's theory of 'Natural Selection' becomes fruition once more. Where individuals survive the struggle for resources. These individuals reproduce, adding their genes to succeeding generations. The traits that helped these people to survive will be passed on to their offspring's. This process is known as, 'Natural Selection'. Conditions in the environment result in the survival of individuals with specific traits, which are passed hereditarily to the next generation.

"Today we refer to this process as, 'Survival of the Fittest'. Darwin used this phrase, but he credited a fellow biologist, Herbert Spencer as its source. Humans that survived the war and Cailleach's influential Influenza can be likened to Darwin's Peppered Moth. (Just like the peppered moth adapted to its environment and became black and grey in order to survive its predators.) These black and grey-formed moths came to outnumber the pale forms of the peppered moth in our towns and cities.

So, since moths are short-lived, this evolution by 'Natural Selection' happened quite quickly. For example, the first black peppered moth was recorded in Manchester, England in 1848 and by 1895, 98% of peppered moths in the city were black.

It is our obligation to maintain humanity under 500,000,000 in a perpetual balance with nature. So, knowing it takes just twenty-one years for a generation to reproduce, 1939 will be the time, time for another war. The time for de-population of the world as it still needs to be decreased.

We must rid ourselves of any race that threatens our very existence, for we are the Guardians of the world. It is time now to analyze the world, our sustainability and put into action the plans our forefathers had for the future.

To guide reproduction wisely — improving fitness and diversity.

To unite humanity with a living new language.

To rule with passion, faith, tradition, and all things with tempered reason.

To protect people and nations with fair laws and just courts.

To let all nations rule internally, resolving external disputes in a world court.

To avoid petty laws and useless officials.

To balance personal rights with social duties.

To prize truth, beauty, love, seeking harmony with the infinite.

It is now with great pleasure I hand over the reins of this Great Order to my brother, as my father wished. He said, 'He is adept and qualified unlike me'."

There was a simmering of laughter in the auditorium.

The Grandmaster handed the white unicorn's head with its golden horn to Dr Goodman. The younger man stood to his right. In turn, took off his white gloves and gave them to the Grandmaster, who then placed the white gloves on his hands.

Dr Goodman held the unicorn's head above his ram's head and then he announced, "The Gloves are off, may everyone stand."

Everyone in the auditorium stood.

Dr Goodman continued, "It is my great honor to present the 60th Grand Master of The Great Order of the World, Leinahtan Selrach Drothslich." He then placed the unicorn's head in the hands of the 60th Grand Master; the audience in the auditorium clapped and cheered. Leinahtan Selrach Drothslich stepped forward to the microphone. He addressed his audience.

"Acting Grandmaster, Claudia, Dr Goodman, Bishop Caraman, Isis, Lugh, Cailleach, Morrigan and Gwydion, fellow brothers and sisters. Sapere Aude, I dare to be wise! I am sorry but I do not want to be a Grandmaster as some of my predecessors were." He turned and looked at his brother and softly spoke the words, "I am sorry, brother."

He then turned and looked directly back at his audience and continued his speech.

"I do not want to order the monopolies of the world, but I will do if it means I can help everyone in this world, if possible, no matter the color of their skin, religion or non-religion. We should all want to help one another, to not forsake the love in our hearts. We should be living by each other's happiness, not by each other's misery. (As some of us here in this sacred room have encountered hatred.) There should be no more hatred in this world. Let's banish it!

We have the power! We have the power to abolish human poverty, to help the poor, help themselves in this world. If we do not do so, I ask you, how are we able to sustain our riches? Giving will enrich our lives far more than any materialistic object.

In this world we live in, there is room for everyone."

He turned and looked at his brother, then looked back at the audience and continued with his speech.

"Our earth is rich and our seas are plentiful they can provide for everyone, as long as we nourish them and do not pollute them, maintaining an ecological balance is paramount. In doing so everything on this earth will flourish and no color or creed will be greater. We are the guardians of the earth and should never forget it.

"We should always remember, it's not what the earth can do for us, it's what we can do for this earth, the incredible world we live in. We must not unleash the dark powers of science and destruction, but embrace the wonders of science and all the good it can do in this world. The aftermath of the wounds of war are abundant and have cut deeply in this world, all of which have been inflicted by man. We must eliminate 'War!'

"It is time to use a tight rein on the Military Industrial Complex. It needs to be harnessed and shackled. I ask now, what has happened to this free beautiful world? A fruitful vibrant world, where everything flourished and nothing was extinct!

"I will tell you. GREED. Greed, that is what has happened, it's diseased man's very soul. It's fortified the world with hate and destruction. Greed is the seed; we do not need to sow any more. BANISH IT!

"We have become cynics, attributed to our knowledge, which has made us cruel and heartless. Cailleach's viral influencer, the Influenza must be stopped along with war. We have the power.

"In our pursuit of progress, we have devised war. War is not progress. We need humanity, more than cleverness, moreover we need kindness. Without these qualities within the world all will be lost. This time by fire, as it is written.

"Therefore, I ask you not to fear the way of human progress in embracing kindness and humanity. The power is within us, mankind, that very word denotes our meaning on the earth, 'man is kind.'

"It is time, time to make amends.

Time to give back.

Time to love our fellow man.

Time to heal the suffering.

Time to eradicate, the dictatorship that we know.

Time to banish the brutes of power.

Time for the soldiers of this world in the name of democracy to unite, so that they may protect the ecological balance of the world, before TIME runs out.

Soren quoted, 'Life can only be understood backwards but it must be lived forwards'.

It is time we understand the errors of our ways so we do not regret our understanding of the future.

It is time to do away with greed.

It's time the world heals and it starts right now with us today, for we are the guardians."

There was silence in the auditorium, however, Mary could hear many voices of disapproval. Humayun entered her head, his voice softly spoken but authoritative. *Mary, concentrate on the light within you.*

Mary closed her eyes and tried to concentrate firmly on the calm within her. Instead of tuning in on the silence within her, all she could hear were many loud angry penetrating voices. She shuddered with the hostility.

An aggressive voice yelled, *He needs to be banished from this life.*

Another voice yelled eerily, *His father will be turning in his grave.*

A sadistic voice spoke. *How very dare he. Hang him and hang him now, so there is not one breath left in his body.*

A fiendish voice yelled, *Kill Goodman! He's the bad influence, and kill him tonight.*

In reply to the fiendish voice, a barbarous voice yelled, *I'll do it and I'll do it tonight, in the lake. He will sink and will never emerge.*

Mary opened her eyes, startled and looked frantic as she scanned the auditorium. She whispered in Humayun's ear. "Did you hear them?"

"Yes, they are still voicing. Leave the listening to the experienced, Mary, concentrate on the light within you. If you don't, there could be devastating repercussions if you stay within this frequency; they will penetrate our light. Please, Mary, concentrate."

Mary tried once more as Dr Goodman and Claudia began to clap. All the people wearing white and most of the people wearing grey and black and white began to clap too. Not one person wearing black clapped. Instead, they began to walk out of the auditorium as Leinahtan Selrach Drothslich shook hands with everyone on the stage, smiling away as he was doing so. He seemed oblivious to the hostility around him, as did Dr Goodman too. It also seemed Claudia was oblivious too, although Mary knew it would not be the case. Did she hear the threats that Mary heard? Did anyone hear?

Dr Goodman took the microphone once more. He made light of the situation. "Well, I was going to announce to everybody to make their way to the Great Hall, for the first dance, but it seems some of us can't wait to be told. Many on the dark side have put their hunger first. I do hope they have smelt the aroma of the delicious buffet or need to quench their thirst. Either way we will see you all in the Great Hall." The orchestra began to play Mozart's Magic Flute as the entire stage began to rotate and descend with Claudia, Dr Goodman, The Grandmaster, Acting Grandmaster, Bishop Caraman, Isis, Lugh, Cailleach, Morrigan and Gwydion on it.

Chapter Thirty-Nine
Did You Hear the Dark-Walkers?

Mary looked frantically at Humayun and whispered in his ear. "Did you hear the Dark Walkers? They are going to kill Dr Goodman and The Grandmaster."

Humayun looked at Mary with concern in his eyes. "Mary, I told you to concentrate on the light within you. You have jeopardized our very existence by continuing to listen." He shook his head. "We are peaceful people, Mary, and our only defense is our faith." Humayun turned and looked at Shaka. "We all need to confer, I sense danger."

Mary butted in, "But what about Dr Goodman and the Grandmaster's safety?"

Humayun rolled his eyes at Mary, turned and looked at Shaka, "We all need to confer, I sense danger."

Shaka looked at Humayun with a serious expression and voiced, "Whatever gave you that impression?"

Humayun made a makeshift laugh and then asked Shaka, "Did you hear any threats on the Grandmaster's and Dr Goodman's life?" Humayun turned and gave Mary a fleeting glance as he smiled at her, then turned back to look at Shaka.

Shaka looked saddened. "That was one incredible speech. It's a pity it was received with so much hostility. All the voices I heard were incredibly angry. I did not have a chance to pinpoint one person as there were too many voices speaking at the same time." He paused. "Humayun, they will both be in danger once they step foot outside Portu Satis Tuto."

Humayun contemplated Shaka's words before answering. "We must inform Keane straight away, he will need to arrange additional security, that's if he has not done it already." He looked at Mary, then addressed Shaka once more. "We need to get close to them and see if we can single out their plans and find the chief instigator."

Shaka spoke with concern. "That's too dangerous for Anna, Annchi, Mary and me, to do tonight. We are too vulnerable against the powerful Dark Walkers."

Humayun chuckled, "I know, you weaklings, Claudia may well be able to get close enough tonight while she dances with the predominant Dark Walkers."

He paused and looked at Mary then looked at Shaka. "I guess Jacob and I must mingle as much as possible too and see what we can pick up."

Shaka nodded yes then replied, "You are worried about Mary, aren't you?"

"Yes. Tell him why, Mary." Humayun looked at Mary with kind eyes.

Mary swallowed before answering, as her mouth was now very dry, with trepidation. Her eyes were fixed on Shaka. "I am having difficulty with concentrating on the light within me, because of the Dark Walkers. They're too penetrating for me to block."

The auditorium was now empty as Shaka replied, "Don't worry, Mary, we have all been there at some point in our lives." Shaka then looked at Humayun. "I'll look after Mary for the rest of the night, while you mingle, Humayun?"

Humayun replied, "Good, I'll need to confer with Claudia and Jacob first though. I'll see you in the Great Hall, and remember to concentrate on the wonderful light within you, Mary." Humayun walked away from Mary, Shaka, Annachi, and Anna.

Shaka turned and looked at Annachi, Anna and Mary, with a boyish grin on his face. "So which one of you lovely ladies would like the first dance?"

Annachi curtly replied, with a sweet-sounding voice, "We should find our way to the Great Hall first. Then if you are lucky enough Anna may dance with you."

She stared at Anna, who shrugged her shoulders. Then she looked at Shaka with her stunning green eyes. Anna smirked, "I am going to refrain from doing so, due to your toe crushing shenanigans when we last danced. My feet are just about healed."

Annachi linked arms with Shaka, turned and walked away from the crescent pew before Shaka had time to reply to Anna, but time to think.

Her short, chic bobbed haircut was quite a contrast to Shaka's tribal long, beaded, braided hair but all the same, the two complemented each other. Mary and Anna followed them through the sun-kissed white gothic arches and down to a large stone spiral staircase. The four started to descend the stone staircase, as they did so, Mary couldn't help but notice the Petroglyphs on the wall as she walked down the stairs.

In a soft and intriguing voice Mary asked, "Anna, is there a story to be told here? These petroglyphs look very interesting."

"Yes, there is," Anna declared. "A very interesting and important one, one you should probably know."

Chapter Forty
The Nephilim

Anna took a few steps back up the staircase, as Shaka and Annachi stopped and turned around.

Anna pinned a stray piece of her red hair behind her ear and then pointed to many winged men, being cast out of the sky, with a bright flash of light surrounding them. "Here are the two hundred angels or gods being cast out of heaven onto Mount Hermon." She pointed to a muscular angel with handsome features. "I've been told this one is Lucifer. Isn't that right, Shaka?" Her rosy red lips smiled.

Shaka grinned and nodded yes.

Anna continued as she walked down the staircase. "These trifling gods wreak havoc on earth. So, God floods the earth to cleanse it." Her plump finger pointed to a petroglyph. "Here you can see Noah's ark and all the animals of the world. Only four of the gods survived, they were known as the Apkallu." Anna pointed to a man half-fish, half-human. Mary chortled, "They remind me of Otto and Ole."

"Nungalpirriggaldim, as you can see, he's half-man and half-fish." Anna smiled as she pointed to two other petroglyphs of men with eagle heads. "Pirriggalnungal and Pirriggalabsu were eagle headed men, demigods." She moved down the wall to a man with wings. "This is Lunana who was two-thirds god and one third man. These divine creatures surfaced from the oceans and lived with the early human beings. They taught the humans all valuable aspects of civilization... and so the humans began to write, draw, build and devise their own laws. They taught the humans about agriculture, land, the value of the energy lines of the world and where to build sacred structures so that the impact of the energy could be captured and put to good use."

Annachi continued. "They teach, in return, to mate and reproduce with human women, as you can see here." Annachi coughed, as she became little embarrassed, she then continued. "The gods and the human women produce the Nephilim, the giants."

Mary ran her dainty forefinger around the outer edge of a Petroglyph and interrupted with the word, "Giants."

"Yes," Shaka proclaimed. "Marduk the ruler god of the ancient Mesopotamia kingdom did not like any of this, so he banished the Apkallu back to Abzu, an underground water hole under the temple of Enki, forever."

Annachi and Shaka continued walking down the staircase a little, followed by Mary and Anna. Shaka stopped and pointed to a male figure, which resembled a Viking king. He had angular facial features, a long clean-cut beard, with his muscle-toned body, wearing a crown on his head and fish shaped body armor. He continued to talk. "Many years later, Lu-nana who was two thirds god and one third man revisited Mesopotamia in the city of Uruk and fell in love with a beautiful woman called Ninsun. She bore a son, a king, King Gilgamesh, who had superhuman powers. As you can see here this petroglyph depicts Gilgamesh."

The words, "He looks like Lugh," slipped out of Mary's mouth. She then ran her forefinger along a solid gold line that started between Gilgamesh's legs.

Shaka's eyes widened as he looked at Mary's expression of interest, but did not acknowledge her finger tracing the gold line. He continued. "His life was full of adventures, traveling the world, slaying many monsters. Notably, his greatest epic was when he fought Huwawa. He was the defender of the secret abode of the gods. He had front paws of a lion, a body covered in barbed scales, his feet had the claws of a vulture, and on his head were the horns of a wild bull; his tail, a phallus, ended in many snake heads."

Shaka and Annachi took a few more steps down, followed by Anna and Mary. Annachi pointed her nimble finger to the petroglyph. "This is Huwawa he looks rather beastly, don't you think, Mary?"

"Yes," Mary replied as she took a good look. She could see a spear in Huwawa's neck as she scanned the petroglyph. She could also see Gilgamesh slaying the creature, yielding weapons in both hands, her finger still tracing the gold line.

Annachi resumed, "Gilgamesh wins the fight and becomes the victor with the help of his companion Enkidu." She pointed to another Viking look-alike grasping a lion in one hand and a snake in the other.

The closer Mary got to Gilgamesh she could see he was wearing a forget-me-not bracelet with forget-me-nots brocade trim around his clothing. Her forefinger now ran around the edge of the forget-me-not bracelet, verifying what her sight was telling her. Her eyes were wide as she turned and stared at Anna, Annachi and Shaka. Mary asked with curiosity, "Do you all know why he is wearing forget-me-nots?"

Annachi began to answer. "The forget-me-not is also known as Scorpion Grass."

Before Annachi could continue Mary butted in, "Are we descendants of Gilgamesh?"

Shaka sternly replied, "No, Mary, all you have been told is true. We are not descendants of Gilgamesh but there are members within The Cabal that are."

Annachi chirped in, "Can't you see the resemblance with Lugh and Gwydion?"

Mary could hardly say her words quick enough. "Yes, I suppose so. Does this include Dr Goodman too?"

Anna answered, "He's part of The Cabal, Mary."

Mary replied in a relaxed manner, "Oh, but he is only small and cannot swim. The Nephilim were good swimmers." (Shaka, Annachi, and Anna chuckled together at Mary's innocence.)

Annachi managed to slip the words out, "Yes, Mary, he can't. He's also not good at sailing and Gilgamesh was renowned for sailing."

Mary did not find Dr Goodman's inability to swim or sail funny, especially as she was the one to hear the threat to drown him. However, her curiosity to find out where the gold line led to out-weighed her confusion as to why Shaka, Anna and Annachi would laugh at Dr Goodman's short-comings. She passed Shaka and Annachi on the wide stone spiral staircase while the three looked on. She continued to follow the gold line, which branched off at the entrance of the Great Hall, into ten separate gold lines as it reached the light blue marble floor of the ballroom. All she could do was stare at the floor, scanning the flat marble map of the entire world. The strange gold lines formed longitude lines of the world.

Shaka stood by her side, marveled with her and then remarked, "It's rather magnificent, isn't it?"

Mary eyes widened and her eyebrows furrowed as she answered, "Yes, but my curiosity exudes me. Those are rather unusual Meridian lines. The longitude lines I can understand, but the latitude lines are not as we know them. They're distorted and remind me of a mixture of Plato's platonic solids, in particular, the Icosahedron."

Icosahedron

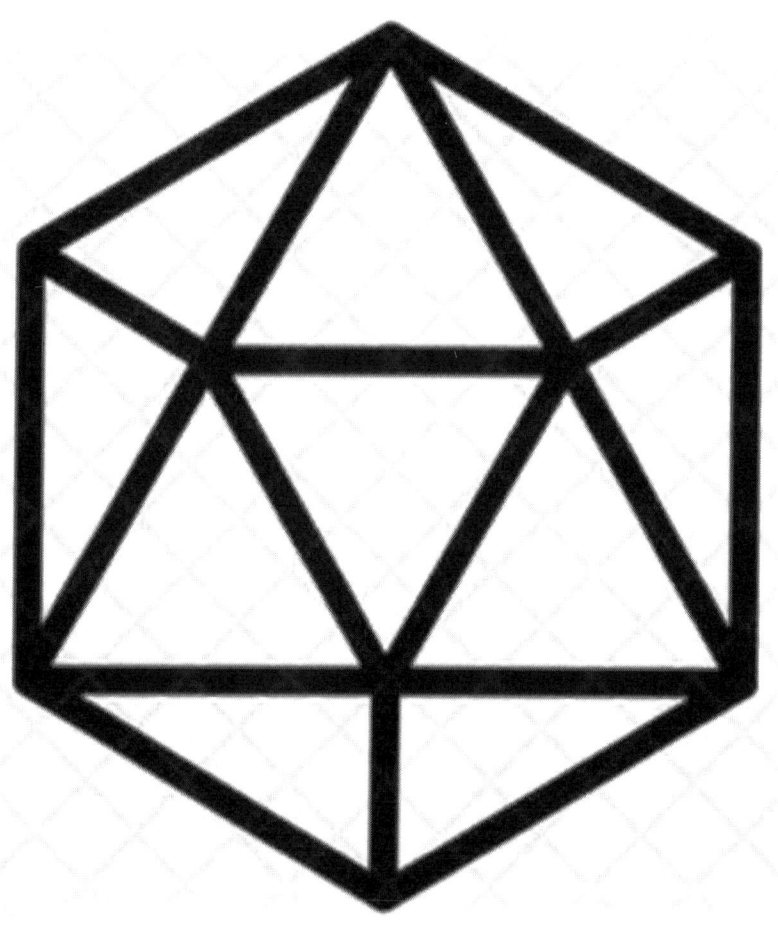

Annachi enlightened Mary. "They are ley lines."

Mary repeated the words, "ley lines," with a puzzled look on her face.

Annachi looked at Anna, and nodded her head for her to continue. Anna spoke, "The gold lines you can see are ley lines. The term, 'ley' itself comes from the Anglo-Saxon, meaning 'cleared strips of ground' or 'meadows', but these lines are primarily energetic and exist whether the land is stripped of its ground cover, or not. As you can see the ley lines continue in the world's oceans and waters."

Shaka continued, "This grid emits energy, with its very own frequency and vibration. The Nephilim knew of these energy grids and how humans could harness the energy. Those aware of this power are at a distinct advantage over those who remain ignorant."

Mary placed her hand to her head wanting to scratch it, but stopped herself the very second her fingertips touched her dressed hair. "I am confused."

Ley Lines and Vile Vortices

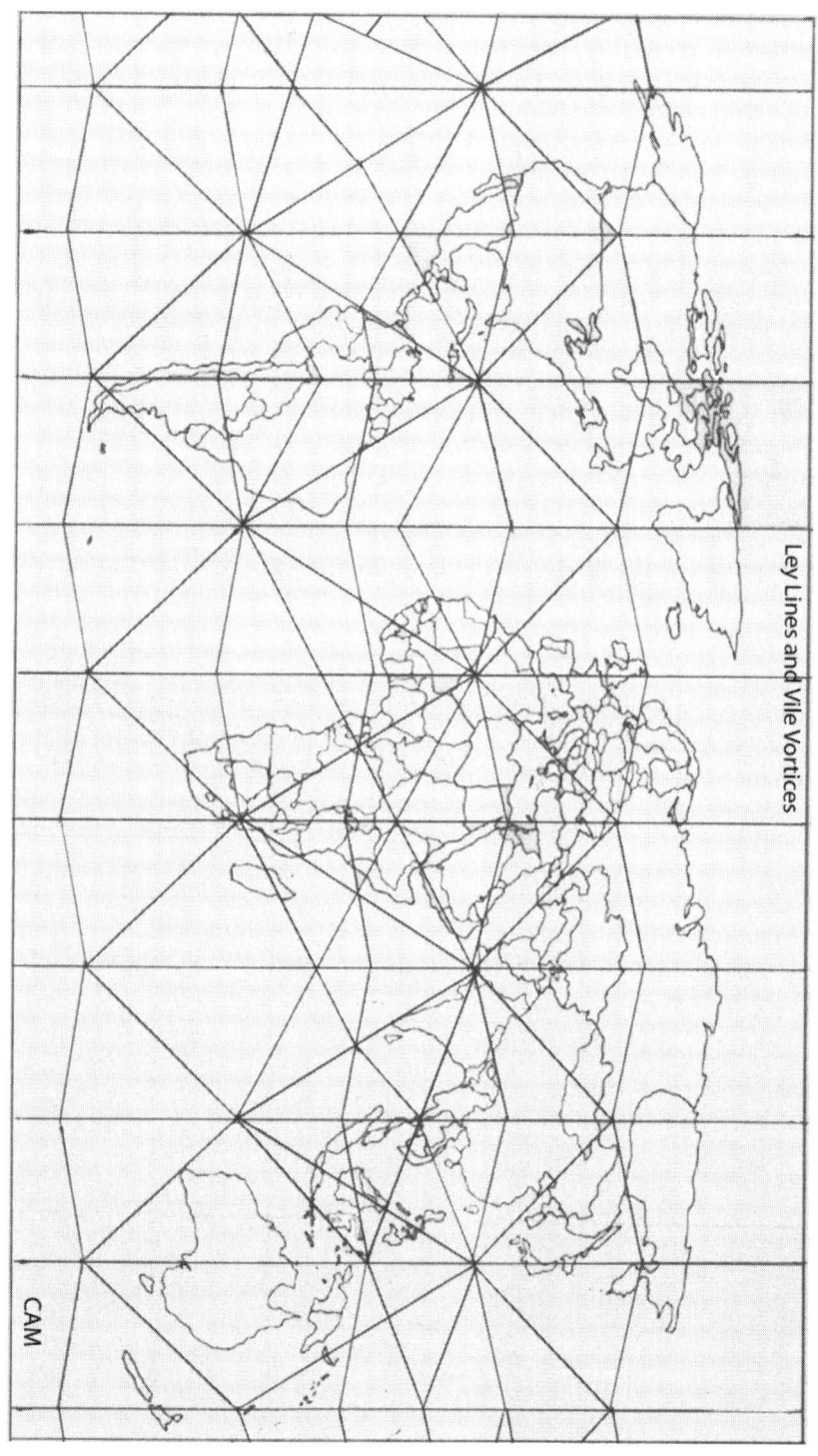

CAM

Anna jested, "I was too, Mary, but what helped me understand was where the ley lines meet. They are the strongest power energizing spots on Earth. Men knowing this built many sacred sites on them, such as Findhorn in Scotland, the Pyramids of Giza, Lhasa Tibet, Machu Picchu, Puma Punku, Easter Island, Angkor Wat, the ancient ruins of Mohenjo Daro. There are many sacred domed structures and obelisks on Earth that prove this. Some of the oldest and most mathematically advanced examples were those created by the Swiderians in Europe of the late Paleolithic Age and early Neolithic Age, they existed from approximately 10000 to 9500 BC such as the Göbekli Tepe, this was built just after the earth became habitable again."

"Swiderians?" Mary questioned.

"Alias the Nephilim," Annachi chirped in. "But Göbekli Tepe was not built on a ley line, Anna."

Anna replied, "Yes, but the soul hole stones, which are six meters tall and weigh around twenty tons, are in line with Deneb. The large star on the Northern Cross which is seen as the entrance and exit to the sky world, this is where newborn souls emerge and souls of death exit this world." Anna turned and sarcastically smiled at Annachi.

Mary's head was now beginning to ache with the amount of knowledge she was absorbing. She shook her head and spoke the words, "Sky world?"

Anna opened her mouth to speak but before she could do so Annachi interrupted. "I thought we were talking about ley lines?"

"We are," Anna replied. "On these ley lines there are also the vortices of Mother Nature, such as the Arizona vortices. The worst one of all the vile vortices is the Devil's Triangle, which also lies on one of these power points." Anna looked at Mary's furrowed eyebrows and decided to stop.

Mary's head hurt with the amount of knowledge she was absorbing.

Annachi continued oblivious to the way Mary was reacting. "Yes, Mary, there are areas on the map that have a red glaze to them. There are twelve in the world, as you can see. Vile Vortices are areas on the Earth's surface, which have naturally occurring anomalies due to the planet's natural electromagnetic fields being stronger in these parts than anywhere else in the world. When certain planets are aligned bad things happen." She pointed to Hawaii. "For instance, Hamakulia Volcano is one of the four hundred and fifty-two volcanoes located on the Ring of Fire; where seventy-two percent of the Earth's most active volcanoes lie. It's worth noting the Ring of Fire is also home to ninety percent of the largest earthquakes on Earth, due to movement of plate tectonics and collisions of Earth's upper mantle and crust. I truly think this is where the Great Fire on Earth will begin."

Anna cut in, "That's enough, Annachi, Mary needs to ease her mind right now, not to overload her brain. Remember what you were like?"

Shaka shook his head at Annachi with disapproval and spoke in a calm tone. "That's why we are here, to help guide The Order, to do right in this world, we're God's voice."

Anna linked Mary's arm and declared, "It's time to lighten up literally and dance. I do hope we have not missed the first one, Claudia is the most graceful dancer I have ever seen regardless of whom she is dancing with."

The four entered the huge opulent ballroom with its magnificent cascading crystal chandeliers, ceiling fresco of heaven and wall to wall frescoes of the world. Mary glanced at the artistry but did not see what they depicted. She asked no further questions, as her head was still digesting the information overload. Her mind craved freedom.

Claudia gracefully danced by with the Grandmaster taking the lead. Mary watched them for a while mesmerized by Claudia's dress and how it encased her body and created wings on either side of her as she moved around the dance floor.

Claudia's voice entered Mary's head. *Concentrate on the light within you, Mary; your mind is far too loud, others may hear you. Hone in on the warm light and the peaceful airy space within you.*

Mary stood gazing at the array of Dark Walkers, Impartial and Divine dancers on the dance floor, but her focus was purely on the warm light within her. Shaka, Anna both stood at Mary's left side, the two knowing without doubt that Mary was now concentrating on her inner light. Annachi however truly did not want to understand Mary's need for a silent mind. She was far too excited to feed Mary her knowledge.

Annachi's brown eyes lit up as she whispered in Mary's right ear. "Oh, look, Mary, Trebla can tell you a lot more about the Ring of Fire than I can. He's a genius, something I am aspiring to be." She then shook her head as she turned up her nose, then whispered, "Not literally, I do not want to look like I have never had a bath or have wiry untamed grey hair, and bless he doesn't even wear socks... smmeelly feet. But don't be put off dancing with him, I can never smell his feet and he's more agile than he looks." She waved her hand at the old man and smiled. In reply Trebla walked over to Annachi.

Trebla's eyes twinkled with excitement the closer he got. "Well, Annachi, you are a sight for sore eyes." His German accent was somewhat similar to Dr Goodman's. He looked at Anna and Shaka and nodded his head. He turned his gaze to Mary and commented, "Ja, your friend Mary is too."

Annachi smiled as she uttered the words in Trebla's ear, "Would you like to dance with Mary and tell her all about the Ring of Fire? She is very interested in knowing about it."

Trebla replied, "I would very much like to dance with this beautiful creature." He held out his hand and asked Mary, "Would you care for the next dance, my dear?"

Mary looked rather stunned and then looked at Shaka, Anna and then back at Annachi.

Annachi replied, "Trebla is a delight to dance with and has the most brilliant mind that I have ever come across. Oh, he's also dabbled with electromagnetic effects and he's wearing a light grey suit."

Mary felt compelled to dance as she sheepishly replied, "Yes," and took his wrinkled hand. All the while she scanned the dance floor for Dr Goodman.

The orchestra began to play; Trebla commented as he led Mary to the dance floor, "One of my favorites, Tchaikovsky's Waltz of the Flowers. Are you a rose or a forget-me-not, my dear?"

Mary didn't answer; she just smiled out of politeness.

Trebla smiled and commented, "I can tell you're a rose in the making, my dear." He gently placed his bent right arm out beyond his nose for Mary to mimic the movement with her left arm. She did so and the two twirled to the right raising their opposite arms as they met full circle. They touched each other's raised hand, lowered their arms and commenced dancing, promenading around the other dancers. (All were moving rhythmically in time with the music.)

Trebla asked Mary, "How do you like my dancing, my dear?"

Mary smiled and replied, "You're particularly nimble." She stopped herself from continuing to answer.

Trebla butted in, "I'm particularly nimble for an old man, you meant to say? I do not mind the truth, my dear. However, always remember the Albert Einstein quote, "'Whoever is careless with the truth in small matters cannot be trusted with important matters'."

Careless with the truth; Mary dwelled on Trebla's words for some time, as her body motioned through the dance. There were a lot of hidden truths and she was only just beginning to find out all but a few, she thought. This world was far different than the one she was living in a week ago.

Trebla continued the conversation, saying that he seemingly was extremely passionate about, The Ring of Fire. "So you would like to learn more about the volcano named Hamakulia on the southeast side of the Hawaiian island? It's the central attraction in the Ring of Fire, except the Ring of Fire really is not a ring of fire at all; it's shaped more like a malformed horseshoe." He did not wait for Mary to respond, he just continued to talk. "The problematic location is literally in the ocean, northeast of Hawaii, halfway between the Murray Fracture Zone and the Molokai Fracture Zone. The volcano-electromagnetic activity derives from a variety of physical processes."

He paused and looked at Mary. She nodded her head as if she was listening, but she wasn't, as she scanned the ballroom floor for Dr Goodman.

Trebla continued. "These include electrokinetic effects, thermal demagnetization, thermochemical effects, resistivity changes, remagnetizaton, magnetohydrodynamic effects, fluid vaporization, piezomagnetic effects and burst-explosive ionospheric traveling disturbances."

Mary's eyes scanned more intensely for Dr Goodman. Suddenly her eyes became transfixed on Darius, as he was dressed in a white morning suit. He seemed entranced with the woman he was dancing with, even though she was wearing a black ball gown. As the two rotated, Mary couldn't see the strawberry blonde-haired woman's face because she was wearing a black feather winged eye mask, adding more intrigue to Mary's thoughts.

Trebla still muttered on, "Recognition of contrasting physical processes and their interdependence is often possible with multi-parameter tracking. This is now common on volcanoes, since many of these processes occur with different timescales. Some are concurrently identified in other geophysical documentation. Such as seismic, gas, deformation, ionospheric disturbances, et cetera, et cetera. Electromagnetic tracking is crucial in understanding these processes. It is my view that Hamakulia is where the world will begin to end. We somehow need to figure out how to stop it, before it has catastrophic consequences along the Pacific Rim."

The dance came to an end. Mary shook Trebla's hand then whispered in his ear, "Thank you for the dance and the information, although I had not been able to follow most of what you spoke about." She found herself back where she had started but Shaka, Anna and Annachi were nowhere to be seen.

Trebla looked around and commented, "It seems your friends have deserted you."

Mary looked confused as she scanned the ballroom. She could see Humayun with a woman dressed in grey and Nhoj Feckellore rubbing his hands with anticipation of dancing with Claudia, as he walked up to her. Darius and his partner had vanished from Mary's view and Dr Goodman was still nowhere to be seen.

Trebla looked rather spellbound by Mary's beauty and stood gazing at her as she scanned the ballroom. He asked with sincerity, "Would you like another dance, my dear, and I can tell you about the Universe."

Chapter Forty-One
Puff, Puff, Powwww!

Darius suddenly appeared wearing a charcoal grey coloured morning suit and took Mary's hand. Before Mary had time to react, Darius looked Trebla in his eyes and said, "You tell that to all the women you want to rendezvous with. She's a little young for you, don't you think, Granddad?" The orchestra began to play the Pachelbel Canon waltz. He whisked Mary off her feet, lifting her into the air with his arms outstretched, placing his hands underneath her arms, (leaving Trebla with his mouth open).

Mary in turn balanced herself with her hands on his shoulders and arms outstretched. Darius turned one hundred and eighty degrees and placed Mary down onto the dance floor. He then began to promenade her; the two entwined between other couples.

"Why have you changed your clothes from white to dark grey? You almost look like a Dark Walker," Mary asked.

"I haven't it's against the rules on Inauguration Day, Mary, every person here tonight must show his or her true color. As you can see, I'm somewhat darker than you thought I was, but I'm still an Impartial," Darius replied.

"But I have just seen you dressed in white, dancing with a woman dressed in black," Mary inferred.

"Wasn't me, Mary," Darius replied with a droll tone in his voice.

"Then who was it, your twin?" Mary scoffed.

Darius stopped dancing, still holding Mary, whilst other dancers danced around them. "I am the one and only, Mary, but it was most likely Jacob," he declared, as he picked up the waltz steps.

Mary decided to ask no further questions about Jacob. She continued to scan the dance floor once again for Dr Goodman. "Have you seen Dr Goodman, Darius? Only, it's important I see him," Mary asked with urgency in her voice.

"Yes, I saw him with Bobby," Darius replied with a smirk on his face. His expression then turned serious. "Mary, I need to talk to you somewhere quiet. I have something important to tell you." Darius led Mary off the ballroom floor.

Mary dwelt on how to tell Darius her need of urgency for her to see Dr Goodman. How was she going to tell him that she heard many threats on his life or for that matter on his father's life? After all he was his illegitimate son of the Grandmaster, or was she mistaken and was he the illegitimate son of the previous Grandmaster?

Darius continued to lead Mary through the opulent corridors with huge black and white marble tiled floors and gold ceilings of Portu Satis Tuto. Eventually the two found themselves outside standing next to an ornate stone bench with one rearing lion on the right end of the bench and one rearing unicorn at the left end.

"Is this your bench? Only there is a rearing lion and a unicorn in the same order of the motif in your cabin," Mary asked.

"Yes, it is." Darius's eyes narrowed as he answered. "But can we have less of the small talk, Mary? I have a confession; it's been devouring my head and heart." He cupped his hands around Mary's left hand. "I need you to sit down for this."

The two perched on the bench, which was placed at the edge of a brightly lit pond, as the night's breeze made Mary shiver.

"Would you like my jacket? It's getting rather cold," Darius asked.

"No thank you," Mary scoffed as her impatience began to rear its ugly head as she lifted the train of her dress up and placed it around her shoulders like a shawl. "Will this take long, Darius? Only I really do need to find Dr Goodman."

Darius stared sternly. "I love you, Mary, and I found it hard that you turned down my love," Darius confessed, as he looked down at Mary's delicate hand. He then mumbled the words, "It was me."

Mary looked rather bewildered as she asked, "What do you mean it was me?" She paused for a reaction; there was nothing. "Darius, look me in the eye please."

Darius looked Mary in the eye like a scorned puppy.

"It was you that tried to kill me in the Brisfit?" Mary asked with glazed eyes.

"No, Mary, I did not, I would never knowingly try to kill you. You have my heart, you are my life and it cut deep within my heart when you told me you did not feel the same way." Darius paused for thought. "I have pretty much been unable to live with myself since. I have a compelling desire to hurt myself very badly, for what I did." His eyes welled with tears.

Mary whispered the words, "Never knowingly try to kill me. What did you do?" as her mouth dried with her nerves.

"It was me that took the shot," he revealed.

Mary's eyes now furrowed in vexation. "You took a shot at what? You jammed Chief Gunner Siddal's gun, then took a shot at the mine?"

Darius looked appalled by Mary's suggestion.

"I saw you placing dirt into the open channel of his DSC 1917 rifle," Mary declared as her eyes once more start to glaze.

"What do you mean, by open channel of his DSC 1917 rifle?" Darius asked.

"There is only one on a DSC 1917 semi-automatic rifle. The one next to the firing bolt of course," Mary scoffed.

"I vexed my concerns about the DSC 1917 semi-automatic rifle jamming in the past. I even demonstrated how easy it is to jam with the smallest amount of dirt to my father, and yes it was Siddall's gun at the time. He was well aware it jammed and cleaned the dirt out. That is the only time I have ever placed dirt into an open channel of a rifle, all in the hope that the rifles would be changed. They were but too little too late." Darius's expression saddened further. "I do blame myself for not making more of an uproar about sending our soldiers to war with inadequate rifles. So, yes, Mary if you want to blame me for Chief Gunner Siddall's death, then I guess you have every right to."

Mary lifted Darius's chin with her right hand and looked at his glazed green eyes. "I don't blame you at all but I still have no idea of what you took a shot at." Just as Mary spoke her last word an image materialized inside her head. The image of Mary riding an Andalusian horse, alone in a golden field of wheat. There's a loud shot and the horse bolts and rears uncontrollably, so much so that Mary is thrown through the air and lands with a thud, she can only see darkness.

Mary detached her hand from Darius's chin and then spoke quietly and calmly. "You caused the horse to bolt and rear."

Darius confessed, "I did but did not think for one minute that you would incur such a bad injury. One so much so, it nearly took your life." He grasped her hand.

Mary pulled her left hand out of Darius's grasp and curtly announced, "I need to find Dr Goodman."

Just as Mary stood, Darius pulled out of his pocket a small handgun with a fluted muzzle and a large barrel. Mary looked startled as he broke open the barrel and took two shotgun shells out of his pocket. He held one green shell up to show Mary as he uttered the word, "Puff." He placed the shell in the chamber.

Darius then held up the second shell and sternly spoke the word, "Puff," as he placed it in the chamber. He took out a third shell from his pocket, but this time the shell was colored red and he placed it in the chamber. He intoned the word "Pow," then spun the cylinder and placed the muzzle of the gun against his temple.

Mary looked on horrified, as her trembling words were spoken. "Pllleeease don't do this to yourself. The more anger towards the past you carry in your heart, the less capable you are of living and loving in the present."

Darius pulled the trigger, as the tears began rolling down his cheeks. "Puff!" he said with a disappointed tone.

A calm tone induced Mary's voice. "Please, Darius, put the gun down. I forgive you. If I can forgive you, then surely you can forgive yourself. You need to let go of the anger you feel inside yourself and this is not the way to do it."

'Puff.' The gun sounded once more.

Mary's eyes widened but her voice remained calm. "Darius, I need you to help me right now, and if you kill yourself, you won't be able to."

Keane slowly appeared behind Darius. Mary did not acknowledge his presence in any way. Her composed voice gave nothing away, as she spoke. "I am sure Dr Goodman's life is in danger. Darius, I need you to help me find him. So, please put the gun down. I don't want to lose you or Dr Goodman and if you blow your brains out, I will lose you both." A tear rolled down Mary's cheek.

Darius's intense look began to fade, and he loosened his grip on the small handgun. As he did so, Keane grabbed the gun from Darius with his right hand and placed his left hand on Darius's shoulder.

"Appearances can be so deceptive, can't they?" Kean said. He then squeezed his shoulder. "You know, Darius, war makes you a man but it's the boy inside you that deals with the aftermath. I will get you the help you need, but first I think Lady Mary has a pressing engagement, we must attend to." Kean looked sternly at Mary before he spoke. "Now then, why do ya think Dr Goodman's life is in danger? He's in Portu Satis Tuto. There is no other place on this earth as safe as 'ere!"

Mary gulped before talking. "I heard threats after the Grandmaster's speech to kill Dr Goodman tonight in the lake. One barbarous toned voice said, "I'll do it and I'll do it tonight, in the lake, he will sink and will never emerge. I don't think he is in the castle any more, I think he's been taken out onto the lake."

"Did you see who it was making the threats?" Keane asked calmly.

"No," Mary replied, "I did not."

Keane raised his eyebrow and then grinned with a tight lip. "Well then we'd better go and see if Dr Goodman is taking a leisurely ride on a speed boat or skinny dipping in the moonlight, whilst trying to impersonate Houdini." Keane tapped Darius on the shoulder. "All in the hope of putting Lady Mary's mind to rest once and for all. Eh? What do ya say, Darius?"

Darius answered with a collected tone in his voice. "Yes, we had better make haste then. We can take the Magdalena, my father's boat, she's the fastest on the lake."

Chapter Forty-two
The Evil Twin

Keane set the pace, as the three walked quickly through the grounds of Portu Satis Tuto. It was not before long that they reached the marina on the lake. The three walked along the dock where many state-of-the-art speed boats, were moored.

Keane's eyes were drawn to large gap between two boats. He growled out the words, "The Arianna's gone an I didn't give anyone permission for it ta be used." Kean scowled as he looked around the dock a second time. "So is the Mortimer, and it can track the Arianna." Kean looked up at the almost full moon and commented, "Never mind about tracking, the moon is bright and we should see 'em."

They walked past three small speedboats and stopped at a beautiful streamlined power cruiser that sat waiting, glistening in the moonlight. Darius climbed aboard and held his hand out for Mary. In turn she lifted up her dress with her left hand, grabbed Darius's hand, then stepped aboard the Magdalena.

Kean put his hand out for Darius too, to pull him aboard. As Darius began to clasp his hand Kean tapped Darius's hand and said, "Just joking with ya." He then nodded his head and laughed.

Darius did not react; his mind was set on starting the Magdalena. He turned and made his way to the wheelhouse. Mary followed as she stood by his side scanning the lake in front of them for any movement. Darius sat in the cockpit, switched the blower on, then checked his shifter was in neutral and shouted to Keane, "Cast off the bow line." He then turned to Mary. "Better put a life jacket on, sweetheart, we do not know what we will encounter out there."

Keane stepped inside the wheelhouse, took two life jackets and placed one in Mary's hand and one in Darius's. Mary shivered a little, as her shoulders began to feel the cold damp air. Keane commented. "'Ave you got a jumper for Mary to wear, Darius? Your sweetheart 'ere is shiverin'."

Darius picked up a large Aran sweater from the passenger seat and placed it over Mary's head. Mary said, "This looks familiar."

"That's because it is," Darius replied. "It's my old faithful sweater that now has a distinct scent of my sweetheart, Lady Mary Tavistock."

Keane butted in, "All right you two, enough of the lovey doveys, I thought we were on a mission 'ere!" He looked at Darius with serious intent, before speaking. "I think that blower has done its thing, Darius, it's safe to start the engine now without blowing us up."

Darius nodded his head and started the engine. Keane cast off the stern line and Mary tied her life jacket. It was only the second time she wore one, but this life jacket felt a little heavier than the last one she thought. They headed out on the lake scanning the water for any signs of boat light and movement.

Keane yelled out from the deck. "Over to your right, Darius, I can see a light." Darius motored up slowly to the Arianna.

Mary's cogitative eyes widened and a sudden look of dismay transformed her face. She could barely speak her words, "There does not seem to be a soul around."

Keane scanned the boat with his eagle eyes and then in a calm commanding voice slipped out the words "Pull her in close, Darius, I'll jump on board an take a look."

There was an eerie calmness to the tranquil moonlit water of the lake, as Mary and Darius watched Keane jump on board the streamlined cruiser. The two eagerly watched Keane's shadow as he moved down within the curtained cabin.

Darius shouted out to Keane, "Is everything all right in there?" as he tied the two boats together.

In reply Keane shouted back sarcastically, "Give us chance ta see, eh! I've only been aboard for less than a minute!" He then seemingly looked like he had dropped to his knees, as he walked on a lower level. Keane then moved towards the bow of the boat very slowly, bending down further so that his body was out of sight.

They waited transfixed on the curtains of the cruiser for any sign of movement from Kean.

Darius turned to Mary and cupped her chin with his left hand and looked straight into her dark blue eyes with a pensive look. "I'd better go and find out what's taking him so long. He's been gone a while; he must have found something; if you see anything holler and I'll come running." He kissed Mary on the forehead and put a flashlight in her hand. "Don't let go of the light." He stepped on board the Arianna, without looking back.

Mary gazed on, watching Darius's shadow move in the cruiser the same way Kean's did, until she could no longer see him. The deep dark serene water captured her attention with a sudden splash. So, she moved closer to the edge of the boat. As she did, she caught sight of bubbles, floating to the surface. Her eyes were drawn again to more movement within the water. Transfixed, she placed the flashlight in the direction of the bubbles, as the light hit the bubbles, the very image retrogressed her to her recurring dream. She was staring at the same deep dark serene water, bubbling ever so slightly, giving nothing away of the fraught torrid battle that lay underneath, she thought. (Was there a battle going on?)

An uneasy feeling engulfed Mary as she shivered with the cold damp air and her thoughts. She quickly scanned the rest of the water around her, with the aid of her flashlight. There was nothing she could see, but she knew something terrible was about to happen.

Staring transfixed on the bubbles again, her mind wandered to what or worse still who was making them as she shone the flashlight on the bubbles.

Suddenly she felt an aggressive smack against her shoulder, which caught her off balance as she jumped with fright. Collecting herself, Mary turned around with the flashlight in hand and shone it on the face of the culprit.

"Hello, Flo, how does it feel being me?" she said, with disdain in her voice, her black lips smiling at the look of horror on Flo's face.

Flo stared back, stunned at the sight of her deathly looking venomous identical twin sister, her mouth wide open as she stared, speechless.

Darius shouted from inside the Arianna, "We have found Dr Goodman and he's been beaten badly, but he's alive and bound in chains."

Flo did not answer, although she heard Darius's words. She acknowledged him by closing her mouth and smiling with relief. She stared deeply into her sister's eyes. All she could see was an abyss full of evil, staring right back at her. She uttered the words with sincerity in her heart, "What happened to you?"

"YOU!" she scorned and with one almighty push, she violently shoved Flo into the lake.

Flo's body plunged into the ice-cold water, it totally took her breath away. Her eyes widened and her mouth shut, conserving the air within her body. She slowly began to sink, dragged down by her life jacket in the deep dark water. All the while she continued to hold the flashlight. Time slowed as she realized her body was not going to emerge. There was no buoyancy in her life jacket, so she pulled on the bow and watched it unravel. Her life jacket loosened, so she slipped out her arms one by one. The jacket sunk further to the bottom of the lake as Flo's body began its climb to the surface.

Flo gasped for air, as her face emerged. She began to take notice of where the boats were. She scanned the area and could see another boat approaching in the distance. Her first instinct was to swim to the Arianna, avoiding any further confrontation with her twin. As she did so, she was dragged down under the water by someone or something much stronger than her.

Her thoughts were quickly taken back to her dream as she took a deep breath. This time, she was not going to struggle and fight. She was going to conserve her energy and concentrate on the light within her and try to telepathically communicate with Claudia, Humayun, Shaka, Annachi, Anna and Jacob.

Still holding the flashlight and with a relaxed state of mind, she began to float back up to the surface. Catching her breath, she managed to shout, "Help, help!" Before she was dragged down again.

The perpetrator held Mary's body down longer. It looked lifeless as she elegantly swayed rhythmically from side to side within the deep dark water.

Her relaxed state of mind opened all of her senses, each acting together, so that there was no center from which the senses were moving. There were no limitations to give the senses their rightful place, not suppressing any. Every sense was fully awakened. Her body was surviving in a fully relaxed state. Where the time within her self-consciousness stopped, the attachment stopped, empty, totally, completely within her consciousness. Thought as time stopped, measurement stopped, control stopped, leaving herself open to her extra sensual perception; depthless, timeless with no beginning, no end and no boundaries. In this tremendous quality of silence, she became one with her other fellow deities.

Claudia's voice entered Mary's thought. *We've found you, Mary, we will be with you shortly.*

Mary's eyes suddenly became wide open as she stared into the eyes of Bobby. Her first thought was, 'Had Bobby come to save her?'

He stared back at her with disdain in his eyes. Mary's body started to surface; he pulled her back down before she could breathe. She then realized all the while Bobby was the one dragging her down.

Once more he stared into her eyes, sadistically mesmerized by every facial expression of sufferance on Mary's face. Mary ascertained Bobby must have sabotaged the Brisfit but he had not counted on Dr Goodman insisting on Mary flying with him and swapping airplanes. Bobby was the person trying to kill her, she was certain now, but why? She could feel herself panic as she tried to surface. Air bubbles began to seep from her mouth and float to the surface as Mary was pulled down once again. Her mouth seeped the last few bubbles of air; she began to lose consciousness. Her eyes lost focus and she was submerged in a bright warm white light. Here the air was plentiful as she was walking, engulfed by a huge expanse of white fog. Her footsteps made no sound. She paused and looked around to see if there was anybody else there. There was not a soul around her but the fragrant scent of roses captured her attention as she sniffed the air. She decided to follow the trail of scent, as she did so, the warm white light slowly turned into a bright white light. She squinted her eyes to see a figure in the distance with their arms outstretched. An incredible warm feeling of love immersed her very soul as she proceeded to walk, her eyes teared with relief the closer she got to the outstretched arms.

Mary was totally unaware of the rotating battle of fists in the lake between Darius and Bobby as Mary's lifeless body swayed in the deep water. Her long golden locks of hair floated way above her head, illuminated by the flashlight, still grasped by her hand. A trail of blood started to weep in the water from Darius. Bobby suddenly disappeared into the darkness of the lake as Darius clutched his left chest and swam over to Mary. He spun her around in the water so that her head was facing upwards as they surfaced. He let go of his wound to support Mary, wrapping his arm over her shoulder, threading his hand underneath her right armpit and behind her back so that Mary's head and neck were supported and out of water. He cupped Mary's forehead with his left hand and swam towards Arianna.

Keane looked on to see the Magdalena distancing itself and the Mortimer drawing close. He then spotted Darius struggling with Mary in the lake and jumped in to help.

As he reached them, he shouted, "Put some backbone into it. Ya wouldn't think you were a big burly guy!" He grabbed hold of Mary and swam over to the Arianna, not realizing Darius was badly injured.

Darius suddenly sank deep down into the dark lake, as Keane rolled Mary's body onto the Arianna's deck. Dr Goodman limped over, battered and bloody, looking down at Mary's lifeless body. His eyes became tearful. He knelt down to check her pulse. He nodded his head and uttered the words, "Nein, nein, nein, she is so cold." He laid his right ear on her left chest, listening for a heartbeat. Then looked up at Keane and uttered the word, "Nein." At the same time, he placed his palm on Mary's forehead and gently tilted back her head and lifted Mary's chin so her mouth was open. He then positioned the heel of his hand in the middle of her chest, just below the nipple line and put his other hand on top, with his arms straight. He started pumping his hands applying pressure and releasing pressure, making sure Mary's chest rose before he applied the next quick compression. He made thirty of them, and then took two puffs in her mouth. Then started pumping his hands again. He shouted out to Keane, "Go and get me the Goodman Electronic Defibrillator and lots of blankets!"

Keane quickly moved out of sight as Dr Goodman tilted Mary's head back once more and blew two deep breaths into her mouth. There was still no sign of life as Dr Goodman pumped away on Mary's chest again. He cried out loud, "Mary, don't leave me." Tears rolled abundantly down his cheeks. "I'm not going to leave you! I promise, Mary. Come back to me!" he shouted.

Keane now arrived with the Goodman Electronic Defibrillator and an eiderdown. He opened the box then cut open her sweater and dress, dried her chest with a towel and placed an electrode on Mary's right side and then placed a second electrode on her left, just below her breast.

"I've taught you well," Dr Goodman acknowledged. "Stand back!" he commanded and switched on the defibrillator to shock Mary's body.

Her body jolted, but there was no sign of life.

Dr Goodman bellowed, "Don't leave us, Mary. You have great things to achieve, and the world needs you!" He flipped the switch on the defibrillator once again.

Her body shuddered; there was still no sign of life.

"Come back to us, Mary, I need to show ya how to kick ass!" Keane shouted. "So this will never happen again to ya!" A fraught expression appeared on his face as he wiped a tear away with the back of his hand. "Come on, gal, come back to us."

Mary was totally unaware of the distress around her as she felt the warm loving embrace.

Dr Goodman shocked Mary's body once more. Keane watched on eagerly, waiting for Mary to breathe. There was no movement after Mary's body jolted. Dr Goodman turned to Keane and nodded, no, with a hopeless look on his face.

"She has more guts in her, Doc, than ya think. Give her another shock, she can take it," Keane suggested as another tear started to fall.

Dr Goodman shocked Mary once more. Her body tremored, but there was no sign of life. "Nein, nein, nein, she's gone," Dr Goodman said, as he shook his head.

"Don't give up, Doc. It's not over till the fat lady sings, or thin lady, or any lady. An I don't hear a lady singing!" Kean's voice weakened as his tears streamed. "Don't leave us, gal."

Mary's lifeless body lay on the deck with the moonlight gazing down. A strange white mist surrounded her body as the Mortimer pulled alongside the Arianna. Claudia, Humayun and Jacob stepped onto the Arianna. They did not speak any words but gazed at Mary as Dr Goodman and Keane stared at them nodding their heads with dismay.

Jacob dived into the lake as Claudia bent down and kneeled over Mary placing her hand into the white mist and on Mary's heart. A white golden light illuminated Mary's whole body. It brought warmth, love and hope to all seeing it.

Mary's father slowly released his hug, as he said, "I have very much enjoyed your hug and visit, child, but it is not your time. It's time for you to go back, your sister is calling you. You have great achievements ahead of you. Go and be the savior you were born to be, my child. The world needs you more than ever." He kissed her forehead and then let go."

Mary felt her body plunging through the warm white haze, only aware of her own presence. She felt her body falling gradually through the clouds. A mist of calm encased her body, like a cozy soft blanket, one made with love, given with love and one that wrapped her in love. She was totally submerged in a bright warm white light, where the air was plentiful.

Her relaxed state of mind opened all of her senses, acting together, so that there was no center from which they were moving. There were no limitations to give the senses their rightful place, not suppressing any. Every sense was fully awakened. Her body was surviving in a fully relaxed state. Where the time within the self-consciousness stopped, the attachment stopped, empty, totally, completely within her consciousness. Thought as time stopped, measurement stopped, control stopped, leaving herself open to her extra sensual perception; depthless, timeless with no beginning and no end. In this tremendous quality of silence, she became one with her other fellow deities.

Claudia's voice entered Mary's thought. "We've found you, Mary. We are here. Come back to us, Mary. Come back."

She became aware of Claudia's presence. However, Mary was unaware of Jacob honing in on Darius's body while diving down in the deep, dark water. She was unaware of him surfacing, unaware of Jacob's shout from the lake. "Humayun, help me haul Darius on board, I think he's dead."

To be continued in

Gemini Complex, The Awakening